JUNE THE TWENTY FOURTH

A novel by

DAVID BRODIE

DEDICATED TO MY FAMILY AND FRIENDS

Published by David Brodie Books

This is a work of fiction. Names, characters, places and incidents either are the product of the author's imagination or are used fictitiously. Any resemblance to actual persons, living or dead, events or locales (except known venues e.g. The London Hospital; Belsen) is entirely coincidental.

First printed June 2021

ISBN: 9798841488040

Cover design by MET1 CREATIVE (www.met1.co.uk)

All proceeds from the sale of this book will be used to support the Nepalese charity Mountain People (mountain-people.org), which aims to help the Nepalese people help themselves.

PREFACE

This novel can best be described as an adventurous biography.

It follows the lives and loves of two boys as they experience a number of events, from birth to maturity. These events, some might say fantastical, are initiated by an unknown mentor.

Throughout the boys' lives, their places in family, society and personal development are contrasted, for no two people walk in the same shoes forever.

Two chapters in the novel (numbers 6 and 14) may be considered, for some, tough reading. They are graphic and disturbing, relating to evil and malevolent practices. They remain, because they are both relevant to the evolving personalities of the characters. Some readers may prefer to skip over these and I have provided a one-line summary of all chapters at the end, so the reader still has an insight into their content.

This summary may also be useful for those who prefer to leave a book unfinished for a time and like to be reminded of what has been read before.

I am extremely grateful to Cecilia Winkett who kindly commented on an early draft of the text.

I have tried to retain a level of authenticity with some of the events in the book, but please, dear reader, appreciate that this is a fictional novel, not a documentary.

Any errors, omissions or grammatical idiosyncrasies are entirely my own and I take full responsibility. The pedants amongst you will, I am sure, have a field day.

If anyone considers that his or her contribution to charity has not been a reasonable investment, I will be pleased to refund the cost in full.

The main purpose of a novel is for the reader to have a few moments of respite from their normal lives. It is the opportunity to transport you from realism of today to dwell in a season of uncertainty. Did this all really happen?

I do hope that I have succeeded.

David Brodie

June 24th 2021

CHAPTER ONE
BIRTHS

It was the day before June 24th, 1944. The explanation for the name of this auspicious date, Midsummer's Day, had been lost in the distant mists of time.

Maggie Breakwell went into labour at the Grange Maternity Home, Hindhead, at 3.00 am on a dark, unfriendly morning. She was already three weeks overdue, but the notion of inducing a baby was of little interest to the staff in this remote backwater.

The Grange was a stark, dismal place. The rows of iron beds were of standard hospital issue. Each mattress was shrouded in brown rubber, under a well worn, stained sheet. Any movement in those beds was signaled by the muffled groan of migrating rubber. It was a constant reminder of institutional poverty.

The Grange had previously belonged to a local family, but they had moved away from Hindhead, leaving it in a state of decay and disrepair. It had been requisitioned to cope with the numerous pregnancies resulting from the temporary liaisons of troops passing through the capital. Most of the women at The Grange had been rejected by their families. Many were totally unaware that these women were giving birth to their own children. Few of the fathers ever saw their offspring, even once.

Prospective mothers were given a thin blanket. Most spread their own coats on top of the bed to give them small comfort during the long, cool nights. All floors had a covering of cheap linoleum. The dominant smell was of cheap disinfectant, used daily to scour every surface.

Some staff brought in the occasional bunch of flowers to try to brighten the appearance of this austere place. In this stale, listless atmosphere, the blooms struggled to survive. The cheap vases, half filled with murky water, mostly contained flowers long dead. Somehow, these mockeries to still life created a mood more like a morgue than a place of new birth. June 1944 was a hot month in the south of England, but the window frames had been painted over and were impossible to open. The women waiting to give birth accepted this discomfort as part of the price they paid for their indiscretions.

The few staff were generally kind, but stretched to breaking point with the large number of women under their care. Most were in the final weeks of pregnancy, with as many as three in labour at any one time. The nurses could do little more than supply fresh water, leave a worn towel by each bedside and check for basic medical needs.

A delivery room was considered a luxury and all the mothers gave birth in the main wards just a few feet from other frightened women waiting their turn. There once had been curtain rails around each bed, but metal was needed for the war effort and they had been removed two years before.

Birth at The Grange Maternity Home was a very public affair and the screams of those in labour kept others in the hospital fully aware of what lay ahead.

* * * * *

Celia Lavenham reclined in her luxurious bed at the Portland Hospital, where the Egyptian cotton sheets were changed twice daily. She had chosen the down-filled coverlet with hand-stitched flowers because it reminded her of the private garden at home.

The Portland was totally different from The Grange. Each mother had an en suite, private room with opening windows and table fans to circulate fresh air. Vases of flowers were changed daily and staff and family flitted in and out of the rooms day and night. You could be forgiven for thinking the nurses had been chosen for their good looks, but they were also attentive and professional. Meals were chosen from a sumptuous menu and alcoholic drinks, although not encouraged, were available. A personal doctor visited at least twice a day. If needed, he would never be more than a phone call away. The atmosphere was calm, relaxed and welcoming. The most advanced medical facilities were available to ensure that childbirth at the Portland was as comfortable as possible. There were three delivery rooms, but rarely was more than one needed. The few patients at the Portland gave birth in a far more organized manner than elsewhere.

* * * * * *

At The Grange, where Maggie lay craving the advent of dawn, there was a single nurse on duty. She was busy dealing with a 16-year-old girl who had been crying softly for most of the night. Maggie struggled with great difficulty to the only toilet. It was no great distance, just along the corridor from the ward, but those few yards seemed endless. There she dealt with the trauma of her breaking waters and waited until the first of her contractions had passed. Maggie felt ghastly, but knew there was worse to come. She steadied herself against the handrail and made her way cautiously back to her bed. As each crippling pain ripped through her distended abdomen, she felt a wave of nausea rising in her tortured throat. She grabbed a dish, but couldn't even manage the comfort of vomiting away the offending bile. She gulped in air and tried to relax, knowing full well that the next contraction would be as bad or worse than the last. Somehow she survived the night without screaming for help. At last, the first light of dawn glanced its welcoming glow around the edges of the blackout curtains.

Maggie, now utterly exhausted, cried out weakly for help. The nurse was slow to respond, but eventually came to Maggie's bedside. As she pulled back the sheets, the nurse was horrified to see the indistinct, but certain crown of the child's blooded head. With one final, agonizing push the baby arrived into a confused, war-torn world. The boy was wrapped in a rough towel and placed against his mother's breast. Maggie felt a mixture of emotions from sheer relief to concern about their uncertain future together. Most of all, the joy of just being with her new son was a moment she could cherish. This brief moment of joy was hers alone, in spite of how the last twelve months had brought her to such a pitiful state.

* * * * * *

Celia's baby was not due for another three weeks. For Celia, every precaution was taken to ensure the whole process was as comfortable and incident free as humanly possible. Her vital signs and the unborn baby's heart were being monitored by an array of the latest medical equipment. Not for her a hospital gown, but a nightdress of Chinese silk in the fashionable style of the time. Professor James McCardle, who was the queen's personal gynaecologist, visited Mrs. Lavenham every morning at precisely 9.00 o'clock. He was always prepared to spend any amount of time with her. The state of her pregnancy was the prime topic of conversation, but political and court activities were often mentioned during these visits.

It was Midsummer's Day. The cancellation of Royal Ascot was being debated when the discussion was interrupted by the harsh tone of a medical alarm. The Professor reacted with the reflexes of a much younger man. He called for assistance as he gently and expertly moved his foetal stethoscope over her distended stomach. The Professor, his assistant and now a senior nurse quickly agreed that immediate action was needed and without waiting for a porter, they wheeled her bed into the adjoining surgical theatre.

"Your baby's in a little bit of distress," whispered Professor McCardle, in a tone that failed to disguise his concern. "We think it best to bring him into the world a little earlier than you might be expecting, but please be assured we have the best team in the world here to do just that."

The look of sheer terror in Celia's eyes lasted for no more than a few minutes as the anaesthetic injection took immediate effect. Very soon, a team of six highly experienced staff was ready to operate. The hospital's most senior surgeon took the responsibility to make the deep incision to expose Celia's womb. A further more cautious incision revealed the baby, now struggling for life-giving oxygen. The child was rapidly removed, cleaned and placed in a nearby incubator. Both incisions were stitched closed and Celia's anaesthetic was very slowly reduced so that some 30 minutes later her eyes dreamily focused on a group of concerned faces surrounding her bed.

Aware of Celia's semi-conscious state, Professor McCardle spoke slowly and deliberately.

"Mrs. Lavenham, your surgery was a great success and you are to be congratulated on giving birth to a fine son. However we do have a little concern that he's in need of special care for a while. This is largely because he came rather earlier than we both expected. With your permission, I would like to have him transferred to where I am confident he will get the best treatment available."

"But surely," responded Celia, not quite able to take in the implications of what was being said, "this hospital must have every possible resource."

"Not quite," responded the Professor with a sigh, "the Portland is one of the very best, but unfortunately your son will need intensive care for a few days. This is only available at Great Ormond Street, one of London's best teaching hospitals. I recommend most strongly that we move him immediately to this specialized hospital for children. With your husband away, I do need your permission and believe most strongly that we should act swiftly."

Celia struggled to absorb this devastating news and although unable to bring herself to speak, gave a slight nod of assent before closing her eyes and sinking back into the comfort of her luxurious pillows.

A private ambulance was quickly arranged and the child, still in his incubator, was sent speedily but carefully through the darkening streets of London. As the ambulance approached the hospital, its progress was slowed down by the carnage in the surrounding streets. The V1 bombs had started their devastating and merciless reign of attrition just ten days earlier. Whole streets were either obliterated or abandoned and the still smoking ruins of tightly packed homes were evident everywhere.

Staff at Great Ormond Street had been primed to treat this new born with utmost urgency and Celia's baby was escorted with care to the lift. At the fourth floor, he was handed to the waiting ward sister. She transferred him rapidly to the intensive care unit and into the pre-ordered high-intensity incubator. Within minutes blood tests were organized, a line inserted and all vital functions were constantly monitored. The whole process was like a meticulous, military operation, coupled with genuine concern for the young child.

* * * * *

At Hindhead there was little time to celebrate a new birth as others were waiting to have their children delivered. Maggie's boy was at least in a nearby cot as she struggled to recover from the traumatic 22 hours it had taken to bring him into the world. The curtains were drawn apart and light streamed in early on the morning of Midsummer's Day. The sun's rays failed to brighten the appearance of the drab ward. It remained worn and weary, reflecting the poor souls within. Those poor souls who had little option than to be incarcerated there until they were strong enough to face the world. Most would be blessed with a part of themselves now in their arms. For some that blessing would be short-lived. A baby born at The Grange had an uncertain future.

Maggie turned her aching body towards her new son, gurgling happily beside her. She smiled at him adoringly; this precious bundle of life that had caused her so much pain. In spite of her strong emotional attachment, she was now just able to take a more dispassionate look at the child by her side. Maggie was concerned that his colour seemed to lack the rosy pink of a newborn. In spite of her pain, she struggled to her feet and examined him more closely. She cradled him in her arms and took him over to one of the other children lying in the packed ward. Her suspicions were right; her son had a distinct yellow tinge to his skin compared with the others. Her professional training told her straight away that he was severely jaundiced. He needed the specialized therapy of a light box, and fast, before further damage was done to his tiny liver. Maggie was well aware that the equipment needed was never going to be found here at Hindhead. Her listless brain, still suffering from the trauma of the night, strived to explore every option. She settled on a risky, but immediate strategy. She needed this treatment for her son - treatment she knew was absolutely essential.

When no staff were to be seen, she packed her meagre belongings in a battered suitcase. She wrapped her tiny son in the only things she had to hand - a towel and a blanket. Without even a goodbye to others in the ward, she crept out of the dismal nursing home and headed into the now sunlit street. Maggie felt, with no good reason, like a thief. It was her child, her decision, and her destiny. She had deliberately avoided calling for a taxi from the nursing home. Her only option was to walk the half-mile to the nearest taxi rank at the station. As she walked, she constantly questioned her motives. All she could do was hope upon hope that her judgment was sound. Deep down in her innermost soul, it seemed right. She prayed that her intuition had not clouded sound wisdom.

Settling into the grubby leather upholstery of the taxi, she quietly asked the driver to take her to central London, to Great Ormond Street Hospital. During the trip, Maggie was desperate to sleep. The trauma of the last 24 hours inflicted a state of lethargy she had never experienced before. It was if a straight jacket was enveloping her whole being. In spite of this, she cuddled her son, knowing that this very first journey together was the start of a very special relationship. A relationship that might, quite possibly, be hers alone to forge over the years to come. With a jolt, these thoughts vanished. Maggie's mind returned to the reality of her baby's urgent needs. The journey seemed interminable as the driver skillfully steered his taxi around the debris left by the recent bombing. Maggie struggled to recognize some of the streets she had recently walked on her way to work. At long last, with Maggie now in renewed pain, the two arrived at Great Ormond Street. Maggie struggled to open her purse. The driver, as he unlocked the rear door, steadied her arm, saluted and refused to take any money. Maggie was unused to such kindness. On sheer impulse, she gave the generous driver a thankful kiss. She by-passed the emergency entrance and went straight to the fourth floor. There, at the east wing designated for intensive care, she handed her son over to the startled staff. Maggie insisted he was put in a light box immediately. The sister in charge took one look at the child. She knew exactly what was needed and gave him absolute priority. Maggie whispered her thanks and was about to request a mattress beside her son, when she collapsed. The floor rose to meet her limp body and Maggie gave in gracefully to the power of gravity. Maggie was taken by trolley to a recovery ward in an annexe some 200 yards from the main hospital. The ward had been insulated from external sounds. It was specially designed to provide a haven of peace in what was becoming a violent and discordant world. She was given a powerful sedative and in spite of Maggie's concern for her young son, she could do little more than drift off to a troubled and fretful sleep.

Two boys, born in the middle of a terrible war on the selfsame day, were now lying side by side in the intensive care ward of Britain's best paediatric hospital. They came from totally different worlds, both born in acutely different circumstances and each very unaware of the other.

The bomb hit Great Ormond Street Hospital at five minutes to midnight. It totally devastated the east wing on the fourth floor.

CHAPTER 2
DEVASTATION

The bomb was one of the first of Herr Hitler's new wave of missiles. Unlike the usual despicable drone of the Luftwaffe's night bombers, these V1 'doodlebugs' sounded like a high-revving lorry engine. Searchlights would probe the darkened skies for these murderous machines, but little could stop their paths of inhuman destruction. On that evening of June 24th, 144 flying bombs were launched with 111 crossing the coast of Britain. There were 93 fatalities on that single night, with another 655 seriously wounded, many never to survive. Precious lives, prematurely lost to these vicious instruments of conflict.

Every ill child at Great Ormond Street Hospital had worried and suffering parents. Each mother had every hope their child would soon recover and return to the love and affection of their families.

The initial blast was as if the world had come to an untimely end. Within one brief second, eardrums were shattered; people and objects were thrown across rooms; eyes were blinded, for the lucky ones, only temporarily.

The immediate aftermath was an appalling scene of death and destruction. The chances of survival were so limited that no rescuer would even consider a successful outcome. A short period of utter silence followed, as if some unknown deity had decided to assess the situation.

People and masonry started to stir. Then came the worst sound known to man, the howl of tortured pain. The cries of the injured; the last struggling breaths of the dying; the ghastly drip, drip, drip of blood from the seriously wounded. A gaping hole in the roof revealed nothing but the black void of a starless, ebony sky. A void so vast it could be the distant entrance to Hades itself. Then came new sounds; the crackling of burning wood: the muffled, distant sirens: people stirring, shouting, ordering, comforting. Slowly, oh so slowly, the sounds of rescue, recovery, release and freedom. For many on the fourth floor, freedom was from pain as they drifted into a never-ending sleep. For others it was release and recovery from the bonds of fallen joists, iron beds or heavy machinery. For a few it was rescue and recovery from the burning debris now falling from the voids in the ceiling above. For most there was no rescue, except into the hands of the Almighty.

Staff nurse Sheila McEvoy fluctuated between unconsciousness and a state of dream-like awareness. One moment she was slipping into the arms of Morpheus and then gradually she would sense an indistinct notion; an extraordinary calm, yet surrounded by the insanity of her surroundings. In one brief moment she thought she sensed a whimper, a cry, a shout. As quickly as it was heard she sank back into a vacuum of oblivion. She was strangely content in this unreal state. She felt no pain, no worldly troubles, no plans, no memories, just a sense of enduring peace.

As Sheila's life ebbed away, her still active mind was punctuated by images of this brief time on earth.

The images of the nurse's dressing-up clothes she'd been given as a child one Christmas. How everyone had said that she really looked the part as she tended her dolls. The way she bandaged them, oh so carefully, with scraps of fabric from old handkerchiefs. The way she worried so much when a safety pin punctured the soft brown fur of her favourite teddy.

These fleeting mental visions reflected the care she gave to her younger brother, unusual in one so young. She seemed to have the gift of empathy to anyone less fortunate than herself. These experiences were gently transporting her to a career of caring for others.

These rapid, dream-like pictures projected her to the age of eighteen. She was so excited when accepted as a trainee nurse at the famous London Hospital. Then followed the joy and relief at becoming a registered nurse. The thrill of being transferred to the acute paediatric department of Great Ormond Street, so widely acclaimed as the best in the country.

For Sheila there was no sense of time. Nothing but images, flashing fleetingly across a faltering brain. Yet those away from her diminishing world were all too aware of the precious urgency of each passing second.

The rescuers knew that speed was the saviour. Those closest to the fourth floor, even though initially rigid with shock, were soon mobilizing every possible aid. The internal phone lines had failed, so people were sent hurriedly to summon any type of assistance. The complex machinery of a hospital was in turmoil. Yet the staff, well trained in emergency procedures, reacted as one. Priority was given to controlling the fire and extinguishers were rushed from other floors. With scant fear for their own lives, doctors, orderlies, porters and nurses, all moved in unison to tend the unknown and disfigured bodies on floor four. Their immediate concern was to save any lives that had survived the destruction. Even the inexperienced could tell that this was for many a forlorn hope.

Amid the chaos, made worse by the Stygian, inky blackness of the ravaged ward, a low moan was heard in a far corner. Quiet was ordered and, in spite of the gentle hiss of doused flames, the source of the tiny sound was found. The rescuers' movements were minimized by caution, but within minutes an ear was placed against Sheila's half open mouth.

"I think she's breathing," were the only words spoken and immediately two other rescuers gathered by her side.

"We can't examine her properly here; she has to be moved. This place could collapse at any minute."

"Keep checking her breathing. We're not giving up on this one yet."

Sheila just knew, in spite of her piteous state that nearby was an even greater need. Every weakened sinew in her body was straining to react. Her leadened state couldn't even muster the most meagre response.

It is thought that at the point of death, the human body shows not only incredible resilience, but also an astonishing heightening of the senses. For one instant in time, Sheila's perception was strangely intensified. Amid the chaos and destruction all around her, Sheila, unbelievably, heard the soft sound of two tiny individuals.

As another ear was placed close to her lips to listen for the tell tale rasping of life, Sheila drew Herculean strength from deep inside her failing body and in almost her final breath she whispered "The babies…. alive…. two."

Quiet was no longer requested, but demanded. The chill, doom and dismay of the night were for the briefest of moments punctuated by the soft mewing of a newborn. It was if a thousand breaths were held in unison, and were rewarded by another sound. It was the almost imperceptible whimper of another child.

From the misery of despair and destruction came the slenderest measure of hope.

CHAPTER 3
PHOENIX

As Sheila lay at the doors of death, she had made one final sacrifice. Her whispered words had alerted the rescuers. Following the muted sounds, they moved cautiously through the charred embers to the far corner of what was once the east wing on the fourth floor. Torches flickered, their beams probing the ebony stillness of the malignant building. As eyes slowly adjusted to the gloom, what looked like a small, upturned packing case was spotted in one corner. This innocuous object was first spotted by one of the rescuers, Willard Boulton.

Willard Boulton was in the final year of medical school and had elected to cover the night shift for the last three nights. This was in addition to his normal duties in the emergency care unit, a posting that was permanently chaotic. The numerous injuries brought in constantly from the ravage of the deadly V1 rockets had made the last week particularly haphazard. The hospital authorities, even in wartime, would rarely allow anyone to work for three days and nights continuously. It was recognized that physical fatigue would inevitably compromise anyone's mental faculties. This, in a busy hospital, could prove fatal.

Willard, his body now blackened by the soot and grime of the surrounding debris, moved with extreme caution towards this uncertain destination. The smoldering spars he moved to reach the end of the room had already blistered his hands. In spite of his pain, he hesitantly turned the case from its side. He was astonished to see what could only be the tiny form of a newborn child. His emotions were in turmoil. He felt elation, but also immense concern for the health of the child and a dread that it may no longer be alive.

"I need help," he spluttered in a rasping voice, numbed by the smoke and powdered grit he had inhaled over the last hour.

Others came. They brought fresh minds, strong arms, but most importantly, they brought hope. With utmost care, they carried the box, now seen as an incubator, away from the imminent danger of the further threat from falling debris. Cautiously, the incubator was moved to comparative safety. It was taken away from the devastation of the east wing to a lower floor where the poor child, still no more than a day old, could be fully assessed and treated.

Back on the fourth floor, the young student doctor collapsed with exhaustion. As he slumped to the floor, his mind was now a near vacuum of distorted senses. Slowly, almost imperceptibly, the neural linkages in his brain returned to Sheila's last words. She said 'two', he muttered under his breath. She said 'two'!

His body could hardly move, but one final surge of adrenaline forced him to respond to the critical word 'two'. He knew that hope must prevail over despair. He dragged his listless and ailing body to his knees. He crawled back into the blackened debris and headed once more into the remains of the hospital he so loved.

As the word 'two' threaded itself into Willard's consciousness, he just knew that somewhere in this infernal misery around him there had to be another child. Someone's son or daughter; perhaps the first child of loving parents; the human expression of their union, devotion and adoration. Willard, now struggling to breathe, had to make one last monumental effort to search for the baby. The baby he now believed, with increasing certainty, deserved his protection.

Willard returned with extreme care to where he a thought the incubator had been found. Another rumble, another fall of rubble from above and immediately any clarity of sight was washed away. A thick miasma of grime and dust rose from the floor. In the impenetrable darkness, which no torchlight could hope to pierce, he could do little more than feel ahead with outstretched fingers. With extreme caution, he swept his hands from side to side, and inched ever forward to do his best to cover the uncertain ground ahead. Each second seemed to stretch to a minute. As he persevered with the intricate task, his focus seemed to ebb but then flow back from the brink of detachment. Now the minutes seemed to stretch to hours. After what felt like an eternity, Willard's outstretched fingers grasped a metal leg. He dismissed it as the base of a chair, but as his grip tightened ready to move it away, he felt a small tremor pass very faintly into the palm of his hand. He paused. Was this almost imperceptible movement just a muscular spasm from his exhausted limb? Was it his now rapid heartbeat echoing through his body to the tips of his wearied fingers? He paused again. No. His heartbeat was certainly giving out a dull, but rapid, thud both in his chest and head. It came again. A short shiver of movement; a message of life; a vestige of hope. Willard pulled gently on the metallic object in his grasp. He struggled to kneel. He could now explore more fully what he'd felt only moments before. It was like a cot, but with firm sides and some sort of cover. He once again shouted for help, surprised that his voice could even be heard after inhaling such quantities of airborne effluent.

Help came just as the miasma settled around him again. Powerful torches could now just about penetrate the gloom. He was soon found; still holding on to the cot like a drowning man would hold a lifeline. Willing hands gently prised his hands from the cot and it was moved to safety. Safety from the certain enclave of surrounding death.

"Come on doctor, let's get you out of here into the fresh air. You look as though you need it," came the spirited words from one of the other rescuers. But Willard could not reply. No part of his conscious state could function any more and he slipped into the death zone, where only rapid and prolonged treatment would save him.

Strong hands lifted Willard away from the east wing. These hands took him as quickly as caution would allow to the intensive care ward, thankfully undamaged by the bomb. He was given priority treatment, with a breathing tube fed down his throat, and numerous catheters inserted to supply him with life saving drugs. Most importantly he was put into a deep sedation. It was expected to last for many days. His vital signs were monitored every fifteen minutes; such was the concern for Willard's fragile state.

In a small side room, the difficult task of treating the seriously ill babies became a priority. The bomb had destroyed the electrical feed to this part of the hospital, but the emergency generators at least provided a dim light to review the casualties.

The duty registrar, Harry Ames, had been on the ground floor when the bomb hit. He examined each child in turn with a combination of diligence and care. The impact must have thrown each baby over the room on the fourth floor, causing extensive bruising and lacerations. He explored the possibility of internal bleeding and organ damage. Their still-soft skulls could well have saved them from severe brain damage, but this still had to be assessed. His examination was rapid, but meticulous. He knew full well that in cases like this, time is of the essence. Decisions had to be made and quickly.

"Does anyone know why these kiddies were up on the fourth floor?" he demanded to no one in particular. Everyone was struggling for answers, but none came.

"All records would have been with them on the ward," answered one of the attendant nurses, "the wrecked light box suggest one them may've been jaundiced."

"Well that's a start," retorted the registrar, more in exasperation than appreciation.

"But for Christ's sake, which one? Have we got no ID on them at all? As they are, you simply can't tell them apart."

"Doctor, I don't think we have time for this right now," said a concerned nurse, more familiar with trauma cases. "We've got fluid lines into both of them and we need to get them to a high dependency unit as soon as possible."

"They can't stay here," replied Dr. Ames, decisively, "they'll have to be transferred to The London immediately. We've done everything possible here for the poor little fellows. I'll arrange transport."

With that, he raced off to the main entrance hall to summon an ambulance.

It was starting to get light on that June dawn as Harry Ames rushed around looking for any method of getting the two barely conscious babies to The London Hospital. The heavy overnight bombing had sucked every available ambulance into the epicenter of the resultant mayhem. The East End of London had been hit particularly hard and this was exactly where the two babies needed to be sent. In desperation, Dr. Ames flagged down the only vehicle passing the hospital, a delivery van on its way to Spitalfields Market. The driver, recognizing quickly the seriousness of the situation, threw out a pile of boxes from behind him, just making space for two adults and their precious cargo. The large back doors flew open and each child, now in makeshift cots, resembling large hampers, were cautiously loaded into the van. Dr. Ames brusquely commandeered one of the nurses just arriving for her shift and together they squeezed into the dark interior. Both children were now linked to catheters, drips, bags of saline and infusion pumps. Paediatric masks and two small oxygen canisters were quickly added to the emergency consignment. The poor nurse, unexpectantly thrust into this life-saving journey was at first mesmerized by the rapidity of the activity around her, but very soon her professionalism came to the fore. Taking the lead from Dr. Ames, she applied all her nursing skills to keeping the tiny babies alive.

Before the war, this journey would have taken no more than 20 minutes, especially in the early hours of the morning. The blitz had changed the profile of London beyond recognition. The driver had to avoid bomb craters, collapsed buildings, barriers and burnt out cars. He threaded his van through the debris, trying every option to deliver this unusual load of desperate humanity to their destination in Whitechapel. He drove from near Russell Square, skirted the City of London with its views of St Paul's Cathedral, passed Spitalfields Market and as he approached the Good Samaritan pub, he at last turned up to the main gates of The London Hospital.

During the drive, Harry Ames apologized to the young lady who endured the uncomfortable, yet essential journey. He explained that he rarely ordered nurses into passing vans without so much as a brief justification, but time was more important than niceties on this occasion. Nurse Bradley, briefly introduced herself as Clare. The rest of the journey was spent in near silence, giving all her attention to the critical needs of the two babies. As they passed the Good Samaritan, a pub that was popular with off-duty medical staff, Harry apologized once more. Somewhat shyly, he offered to take Clare for a drink when things calmed down. Looking at him properly for the first time, she smiled, and in a spirit of conciliation, accepted.

As the van crunched its way up the lightly graveled drive of the hospital, the grand doors, originally opened over 200 years before, re-opened again to admit two almost lifeless bundles of humanity. With utmost care, the babies were transported into the depths of this ancient building and were soon receiving every attention the war-torn facilities could offer.

Two babies, totally vulnerable as they lay side by side, did, by the grace of God, survive, despite the nursing staff holding out little hope. They were both fighters. Their little bodies, now both in incubators and light boxes, almost imperceptibly gained strength. Their external wounds healed, their bruises slowly faded and they soon became the two miracles of the only bomb ever to fall on Great Ormond Street. No one knew their names, their parents, or their backgrounds. In the wonder of survival, these things, for now, seemed not to matter.

For two mothers, though, it did matter. They were both desperate for news of their newly born children. Two mothers, separated by class and situation, were recovering in two very different hospitals. Maggie, in the soundproof annexe near Great Ormond Street Hospital and Celia in the seclusion of the Portland Hospital, were still unaware of the fate of their children. Neither could know that a bomb had obliterated the fourth floor of the very hospital into which their babies had been entrusted.

CHAPTER 4
RESTORATION

In Great Ormond Street Hospital, the damage from the bomb was largely confined to the fourth floor, but its horrendous impact was seen and heard throughout the building. It was as if a giant hand had shaken every room and clenched its fist on the fourth floor. As every effort was given to help those in greatest need, Maggie, who was sedated in a soundproofed annexe some 200 yards away, was left largely unattended. Nursing staff had been rapidly redeployed to assist with the injuries in the main hospital building. Over time, the devastating news of the bomb's damage spread to the annexe. The few patients in the recovery ward slowly became aware of the nearby carnage.

Maggie's mind, still exhausted from giving birth the day before, painstakingly tried to make sense of the last twenty-four hours. She struggled to find order in the sequence of events that had brought her here. Slowly the mist in her mind cleared and she recalled the pain of giving birth in that awful nursing home. The tender moments she shared with her son. The realization that all was not well and that only she could have initiated the action needed. The decision she made to take the taxi into London and make her way to this hospital. She knew that her child would be in the best place. That he would improve and, given time, would recover fully. She struggled to recollect what he needed. A special box. That was it, he needed a special light box, but where was it? Was it here? Is it by my bedside? She fluctuated in desperation between the past and the present. Slowly, oh so slowly, the realization came to her. Her son was not here. There was no life-saving box beside her bed. Her jaundiced child was elsewhere. But where? Then her still hazy brain cleared to unmask the awful truth. Her child had been taken to the fourth floor. The upper floor, the floor of the bomb. Her tortured scream brought the duty nurse to her bedside and she laid a calming hand on Maggie's arm.

"My baby," she whispered, "where is he?"

"I'm not sure," came the professional reply, "but I will try my best to find out."

"But the bomb, the fourth floor, surely…" Maggie's voice trailed off in distress and despair.

"Leave it to me," the nurse stated quietly in a tone of reassurance. "As soon as I can get some cover here, I will personally get you any details I can. Please just rest. You've had a terrible night yourself after what you went though yesterday. Let me get you something to settle you."

"You're very kind," Maggie replied weakly, "but that's the last thing I want right now. I want my baby back. Please help."

The nurse gently released her grip on Maggie's arm. Smiled and turned away, determined to help in any way she could. She knew what Maggie needed immediately was reassuring company and she returned within minutes with some strong, sweet tea.

Maggie responded with a half smile, knowing she was in good hands. Her heart still yearned for news, even though doubts in her mind were starting to form. She sensed a void, an ache, a rift from reality, but most importantly a separation from her very soul. The unborn child that so recently was part of her physical being had melted away. It was if a heavy door had been slammed shut, separating Maggie from reality.

Maggie's imagery suddenly came into focus as a smiling nurse knelt beside her.

"Well done," she said, "you slept for over an hour. I have some news for you. As you heard, the bomb hit the fourth floor of the main hospital and caused serious damage. However two newborn boys were rescued. They were both in a grim state and needed urgent attention. Both were transferred to The London Hospital in Whitechapel during the night. I'm afraid that's all I know, but we are trying to make contact right now. It's not easy because the bombing last night hit that area badly. As soon as I hear anything, you'll be the first to know."

Maggie relaxed visibly. As the nurse was relaying the news, Maggie had sat half upright in anticipation. The nurse left and Maggie sunk back into her thin, crumpled pillow. A small wave of hope swept over her. Still physically weak, the news had given her renewed energy. She drew the curtains around her bed and dressed. Pulling her meagre belongings together, she stuffed them haphazardly into her small, battered suitcase. She found a scrap of paper and wrote a brief note of thanks, leaving it propped against her pillow. Maggie checked that the nurse, the one who befriended her, was at the far end of the ward. She crept silently out of the door and down the stairs to the ground floor. As she walked down the outside steps, the fresh, warm breeze of that summer morning hit her with a combination of joy and anticipation. Her newfound vigour had but one purpose. Her intention was unassailably clear. She needed to know if her baby was still alive. The fear and dread was overlaid with the most powerful of emotions – hope. It became her guiding star as she walked with renewed purpose along the route she knew so well to the East End. It was that same route, used just a few hours earlier to take her child to a place of care and protection. Within the realism of war, protection was the expectation of all, but care was a privilege of the few. Maggie walked on, her mind focused on the protection and care of the one place where she hoped to find her son. It was all she could do.

If you'd been a bystander that June morning, you might have thought you were watching a weary woman, perhaps returning from the nightshift in a local munitions factory. Few would appreciate that this same woman had suffered the agony of childbirth only the day before. She was scarcely fit to leave her bed, yet alone be walking the streets of London totally unaided. Yet that same bystander would not appreciate Maggie's sheer tenacity. Every single fibre in her body was directed to one specific goal. She must find her son.

*   *   *   *   *

Celia Lavenham, meanwhile, was starting to feel better. The first class treatment she was receiving at the Portland Hospital gave her and the medical staff every confidence that she would soon be fully recovered. Before she went to sleep that evening, her personal doctor had given her an optimistic report on her baby, expecting them to be reunited very soon.

"The incubator was purely a precaution," he had said. As you know, your child was three weeks premature, so a little time with extra support and he'll be as right as rain."

When Celia woke the next morning, she was surprised to find Professor McCardle by her bedside. Taking her hand in his, he tried to remain calm as he asked how she felt.

"Much better for that sleep," Celia replied dreamily.

"Good," the professor responded, "it's just that there have been some developments."

"Developments?" questioned Celia, "but I feel fine."

"Yes," he replied, "but it's not you we are concerned about. There has been a sort of incident at Great Ormond Street, where your son was being treated."

Celia sat up, part in shock and part in disbelief.

"Yes, we believe everything is now under control, but early this morning a bomb hit the fourth floor of the hospital causing substantial damage."

"You mean…"

"Yes, this is where your boy was being incubated. I am sorry to bring it to you like this, but the latest news is more encouraging. It appears that two babies were brought out, badly injured, but both alive. We are optimistic that one of these babies is your son. We have an unconfirmed report that both babies were taken elsewhere early this morning, but we are still trying to piece the information together. The bombing in that part of London was pretty bad last night and communication is difficult. I have one of my staff ringing around all the local hospitals right now and will be back to you as soon as we have further information. I am so sorry, Mrs. Lavenham, but we are trying our best."

Celia smiled weakly. Slowly the situation sank in. The full impact of Professor McCardle's news bore into her weakened mind. She tried to speak, but no words would come. She sank back into her oversized pillow and nothing could stop tears of fright forming in her enquiring eyes.

"It's quite alright," intoned Professor McCardle. "I suggest I give you something to make it a little easier. I promise I will wake you as soon as we have some more news."

Celia half nodded her head and closed her eyes. A nurse brought her a glass of water and two oval-shaped pills in a porcelain dish. Celia took the pills, swilled the water around her mouth and swallowed. She felt nothing but resignation. Opening her eyes momentarily, she saw no sign of

Professor McCardle, just an attentive nurse smiling at her. Then she drifted off, to dream fitfully of bombs, fire, young love and her home away from the mayhem of London.

Several hours later, Celia was gently shaken awake. Professor McCardle, true to his word, had returned to bring her his recent news.

"Mrs. Lavenham," he stated quietly, "we are pretty sure we've located your son. He was taken to The London Hospital and is now in intensive care. He seems to be stable, in spite of his traumatic introduction to the world. If you feel up to it, I see no reason why you shouldn't go to see him as soon as we can arrange transport. My preference would be for you to stay with us for a few more days following your difficult birth. However, in view of the circumstance, and as long as you agree to travel by ambulance and with one of our staff to accompany you, I will agree to release you."

"Thank you, Professor, that would be wonderful. I very much appreciate everything you have done, but it would be thrilling to be with my son as soon as possible."

"Right. I will make the arrangements but in the meanwhile please continue to rest."

Celia's body visibly relaxed, but she still felt that sharp dagger of concern. What if he were badly injured? What if his little body had been starved of essential oxygen and other nutrients overnight?

What will he look like? Will he be scarred permanently? Will he have internal injuries? What about his tiny brain? Will he be affected by the trauma he must have suffered? Celia had these and other more frightening cares troubling her as she lay waiting. Once again, she drifted into an unsettled sleep. This time her dreaming illusions were of tiny charred bodies, of scarred limbs, and of a bright nursery, but strangely empty.

She woke with a shudder, relieved to leave her nightmares behind. The sun now streamed through the window, with fresh flowers welcoming the day. The same smiling nurse, whom she recognized from the previous night, helped her to dress. Her clothing and personal belongings were packed into two smart, matching, leather-bound suitcases. Celia was escorted to the lift, and then taken to the Portland Hospital reception area, where a uniformed driver helped her into the waiting ambulance. The nurse who had been with her for the last few hours had now pulled on a bright red cloak and was encouraging Celia to lean on her for support. Celia was grateful and on the ambulance journey learned that Nurse Davies was originally from West Wales, an area she knew well from family holidays, The ambulance was driven with care, in part to minimize any discomfort for its occupants, but also because of the state of the roads. Overnight, debris had been scattered around. It was as if some unseen hand had randomly sown not seeds, but pieces of masonry, tarmac and other rubble.

The ambulance pulled up outside the doors where two babies had been carried in much earlier that day. Nurse Davies helped Celia out and together they walked purposefully towards the reception area.

"Nurse Davies, would you mind taking over for the moment? All I want to do is see my son, but I still feel a little delicate, so if you could just…."

"Of course. Leave it to me. I'll find out just where he is and then we can go up together."

"Your so kind," Celia sighed, and she collapsed into a nearby chair, grateful she had an understanding person with her at this difficult time.

*   *   *   *   *

Maggie Breakwell eventually found her way to the front door of The London Hospital and immediately went to paediatric intensive care unit on the second floor. She knew the hospital well, having spent nearly two years training there along with other associated hospitals.

As she turned the corner at the top of the stairs, a nurse she knew by sight, if not by name, greeted her.

"Can I help," she said, "Hang on, don't I recognize you?"

"Nurse Breakwell, Maggie replied, "I did two rotations here earlier in the war."

"Of course, well how you?"

Maggie ignored the pleasantries and asked quietly, "I believe two babies, both boys, were brought in here last night. They had been injured in a bomb blast over at Great Ormond Street."

"But of course, the twins. They came in at about five hours ago. You're heading in the right direction. Just along the corridor on the left."

"Twins," interrupted Maggie, "you said they were twins!"

"They might as well be. Impossible to tell them apart. No records came with them. Nothing. Not even a name for either of the poor little mites. It'll be a miracle if they survive. Did you nurse them at Great Ormond Street?"

Maggie turned away, just nodding her thanks to the nurse in her urgency, and rushed on.

She almost ran through the door marked 'Intensive Care' and was momentarily checked by an austere looking nurse, who rose to meet her.

"Can I help?"

"My baby, my baby, where is he," Maggie gasped.

"The only babies we have here are the two little ones brought in this morning after the bomb blast, but surely…"

Maggie interrupted by running to the two incubators in the middle of the room.

"One of them's mine," she screamed and sat down between the two children.

The two babies both had multiple leads trailing from their cots and both had oxygen masks over the lower half of their faces. They wore identical clothes – cotton bonnets, mittens and tiny all-in-one garments. This swaddling hid the worst of their injuries and Maggie gazed rapturously from one to the other. In her heart of hearts she was desperate to know which baby was hers. Reason prevailed and in truth she was unable to distinguish one from the other. She could just make out a gorgeous pair of blue eyes below the lightest of blond down poking out from their bonnets.

She sighed in affection combined with exasperation, but the smart lady who breezed into the room interrupted her reverie.

Maggie looked up, smiled wanly and then returned her loving gaze to the two babies.

"Which one is mine?" Celia enquired to no one in particular.

This was the moment; the dreadful moment in time that seemed to last for ever; that eternal moment both women would never forget. The moment of uncertainty; the moment of doubt; the moment of perception. For both it was impossible for this moment to be one of acceptance. Only time had the power to convert anxiety into acceptance. But this was not the time.

The austere nurse, who had been observing the situation from a respectful distance, now felt she could intervene.

"I wonder if it would be helpful if we all introduced each other?" she enquired. "I am Nurse Tromans, currently responsible for the care of the little ones, and you are ladies are?"

Celia was the first to reply. "Celia Lavenham. My baby was born yesterday and I was told that he was being cared for here, in this hospital."

"And I am Maggie Breakwell. I'm in exactly the same situation."

"So," interjected Nurse Tromans, "both of your babies must have been at Great Ormond Street overnight and, thank God, both survived the terrible bombing there."

"Exactly," responded Celia, somewhat curtly.

Maggie initially nodded, but then added, "Is there much hope?"

Nurse Tromans was cautious in her assessment, but decided to be honest.

"Both babies have been through significant trauma from the bombing, complicated by the fact that all medical records on the fourth floor were destroyed. We had no detail of their situation before the bomb hit. Perhaps both of you would be able to assist, in spite of both of you only giving birth so recently?"

"My little boy was born by Caesarian section at the Portland and was about three weeks premature," stated Celia, rather flatly. "I was told that he was going to Great Ormond Street as he needed to be in a special incubator for a while."

"I was in a rather different situation, Maggie said quietly. " I was overdue and my little boy was at Great Ormond Street because he was jaundiced and needed specialist equipment."

"So was he born there?" Nurse Tromans enquired.

"No," Maggie replied, "he was born at a nursing home in Hindhead."

"I see," said Nurse Tromans, not fully understanding the situation. She then tried to review the situation.

"So both your boys were at Great Ormond Street. They came here after they were rescued from the wreckage of the bomb, and we seem to have no record of which of the little fellows belongs to each of you. Can either of you help me here? Were there any form of identity marks or anything that could help tell which child is yours? Both mothers shook their heads in disbelief. The shock of such a situation fanned the flames of doubt. The two women slowly began to appreciate the dramatic consequences of their predicament. How could this be? How could any child, let alone their own first born sons, be subjected to this state of unknowing?

Nurse Tromans was equally at a loss, but she recovered quickly enough to try her best at suggesting a way forward.

"For now," she said, "we all need to concentrate on getting them over their injuries. As they recover, as I'm sure they will, we may find some clues to their true identities. The fact that one was prep and the other late may well give us a clue. Meanwhile, I suggest that both of you stay nearby as long as you can. You both have been through a hard time and need to build up your own strength. In view of the bombing in this part of London, we cannot offer you accommodation in the hospital here, but you are more than welcome to come in every day. At this stage there is nothing you can do to help them, but I can assure you they'll receive the best possible care. It's impossible to give a precise time scale, but I am confident that within a couple of weeks, they should both be well enough for you to feed them yourselves."

Both Maggie and Celia were distraught at the idea of leaving their babies in the care of the hospital. Their recent experiences gave them little cause for confidence, but realism prevailed. With a final loving look at the two babies, encased in their strange, artificial surroundings, they both left the room. The room that contained their hopes and their dreams; the room of uncertainties, of a future unknown, of survival wrapped in optimism. Most of all, it was a room full of potential, of possibility, of opportunity. No one could predict the impact that these two babies would one day have on the world. This was of a time yet to come.

As the two women went down the stairs, Maggie suggested that they spent a moment together in the teashop run by the League of Friends on the ground floor. Celia was at first unsure, but on reflection she relented and very soon they found themselves seated together at a small table in the corner of the tearoom. Their conversation was stilted because the situation was so difficult for them both to comprehend. They learned a little of each other's background. Celia explained that she was very soon hoping to be married. This came as a shock to Maggie. She had assumed that Lavenham was Celia's married name.

"No," confided Celia. "My fianc e has been working especially hard over the last few months and then when I became pregnant, it was felt best to wait. My family was distraught at the news of the baby, but now I hope we can settle down quickly and get married next year. And you?"

Maggie hesitated, but felt able share a little of her story with Celia.

"I met a boy about a year ago and we soon fell very much in love."

"So will you get married soon?" Celia asked.

"It's a little complicated," Maggie replied. "My situation is far from straight forward."

Celia sensed that it would not be wise to pursue things further, so changed the subject.

"Will you be staying locally while the babies recover?" she enquired, and then without waiting for an answer added, "I shall be living with my parents in Surrey and travel up to London whenever I can."

Maggie felt able to confide a little in Celia and answered her question honestly, but with a degree of caution.

"I will be living locally, in one of the hostels for nurses, at least until I can take the baby home."

"I'm sorry," said Celia, "I had no idea you were a nurse."

"Well not quite," Maggie corrected gently, "I just need to finish my training and then I'll be fully qualified."

"I see," said Celia, "will that take long?"

"Actually, no," Maggie replied. "In fact I take my final exams very soon."

Celia was keen to probe deeper, but felt this was not the time.

"Do we need to make any arrangements for visiting the babies?" Celia asked. "I'm sure we could get a progress report every day and I will certainly be coming to town as often as possible."

Maggie sensed that 'as often as possible' did not necessarily mean every day and she found this strangely calming. It wasn't that Maggie disliked Celia; there had not been time to form such an opinion. It was just that she found the idea of the two of them being side by side with their babies in that tiny room slightly unsettling.

"In view of the travelling," announced Celia breezily, "I shall probably visit them in the afternoon."

Maggie said nothing, but knew that as her study leave gave her flexibility, she would try her best to see the children every morning. As this thought went through her head, the word 'children' brought everything into focus.

"Celia," she said, looking her straight in the eye, "how can we possibly resolve which child is ours?"

"I'm sorry, Maggie, but I just can't see a way forward just now. From what you said, your boy was late and mine was early. This is bound to help. I can only think that we must take Nurse Tromans' advice."

Maggie was unconvinced that the timing of their births would make a great deal of difference, especially as the two boys were recovering in intensive care.

"But Celia," Maggie replied, "Nurse Tromans didn't actually give us any advice. She simply said that in time we might be able to start feeding the babies ourselves."

Celia thought for a moment. "Then perhaps this will be the answer. Perhaps one of the babies will respond better than the other. I just don't know. I'm as confused as you."

Maggie's training as a nurse left her with serious doubts, but she knew she had little option. Perhaps time would be her friend and for the moment the two mothers had little else to offer.

Over the next two weeks, Maggie visited 'the twins' as they were known at the hospital on a daily basis. By the end of the second week, it was agreed that their injuries had healed sufficiently for them to be taken out of their little incubators. Maggie took great joy in cuddling them both and less than a week later she was able to feed them herself. As first one, then the other was put to her breast. She loved the feeling of the gentle sucking on her nipples. It was for her a heavenly experience; she delighted in the sheer ecstasy of true motherhood. She felt a lightening of the soul, a wonderment. Deep down, in these brief moments, she could detect the unmistakable feeling of nothing short of reverence. Every day, it was becoming harder for Maggie to leave the helpless babies. With her exams approaching and the grim reality of her uncertain future, she knew that she had little choice.

Celia also came to visit the boys periodically and would feed them as best she could. At first she struggled, but in time, and with the patient support of Nurse Tromans as her tutor, she also gained immense satisfaction in seeing the boys thrive.

It was a slow process, but five weeks after their birth, both boys were ready to leave the hospital. Their physical state had changed dramatically since they were admitted. Their injuries had almost healed and no longer needed dressing. Both boys were now more animated and responsive. Their earlier lassitude, due largely to the traumas of their births, had disappeared. Although still small, the staff at the hospital were confident that the two miracles were ready for the next stage in life's journey. A journey away from the necessary care of the children's ward. A journey into the exclusive care of their mothers.

There was, however, still the overriding issue that troubled the minds of both mothers. The boys still looked identical. There wasn't a dimple or a freckle that could set them apart. Hospital records had been checked and double-checked. It was simply impossible to tell which baby belonged to which mother. It was an insolvable dilemma. An enigma worthy of a Greek tragedy or a Shakespearian play. It was a foretaste of the future.

Maggie was more excited than usual when she next visited the babies. She had sat her last exam the day before and was looking forward immensely to spending more time with the boys. She happily turned into the corridor on the second floor to be greeted by a tall, middle-aged doctor, whose serious face caused Maggie's heart to miss a beat.

"Miss Breakwell," he said in a voice which betrayed no emotion, "I wonder if you could come with me for a moment?'

"The babies," Maggie cried in alarm, "are they both alright?"

The doctor took her arm and steered her gently but firmly into the family room.

"Please sit down," he requested.

Maggie, now visibly in the early stages of shock, could do little but agree to the request.

"As far as we know, the babies are fine. You can be assured of that. We do, however, have a serious issue on our hands."

Maggie became immobile. She knew that words like 'serious issue' were usually a foretaste of doom. She could do little but watch the doctor's lips move, taking in very little of what he was saying.

"Miss Breakwell, do you understand what I am saying?"

"I'm sorry. I'm having some difficulty. Could you just start from the beginning?"

"I'm afraid the hospital must take some responsibility. It is most unfortunate."

"Unfortunate, but what…"

The doctor now took a different approach. "Perhaps you would like to come in and see your boy?"

"My boy, but yes, but how do you know?"

"This is the issue, Miss Breakwell. No one can actually know. It's just that we are left with no choice."

"No choice. I'm sorry but I just don't understand."

"Miss Breakwell, the fact is that Mrs. Lavenham has taken the other child. As I said before, we are deeply sorry. She took it upon herself to choose one of the babies and without any form of consultation, took the child away from the hospital. As you are aware, we had no records on either of the children, beyond their mothers, and Mrs. Lavenham left no forwarding address. Assuming that she is still in the country, a reasonable assumption in war time, then it may be possible to trace her."

"How do you propose to do that, doctor," Maggie enquired, still not grasping the full significance of what had happened.

"She may register in a postnatal clinic or register the birth of the baby, but I concede that tracing her will be almost impossible at this time."

"So," said Maggie, now starting to appreciate what had been said, "The baby that is left will be registered as mine, even though none of us can be sure it really is my baby."

The doctor looked relieved and added, "This seems to be the only option, in fact the best option."

Maggie's disquiet at this turn of events dissolved the moment she looked in on the remaining baby. As she peered over the side of the cot, Maggie detected what could only have been the start of a smile. This was the infant's first gesture of warmth, his first recognition; his very first bond with the adult who was to care for him as he grew into maturity. It was enough. Maggie was entranced, delighted and for the second time in a year, in love.

Maggie ceased to care about the way her baby boy had become hers. To her it was providence. She knew she would have no regrets. Providence, for Maggie, had presented perfection She was overjoyed and showed her love in the most practical of ways. She put her child, her very own child, once more to her breast.

Now he was hers, she could name him. "I will call him David," she said to herself, "it means the one beloved of one." She often reflected on this choice. David was one of two, and in his young life could only be loved by one – herself. It was sufficient.

Arrangements to leave the hospital, mother and baby, were quickly made,

While waiting for a taxi to take her and her lovely baby home, Maggie had a last cup of tea in the cafe of the League of Friends on ground floor.

In the opposite corner were the two people who had brought the two babies to The London Hospital only five weeks previously. Dr. Harry Ames and Nurse Clare Bradley were enjoying each other's company, not for the first time.

"You know, "said Harry Ames, "I still cannot get that scar out of my mind."

Clare, somewhat distractedly, asked him what he was talking about.

"Don't you remember, Clare? The two babies we brought here during the night of the bomb at Great Ormond Street. I asked to examine them a couple of weeks ago as you and I had seen them earlier in such a pitiful state. They were both coming along famously. The strange thing was that one of them had a scar on the inside of his right foot. It hadn't healed like their other injuries. It was almost as if it had happened since they came to The London. It just didn't seem right. It doesn't make sense."

Clare put her hand gently on Dr. Ames' arm. "You worry too much Harry. Come on, or we'll be late for our shift."

Before Maggie could travel to her parents' home in Gloucester, she had one last task to do. It meant making the tedious journey to Haslemere in Surrey. She knew the experience would be uncomfortable but necessary.

CHAPTER 5
CERTIFICATES

Maggie Breakwell had just forty-two days to register the birth of her baby. Time was running out, but she had little choice in the matter. She'd been given a small carrycot and David was wrapped in a light cotton blanket, quite sufficient for the warm weather of that July morning. She took the mid morning train from Waterloo Station and arrived at Haslemere forty minutes later. The journey was made easier by the friendly help given by other passengers on the train. She was encouraged by the complimentary comments about her new baby. For Maggie, this totally new experience was one she couldn't help but enjoy. It was the first public recognition of her private thoughts. She smiled in thanks when anyone commented on her pretty baby; her inward smile was much deeper, more profound. The past had given her moments of pride – exam results, swimming galas, nursing prizes – but this was special. This was no longer a personal pride in transitory achievements. This was something unfathomable, private, and rare. He was a living part of her flesh. The baby was a vital extension of herself.

It was a short walk to the High Street in Haslemere from the railway station. The tired, brick built Register Office was up a short flight of cold, stone steps. Maggie struggled to open the swing doors; those same doors that guarded the records of births, deaths and marriages in the surrounding area. A tall man, dressed in a black suit, seeing her plight, held the door open. With the carrycot ahead, she stepped into the dimly lit edifice. Maggie reflected on how all of life was cocooned in this austere building. She was there to register a life of the future. The man just leaving looked as though his task had been far more final. He had probably been registering a life spent. Maggie wondered if it had been a life spent in glory or in shame? A life spent in service or in treachery? A life of distinction or of reticence? She would never know. Looking down at her own child, she couldn't help but wonder for him. Had he a future of honour or of infamy? All she had were her hopes. For now, it was enough.

The spacious lobby had a number of un-named, but numbered doors. A small, hinged window was opened from within. A woman of an undistinguishable age looked out at Maggie and raised enquiring eyebrows.

"Can I help," came a bored voice. "Oh I see you have a baby. You need to go to room number three. There should be someone there to take your details."

With that the window closed again and Maggie was, once more, left alone. Alone with her thoughts and her beautiful baby. She walked the few steps to room three and knocked on the door.

"Come!" came from within. Maggie opened the door to reveal standard utility furniture, so typical of the civil service. From behind a dark mahogany desk, a middle-aged man stood up and came over to help her with the baby. His limp was pronounced and Maggie felt a degree of sympathy. Here was a man, either wounded in conflict or who couldn't fight for his country because of a previous injury. Maggie smiled and in so doing wondered why she even had such thoughts. For a moment her attention was elsewhere. It was for a man overseas; a man fighting for his country. She momentarily prayed that this man was not injured, not like the one walking towards her.

"Do sit down," he said kindly, taking the carrycot from her.

"Thank you," Maggie replied, "it's been quite hard carrying him in this heat."

"Can I get you a drink? Water perhaps, or even tea? I'm told tea is very refreshing on a hot day."

"That would be wonderful."

"I'm afraid the milk is only powdered, but I've got used to it by now."

"Perfect," said Maggie, "that would be lovely."

The official busied himself making tea, to Maggie's surprise right in front of her.

"Yes, we used to have a small canteen here before the war, but you know how things are. I find it easier just to sort out drinks for myself. I'm sorry, I haven't introduced myself. Jennings. District Registrar. And you are?"

"Maggie Clarke. My baby was born nearby in Hindhead."

The registrar gave Maggie her tea and apologized for the lack of sugar. Putting his own on top of a four-draw filing cabinet, he opened one of the top drawers.

"Then you'll be here to register the little one, I assume."

"Please."

"Should be pretty straight forward. I assume you've all the relevant documents."

"I believe so," said Maggie, opening her handbag.

The registrar took out a file and sat down behind his desk. He carefully moved his tea, placing it on an old beer mat to his right. He took a fountain pen from his inside right pocket. For some reason Maggie noticed he continued to use his left hand, not just to reach his pen, but also to write. His movements were slow and deliberate, yet with a gentle touch. Maggie wondered if his gentle touch extended to others; a wife perhaps, children or even a lover. The slight scratching of pen on paper interrupted Maggie's curious thoughts.

"Before we start," said the registrar, "I do need to remind you that it is an offence for any of the particulars on this certificate to be false. If this were to be the case, then you would be liable to prosecution. I'm sorry if this all sounds a little harsh, but it is my duty to tell you. Do you understand?"

"Of course, Maggie replied, not quite understanding why she should feel a little nervous.

"Good, then let's start. I've already filled in the year and the registration district of Surrey South Western. The birth was in the sub-district of Haslemere in the County of Surrey. When and where was the baby born?"

"Twenty fourth of June, at The Grange Maternity Home, Hindhead."

At this, the registrar raised his head momentarily.

"The Grange," he said, "how was it?"

Maggie was inclined to relate her dismal experiences, but chose to put them in the past.

"Acceptable," she said.

"I see," came the unconvincing reply.

"Do you have a name for the child as yet?"

"David, she replied.

"Just David?"

"Yes, for the moment."

"It's not a problem. If you choose to add any other names, it can be done later. A strange thing to ask in view of the name, but I assume he's a boy?"

"Yes"

"And the name and surname of the father?"

Maggie hesitated. She knew the question could not be avoided, but it still left a slight chill and a note of anxiety.

"I prefer not to say."

The registrar's pen was raised momentarily. He looked up from the certificate he was completing so laboriously.

"Slightly unusual," he said, "but totally admissible. Shall we move on? Your name, surname, maiden name and address?"

"Maggie Clarke. My maiden name was Breakwell."

The registrar wrote with care. 'Maggie Clarke formerly Breakwell'

"And your address?"

"Garthfell, 199, Elm Road, Gloucester."

The registrar continued to write and then looked up again.

"Can I assume you wish to leave the occupation of the father blank, Mrs. Clarke?

"Please. Do you need my occupation?'

"No, that's not necessary. The next box is for your signature. I will repeat your address here and leave space at the top for your signature. Then I date it, today the fourth of August 1944 and sign it in the last box. There, done."

He carefully placed a large piece of blotting paper over the certificate and applied gentle pressure from the right to left, still using his left hand. Maggie's thoughts went back to his delicate touch. Would any man show this degree of sensitivity to her? He lifted the blotting paper, checked that all was well and walked round the table with the certificate.

"If you would sign just here," he said, pointing to the appropriate box.

Maggie took his pen. It was more than a signature. It was a life-long commitment. She was signing to show the world that this was her child. It was a document of his birth. Unknowingly she shuddered. For a fleeting moment, her mind returned to that room in the hospital. The room where the tall doctor with the serious face had told her about the one remaining child. The one she had just registered as hers. Jumbled up with these thoughts were the words of the registrar. Her mind replayed 'false, offence and prosecution', but such thoughts could only be destructive, negative, and illusionary. She knew David was hers. How could there be a fragment of doubt.

Maggie, taking a deep breath, signed her name. The deed was done. It was over. She visibly relaxed, turned to the registrar standing by her side and smiled.

"Excellent," he said. "Now you look after that little boy. He's a long way to go in this world and when this war is over, things have got to improve. I wish you both well. Before you go, can I just have a closer look at him?"

Maggie was a little surprised at this sudden interest, but happily agreed. The registrar lifted David up from his carrycot, held him with slightly bent arms, gave him a long searching look and carefully placed him back in the cot.

"He'll be fine," he added. "Have a safe journey home, Mrs. Clarke."

With that, this gentle man carried the cot out of the room, shook Maggie by the hand and returned to his office.

Maggie was strangely moved. She walked back to the station with a certain lightness in her step and in her mood. She leant back in the relative comfort of her seat in the third class compartment and took out the certificate. She looked at his signature, but it was slightly smudged and the name indistinct. It was probably for the best.

*   *   *   *   *

For Celia, things were very different. Dr. Willard Boulton, who so unstintingly had rescued the two babies from the fire, had kept his promise to marry Celia. They had been engaged a month before Celia's baby was born. Before that, they hadn't seen each other for some time. The difficulty of travel and communication during the war was a factor in their separation. Willard's intensive clinical schedule, coupled with his final examinations was usually given as the main reason. Willard graduated from medical school in September 1944 and their marriage was set for early April of the next year. Immediately after graduation, Willard enlisted in the Royal Army Medical Corps and was sent for training at Church Crookham in Hampshire for six months. Celia was far from happy that Willard had spent so little time with her, but accepted that someone with Willard's skill and training was essential in these final stages of the war. He was granted leave to be married as planned, with all the arrangements being left to Celia.

Celia struggled with the demands of a young baby and planning their wedding. Her parents were generally supportive, but in view of the situation tried to keep Celia and the baby out of sight until after the wedding. It was not a happy time. The way the war had dragged on meant that the fripperies of a wedding day were abandoned. Even the arrangements for the wedding reception were kept to a minimum, especially with food and petrol being in such short supply. They were married in a small church near Celia's home in Surrey. A few, carefully selected guests attended. Those close to the family, the ones aware of the baby, were invited, but sworn to keep the unfortunate sequence of events to themselves. Few came from a distance. Those who did were totally unaware of the child, now some nine months old. A nanny, who came down from London for the occasion, looked after him on the day of the wedding. In rural Surrey, it was still considered inexcusable for a woman to have a child before marriage. Celia was all too aware of the local strength of feeling. Marriage would soften this, but far better just to allow things to settle before introducing her baby to the world at large.

Dr. Boulton had now fully recovered from the injuries inflicted in rescuing the two babies. His strong, but boyish looks had returned. The muscular tone when playing rugby for the college was still in the past. This was in part due to the wartime rationing, but mainly as the opportunity for exercise was limited during his current training. At the wedding, he looked resplendent in his military dress uniform. The dark blue coat and trousers were faced in a dull cherry colour, worn exclusively by the Royal Army Medical Corps. His great friend and colleague, Jim Driver, was Willard's best man. Jim was also dressed in the same military uniform and, together with Willard, they made a handsome pair. Jim had graduated at the London Medical School at the same time as Willard and they had enlisted together. In the past, the two of them had worked, drunk and played rugby together. It seemed perfectly natural that they should join the army as soon as they qualified. They were both looking forward to making their own contributions to fighting the foreign tyranny. The optimistic intelligence that the war was coming to an end did nothing to dampen their enthusiasm for action. Celia and Willard decided, quite understandably, to delay any prospect of a honeymoon until after the war. They both accepted the inevitable time of separation. Two days after the wedding, Willard, with his best man Jim, returned to active duty. The two men went to war as many of their comrades and friends had done so bravely and without question. They had both been drafted to one of the most horrific assignments outside of direct, armed conflict. They were sent with a large medical team to a place in Northern Germany. It meant nothing to them. It was called Bergen-Belsen.

CHAPTER 6
LIBERATION

Willard and Jim arrived at Bergen-Belsen on April 16th 1945, the day after it had been liberated by the British and Canadian troops. The officer commanding the camp, Brigadier Glyn Hughes, met them at the gates. He warned them, they were about to witness some of the most loathsome horrors they were ever likely to see. This hell on earth was discovered, almost by accident. An SAS officer and his driver had been on a reconnaissance mission in the heavily wooded area. The troops from the 11th Armoured Division were still in the early stages of trying to assess the squalid conditions in the camp. None of the soldiers had seen an SS concentration camp before. Most could not begin to appreciate the despicable conditions all around them. It had taken time for the pitiable inmates to understand what was happening as the gates of despair opened. Soon the words liberation and freedom were being spoken in hushed tones of disbelief by the scarred and cracked lips of the survivors.

As the two doctors walked, with some trepidation, into the camp, they were numbed by the horrors seen all around them. They were surrounded by thousands of grotesquely emaciated bodies, most in the final stages of a miserable and prolonged death. It was impossible to register the revulsion that met their incomprehensible gaze. The two men wept openly, holding each other to stop them collapsing on to the corrupt soil around them. Together they cursed the depravity of man. Dropping to their knees, they cried out to the unseen God who allowed such things to happen. Every one of their senses was tainted with the obscenity of death. The stench of atrophy forced itself unwillingly into Willard's lungs. He choked as his gut emptied on the evil ground. His vomit mixed with the odious faeces of a thousand inmates who were unable to move to a place of privacy. Tens of thousands of men and women had succumbed to a grotesque imitation of Dante's inferno. But such appearance was illusionary. These were far from Dante's hellish souls who had rejected spiritual values by yielding to violence. These poor souls had never perverted their human intellect by wicked acts against their fellow men. These were the blameless ones. They had been enmeshed in the brutalizing lunacy of Aryan supremacy.

Most were no longer capable of crying. Tears were impossible for those deprived of water or food for days, weeks, and months. Their dehydrated and starved bodies failed to respond to what was happening around them. They could only stare; a vacant, silent, an unbelieving stare at the few, concerned soldiers who looked on with undisguised horror. As Willard and Jim continued to walk deeper into the camp, they were both struck by another ever-present feature. It was the quiet. There were thousands of deathly mortals in this God-forsaken place, but there was no sound. The few, who could move or walk, did so in complete silence. Those who tried to walk did so with a slow, meandering gait. It was if they were sleep walking. Sleep walking to oblivion. Soundless, the world seemed to be coming to a hesitant but inevitable stop. The whole place was enveloped in a monochrome haze. There was no colour. Everything was dull. The filthy, striped clothes worn by the inmates formed an image of dismal monotony. The earth was bare and lifeless. Even the April sun, trying its best to warm the acres of pain, could do nothing to lift the gloom. No other place on earth, so full of people, could ever be so barren.

Jim and Willard had seen death and destruction during their time in the blitz. They had seen death come quickly. They had seen death come painfully. They had seen death come between clean sheets and in hospital corridors. They had seen death come on the operating table and in the quiet of homes for old people. This was different. They had never seen death by starvation, by disease, by cruelty and by neglect. The biggest difference, by far, was the scale of the wickedness they were seeing with their own eyes. Never had the two young doctors witnessed such a depth of human depravity. Witness to such loathsome treatment of human beings was almost too much for them both. They felt unable to express their mutual disgust. Their normally outgoing personalities mutated into introspection and almost to ravages of despair. Dead and dying men, women and, sadder still, children, covered acres of the polluted land. In several cases it was impossible to tell the difference between men and women, such was their emaciated state. The dead lay not just next to the dying. The dying were resting their heads and feeble limbs on the dead. They were unable to move, frozen in an aimless state of being.

The worst was the wooden huts, surrounded by barbed wire. Built to house some 60 people, each hut contained well over 400 skeletal mannequins of mankind. The doors were open, but no one moved. It was almost impossible to get into the huts as the tangled bodies were piled up, five or six deep. Such was the heinous sight that at first the wooden bunks were indistinguishable from the mound of putrid and decaying humanity. None wore clothes and most were dead. Yet in the piles of human bones, wallowing in their own vomit, faeces and urine, Willard and Jim found a few still alive - just. It was a twitch of a hand, a blink of an eye, a cough, or bowels emptying. These were the signs the two doctors sought when trying to determine life.

It was these tiny vestiges of hope that gave Willard and Jim the will to control their anger and disgust at the loss of humanity. They threw themselves willingly into the relief effort.

In spite of the unimaginable stench from these huts, the fetid bodies were slowly moved to the burying pits. The scarce survivors in the huts were mostly suffering from dysentery, leaving them unable to move. Willard and Jim examined the few living inmates and quickly established that all were ridden with lice. Every part of their miserable bodies was covered with the tiny creatures, causing painful sores and spreading infection even further. Typhus, tuberculosis and typhoid fever were everywhere. Little could be done at first to contain these awful diseases. Every effort was made to move the barely living from this epicenter of death.

Then came the sound; a sound that Willard would never forget. It was the mewing of black kites as they circled overhead. The kites knew no humanity; the kites saw nothing but carrion. Yet it was the kites that jolted Willard and Jim out of their inanimate despair. The kites were acting without compassion and care. Yet the same truly human qualities gave purpose to these soldiers and doctors. They replaced immobility with action.

Their initial revulsion was replaced by purposeful commitment to the gruesome task ahead of them. On that first day in Bergen-Belsen they found over 13,000 unburied bodies. The task of placing them in mass graves was given, with reluctance, to any remaining captured Nazi troops. These defeated guards dragged the bodies to their final resting places in the unwelcome ground. The few living inmates watched with undisguised contempt.

Willard and Jim now took over the main task of preventing further death, but the state of the inmates made this almost impossible. Typhus was now the main killer. In spite of every effort to provide water and any army rations, the death continued. Five hundred were dying daily. They were sadly too ill to respond to any effort to provide assistance.

For those still alive, Willard and Jim set up a form of human laundry. It was designed to make every effort eliminate the scourge of lice. It was little more than a trestle table surrounded by two piles of clothing. One was the pile of discarded clothes to be burned. The other was fresh clothing, thankfully now free of the dreaded insects. Everyone was soaked in water, deloused and cleaned as best they could. These miserable, exhausted specimens were little more than empty shells of emaciation. The white covering of delousing powder gave each one a skeletal spectral appearance. They left the human laundry looking like shambling ghosts. But they were alive. It was only then that they were moved away from the field of despair. Jim and Willard had established a temporary hospital in the nearby Wehrmacht barracks. These buildings were far from adequate, but moving these sad but grateful people away from the main camp gave them a new beginning. They managed, with the help of the many medical students who had arrived from London hospitals, to move almost 29,000 survivors to the old barracks over a period of four weeks. For the first time in years, those people, who had faced and experienced death on a daily basis, were now given the feeble promise of optimism.

Willard walked with immense care on the few square yards unoccupied by the ghostly apparitions of abject misery. He was looking for hope, but there was none. By far the worst was the babies. It was incredible to imagine that babies had been born in this hell, but the evidence was there in front of him. Tiny bundles of stinking, skeletal tissue were hardly distinguishable from the rags surrounding them. Here was the silhouette of a child; a child yet to cast a single shadow on this tormented earth. A pitiful figure crawled up to Jim, kissed his boots and thrust a bundle into his arms. Jim was unable to tell whether the gift was from a man or a woman. The living skeleton said just one word, "Please" before moving away. Jim unwrapped the bundle with care and was horrified to see a baby. A child, clearly no more than a week old, but with ghastly green skin and long since dead. No child was ever found alive in Bergen-Belsen. Jim's thoughts were with the mother. He struggled to imagine how a woman, so far gone in pregnancy, could have been forced to march into this vision of hell.

To add to the horrors of Bergen-Belsen, the Nazis attacked with four warplanes, strafing the helpless survivors. The attack killed three of the medical students brought out from London. Jim struggled to understand this willful act of aggression. He was unable to accept how such a futile act could be inflicted on a defenceless camp, where every day hundreds of people were dying of disease and starvation. Jim took personal responsibility to write to the families of the three medical students. These young men had volunteered to interrupt their comfortable studies in London to face the torment of Bergen-Belsen. Few of them, when they volunteered to come to Germany, could have had any idea of the horrors they had witnessed.

Jim, although surrounded by death on a minute-by-minute basis, was deeply angered by the merciless killing of these three students. Three young men, just a year or two younger than him and each from his own college, had paid the ultimate price for their simple humanity. Jim was not normally a revengeful man, but at this moment he felt so wronged that he totally lost his normal self-control. Even with his eyes closed, Jim could not stop seeing the staring eyes, the pallid skin, and the haggard yellowish faces of all the people around him. Jim found himself absorbed in a maelstrom of resentment for what he had seen. Whether it was the atrocities of the camp or the air raid he couldn't tell, but he totally lost all restraint. He grabbed a pistol from the store and marched purposefully and unknowingly to where the bodies were being pushed into the graves at the perimeter of the camp. Willard, watching from a distance, took time to register what he was seeing. Then Willard, realizing what his good friend was doing, ran towards him, but couldn't get close enough to intervene. Jim's mind was filled with the image of the dead child pushed into his arms and the three young doctors who had died by a senseless act of cowardly hostility. He lost control. Jim raised his weapon and pointed the muzzle at the back of the nearest SS guard as he bent to shove another poor victim into the pit of the dead. As the safety catch clicked, the guard turned. Facing death, he felt fear but no remorse. He was resigned to his imminent fate.

Willard was aghast, but still distant from his friend, felt impotent. Without thought or understanding Willard found himself shouting to Jim. His words rang out clear and true, silencing the 'mew mew' of the circling kites. "Primum non nocere!" shouted Willard. Jim hesitated, just hearing the strange incantation from afar. His mind registered the strange words and slowly processed what he heard. "Primum non nocere, primum non nocere." His brain unscrambled the words and Jim slowly recognised their meaning. "First, do no harm". It was the basic tenet of the oath he had sworn at the time of his medical graduation. Jim sank to his knees in silent supplication. He pointed the pistol to the ground and fired. Those burying the dead, stopped, turned and stared. The SS guard, so close to death, exhaled a deep sigh and continued his unremitting task.

Willard, still some fifty yards away, raised a single hand to his friend and waited. Jim walked over and the two embraced. Willard gently took the pistol from Jim and together they walked back to the main compound. It was over. It was in the past.

Willard and Jim focussed all their energy on the relief of suffering. It was an impossible task as the few painkillers they brought with them were used up within days. On their third day in the camp a group of the more able inmates raided a pigsty at the edge of the compound. The pigsty was undefended from looting and almost fifty pigs were slaughtered. Some may criticize this action as verging on anarchy. Yet those critics could never appreciate the effect of starvation on these tragic individuals. The sadness is that the act gave little benefit to those in greatest need. The effects of dysentery had caused heir digestive juices to fail. Their stomach linings were like leather and it was impossible to digest the fresh meat the pigs could provide.

Willard and Jim worked tirelessly to save the lives of the ill and dying all around them. Their options were limited because they could only offer army rations, mainly bully beef. They found that people in this state of distress could tolerate very little solid food. They also tried skimmed milk and this was helpful, but still the dying continued at an alarming rate. Willard remembered reading about a rice and sugar mixture, which had been tried out during the Bengal famine two years earlier. He suggested this and although many were too weak to take in anything solid, this proved for many to be a life saver. For those who couldn't eat anything, the doctors tried intravenous feeding. They would set up the solutions in a bag, but as soon as the emaciated inmates saw the needle, they became uncontrollably hysterical. They learned, from those inmates able to speak, that the SS had murdered countless prisoners by lethal injection using petrol. The morbid fear amongst the prisoners of the intravenous needle meant this method of feeding was soon abandoned.

The atrocity of the air raid had damaged the water supply badly, with no prospect of immediate replacement. Without a regular supply of water, dehydration and sanitation continued to be a serious issue. Further pockets of dysentery started to occur throughout the camp. Jim had the idea of pumping water from the nearby River Maisse. Over the next few days, any engineers in the camp were put to use setting up a pipeline to the holding tanks by the kitchen. It was a long job and took two weeks before a regular supply could reach the camp. The health of the inmates deteriorated further and the death toll continued at the same appalling rate.

It was a revolting and onerous task to move the numerous bodies to the mass burial pits. Reluctantly it was agreed that a bulldozer would be used to help push the bodies into their final resting place in the earth. After two days, this barbaric practice was stopped. No-one could countenance the lack of respect shown to the nameless dead by using a machine on the mangled and putrifying corpses.

It was not only the inmates of Bergen-Belsen that were buried in the open graves. Two SS officers committed suicide and were pushed unceremoniously on top of their former prisoners. A further two guards were shot trying to escape and they met the same fate. Some said they were the lucky ones because at least they had a name. Not so the thousands of inmates who were interred in those huge pits of despond. They had no name. The SS had destroyed all records as the allied troops advanced. No distant families could ever put their loved ones to rest, even in the echos of their minds. They were missing. Gone. Remembered, but never given the respect of a personal burial. Their only tombstone was a mound of earth in a far off land.

Jim and Willard, along with the medical students and staff snatched no more than a few hours rest on a daily basis. The work was grim, squalid and offended every aspect of humanity. No person of any rank or religion should be carried to their burial place in a wheelbarrow. They had little choice. Any material, whether a garment or a piece of cloth, was used for warmth or dressing. There was no civility at Bergen-Belsen. The dead were taken as rapidly as possible to the burial grounds just beside the camp. With typhoid rampant, every dead body was moved as quickly as possible to avoid further infection. As they were buried, a small measure of respect was given, but expediency ruled. No individual funerals were possible in those conditions. The remaining Jews, those that cheated death by their own fortune and by the efforts of Willard, Jim and their team, had words for it. They called it 'sclerosa duse', the sclerosis of the soul. They knew there was no choice but to see their family, friends and fellows be treated to an inhuman burial. A burial losing all individuality. A burial without a eulogy. A burial where no mourners would ever gather. No reminiscences would be shared. No time to ponder, reflect, cry and console. Their souls hardened – sclerosa duse.

A week after the camp was liberated, a patrol found a cache of German stores containing tons of potatoes, floor, tinned meat, sugar, cocoa, some grains and even Red Cross parcels. This find gave some hope to those that were still desperate for food. Sadly, as they had found before, this extra food was as of limited value. Most were still too ill to tolerate any solid food. On the same day, some Canadian troops found a damaged bakery in a nearby village, but it took another three weeks to repair. Now, the bread, softened with water, could be tolerated for most of the desperate survivors. It was pitiful to see a meal, normally put out for hedgehogs in winter, could be such a source of comfort.

Willard and Jim, along with the many medical personnel who had recently arrived, worked unceasingly to care for any that could be saved. Dysentary was still the biggest killer. yet in spite of every effort, the unremitting death rate was the same. The barracks that Willard had commandeered just outside the camp, became within weeks the biggest hospital in Europe. It now contained some 13,000 ill and hungry patients. Willard and Jim were both promoted to captain and put in joint overall charge of the hospital.

On May 19th, only one month after Bergen-Belsen was liberated, the process of burning the camp to the ground was started. Jim and Willard watched as a group of soldiers used a modified bren gun carrier to throw flames 20 feet into the huts of indescribable misery. It took little more than two days to finish the grisly job. Only those few buildings still needed as hospital annexes were spared. Some argued that the buildings should remain as a memorial to the atrocities committed there. Of much bigger concern was the prevalence of dysentry and typhoid, Willard and Jim argued that the only way to eliminate these joint scourges was to remove every evidence of the site by burning. The mass graves remained as a memorial to the thousands who died in such inhumane conditions. Those graves were a sad testament to the evil of war. Most especially, they reflected the evil of a nation caught up in the misguided obediance to the Nazi cult of supremacy. The Germans had systematically depersonalised and degraded the occupants of Bergen-Belsen. They had dehumanised them in a cruel and deliberate manner. A manner that few could ever forgive.

Willard resolved at that moment, when the charred embers of the camp were still glowing, to return. One day he would commission a fitting memorial to the lives lost in this place. For Willard and Jim their future was uncertain and unknown. The short time they spent together in that squalid place was to change their attitudes, change their motives and above all to change their lives.

Captain Willard Boulton and Captain Jim Driver were ordered back to Britain and to prepare a full report on their experiences. Their contribution to the medical emergency in Bergen-Belsen was recorded in despatches. They sought no reward and none was given. It meant little to them that the war in Europe was already over. Their small contribution was to live in their minds for ever.

They arrived back in London on June 24th. It was the day that Willard's son, Peter, was exactly one year old.

CHAPTER 7
SEPARATION

Captain William 'Bill' Clarke returned from the war in the Far East in January 1946. He'd been with the 14th Army, the 'forgotten army' under the command of Lieutenant-General William Slim. Final victory over the Japanese was several months after the war had ended in Europe. The men of the 14th Army had fought on, mainly in Burma. It was a campaign that received little publicity. Yet it was probably the bloodiest and most challenging of all operations in the Second World War. The bravest of all in the 14th Army were the Chindits. They haunted the Japanese as 'the green ghosts'. Chindits lived in the jungle behind the enemy lines; they struck in the dark. They carried their wounded with them. They fought a battle unlike any other in the war. Captain Clarke's war was to resupply these brave men. He now lay on his worn and sweat-drenched camp bed, waiting for his name to be listed for the return home. He put down his battered pipe, still alight with the dregs of cheap tobacco. He placed his hands behind his head, contemplated the recent past, and desperate for the restorative powers of sleep.

By 1944 they had fought their way across the Irrawaddy River and driven the Japanese forces back. It had been hard. They had endured insufferable losses. Friends who had been alongside were no more. Captain Clarke twitched in his sleep as he dreamt a vivid dream. A vivid dream of recent memories. Recent memories of pleasure tinged with regret.

'The bombed out buildings were still smoking, competing with the humid vapours rising from the over-heated blackened and defiled ground. The acrid smell of the devastation hung limp in the polluted air. The street was packed with gaunt coolies scurrying to unknown destinations. They touched, they hustled, and they collided. This sea of humanity was awash with people almost fighting for their own little space in the anthill of Mandalay.

Then she appeared. The crowd parted. It deferred to give her the path she demanded. She was a rarity, a Burmese Geisha. She sashayed with a languid poise, in a free-flowing motion, ever forward to her chosen destination. Her kimono was iridescent with every hue of purple, from African violet to a soft lilac. Her jet-black hair was beautifully arranged. She had a lotus flower pinned delicately over her left ear. She stopped at the imposing wrought iron gates, guarded by two brass dragons. She pulled the chain to the bell. It summoned the gatekeeper from deep within the bowels of the imposing mansion. She entered and passed deep into the dark rooms. She stepped carefully over the raised thresholds, raising her kimono, to expose for a moment, her tiny feet.

She was expecting an important client, one whose every need must be satisfied.

But first the foreplay, the chanoya, the ritual of the Burmese tea ceremony.

Everything had been prepared. The room, its floor covered in tatami mats, was sparsely decorated. A simple flower arrangement was on a low table, inlaid with cherry wood. The fragrance of the flowers enhanced the atmosphere and the expectation of what was to follow. The table was set with the most exquisite ceramics, each embossed with seasonal motifs. The soft light from the open window reflected off the gold filigree on the tiles, each one marking the corners of the table. Two, highly embroidered cushions were placed either side of the table.

She knelt and waited.

In the temporary military base, just behind the mansion, the four of them also waited. They were the only four from the platoon that had been together since the 14th army had returned from that terrible defeat in the jungles of Malaya.

They knew the time and the place, but no one knew who was to go. The four, short bamboo sticks were folded inside a grubby handkerchief. It was all they had. In turn they chose and the winner shook hands with the others.

In the mansion, he was led to the room set aside for the ceremony. Outside he washed his hands, a symbolic cleansing of the dust and turmoil of the outside world. As he stepped over the high threshold, he bowed to protect this head from the lintel above. It was taken as a mark of respect and she smiled knowingly.

He knelt and was captivated by the grace of her movements. She took a silk cloth from the sash of her kimono. It was symbolically inspected, folded and unfolded and used to lift the iron kettle from the stove sunk into the floor. She cleaned all the china from the purified water in the iron kettle. With utmost grace, she added a fine powder of green tea to a bowl and whisked it in a series of gentle strokes. She passed him the bowl and a linen napkin, embellished with the same seasonal motifs. He took the bowl, but uncertain, he looked towards her. She cupped her hands and lifted them to her mouth in a gesture that could only mean drink. He then started to pass the bowl back to her but she shook her head and gestured again. She took her napkin and mimicked wiping the bowl. He wiped the bowl and she then held out both her hands towards him. She turned the bowl from where he had wiped it and took a sip of the tea. She wiped her side of the bowl and it was passed back to him. This happened twice more and then she took the kettle again. With slow, delicate movements, everything was washed. She sat in repose for what seemed like an eternity. His eyes closed and he relaxed, enjoying the peace. Peace, which had been so distant over the last few, ghastly months. His eyes opened to the sound of her soft breathing and the sight of her breasts rising and falling within the confines of her kimono.

His eyes closed again but this time it was not the sound of breathing that disturbed him but the rustle of a slight movement. She was standing and was walking slowly towards a hinged partition in the room. She turned to look at him and trailed a single arm in his direction. He followed, taking her hand in his. She led him to another door, hidden behind the room divider. She opened it, let go of his hand, and gestured him to stand in the doorway. A single oil lamp lit the room and as his eyes adjusted, he could see a futon covered in silk brocade. She walked forward no more than three paces, looked back at him briefly, and then turned away. Her kimono dropped to the floor, revealing her flawless skin from the arch of her shoulders to the base of her heels.'

Bill gradually came back to the present. His pipe was where he left it, no longer smouldering. Were these distant memories really regret or something deeper? He, a married man, who had sworn to be faithful. In times of war, many things were different; many things changed, but regret still lingered.

Bill Clarke was lucky, one of the first to be demobilized. He had hoped to spend Christmas with his wife of just three years, but was allocated to the five-week voyage back from Rangoon. In the Burma campaign, leave was restricted to the immediate locality. Most in the 14th Army had not seen Britain in about two years. In the case of Bill Clarke it had been longer. His only leave had been cancelled as he'd been hospitalized with malaria.

On arrival in Southampton, Bill took a train to London and the next day went from Kings Cross straight to Cambridge, where he'd booked a hotel in the centre of town. As the train journeyed north, Bill sighed with pleasure at the anticipation of seeing his wife after so long. His army uniform had been cleaned overnight in London and he wore it with understandable pride. In spite of losing so much weight in Burma, the outfit looked good on him and gave him a distinguished air. His wife, Maggie, now lived in the small village of Witchford, just outside the pretty cathedral town of Ely. The move to Witchford had not been easy and she hoped it would only be temporary. She'd chosen to take an advanced course in midwifery at nearby Cambridge University. At first she thought she'd be able to keep David with her. It was an illusion. The course was structured in such a way that having an 18-month child around, even a reasonably well-behaved one, just wouldn't work. Maggie had little choice. She would have to give up the course or ask her parents to look after David. The arrangement of semi-permanent child minding was far from ideal. Fortunately, Maggie had a much younger sister who just loved to play with David, when she came home from school. The course was only for three months and Maggie was able to get back to Gloucester at weekends. She missed being with David, but knew that there was no other option. She may need to become more independent in her future life.

It was no more than half an hour by bus to get to Cambridge. Maggie was almost numb at the prospect of seeing Bill. She had no idea how this meeting could possibly develop. She had rehearsed her words constantly, but it never seemed remotely right. How could she do this to someone she had once held with such affection? She knew it would cause upset, grief, even recrimination. Her anxiety spilled over into a form of paralysis. When the bus drew to a stop at the main bus station in Cambridge, she just sat there, totally immoveable.

"Terminus, Miss," shouted the driver, looking around at his one remaining passenger, "all change here Miss, unless you're paying to go back."

Maggie's reverie was interrupted by another shout from the driver.

"Are you alright dear," he called out as he started to move from the front of the bus.

"Yes," she replied. "I'm sorry, just a little distracted."

"Well if you're sure," he said kindly and helped her down the steps. "Now you take care," he added, "everything will be fine."

Maggie appreciated the gesture, but was truly terrified at the prospect of the meeting awaiting her. She walked in a trance-like state the short distance to the hotel, every step filling her with increasing dread. As she turned the final corner into Regent Street, she paused. Why go on she thought? Is there no other way? Do I have to tell him like this? But she knew that she owed him this at least. There was no going back. Not now. The Cambridge Arms came into view and her resolve and her pace quickened. She pushed the heavy door open. Before the war, there would have been a uniformed doorman to open this door. Nowadays, most men, at least those that survived, were in a different uniform. Would Bill be in uniform, she pondered as she headed for reception? Her answer came immediately, because he was there. He was thinner, gaunt even, but it was still the same Bill. The Bill she'd married. The Bill she expected to be with for the rest of her life. He smiled. She responded, perhaps a little weakly. They hugged and moved to a quiet alcove next to the library. As they sat together, Bill seemed a little nervous.

"Maggie," he said, 'there is something I need to tell you, something that has been troubling me. While abroad I was unfaithful." He was unable to stop. The words just flowed from his lips like a torrent.

"I was on leave in Mandalay. I just needed company. She meant nothing. I paid for her services."

"Bill, slow down, it's OK," Maggie interrupted, whilst putting her hand on his arm.

"It's of no consequence. I quite understand."

"You do?" said Bill. The relief in his voice was apparent. He responded by putting his other hand on top of hers.

"But Bill, I also have a confession."

Bill was taken aback. This was not what he was expecting.

"A confession, how do you mean?

"I have also been unfaithful, Bill. To you. I'm sorry, but this is far more serious."

Bill looked confused. He straightened up visibly as he looked at Maggie. She detected the beginning of a look of concern on his face.

"While you were away, I fell in love with someone else. I'm sorry but….

"But that's in the past now, surely," Bill exclaimed.

"No, Bill. I'm sorry but it's not that straightforward."

"You mean you're still in love. Is that it?"

"In part, yes," said Maggie, no longer able to look Bill in the eye. " You see he didn't know I was married to you."

"But surely you can put this all behind you now we're back together?"

"It's not that simple, Bill. You see I realize this is terribly unfair to you, but I had a baby."

"You mean it wasn't mine?"

"No Bill, the baby is only 18 months old. He's not yours."

"And this person, your, how can I put it, your lover. Is he involved with you both?"

"No Bill. Once he found I was not free to marry, then things changed. I went home to Mum and Dad soon after the birth and he never wrote."

"Maggie, I just can't take this all in right now. I need time to think. This changes everything. You'll just have to give me time."

He then, surprisingly, changed tack.

"Your parents, what do they think?"

"They were horrified at first. I suspect that Dad may have prevented any contact from the father, if there was any that is."

"I just wish I could understand"

"I'm sorry, Bill. I never expected………"

"Maggie, I'm at a complete loss. It's just too sudden. Yes, too sudden. I need time."

"Of course, Bill. I can't see how we can carry on as things are just now."

Almost as an afterthought, Maggie took off her wedding ring and handed it to Bill.

"Bill, this all feels wrong, but I think it best for you to have this."

Maggie got up. She bent over to kiss Bill on the cheek and turning to one side, he let her. She walked out of the alcove, out of the library, out of the hotel and most likely out of Bill's life.

Bill sat very still. He contemplated the notion of infidelity. Was his one night stand any different from his wife taking a lover? He believed so, but one thing was sure. The consequences were very different. Consequences, which could last a lifetime.

Maggie received the petition for divorce two months later. She didn't contest the fault, which was stated as 'adultery with a person unknown'. The process was uncomfortable and caused Maggie some considerable distress. She recognized that her relationship of over a year ago could be interpreted, at least by Bill and her own family, as totally unacceptable. She still had deep feelings of respect for Bill, but, for now, this was not enough. Her love, the love that gave her a child, was in the past. Maggie struggled with these mixed emotions and knew she would face an uncertain future. Only time could possibly provide the answer. Yet few people in Maggie's difficult position were able to give time alone the chance to reveal its destiny. Time needed to be challenged with action. For Maggie it was giving her newborn child a refuge, a home and a place in a war-torn society, however temporary.

After her brief studies at Cambridge, Maggie had little option than to return to her parents' home in Gloucester. It was not a comfortable time living with disapproving parents, but she had a supportive younger sister who would help out whenever she could. Her sister, Janice, was ten years younger than Maggie and in her final years at the local school. She doted on David, would take him for walks and meet him from the local nursery. Maggie needed the help as she was extending her midwifery qualification to train as a health visitor. It meant a difficult journey by train to Bristol where she had enrolled at the University. Her mother also helped with the growing child and David enjoyed a carefree life, untroubled by the circumstances of his birth. Maggie's father, although a strict disciplinarian, was tolerant of the unusual family situation. His great love was rugby and although his playing days were over, he spent hours every week administering the Gloucester county rugby referees association and the insurance arrangement for all regional clubs.

The house in Elm Road was a typical Victorian semi, sitting alongside a small, suburban diary. The sounds of the diary - the clattering of milk churns - must have been the sounds that young David first associated with his grandparents' small, but tidy, home. Once David was able to walk, he loved to explore every nook and cranny of the house. The solid front door opened onto a bright red, quarry-tiled passage, which ran right through to the dining room near the back of the house. The first room on the right as you moved from the front of the house was a rarely used sitting room. Typical of the 1940s, this room was 'kept for best', although no one seemed sure when 'best' was justified. David just loved this room, as adults hardly ever ventured there. It seemed to be his private domain and although usually quite cold, he loved to examine the little treasures on display. These included a model bear made of wood and lying on its back. Between the paws of the bear was a brass cup. It was quite possibly a souvenir from Bern in Switzerland, representing the bear from which the city was reputedly named. According to the local legend, the founder of the city of Bern vowed to name the city after the first animal he met on the hunt, and this turned out to be a bear. In those days there was still a bear pit in Bern, with two live bears.

On David's second birthday, a parcel came through the post, addressed to him. The parcel had been carefully wrapped in two layers of brown paper, tied with string and sealed with wax over the knots. It was a struggle for David to unwrap this unexpected present and he needed help to loosen the string. To David's amazement it was a beautiful, dark brown bear. It was about fifteen inches tall, covered in soft fur and had a quizzical face. There was no card or note with the bear. Hidden in one ear was a little bell and in the other, rather strangely, a small button. David now had his own bear. He loved this bear and wouldn't be parted from it for days. He took it to the bottom of the garden to show the old, rather portly man, who spent much of his time sitting in a deckchair just over the fence. The old man gave David a juicy plum from his own tree. He insisted David took the plum home to see if his grandparents wanted more. Such was David's enthusiasm to show everyone the plum that his birthday bear was left by the fence. Back at the house, David was mortified at his loss. He cried for his bear, now named Grizzly, and could not be consoled until steps were retraced and Grizzly was found.

Maggie knew the bear was from the Steiff factory in Germany. She was intrigued about the gift from an unknown giver. She thought long and deeply as to who could send such a wonderful and appropriate present to her son. She had no firm conviction. Even if she had, she would, without question, keep it to herself.

One of the other items in the front room, which had a permanent fascination for David, was a large radio receiver. It stood fully four feet high with an intriguing glass panel. Etched into the glass panel were two vertical lines covered with names and numbers. Once switched on, this radio was a source of wonder to young David. By slowly turning a knob in the centre of the radio, he could produce all sorts of sounds. There would be whistling, whooshing, music, songs and speech. It was the singing and spoken word that fascinated David most. Sometimes it was the measured intonation of the news. On other occasions it would be the multiple voices of a play. Once his grandmother watched from the door as David was captivated by the beguiling voices of the duet "Sull'aria... che soave zeffiretto" from The Marriage of Figaro. He was sitting in the chair next to the radio, with his head turned slightly to one side and deep in concentration. That evening, Maggie was told what her mother had seen. She gave an enigmatic smile and said nothing. Her thoughts went back to earlier times before David was born.

The next room off the central corridor was the study belonging to Maggie's father. The long wall was lined with a wonderful selection of fishing rods and reels. In most cases they were fly fishing rods of various vintages and conditions and were hung vertically, spaced about ten inches apart. The large oak desk was always full of papers dealing with Maggie's father's work and many interests. At the back of the desk were six cubbyholes, stuffed with a variety of bills, receipts and other items. On of them contained a bundle of letters. All of them were unopened.

The room at the end of the ground floor corridor was where the family would sit and eat. It was furnished with little more than a table, four dining chairs and two sitting chair either side of the coal fireplace. The fire was stoked with a First World War bayonet, brought back from the front by Maggie's father. David found the bayonet fascinating and would occasionally be given permission to stoke the fire himself, most often with the guiding hand of one of the others. The other thing Maggie's father brought back from the war was his military medal inscribed with 'for valour in the field'. When asked, he was always self-effacingly vague about his medal; usually claiming "they had a few to spare and gave him one." Maggie knew that this wasn't true, but she and her father just left it at that. Certain topics were not to be pursued.

The only other room in the house was a scullery where all the food preparation and cooking took place. It had a large stone sink, used for washing up, laundering clothes and for Mr Breakwell to have his daily shave. The gas geyser just above the sink, with its visible flames was something that young David would watch with interest and concern in equal measure. The spluttering and whooshing of the gas, before it settled down to a more regular hiss was, to David, always unpredictable and a little frightening.

The large garden to the rear of the house was a joy for a two year old. It had various outhouses, including David's favourite room, the woodshed, where his Grandfather would build or mend numerous items of furniture. David didn't know what he was doing, but the smell of a pot of woodworkers' glue was just heaven to the young boy. He loved to just sit and watch as the wood shavings fell on the floor, as the joints were inserted and the clamps were applied.

The garden was also an endless fascination. The fruit trees were largely out of bounds, but in season even a small boy could pick the extensive, south-facing blackberries. It wasn't without its hazards, but David soon learned to choose the berries that were on the edges of the plants and avoid the painful thorns.

The only building that was out of bounds to an inquisitive two year old was the garage. This was mainly because it was only just big enough to house his grandfather's Morris Oxford Bullnose, now over 20 years old. David could hear it leave the garage when his Grandfather went out, usually after a lot of effort with the starting handle. David would wait to hear the low rumble as it returned every evening.

For David, life at his grandparents' home was comfortable and secure. He knew no other. Maggie struggled with the responsibilities of looking after him, but survived with the support of her family. She had by now qualified as a health visitor and was fortunate to find work in the Gloucester area. She still found it a struggle to work full time, yet take responsibility for David's upbringing. Soon she would have to consider sending him to school. This worried her, as her unconventional family arrangements were still not easily accepted in the close community of the Gloucester suburbs. Was she always to be bound to her parents, or did the future offer more?

CHAPTER 8
RESCUE

Occasionally Maggie would walk thoughtfully along the local canal. It gave her time to contemplate her current situation and to explore the numerous possibilities for her future life with David.

In the November of 1947, she was walking near the canal, taking a short cut between her appointments at work. Her reverie was startled by a scream, which seemed to come from the opposite bank of the canal. Maggie rushed to the canal side and saw to her horror that someone had slipped into the water on the far side. It was impossible to see whether it was a man, woman or child. Instantly Maggie could see that the person was in deep water and in serious trouble. Maggie slipped off her shoes and coat and dived into the water. The impact of the cold November water was instant and Maggie was temporarily stunned, fighting for every breath. Trying desperately to remain calm, she struck out forcibly for the opposite bank, now feeling the menacing drag of her remaining clothes. The person in the water ahead of her gave one last piercing scream and disappeared under the filthy scum of the canal. It seemed like forever, but Maggie, now tiring, reached the spot where she thought the turbid water had been disturbed. An occasional bubble broke the surface and Maggie, taking a deep but difficult breath, dived under the murky surface. Visibility was poor, but Maggie could just see a dark figure under the water. Grabbing hold of what seemed like a loose bit of clothing, she kicked hard to bring the motionless body to the surface. Gasping for air, Maggie now saw she had a woman in her arms; a woman whose ashen face told that her life was slowly ebbing away. Maggie, spat out the foul water from her own mouth. With one hand, she managed to pull the limp shape to the bank. To her horror, Maggie now saw that the bank was too steep at this point to drag the woman out of the water. Near to exhaustion, she had to swim a distance of ten yards, with the woman in tow, to a place where the bank sloped more gently. Maggie's feet now touched the canal bottom and she was able to pull the women to the canal side. Thankfully, a man further down the bank had heard her struggles. With his help, they were able to drag the woman to dry land. Maggie soon realised that the woman was reaching a critical stage and unable to breath. Maggie's basic training launched into immediate action. Finding a weak pulse, and having checked for any obstructions, she pulled the woman's head back and blew forcibly into her mouth.

At first there was no response, but after several minutes of continuous artificial respiration, she suddenly spluttered and seemed to draw a half breath. Maggie quickly turned the woman on her side. She immediately vomited a mixture of canal water and bile on to the canal bank. She then started to take gulps of air and, in spite of her wet and bedraggled appearance, the colour slowly returned to her face. It took time for the bluish tinge of her lips to take on its normal pink, but slowly the woman started to breath, fitfully, but unaided.

It seemed like forever, but within ten minutes an ambulance arrived and the women was quickly stretchered into the waiting vehicle. Maggie, now thoroughly exhausted, just felt the need to get dry and warm. She was perfectly happy to go home immediately and change out of her sodden clothes. At the insistence of the ambulance staff, Maggie also travelled with them to the hospital.

That decision was the one to dictate the next stage of her life. The visit to the hospital inevitably meant giving her name and address to the authorities. Maggie could not remain anonymous. Although she was discharged almost immediately, her brave action earlier in the day was now a matter of public record.

It was several months later that Maggie received a recorded delivery in the post. It was a letter from the Royal Humane Society recommending her for the Bronze Medal. Some weeks later, the Lord Mayor of Gloucester, at a ceremony in the Town Hall, presented the award. Maggie was able to meet the lady, a Miss Mansell of nearby Quedgeley, whose life she had saved. The local paper, the Gloucester Echo, reported the event under the headline 'Gloucester River Rescue Earns Award'. The paper published a photograph of the Lord Mayor presenting the certificate to Maggie. Miss Mansell and Maggie's son, David, now three years old, were also in the photograph. It was a special day, although Maggie tried her best to play down its importance. She modestly took the view that she happened to be in the right place at the right time.

No one really knew how Bill Clarke found out about Maggie's award for saving Miss Mansell's life. He was by now living in the town of Ely, a few miles out of Cambridge, where he had found a job with an insurance company, An insurance clerk is fairly unexciting, but these were the years following the war, when opportunities were limited and aspirations frustrated. He had always yearned to be an architect, but the war had interrupted any prospect of training in that field. He had reluctantly settled for a mundane, safe and uninspiring position at the headquarters of a large company in the motor insurance world. After the uncertainties of the war years, he was, for now, content to have reasonable security. After all, he reasoned, everyone needed insurance and the motorcar was a commodity that would grow in popularity, albeit at a slow pace.

Importantly, Mr Bill Clarke (he'd abandoned the military title of Captain) did find out that his former wife, Maggie, was back living in Gloucester. He assumed that she was living with her parents and wrote to her at her old address of 199, Elm Road. Bill Clarke's distinctive writing style of a rather prosaic copperplate was instantly recognised. Maggie, somewhat intrigued, took the envelope, unopened, to her room. She hesitated before opening it, not sure if she felt able or willing to re-establish any form of contact with Bill. Such was her uncertainty, that Maggie left the letter, still unopened, until she returned from work later that evening. Maggie enjoyed a quiet dinner together with her parents, her younger sister and David.

Maggie, revived from the simple, home-cooked meal, enjoyed the hour spent with David. They played endless games of hide and seek and she helped him with a simple jigsaw, made by cutting up photos from the Picture Post. She bathed David, washed his hair to much protestation, and dressed him in his favourite pyjamas. The two of them, cuddled up in David's bed and reading his favourite story of Purple Pup, looked the picture of contentment. But for Maggie there was still an element of doubt in her mind. Could her future really be nothing beyond working to look after David? Was her life to be set in a pattern of such limited scope? Could any of her ambitions ever be totally fulfilled? Would she always live within the confines of relying on others to share the responsibilities of caring for her only son?

"Mummy why have you stopped reading," came the plaintiff voice from beside her.

"I'm sorry darling," she replied, "I must have fallen asleep for a moment."

Maggie knew this was hardly true, but to be lost in thought would take some explaining to an inquisitive three year old. She tucked David up and together they sang 'Gentle Jesus' followed by an equally gentle kiss. She drew the curtains a little to let in some light. It gave the bedroom a warm, cosy feeling of embrace.

With a degree of hesitation, Maggie then went to her room. Slowly and carefully she opened the letter that had been a source of trepidation all day.

My Dear Maggie,

Congratulations on your medal from the Royal Human Society, richly deserved. I read about it in the Gloucester Echo, sent to me by an old army friend. I was so pleased that your bravery had been rewarded in this way. I was quite surprised to see from the photograph in the paper how your son has grown. He must be quite a handful.

After demobilisation, I was unable to pursue my interest in architecture, but have now moved to near Ely, a pleasant place and quite a change from my parents' place in Middlesbrough, let alone the Far East. I work for a large insurance company at its headquarters in Ely. At the moment I am a fairly junior clerk, but hope that if all goes well I will get promotion in due course.

In the 18 months since we've been apart, it has given me time to think, mainly about us. I accept that we both made mistakes, but you know that the short time we were married was quite special.

I find it difficult to put my feelings down on paper, so wondered if you might consider us getting together – even if it was just to catch up properly on all the news. If you will agree to this, I would welcome the opportunity to meet your son.

Dear Maggie, please forgive the rather cold formality of this letter, but it doesn't represent the way I genuinely feel. If we met, perhaps I could be more expressive.

With kind regards and love

Bill

Maggie turned the letter over in her hands. Was she half expecting some added words of undying love? A Shakespearean sonnet or some well-chosen words from Lord Byron? Not really. She knew Bill too well. He was the steady, reliable, honest sort; not one given to romantic gestures. But she liked him; she liked his uncomplicated, fair and open-minded approach to life. She also held an unproven belief that he would make a good father. She sighed a deep sigh as she mused in this way. After all, if a sin had been committed, which was the most sinful? Was it his short time with a prostitute or her taking a lover? She found no immediate answer. She would reply to his letter, but just as Bill had said when they last met, it was she who now needed time to think.

Maggie's thoughts kept going back to Bill's letter over the next few weeks. More importantly, her thoughts kept going back to Bill. She had loved him, of that there was little doubt. But her affair had been far more than a temporary fling to suit the moment. She had been deeply in love for those precious few months. Had things been different she would have happily married that man. In him she had seen tenderness, warmth, desire and passion. In Bill she saw fondness, devotion and affection. She knew that the man of her affair could cherish her, but with Bill she was less sure. Perhaps they could both, but express it in subtly different ways. As she wrestled with these thoughts, she started to recognise her own fallibility and how she'd become self-indulgent. Why was she even capable of making this comparison? She had not heard from the man of her past affair. No visit, no phone call, not even a letter or telegram. He was no longer a part of her life … and yet. Maggie took time to recognise that there was no 'yet'. He had gone. She was probably forgotten. This realisation hit hard and initially the truth of self-discovery left Maggie troubled to the core. She lost her usual enthusiasm for family or work. She enjoyed her moments of intimacy with David, but in other respects she was severely dispirited. It wasn't what Winston Churchill referred to as the 'black dog'. It was in part an unspecified longing. Maggie was unable to be more definite in her personal analysis. Members of her family tried to help, but were generally met with a wall of silence. This was not the Maggie they knew and loved. During this time, she felt unable to even respond to Bill's letter. Such things would have to wait. She recognised that time cannot always heal, but she hoped it could at least put things into perspective.

There was perhaps a single incident that helped Maggie to regain some sort of a positive outlook. For most it would be meaningless, but for Maggie it seemed to chime with her deeper thoughts and reveal a new direction. It was through a single verse of poetry. Her father had lent her his copy of The Oxford Book of English Verse. It was bound in a deep blue vellum, a first edition and dedicated by the editor, rather strangely, to 'The President, Fellows and Scholars of Trinity College Oxford' and 'My Most Kindly Nurse.' The book itself was quite probably of some considerable value, but the real value was in the chosen poetry. One verse by Wordsworth had been marked. Maggie assumed it was part of her father's education at College. It read:

> Enough, if something from our hands have power
> To live, and act, and serve the future hour;
> And if, as toward the silent tomb we go,
> Through love, through hope, and faith's transcendent dower,
> We feel that we are greater than we know.

As Maggie read and re-read this single verse, her eyes opened to the possibilities ahead. She started to appreciate the prospects for 'the future hour.' That evening she decided that at the very least she would meet Bill. It would be a small step for them both; one without commitment or promise; one that may even clarify her current uncertainty.

Her note back to Bill was brief and business-like. She felt no need for detail. As they were to meet, this could wait. She had always been more comfortable talking face-to-face and she rather felt that Bill was the same.

The meeting was arranged and, as requested by Bill, she took David along to meet him. They met two weeks later on a Sunday. It was a day when single people felt more vulnerable, but at least it would be quieter. All the shops and most restaurants were closed, so they met for a late lunch in The Metropole Hotel in the centre of Gloucester. Commercial travellers mainly used the hotel, so it had few customers. The dining room was spacious and airy and was far from ideal for any sort of intimate discussion. David had never been to a restaurant before so was very excitable. The staff, the table setting and the general luxurious ambience of the place were all a constant source of fascination for a three year old.

Maggie and Bill talked guardedly at first about the last eighteen months, but as the meal progressed Maggie sensed a genuine interest in Bill's questions about David. They both relaxed more and towards the end of the meal, Bill suggested the three of them walked down to the docks. The swans swam optimistically towards them, ever hoping for a few bits of stale bread. David was delighted when Bill produced a bread roll from his pocket and broke it into pieces for David to throw for the swans. The squabbling of the swans for each piece caused David a little alarm, but he was comforted when Bill held his hand and showed him how to throw each piece away from the main group of swans and into calmer water.

As they strolled along the side of the docks, they moved from the sun into the shadow of the huge warehouses that lined the ancient Gloucester wharfs. Warehouses that would once have stored tobacco, rum and cotton from the Caribbean. Those days were long before the war changed the trade routes, possibly forever. As they sauntered into the shade, the temperature dropped noticeably. Bill appreciated that Maggie, wearing a light summer suit, would soon feel the cool of the late afternoon. He put a protective arm round her shoulders and she responded by slipping her arm around his waist. David, noticing the subtle change in posture, insisted on squeezing between the two of them. Maggie had little option but to let her arm drop and felt a pang of disappointment. She had enjoyed the short-lived moment of affection, and sensed that Bill felt the same.

Before long, David disentangled himself from between the two and opted to hold Bill's hand. Maggie, once again, put her arm around Bill's waist and the two cuddled together like young lovers, content in each other's silent company.

The late afternoon became early evening and David showed signs of tiring. Maggie knew she should soon be heading home to put him to bed. As they strolled towards the bus station, David chatted excitedly about the journey home. He was desperate to have the front seat on the upper deck. As soon as the bus arrived, he went ahead to claim his favoured spot. Bill and Maggie let him go ahead up the stairs, turned to each other and kissed. It was at first an uncertain kiss; it was a kiss that asked a question; they broke apart for a moment and then kissed again. This time there was no misgiving; it was a passionate kiss; a kiss of assurance; a kiss of absolution; a kiss to 'serve the future hour.'

David looked down from the front seat of the upper deck and waved.

Bill and Maggie met just three times more, each time with David and always on a Sunday. He looked forward to these meetings, mainly, if the truth were known, because it meant he could avoid going with his grandmother to Sunday School. David found her strict and uninteresting church rather forbidding and a little threatening. The meetings were planned around the needs of a young boy and included a boating lake, a play park and once to have an ice cream sundae in the Kardomah cafe near the Cathedral.

Their next meeting was arranged without David. Maggie agreed to see Bill back in Cambridge, not far from where he now lived. Maggie worked most of Friday evening, so travelled to Cambridge the following day, arriving late in the afternoon. Summer was nearly over, yet Maggie wore a light dress. It was a pale shade of yellow, covered in a pattern of light blue flowers, as if forget-me-nots had been strewn randomly over her. The dress, in the post-war fashion, had a row of large white buttons running centrally from the neck to the hem. Bill's eyes danced over her, finding it impossible to hide his admiration for her elegant look. There was still some warmth left from the setting sun, so the two of them walked around the city centre. They had a shared love of the various colleges; Bill more from an architectural view and Maggie admiring the distinct colours as the setting sun played on the brickwork. Maggie, for reasons unknown to Bill, was especially keen to see Trinity College. She wondered if poetry was as influential here as its namesake at Oxford.

They had a pre-dinner drink in the private library of the Cambridge Arms. Bill was unsure about choosing the same place that had been so ominous two years earlier. He knew the risks of association, but decided this was the time to face any demons still lurking from the past. He'd learned from his time in Burma the importance of an auspicious place in local culture. He just hoped that this particular place would prove as favourable. Maggie was initially surprised by the choice, but was willing to be open minded. She let Bill take the lead on trivial matters such as where they were to eat.

The two chatted amiably at first and as the evening wore on the conversation became more affectionate. The issues that separated them were not ignored, but not dwelt upon. They seemed to reach a state of settlement. The past was not resolved by agreement, but it was by acceptance. For both, they could agree on a more promising future. Maggie summarised the moment by saying that she "felt that we are greater than we know." Bill, taking his time to absorb the comment, agreed.

"That was almost poetic," he added.

Maggie just smiled.

They enquired if the hotel could find them a room for the night. The night manager was at first a little unhelpful, but eventually offered them a room above the kitchen. He warned them that the bathroom was a little way down the corridor. With an air of resignation, he politely informed them that breakfast was not served after 10.30am, even on a Sunday. Once safely in their room, Bill did a passable impersonation of the night manager and Maggie giggled her appreciation. They both hung their overcoats in the wardrobe and made no further effort to unpack, apart from opening the lids of their small cases. Each case fought for space on the small amount of threadbare carpet that surrounded the bed. There was just room for a mirrored dressing table and a single chair. Maggie laid claim to the dressing table, by laying out her hairbrush and a few items from her handbag. Bill responded by throwing his jacket on the back of the chair. Maggie went first to the bathroom along the corridor. Bill waited patiently, but in private anticipation, for her to return. This simple routine was too reminiscent of the previous, brief time they had lived together. Before Bill had been posted abroad. Before things had happened to them both. Things now unsaid, yet never fully forgotten. Bill came back to the room to find the light of a single lamp making sweeping shadows on the wall. Maggie, still in her dress, was brushing her hair in slow, fluid strokes and the shadows were dancing to the same rhythm. Bill looked at her muted reflection in the mirror and felt both warmth and affection, something much deeper than mere longing. He firmly, but tenderly, took the hairbrush from Maggie's hand and gently brushed her hair, just as she had done. It was now with an intimacy that can only come through genuine love.

Neither wanted the other to stop, but in time Maggie held up her hand and took the brush from Bill. It was placed with purpose on the dressing table. She stood to face him, put her arms on his shoulders and kissed him very gently on his lips. When they broke apart, Bill looked down at her. Slowly and excitedly, he undid the row of buttons on her dress, moving downwards from her neck. When he reached the last button at the hem of her dress, it slid from her shoulders, dropping soundlessly to the floor. The forget-me-nots now in a crumpled heap. She was wearing nothing underneath, her naked body both inviting and welcoming.

Bill and Maggie re-married that December at the Cambridge register office. It was a quiet affair. Maggie wore a dark blue suit over a white blouse. Around her neck was a necklace made with a single row of pearls. It was an extravagance they could hardly afford, but Bill insisted. He wanted her to wear something they had chosen together. Bill wore a charcoal grey suit, a white shirt and his 14th Army tie. They decided not to invite either of their families. It somehow gave the wedding an air of mystery. It was as if they were in a hurry, almost an elopement but entirely legal. Sheila, a nursing friend of Maggie, and one of Bill's colleagues from his work, witnessed the wedding. They spent a pleasant, but rainy weekend in a small hotel in Glenridding on the western shore of Lake Ulleswater. The large picture windows in the dining room of the hotel faced a mountain the Romans called High Street. They could see a pair of buzzards soaring gracefully over the steep crags. As they watched, both wondered, independently, whether the relationship of these birds was a metaphor of their own. It was to be a marriage built on contentment more than passion.

Two years later in May 1950, Maggie gave birth to a second son, Iain, her first with Bill. David, now aged six years, doted on his baby brother and the family settled down to a simple, yet relaxed life. With Bill now working in Ely, the family had resettled to the village of Witchford. It was the very village where Maggie had lived when she was studying for a short time at Cambridge. It was like coming home.

CHAPTER 9
AFFAIRS

Celia's adventures with other men were at first innocent. She loved the attention and, with Willard away in the Royal Army Medical Corps, it was no real surprise that she found flirting a welcome distraction. She was an attractive woman. Her blond, well-groomed hair complemented a pretty face and her eyes particularly had a bewitching charm, which many men found irresistible. Added to this, her rather vivacious personality meant that she was enchanting company and seduction was rarely far from the minds of the men she met.

Willard's tour of duty in Germany was inevitably a contributory factor in their marriage. He was offered married quarters so they could live together, but Celia refused. She hated Germany and the German people in particular. She had seen how the war, especially the time in Bergen-Belsen, had affected Willard. She wanted to have nothing to do with people who could commit such crimes.

At first, Willard's periods at home on leave were happy enough. He enjoyed seeing Peter grow up and would spend long periods of time with him, taking him on adventures in the local woods. Their adventures were simple, damming streams, building dens or simply lying on their backs in the grass watching the changing formations of the clouds. Relations with Celia were sometimes a little strained, but they both accepted that this was normal with young married couples. They rarely went to sleep without resolving any personal issues. Life for them both was considered acceptable, if unexciting. Willard's time in the army was uncertain, so they made no great plans for their future.

In the deeper layers of Celia's personality, she was a risk taker. She enjoyed the odd flirtation when Willard was away. In most cases it was harmless, but opportunity is the greatest seducer. Celia, without question, had that opportunity, especially with a husband who was abroad for months at a time.

Celia's bubbly nature made her an ideal dinner guest, and Celia was more than happy to attend. Peter was now at school and with help in the house and garden, Celia had time on her hands. The post war rationing and the rather austere nature of the country in general, made a dinner party a welcome diversion from her otherwise dull existence. The relaxed nature of a dinner party, with old friends and a growing set of new acquaintances, was, for Celia, a short spell of excitement and sometimes intrigue.

At one dinner party, she was partnered with a young, rather dashing businessman called Paul Carran. His radio company had profited considerably during the war, switching from the domestic market to producing radio equipment for planes. As his company was considered an essential service, he had been excused military service. This way he had avoided any of the experiences of active service, common to most men of his age. He was slim, and his expensive suit was well cut, showing off the best of his physique. Some would call him suave, but he had a pleasant air, which was not unattractive, especially to a lonely woman with a husband far away.

He offered to take Celia home, which was readily accepted. The two of them chatted amiably as he drove steadily through the quiet lanes of Surrey. As they arrived at Celia's house, Paul walked around the car to open Celia's door. Helping her out, he held her arm for a fraction longer than was necessary and Celia smiled her thanks.

"Would you do me a big favour?" Celia asked, "I think I rather overdid the drink and my babysitter could do with a lift home."

"Of course, " Paul replied, and leaving the car door open, he went in with Celia. The babysitter, one of the local girls who served behind the bar at the golf club, was soon ready and Paul escorted her to his car. She lived less than a mile away, but appreciated the lift, as she often had to walk home if Celia was not in the mood to drive. Paul dropped her off, turned his car around, hesitated, but then drove back to Celia's house. A light was on in an upstairs room, but Paul drew his car up close to the front door and rang the bell. A face appeared at the bedroom window. After a short time, Celia opened the front door, leaving the internal chain firmly in place.

"I fancied one for the road and thought you might join me," Paul whispered through the small gap between the door and the frame.

Celia paused, unsure of her response. Still in a state of indecision, she found herself unlocking the chain. She was dressed in a long, white, cotton dressing gown, held at the waist by a gold-coloured cord tied in a bow. It showed off her slim, firm figure well and Paul took a sharp breath of appreciation. Celia led the way to the lounge and settled at one end of a small settee by the window.

"The drinks are over there, in the walnut cabinet," she intimated, waving her hand generally in the direction of the far wall.

"What can I get you," Paul asked, as he opened the double doors of the cabinet.

"Oh, whatever you're having," came the reply as Paul moved the few bottles around until he found something of interest.

"Ah one of my favourites, " said Paul, " a bottle of Calvados, and already opened."

Paul expertly poured two large glasses of the apple liqueur, and giving one to Celia, settled himself on the same settee. Their words, a little stilted at first, soon became more animated as the drink worked its carefree charm. The conversation came round in time to the topic of loneliness and how Celia was coping with living alone. Celia was not naïve. She knew where this was leading, and right now it was exactly what she wanted. Paul leant forward and kissed her gently. Whether it was the effect of the brandy or simply desire, she enjoyed the moment immensely. Paul slowly undid the gold cord around her waist, parted her gown to reveal nothing more than a deep pink, silk camisole with matching silk, French knickers. He skillfully, carefully and salaciously undressed her to reveal a woman in her prime. Celia could have stopped him at any time, but was totally entranced by the way he explored every part of her with his fingertips, his lips and his tongue. She let him take the lead in every aspect of their lovemaking, not wanting for a second to interrupt the flow of the sensual pleasure he gave her. He brought her slowly, deliberately and deliciously to total ecstasy, Celia arching her hips in time with his powerful rhythm. They took time to part, enjoying the state of total relaxation and tranquility that followed the consummation of the affair.

A hazy dawn was bringing a pale light across the cloudless sky as Paul drove home. Celia lay in her bed, unsleeping and uncertain. Was this the life she craved or was she seeking something else? Had the risk taker, taken a risk too far?

The next morning, Celia decided to bring the affair to a close before it went any further. She wrote to Paul making it clear that what had happened was, for her at least, out of character. She didn't expect a reply and none came. In all honesty, it was something she'd enjoyed. In her current state of mind, she was perfectly happy to bring the relationship to an end. The trouble was that memories remain and Celia was unable to erase the moment from her thoughts. The apple had been tasted and the taste lingered.

Celia's garden was unmanageable at the best of times and she employed a local lad to help out for a few hours just once a week. Jack was young, strong and willing to tackle anything in the garden from simple weeding to keeping the many trees in the garden under control. He was more of a labourer than a gardener, as his knowledge of plants and shrubs was limited. Celia would usually set him a specific task and he would get on with it until his allotted time was up. He would disappear back to the village; often not even bothering to tell Celia he was leaving. If a particular job were arduous or lengthy, then he would leave it unfinished and continue it the following week. One morning, he turned up at Celia's house unusually early and started work cutting back a large rhododendron that had started to spread over the back lawn. Celia woke to the sound of a handsaw fighting its way through the lower branches of the invading shrub. She looked out of the bedroom window and as she looked down, Jack looked up, saw her and waved. In spite of the early hour, Celia was now full awake. She went downstairs to make her morning drink of green tea, made more palatable with a slice of lemon. She stood a little away from the kitchen window and could see Jack struggling with the profusion of tangled branches. He stopped, wiped the sweat from his brow with the sleeve of his loose fitting shirt, and started to make his way to the back door of the kitchen. Celia reached for a glass and filled it with clear, fresh, cold water from the kitchen tap. He knocked gently, almost asking an uncertain question. Celia opened the door, smiled and handed him the glass of water. She stepped back; he stepped into the kitchen and slowly, silently, tipped the water into his open mouth. Nothing was said. Celia turned to refill his glass from the tap. It took a moment and in that moment Jack was close behind her. He put one hand firmly around her waist and with his free hand he took the glass from her and placed it steadily on the side of the sink. Celia momentarily froze. His hard body was held firmly against her back. She could smell the odour of his breath combined with the sweat of his labour. She felt her own breathing deepen and the sound of her heart seemed to pulsate in her chest. He kissed the side of her neck and moved his free hand to her breast. Her natural impulse was to resist, but the memory of other times returned. She felt no particular desire, but the feeling of need was overpowering. She moved his hand from her waist to her other breast and slowly relaxed as she and Jack enjoyed the odyssey of exploration together.

Peter could be heard moving from the bedroom above. Jack picked up the glass, abandoned so willingly, and took it back outside. Soon the sound of the handsaw was heard again. It joined the shrill of birdsong and the hum of bees, as each returned to their early morning tasks.

Jack took to arriving at Celia's house, still once a week, even earlier than the last time. At first they continued to meet in the kitchen, but progressively the affair moved to the bedroom. Jack was an inexperienced lover, but Celia still enjoyed his rather urgent, direct, almost brutal lovemaking. It was a far cry from the subtleness of Paul and the tenderness of Willard.

Peter awoke very early one morning and was heard moving from the room next door. Jack had the presence of mind to slip from between Celia's sheets to the en-suite bathroom, just as Peter came in to the room.

"Is someone in the bathroom?" Peter enquired as he dreamily rubbed his eyes, while climbing into bed with his mother.

"It's Jack, the gardener," Celia replied, pulling Peter close to her. "He's been fixing a problem with the drain in the bath."

"Can I see?" Peter asked excitedly, jumping out of Celia's bed and running into the bathroom.

"Hello, Master Peter," said Jack as Peter bounded in, "It's all fixed! You shouldn't have any more trouble with that."

Peter and Celia thanked Jack in unison as he left the bedroom. Celia was relieved and Peter was perplexed. The six year old couldn't quite understand why his mother was not dressed, but snuggled up to her back in bed and was soon fast asleep. Celia was far from asleep and resolved to find another gardener, someone older and less interested in things outside of the garden.

Willard returned from Germany on leave for three weeks. He found his relationship with Celia was cooler, less intense than in the first flush of their marriage. He couldn't be sure of the reason, but just felt less comfortable with the way the partnership was progressing. They socialized with the same set of people, enjoyed meals out together and long walks in the local woods, but something essential was missing. Neither would admit that anything was wrong, but there was always a slight undercurrent of uncertainty.

It was towards the end of his leave that Willard's concern intensified. He was having a quiet drink with an old friend in the local pub and the evening was drawing to a close. They had enjoyed an hour together, chatting about the local cricket team, how it was now easier to get certain things now rationing was ended and inevitably the weather. As they parted to go home, they shook hands and promised to meet up next time Willard was on leave. Almost as an afterthought, Willard's friend casually mentioned Celia.

"How is she coping with you being away so much?" he said.

"Oh she seems to occupy her time pretty well, " was Willard's reply. "She has Peter to keep her company and there is always the tennis and golf clubs."

"Well just you keep an eye on her," said his friend teasingly. "An attractive woman like Celia shouldn't be left alone too long."

Willard was intrigued. "Any reason you should come out with a comment like that?" he demanded of his friend.

"No, not at all, but in a small village like this there are always rumours. Nothing specific, just the usual rubbish that people with nothing better to do like to start. Honestly, I was only teasing. You enjoy her company while you're here."

With that the two friends parted. One was smiling, but Willard's initial intrigue was now replaced with concern. He was not smiling as he headed for home.

Celia's third affair was different. It all started as innocently as any affair can be. Celia first met Neil Culham at the golf club's annual dinner dance. Celia had attended unaccompanied as Willard was abroad in his new posting to Korea. Neil Culham was tall and had the distinguished air of someone who was comfortable in his own skin. He exuded confidence and this, coupled with his natural good looks, made him a popular dancing partner. Celia danced with him twice before returning to her table with the other friends who had made up her party. Towards the end of the evening, Neil invited her to partner him on the small dance floor again. Celia was an inexperienced dancer, but with Neil she seemed to grow in confidence. As the music changed to a slower rhythm, they both found it natural to be closer together and Celia found his firm hold enchanting and a little exciting. As the dance came to an end, Neil escorted Celia back to her table. He pushed a crumpled paper napkin into her hand, saying "Keep this, you may need it."

Celia was intrigued and, quickly put the napkin into her handbag. She turned her attention to the others, all making arrangements for last drinks to round off the evening. Later, as Celia collected her coat from the cloakroom, she couldn't help a quick, furtive glance at the paper napkin. She opened it carefully to see a single line of numbers, clearly Neil's phone number. She put the napkin away once more and looked around for Neil, hoping to acknowledge with a smile that she had read the secretive message. There was no sign of him, so joining her up with her friends once again, the now noisy party headed for home.

Over the next few days, Celia was tempted to ring Neil, but for some reason held back from taking the fateful step. While still in this state of uncertainty, she was a little surprised to receive a call from Neil himself.

"How did you know my number?" she enquired, after recovering from the shock of his voice on the line.

"As you're a member of the golf club, it wasn't too difficult to talk the club secretary into a little indiscretion over members' details," he answered with a pleasant, suppressed laugh in his tone.

Celia could imagine his smile and they soon made arrangements to meet for a drink in nearby Guildford. At first, their meetings were kept well away from Celia's village. As the weeks progressed, and the two became closer, they became less cautious.

Celia's mind was in turmoil. By now she had developed quite an affection for Neil, yet she was still married to Willard, the father of her only son. Over the years her feelings for Willard had cooled, but she was still in love with him in her own peculiar way. She wrestled with the notion of being in love with two people at once. She questioned whether love had to be one hundred percent for one person, or could it be shared? Did love stop at one hundred per cent or could it be a greater number, divided between two people. Added to this was her strong Catholic faith. She knew she was a sinner in the eyes of her church, but her sins could be forgiven and absolved by a weekly confession. The notion of divorce was still unacceptable to her religious upbringing, especially to remarry following a divorce. Her developing relationship with Neil took time, but with Willard abroad, she soon found in Neil a willing and satisfying sexual partner.

It was only after Celia and Neil had first made love that Neil revealed something of his heritage. His father was very ill and Neil admitted that on his father's death he would inherit substantially more than money. Neil would become the tenth Viscount Culham and with that ownership of Hadleigh Hall in the County of Shropshire. Celia was at first surprised and even shocked, as Neil had carefully omitted such important details in all of their earlier trysts. Deep down, Celia was excited and a little enthralled by the news of Neil's situation. She could see herself enjoying the position and privileges of being involved in the family's noble aristocracy. In a different world she imagined herself married to Neil and becoming chatelaine of Hadleigh Hall. But this was the real world and she was married to Willard. Her affair with Neil was a most enjoyable amusement for a woman in her position, but realism shed its shadow on their time together.

It was almost inevitable that some detail of Celia's most recent affair would make its way back to Willard's regiment in Korea. Nothing was ever said openly, but like the time he met his friend in the pub, rumours circulated. Colleagues hinted to Willard that things were far from straightforward at home in Surrey.

At about this time, Willard was due a short period of leave, so he telegraphed Celia to expect him in about a week's time. Unexpectedly, Willard was offered a much earlier flight with an RAF transport plane. He had no hesitation in using the opportunity to add a few extra days to his leave. Soon after the Hercules touched down at Brize Norton, Willard hired a car and drove east to his home in Surrey. He stopped at a florist in Witney and bought a bunch of roses for Celia. He took care in choosing them, as he knew that she particularly liked the colour of pale pink. Parking the hire car at the front of the house, Willard was surprised to see a car he didn't recognize sitting half hidden in the shade of a large beech tree. Willard went in the front door and seeing no one around, he made his way upstairs to unpack, his free hand still clutching the roses. As he quietly opened the door to his bedroom he was surprised that the room was in semi-darkness during the mid afternoon. His eyes took a short while to adjust to the dim light. It was then he saw Celia's back gently rocking on the bed. It took but a moment to realize that she was not alone and the man beneath her was groaning with the obvious pleasure of her movements. The two failed even to notice him as he stood there watching. Willard's immediate emotions were a combination of horror and understanding. Willard dropped the flowers on the floor of the room, closed the door just as quietly and headed downstairs.

Willard left the house and headed into the nearby woods. He needed time to think. His mind was in relentless turmoil. Here was a man who made life and death decisions in his professional life, but failed to be capable of seeing a solution to what he had now seen. He had returned to find a salacious wife, clearly taking selfish delight in the opportunities of his absence. Before returning to England, he knew his relationship with Celia needed serious attention, but had every hope that things would improve. Such hopes were now dashed and palpably reflected in the couple still making love in his own bed. He walked briskly and with apparent purpose for over two hours. The truth was that his strides were purposeless. It exercised his body but failed to exorcise the image of his wife's blatant gratification. He was totally incapable of resolving the confused sentiments coursing through every vein in his body.

He returned to the house, unsurprisingly finding no evidence of Celia's lover. The pale pink roses were displayed to perfection in a cut glass vase – a wedding present from the regiment – and now a distant memory of better times. Nothing was said and nothing needed to be said. Willard spent a few precious moments with Peter when he came in from school. He explained that he needed to return abroad soon. Reluctantly, he told Peter that this visit, although short, was special to him and they arranged to spend the next day together.

Willard and Peter, disconsolate father and excited son, met early the next day. They set out with sandwiches and drinks, back to the same woods that Willard had tramped the day before. Willard hid his inner feelings from his son and the two enjoyed playing hide and seek and building a magnificent den from the piles of brushwood scattered around. They enjoyed their lunch sitting in their own special den and listened intently for the sound of birds around them. Through a gap in the roof of the den, Willard first heard and then spotted a woodpecker, totally oblivious to the two inside. He pointed it out to Peter, who was equally captivated by its bright colours and the rapid movement of its head as it tapped on the bark of the tree above.

As they walked home, hand in hand, Willard explained gently to Peter, that he might not see him for a little while as there were many important things he needed to do. Willard reminded Peter of the time the teddy bear that he gave him for his second birthday went missing.

"Do you remember, Peter, you were heartbroken when you couldn't find him? Then over time you found other things to play with and your teddy was almost forgotten."

"But daddy, I never, ever really forgot about teddy."

"Of course not," Willard was quick to respond, "and remember how happy you were when we found him in the garden shed, although he was a bit dusty."

"Yes, daddy, but we soon cleaned him up and he was as good as new."

"He was," said Willard, deep in unsmiling thought.

Willard promised that while he was away, he would always be thinking of him. He would find ways to keep in touch; find ways to support him; find ways to help him make the right decisions and to guide him in life. Peter couldn't fully understand what was being said; simply enjoying the time he was spending with his father. Years later, Peter remembered that day, not the details, but the sheer pleasure of time spent together. He especially remembered, with surprising clarity, his father's promise to help him. As a six year old, he was unable to know how.

Willard knew full well the marriage was over, but with Celia's trenchant Catholic views, there seemed little option but to continue the façade. Willard wondered if there was any other way. The situation was demanding a more satisfactory resolution.

CHAPTER 10
DEATH

Celia was at home with Peter when the telegram arrived. It was a miserable, rainy day, typical of April. Her thoughts were more concerned with Peter and how he was coping at the local school. The consequences of Willard's unexpected return last year were still raw. He had returned to the army, because at least that gave him some semblance of normality. He wrote regularly and separately to Celia and Peter, but mother and son often shared his letters. To Peter they were encouraging and uplifting, telling him about travel and comradeship. To Celia, the letters were more factual and guarded, doing little more than keeping the lines of communication open. She knew that Willard had been seconded to the Canadian Army. His division was now involved in the Korean campaign, a conflict that had escalated over the last year.

The telegram came from the War Office. It was brief and to the point.

War Office, London

Recipient: Mrs. Celia Boulton

I regret to inform you that your husband, Captain Willard Boulton has been seriously wounded. Stop.

More information will follow. Stop.

I apologize that national security prevents me giving further details at present. Stop.

Sender: Major Joe Moran, Canadian Armed Forces.

Celia was numbed. She couldn't believe that an officer working for the Medical Corps could be involved in front line action. She had assumed that doctors were kept well away from the heat of the battle. Perhaps there had been an accident back at the base. The worst part was the unknown. What does 'seriously wounded' mean? She moved around the house in a semi-daze, not knowing what to do or how she could share the grim news. Perhaps it sounded worse than it was and he would soon be home. He may have to convalesce for some time, but surely he will be fine. Willard was a fighter. Wounds will heal. Perhaps even the wounds she had inflicted. Two days later a further telegram arrived. It also came from the War Office.

War Office, London

Recipient: Mrs. Celia Boulton

It is with considerable regret that it is my duty to inform you that your husband, Captain Willard Boulton, has died following his recent injuries. Stop.

Please accept my sincere condolences for this appalling news. Stop.

Captain Boulton was a highly respected member of my team and is considered a great loss. Stop.

I am sorry to report that it is impossible at present to repatriate his body due to ongoing military activity in the existing theatre of war. Stop.

I have instructed his close colleague and friend, Captain James Driver, to take immediate leave and to visit you. Stop.

I apologize that national security prevents me giving further details at present. Stop.

Sender: Major Joe Moran, Canadian Armed Forces.

Celia was devastated and struggled to know how to react. She appreciated that following their marriage, she had become his next of kin, but knew it was her duty to let Willard's parents know the situation. They were not easy to contact, but with help she managed to reach them to break the horrendous news. They both lived abroad, but promised to do everything in their power to help. Inevitably, she turned to Neil Culham for support. He was understanding and encouraging, but could do little to limit her distress. Celia felt responsible. Willard was in a wretched state when he left her. Could it have been worse? Could he have left her with the intention of suicide?

Within a week, Jim Driver phoned her to say he was back in the country and could he visit. She was desperate for details, but at the same time was deeply anxious that her worst fears would prove true. Had he taken his own life and had she been the one to cause his malignant state of mind?

Jim came later that day. He had deliberately timed his arrival when he fully expected Peter to be in bed. Celia had managed to settle Peter a little earlier than usual to make sure of no interruptions. Jim had changed out of his service uniform. It was his attempt to spare Celia the inevitable association of the uniform. They had not seen each other since the happier times of Celia and Willard's wedding. They both knew that it would be a difficult meeting, but for totally different reasons.

Jim was offered and took a small whisky, but even that gave rise to an awkward moment between them. It was Willard's favourite drink and both knew it. The main feature of the room was a baby grand piano and Jim was tempted to perch on the piano stool. Once again, the association was too distressing for them both, as Willard loved to relax by playing this splendid instrument. Jim sat down with his back to the French doors, the setting sun leaving him little more than a silhouette. Celia busied herself at first making a long gin and tonic, but eventually settled down opposite Jim. The situation was tense. Both, in their own individual ways, were concerned about what was to be said and what was to be heard.

Celia broke the ice by asking Jim about his journey and Jim reciprocated by asking after Peter. They both knew that the purpose of the visit could not be delayed further. Jim, putting his drink down, was the first to come to the point.

"I'm so sorry, Celia, about Willard," his voice only just under control. "You know he was a good friend to me, the best. I was horrified, like you must have been, when I heard the news. Quite tragic..." his voice trailed off.

Celia sat motionless, but managed "It was good of you to come, Jim, so tell me..." then her voice cracked and she stopped abruptly.

"Are you sure you are ready?" Jim asked, "I'm afraid it's not easy for me either."

Thoughts of Willard's suicide flooded Celia's mind and she found it difficult to focus on Jim's words.

"He was in a forward position. The truth is he shouldn't really have been there. Casualties were expected and he wanted to be close by in case he was needed. It was in a place called Hill 677, part of the defence of the Kapyong Valley. He was bringing two injured Canadian soldiers back from just behind the front line when a small land mine was detonated. We don't really know how it happened, but the next we knew, he was seriously injured, mainly in the face. Celia, are you quite sure you want me to carry on? I could write this all down and leave it with you."

Celia took a gulp from her drink, composed herself and quietly and hesitantly said, "Please carry on."

"He lost an eye and one side of his face was in a really bad way. At first we thought he would be all right. But when we got him back to base, I'm afraid septicaemia set in very quickly and within a couple of days his internal organs just packed up and he died."

Celia sat motionless. She felt a mixture of emotions. On one hand she was relieved her actions hadn't caused Willard to take his life. On the other hand a level of grief that such a thing could happen to anyone, let alone her husband. Jim left her with her thoughts, not wishing to interrupt her as the details sunk in.

"I'm sorry, Jim," Celia said, wiping a single tear from her cheek, "It is all so sudden and I wasn't able to be with him."

"I'm sorry, Celia," said Jim, "I'd give anything to bring him back. You know he was a dear friend. The best."

Jim gave Celia a little more time in silence. All that could be heard was the soft cooing of a pigeon outside and the more strident and tuneful song of a blackbird.

"Are you ready for me to carry on, Celia?" asked Jim, "There are more things I need to tell you."

"Of course," she replied, "Please carry on."

"As you're aware, Celia, under normal conditions, Willard's body would have been repatriated back to the UK. Unfortunately, the defence of Kapyong Valley meant that the Canadian troop movements were very fluid. There was no option but to bury Willard immediately. He was given full military honours, but then we just had to relocate to another position. I realize that nothing can help, but he was not the only one in that situation. We were forced to do the same thing for seven other colleagues. In the short time I had before coming to see you, I was able to collect a number of Willard's personal things from back at base. They are all in his trunk in my car. If you wish I could bring them back another time…"

"No," Celia interrupted, "I think it best if you let me have everything now. Did you say the trunk was in your car?"

"Would you like me to bring it in now, Celia, or….?"

"Please."

Jim stood, made his way outside, and went back to his car. He hesitated. It all seemed so final. It almost felt contrived to make this one visit and leave the memory of Willard in this way. He hesitated again and then lifted Willard's trunk from his car into the house, placing it carefully in the front hall.

"Jim, I don't think I am ready for anything further right now. Would you be so kind as to put the trunk upstairs for me? There are stairs to the loft and I would be much happier if the trunk was out of sight for now. I will need to talk to Peter and the trunk would just be too much to bear."

"Of course. I quite understand. Sometimes memories are best shut away until you are ready. But Celia, there is just one thing. I know that Willard would have particularly liked Peter to have his old microscope. He often talked about the day when he was going to give it to Peter and it would be a shame for that to be stored away upstairs."

"Of course, Jim. If you think Willard would want that. But if you don't mind, could I leave you to find it for me?"

With that, Celia went out of the hall and into the kitchen. Soon the sound of her mixing another drink could be heard in the background. Jim, with some reluctance, undid the straps of the trunk, opened the lid and took out the microscope. It was in a polished walnut box, a little battered from its travels and a stark reminder of better days. Jim lifted it by its brass handle and took it into the lounge.

"Where would you like me to put it?" he called to Celia, who was still in the kitchen. Celia came into the lounge, fresh drink in hand, and shook visibly as she stared at the box, now cradled in Jim's arms. She steadied herself against the arm of a chair, took a moment to compose herself and then answered,

"I'm sure Peter will treasure it one day, Jim, but he's still very young. Please will you make space at the back of the piano? It will be fine there."

"Celia, you know that Willard was my greatest friend. I can assure you that everything was done to try to save him. He was a trusted colleague both in the British Army and to the detachment of Canadian soldiers he was with in Korea. I'll miss him tremendously."

"I appreciate you coming, Jim, and I can assure you I'll miss him even more."

"Of course," replied Jim, a little uncertain as to whether this was how she really felt.

"Is there anything else I can do for you, Celia? I will be around for a few days and more than happy to help you come to terms with things."

"It's very kind of you, Jim, but I think I can manage. If I need you I will certainly get in touch."

"There is one other thing we need to discuss, Celia. I am sorry to bring this up, but you are entitled to an army pension."

"I suppose so. I hadn't thought of that. I assume I'll need to apply for it some way?"

"Well, actually no, Celia. I took the liberty of making the arrangements myself. I thought that the last thing you needed at this time was to get involved in such matters, so I've managed to sort it all out for you. All I need is your bank details and then, all being well, payments should come to you automatically."

"Thank you again, Jim. You're most kind."

"Well, Celia, if you're sure there's nothing else, I'll get on my way and leave you in peace."

Celia sat for a moment, finished her drink and stood to see Jim out. She stopped momentarily, as if trying to recall something important. She then went to a mahogany bureau at the far side of the room. She unlocked and opened the sloping front of the bureau to reveal a row of pigeonholes, each containing an orderly pile of papers and notes. From the top, left hand pigeonhole, she took her chequebook. She opened it and carefully wrote down the details of her bank, giving them to Jim. He folded the piece of paper and put it in his wallet.

"Thank you," he said, "just leave all the arrangements to me. I won't let you down."

"I know you won't, Jim. You've been a good friend."

"Just in case you think of anything, Celia, here is my address for the next few days," and he handed her a handwritten note.

They hugged each other. Celia with genuine fondness. Jim with relief that the visit was over and without complications.

Jim returned to his car, turned, waved and drove slowly away, lost in his own thoughts and grateful that he'd done what was asked of him.

Celia turned, went into the house and immediately phoned Neil Culham.

"Could you come over for the evening?" she said. "I need the company."

Celia dreaded the moment when she would have to tell Peter. As dawn broke, she untwined herself from Neil's arms, kissed him gently and asked him to leave. She had decided that there was no option but to tell Peter the truth. He was six years old and in some ways mature beyond his years. Over breakfast she broached the subject indirectly by talking about Willard being away a lot because of his work in the army. Peter listened without comment; his natural intuition somehow knowing that there was more to follow. Celia went on to explain that soldiers who work in the army sometimes get injured or even killed.

"But not Daddy," interrupted Peter," because he's a doctor."

"Even doctors, Peter, can sometimes get injured or even killed."

There was a long pause, while Peter took in his mother's statement.

"In fact, darling, I'm afraid to tell you that Daddy was badly injured in some fighting a long way away."

"But he's a doctor, he will know how to get better," Peter said with calm assurance.

"Unfortunately not everyone does get better, Peter. I'm afraid in Daddy's case, he didn't get better."

Celia's words faltered and then stopped.

"You mean he will always be ill when he comes back" said Peter, showing real concern in his voice for the first time.

"No, darling, I'm afraid it's even worse than that. You see he won't be coming back."

"You mean not at all?" said Peter. "Not even to show us his injuries?"

"I'm afraid not, Peter darling, not even to show us his injuries. You see his injuries got so bad that even the doctors couldn't help him and he got worse and worse."

Peter hesitated, his young mind trying to make sense of it all.

"Do you mean like Chippy, when he was hit by that car and you took him to the vet?"

"Just like Chippy, darling. You remember we hoped he would get better, but the vet couldn't help him and poor Chippy died."

"And then we buried him down in the orchard," said Peter and we said a prayer.

"That's right, darling. And do you remember what else we said at the time. We said the best thing to do was to remember all the good times we had with Chippy."

Peter sat silently for a while, once again working out in his mind what was being said to him. After about a minute, with Celia watching the worried expression on his face, Peter turned to Celia and surprised her by saying,

"Will we be burying Daddy in the orchard with Chippy?"

"Oh that would be lovely, darling, why don't we plan to do that when the blossom from the apple trees lies on the ground?"

"Yes," said Peter, "I would like that."

Celia's relationship with Neil Culham was at first kept discreet. She exhibited an appropriate level of public grief to her family and friends, whilst privately she enjoying the developing relationship with Neil. She insisted that arrangements for marriage would not be considered until after a suitable period of mourning and he accepted her wishes. Six months was the period of time that Celia thought appropriate. After that time, they started to be much more open about their time together. They then made wedding plans, she a widow and he a bachelor, albeit one with a history of dating some of the most eligible and attractive women in the county.

They married in June 1952, just over a year after Willard had died. The blossom from the apple trees was no longer on the ground. Celia's promise to Peter was left unfulfilled. There was no burial in the orchard. There was no body to bury.

The wedding was a grand affair and caused considerable interest in the locality and further afield. A substantial marquee had been erected at the side of the Hadleigh cricket field that was next to the Church of Our Lady the Virgin. The Culham family had always been staunch Catholics, although in certain periods of history, their religious zeal went, quite literally, underground. Hadleigh Hall still had at least one priests' hole; a place of refuge during the Catholic purges. The hall itself was built in the grand Palladian style and set in extensive parklands.

Celia loved the prospect of becoming a Viscountess, perhaps even more than she loved Viscount Culham. Nonetheless, the couple was well suited and family and friends thought them an ideal match.

The church had been decorated lavishly. The lych-gate leading to the church was covered in an array of arum lilies, all collected from the margins of the ponds in the grounds of the hall. The guest list included many of the great and the good from the County of Shropshire. Included amongst the guests was a number of the present and previous MCC cricket team. Neil Culham's father had been a great supporter of the MCC and even had the great Leonard Hutton to stay at the hall on a number of occasions. The best man's speech reminisced about the time that Neil, as a young boy, had practiced cricket with Len Hutton. They had played in the Long Gallery, much to the detriment of several paintings and one precious chandelier. Such was the family's love of the game of cricket, that a match against the MCC had been arranged for the day before the wedding.

Celia looked radiant as she emerged from the sunshine into the quiet solitude of the church. She walked purposefully to the front of the church and stood alongside Neil at the alter rail. The wedding ceremony took the form of a nuptial mass, which included exchanging the vows and rings. Peter was delighted to be asked to present the rings and did so with a self-assurance way beyond his years.

At the point in the service where the priest shook the hands of Celia and Neil, he was able to say for the first time, "Viscount and Viscountess Culham, peace be with you." Celia beamed with delight.

The service finished with Mass. For a number in the congregation, this caused a little embarrassment, as it was, for them, a new experience. The priest, anticipating the problem, graciously excused any who were not regular participants. This settled the congregation considerably. The newly married couple soon emerged into the sunshine to process to the cricket field and enjoy one of the best cricket teas ever seen at Hadleigh Cricket Club.

Peter's life now changed. He now had someone he was encouraged to call 'Father', never 'Dad'. Neil was, if not devoted, a supportive parent. Peter settled into life at Hadleigh Hall with the interest and excitement to be expected of a young boy living in a large and often mysterious home. Peter enjoyed nothing more than exploring the hall and was thrilled when he first found the old priest holes, one under the stairs and the other behind a fireplace. He loved to explore the extensive grounds of

Hadleigh Hall, at first in the company of the local gamekeeper, but then alone. Neil taught him the elements of fishing in the Hadleigh Park's main lake and Peter would spend many hours that summer tempting the elusive carp with a variety of baits. In many ways living with Celia and Neil was an idyllic life for Peter. He still remembered his father, but over time the detail faded. The two years since he saw him last, gave time for any image he had of Willard to grow pale. As the summer came to an end, so did Peter's Arcadian life at Hadleigh Hall.

CHAPTER 11
LOST CHILD

Celia and Neil Culham were now very involved in social, sporting and domestic life of Hadleigh Hall. They decided that Peter should be sent away to be a boarder at a prep school. Tradition overruled affection. They found reasons to justify their decision, but, in truth, they preferred a life without the encumbrance of an eight-year-old boy. The prep school they chose, Langtons, was on the south coast of Dorset, in the area known as the Isle of Purbeck. Langtons was the type of preparatory school that the royals, even the minor royals, would avoid. This gave it total freedom from intrusion, whether from the security services or the media. It gave it anonymity, yet it retained respectability among the 'county set', especially those steeped in the Catholic faith.

Before leaving Hadleigh Hall, Peter helped pack his trunk. It was full of clothes, some old and some brand new. He had special clothes for PE, special clothes for sports and a complete school uniform with several extra shirts. Celia suggested he took something memorable from home, perhaps a photograph or a favourite book. Peter chose the teddy bear he had been given by his true father all those years ago. Celia picked it up at arms length, sighed reflectively, and gave it to Peter. He put it carefully in the trunk and closed the lid with a degree of finality.

Celia and Neil drove Peter to Langtons in early September. As the Bentley swung into the long, tree-lined drive leading up to the school, Peter idly wiped the car window with the back of his hand to get his first view of his new term-time home. He first saw a pleasant house, which Celia guessed rightly to be the home of the headmaster. Langtons itself looked forbidding, made especially so by the light sea mist. The haze surrounded the large Edwardian building, set well back from the road. Peter's emotions were a mixture of anticipation and trepidation. Celia, and especially Neil, had made an effort over the last few months to bring a degree of normality into his life. Yet, in truth, Peter had been lonely. It had developed in him a degree of independence and even self-sufficiency. Peter hoped, beyond hope, that he would make friends at his new school. He was optimistic that some of his anxieties would ease in these new surroundings.

The introductions to his housemaster were formal but friendly and he was then shown to the dormitory he would share with five other new boys. It appeared stark, but clean, with the ever-present odour of cheap disinfectant. The dormitory had six narrow beds, three to each side of the room. Alongside each bed was a wooden locker and at each end of the dormitory was one large wardrobe.

Peter was told that the beds on one side of the room shared one wardrobe, leaving the other wardrobe for the other three boys. There was a further storage area in each corner and this is where Peter's trunk was put once it was emptied. Peter had never been in a hospital ward, but he imagined this is what it would be like. For Neil it was reminiscent of the short time he spent in a barracks during his national service. Celia just wanted to leave and continue her gilded life back at Hadleigh Hall.

Above each bed was a small, plate so that a card could be inserted for his name and he soon found the single word CULHAM above the bed nearest the door. Peter was the second new boy to arrive that afternoon and it was clear that a boy called PEARSON had already taken the bed next to his.

Peter took out his beloved teddy and propped it up on his pillow as he had done for the last four years. The boy called Pearson did not appear to have a toy on his bed, so Peter, with some misgivings, moved the bear to the drawer in his bedside locker. Neil had told him that in a new school it might be a good thing, at least at the start, to conform and not be seen as anything too different. Peter remembered this as he moved the toy bear out of sight. If he needed comforting, he knew the bear was close to him.

The rest of the day was spent being shown around Langtons. The main building had the dormitories, the kitchens, a dining room, a sanatorium, some offices and what was called a common room. The classrooms were attached to the main house and were all single story buildings. They were originally in the same Edwardian style, but had been converted internally to make them into small teaching rooms. One was clearly an art room, another a small science laboratory and yet another a library. Peter was told that the library was originally the stable for Langton House before the name was changed to Langtons. This room was light and airy and Peter looked forward to choosing from the extensive collection of books on the shelves surrounding the room. There was an old, wooden gym with a polished maple floor, wall bars and a collection of strange, leather-covered equipment that Peter had never seen before. In time, Peter became quite proficient at exercising on the vaulting and pommel horse. Behind the gym was a stone built building, with a heavy door at one end. This was the school chapel and was used daily. It was just big enough for all the boys at the school to use at one time, with the children squashed together on the hard wooden pews. The staff at the school, numbering only ten in total, would stand at the front of the chapel facing the boys, always watchful for the slightest misdemeanor.

After the evening meal, all the new boys were told to change into outdoor clothing. They were about to take part in a tradition that had been part of Langtons since before the school was established. It was known as the 'Lost Child Search' and, with due solemnity, the headmaster told them of the legend of the lost child. He explained that before the house became a school, a child had gone missing from the family living there. The search party had gone out with lanterns into the gathering gloom and a light sea mist. The child, the same age as they were now, had eventually been found dead between here and the sea. The family, unable to cope with their loss, had moved away and the house sold to become the school it was today. Each boy was issued with a torch and a stout stick. They were told on no account should they ever walk alone in the area. Peter was partnered with Colin Pearson and they all set off together in the dark, heading south towards the sea. After about a mile the teacher with them, a Mr. Gray, explained that they were crossing an ancient footpath called the Priest's Way. It was here that the group stopped and the teacher gave clear instructions.

"From here on you will head towards the sea. Each pair must always keep in sight of another pair, so there must always be a chain of torchlight as you search for the lost child. No pair must be further than 20 yards apart from another pair. You can search any way you want, but my advice is that one of you searches while the other watches for the next pair in the chain. Then you can change over so you get a rest from searching. There will be a master at both ends of the chain as you move towards the sea. After about half a mile, the land will start to drop away more steeply. This is the point that you must stop. If you haven't found the lost child by then, you will have missed him and must wait until called together. The 'call together' sign is three blasts on my whistle. When you hear the whistle, you must all group together. The pair at the ends will move towards their nearest pair and this means that you will all end up together in the middle. Does everyone understand?"

The boys stood in silence. Some were excited, some curious, but most were terrified.

"Pearson, repeat the instructions, please."

Colin Pearson made a good effort at repeating the teacher's instructions, but was a little confused over the final statement following the whistle.

"OK," said the teacher, "let's practice it right here. All spread out along the Priest's Way."

The boys spread out. Even on a clearly marked path, they quickly realized that each pair felt very isolated. The teacher had stayed in the middle of the line of boys.

He shouted, "Right, now everyone stand totally still and switch off your torches."

One by one the lights went out and soon the boys were in total darkness, strung out along the path. The boys, now standing in total darkness, started to be really concerned. One boy was worried he might cry and blew his nose to cover his distress.

"Great, now switch them back on again," he shouted. Soon each pair could be identified by the row of lights along the path. The boys were relieved to see the darkness punctuated by the torchlight, but most jumped in surprise at the unexpected and piercing sound of the whistle. At first no one moved, then slowly each pair recalled the instructions and moved towards the nearest pair of lights. Soon they were all back together. The earlier fears were gradually being replaced by their enthusiasm to take part in the search to come.

"OK boys, well done. You will be on your own now. Remember you will have no more than half a mile ahead of you before you must stop. You're OK on flat round, but as soon as it starts to slope, you must stop and listen out for the whistle. The lost child will be at ground level. He may be hidden behind a rock or bush. Remember you must always be able to see the next pair of lights. If you can't, just stop and I will find you. Good hunting."

With that, the teacher's light went out and he seemed to disappear. Each pair stood in silence for a moment, then carefully and cautiously they moved away from the path into the unknown. It was no easy task searching the ground ahead as it was uneven and sometimes rocky. The undergrowth was fortunately not deep, mainly made up of bracken and the odd stand of willow herb. The boys could easily be heard in the dark, mainly from the swishing of their sticks as they flattened the rough ground. The high-pitched, excitable voices gave comfort to the more anxious boys as they made their way progressively towards the distant sea. The noise they were making in the search drowned out the sounds ahead of them. Had they all stopped to listen they would have heard far away the sound of the sea crashing on the rocks. The other sound they might have heard was from the line of staff and older boys carrying a long rope ahead of them. After about half an hour the ground did seem to start to fall away more steeply. The boys remembered the warning and one by one the pairs came to a stop. As they stopped, they heard the three blasts on the whistle and the relieved boys were soon together in one group. A number of other older boys and a few members of staff soon joined the boys. The rope that had always gone ahead of them was now coiled up and one of the older boys put it over his shoulder.

"So did anyone find the lost child?" enquired Mr. Gray, the teacher who had given the original instructions. The boys were silent.

"I thought as such," he said, "that's because the lost child was not found in these parts, but further on. We're going there together right now."

The whole group were then reorganized into a single line and set off towards the sea. The sound of waves crashing on the rocks soon became quite distinct and some of the young boys, once again, started to become really concerned. The group was told to stop. The rope was uncoiled and a teacher took one end down a steep section of rock. Soon the older boys and the teachers formed a chain down the rock with the rope between them. The new boys were told to hold on to the rope with one hand and scramble down the rocks to the flat area just 15 yards below. With the support of the rope, the descent was not difficult, even in the dark. Each boy was relieved and pleased when reaching the bottom. Finally all the new boys were gathered at the base of the steep slope and formed a tight circle around the teacher.

"Well done boys. You have now found the place of the lost child. It is known as Dancing Ledge. The small swimming pool blasted out of the rocks just here is where the lost child was found. I congratulate you all on your search and take pleasure in awarding you the lost child medal. I know that every one of you has overcome personal fear in your own way. You have learnt a great lesson tonight and I assure you, you will never forget it"

Mr. Gray then took from his pocket a set of roughly carved wooden medals, each one attached to a leather strap. Solemnly he placed a medal over the head of each boy.

"Wear these with pride, lads. You deserve them."

That night each exhausted boy wore his medal as he slept, some soundly, some fitfully. A few dreamt of the Dancing Ledge. All wondered what other lessons they would learn in this strange school. This nocturnal visit to Dancing Ledge was the first of many night time expeditions. The staff at Langtons would often take groups of boys swimming in the pool, but always during daylight, and always under strict supervision.

Peter did not find it easy to make lots of friends, but he soon found one in Colin Pearson, the one he had partnered in the Lost Child Search. They found that they both enjoyed running and would enjoy the various running activities organized by the school. One of Langtons running sessions was 'hare and hounds'. It involved one person, the 'hare', going ahead, armed only with a large bag of sawdust. His job was to drop a handful of the sawdust at regular intervals along the trail. The master in charge would give him vague instructions, tell him which areas were off limits, but the route was his choice. Then about ten minutes later, the rest of the boys, the 'hounds', would set off in pursuit, accompanied by a lot of shouting, barking and generally having fun. Although it was only a form of running game, the effect on the 'hare' was often quite frightening and he would do his best to avoid capture. The 'hounds' would take great delight in spotting the 'hare' for the first time and the better runners would chase him down with huge prestige given to the first to touch him. It was always taken in an eager spirit and the boys would jog back to school together, having enjoyed all aspects of the chase. Peter and Colin both looked forward to being chosen as the 'hare'. They would try to outdo each other in the routes they chose.

Another favourite with the boys was hashing. In this running game, one boy would set off much earlier than the others and lay a trail using sawdust or flour. He was also given a piece of chalk, which was used to mark the trail. In hashing, he could lay false trails, which after some way would be marked with a chalked cross. All the boys, finding the cross, would have to turn back. The chasing boys didn't have to stick together and the slower ones would wait where the trail split. They would then all meet up after the false trails had been eliminated. Hashing had its own special language, which the boys learned very quickly. "Are you?" was a question to other hashers ahead looking for the route. The answers were either "On-On," meaning follow this trail or "Checking." If the boys heard "Checking," they could then have a rest until "On-On" was yelled from ahead. Every now and then, the leader of the chasing group would call "Circle Up," and everyone would come together to check on numbers and to share any information on the false trails. Then at the end, the final 'Circle Up' would be used to thank the boy who set up the trails. The boys would set off back to school to enjoy tea and toast, a tradition that always followed hashing.

A particular Langtons' tradition was the Sherriff Hunt. It was named after the Sherriff of Nottingham, the person who always confronted the legendary Robin Hood. It started without warning, usually timed to coincide with the end of a Friday chapel service in the summer term. The boys of the Sherriff and his gang of henchmen would sweep through the school in minutes, causing as much disruption as possible. The Sherriff and his gang would then disappear. All the other boys from the school would then be formed into groups of about six to hunt for the Sherriff. They were supplied with the basic needs for two nights in the open air, usually little more than a blanket each, a piece of tarpaulin, some food and matches. The hunt was designed to be 48 hours of living outdoors with the added excitement of trying to capture the Sherriff, whilst avoiding capture. The groups were always made up of younger and older, weaker and stronger boys, so looking after each other was important. It was a test of group cohesion with the common goal of survival. The game was continuous with no respite. The boys had to find suitable camping spots, cook for themselves and watch for the Sherriff and his men continuously. Hunters were allowed to collaborate, but in so doing would be easier to find by the Sherriff. It was exciting, tiring and with only limited structure. The only boundaries in the game were the physical boundaries set by the teachers in advance, but this was spread over many miles and included woodland, open fields and rough heathland. The school was out of bounds during the whole game, adding considerably to the whole adventure. No boy at Langtons ever forgot the Sherriff Hunt.

By the time Peter reached the final year at Langtons, he and Colin had become inseparable. They shared many adventures together and had visited each other's homes during the summer holidays. In their schoolwork, they were mildly competitive, but compared test and homework results more out of interest than rivalry. The one thing they did contest seriously was their running. The two of them were always vying for the best position in races, which at Langtons was mainly cross-country. They were both always in the Langtons team against other schools and although they seldom won, they were consistently the best two runners for their own school. The two boys would keep a tally of their positions in inter-school competitions, each one aiming to score best over the complete cross-country season. In their last year at Langtons, they both finished with the same points when all inter-school races were over. They decided that the school cross-country race, always held near the end of the summer term, would settle the competition between them. They both trained hard, often together, and it was difficult to know who was the better runner.

The weather on the day of the annual school cross-country race was a great disappointment. A dense sea mist had rolled in from the English Channel, reducing visibility to no more than a few yards. The headmaster was concerned, but at the last minute the mist lifted and it was decided that the race should take place as planned. The start was at three o'clock and 15 minutes beforehand the headmaster called all the whole school together to give them a stern warning.

"Be careful boys. The weather is a little uncertain, but should be fine for the next hour. As an additional precaution, please ensure you can always see another runner, either in front of you or behind. I realize that in a race, especially one as important as this, it will not be easy, but do your best. Now, please all walk to the start, where Mr. Gray will start the race."

All sixty boys in the school made their way to the start alongside the chapel. Tradition dictated that every runner should have one hand on the chapel walls and it took a little while to ensure that every boy was ready. Mr. Gray held the starting pistol above his head, wished them all good luck, and fired the pistol much to the consternation of the roosting swallows. The boys took off down the lane towards the Priest's Way, the less experienced sprinting hard. Within a mile, those that had sprinted from the start were suffering. The members of the cross-country team, who were better judges of overall pace, picked off the front-runners one by one and a small group of five runners were soon at the front of the pack. Peter and Colin were with them, both feeling comfortable and matching each other stride for stride. At the turn, the two boys were still together, but now had built up a gap of some fifty yards ahead of the others. Every now and again they looked behind and could always just make out the next boy in the race. As the route turned off the Priest's Way towards the sea, the two boys slowed down slightly to make sure they could still see the others behind. Once they could, they pushed on a little harder, making sure that the gap remained. Peter and Colin were now starting to feel the strain. They were breathing heavily, too much even to speak to one another. In their individual minds, they were both thinking the same thoughts. Which one could hold out the longest? At what point should I try to pull ahead? Would I have enough left in me to sprint at the end? Then disaster struck. Colin, not seeing a small root across the path, tripped and fell. He landed awkwardly and twisted his left ankle. He stood up quickly and started to run again, but the pain shooting up his leg stopped him dead. Peter, stopping to help his friend, asked how bad it was.

"It's nothing," said Colin, "just a minor twist. I'm sure I can run it off soon. You go ahead and I'll catch you before the end. Guaranteed. You just wait and see."

Peter was uncertain. The two of them had come a long way together and it didn't seem right to leave his friend behind, even for a short while.

"Honestly, Peter, I'll be fine. You get along before the others catch up. Even if I have to walk from here, we cannot let anyone else win the race."

Peter hesitated. "Are you sure," he implored his friend. "It just doesn't feel right me going ahead with you like this."

"Peter, I would have left you behind at the finish, so it's honours even. Just get going!"

With that exclamation ringing in his ears, Peter set off again. He was concerned for his friend, but above all, he was still desperate to win the race. Anyway, he justified to himself, Colin could catch me at any moment. Then there would still be the ultimate struggle, perhaps even with the finish in sight. Peter took another turn, this time quite close to the sea. He knew that just a quarter of a mile ahead was the final turn inland and, although uphill, every step would bring him closer to touching the chapel wall.

Then the second disaster struck. As he turned, he hit what seemed like a thick wall of cloud. The sea mist had suddenly returned with a vengeance. It was so dense that momentarily Peter stopped in his tracks. He was totally disoriented, not knowing whether he was still on the path. It was a complete white out, with visibility near to zero. Peter slowly inched forwards, just able to make out the track beneath his feet. Peter then became seriously worried. He could hear the sea pounding the rocks to his right and knew the turn inland would take him to safety. But where was the turn? Peter then stopped. He was getting increasingly anxious, but knew he had to make a plan. This is what the school had taught him. In the school cub pack, he had learned how to pace distances and remembered that two of his paces measured a yard. The distance from the turn he'd just taken to the next turn was close to a quarter of a mile. He knew this from the number of times he'd run it before. Peter started to count, moving forward slowly, but steadily. He counted off the paces in hundreds, raising one finger from his clenched hand for every hundred paces. He reached 800 paces and was certain that the turn must be within the next hundred paces. Now he became desperate, searching cautiously at every pace for the left hand path away from the sea. He could feel his heartbeat drumming on his chest as if he were still running. Then he saw it. I narrow track through the high tufts of grass. He was so relieved and let out a long breath of sheer delight in seeing the path. Within a hundred yards uphill, he broke through the barrier of the dense sea mist into fresh, clear air. He thought he heard the sounds of boys shouting behind him, clearly following him on the upward path back to school. The goal was near. The prospect of winning the race was uppermost in his mind. He forged on, occasionally glancing behind him to look out for his pursuers. Most especially he was looking for Colin. By now Peter was reaching a state of total exhaustion. He knew that Colin could quite possibly out run him over the last few hundred yards. It became a race of survival. Time seemed to stand still as Peter struggled on. Then he saw it, some hundred yards ahead. It was the gate to the orchard at the side of the school. Through that gate he had just 150 yards to run to the chapel. He reached the wide-open gate, looked back once more and then dragged his tired legs to the very end. Mr. Gray was waiting for him and congratulated him as he touched the chapel wall. It was a glorious feeling. He could hardly stand and his legs gave way as he slumped to the soft grass. He had won.

"Well done, Culham. I knew it would be a tough one between you and Pearson, but you were clearly the stronger. I'm surprised you weren't closer together."

"Colin, I mean Pearson, sir, twisted his ankle, sir. He'll be in soon. He was just behind me before the turn at bottom. But then after that, the sea mist rolled in very quickly. I couldn't see a thing for a good way."

"Really," said Mr. Gray, "I thought we'd seen the end of that mist for today. How bad was it?"

"Terrible, sir. I had to walk for a good way."

As he spoke other runners started to come through the orchard gate and finish by touching the chapel wall.

"Where's Pearson," enquired Mr. Gray, "I would have expected him in by now. Which of you saw him?"

The exhausted runners, now slumped against the chapel walls, were surprised at the question.

"He was ahead of us," one of them answered, "we saw him way ahead with Culham."

"But what about the sea mist?" demanded Mr. Gray, his voice showing a new level of concern.

"We saw that ahead of us, sir. It was like a thick cloud, but it rolled further away as we got near it."

"So let me get this clear. It was only Culham and Pearson that were caught in the sea mist. The rest of you were all right."

The boys were now finishing in increasing numbers. Mr. Gray asked each one as they came in if anyone had seen Colin Pearson. None of them had seen him. Mr. Gray was now seriously worried.

"Culham," said Mr. Gray, "I want you to go into the school right now. Tell the headmaster that there may be a boy missing and don't come back 'till you find him. The rest of you stay right here. You may be needed for a search party."

Peter, now fully recovered, ran into the school. As it was a Saturday afternoon, no other staff were around, so he ran up to the front door of the headmaster's large house at the top of the school drive. He had never been to the headmaster's house and it was with a degree of trepidation that he opened the front garden gate. He walked, a little nervously, up to the front door and rang the bell, hearing its distinct chimes from inside the house. He waited, but there was no answer to the sound of the bell, He tried again, now getting increasingly alarmed as he recalled Mr. Gray's clear instructions to find the headmaster. Peter was now starting to panic as he hammered on the large front door. Still with no reply, Peter found the courage to go round the side of the house to the back garden. It was there he found the headmaster having tea with his wife on the back lawn.

"Hello Culham," said the headmaster, "I thought I heard a noise from the house, but wasn't sure. Is everything all right?"

"Mr. Gray sent me to find you, sir. Pearson hasn't returned from the cross-country and he's concerned. He's even talking about a search party."

"Right, Culham, I'm on my way. Better still, you take my wife's bike to get down the drive quicker and I will follow as soon as I'm changed. Please tell Mr. Gray to get the whole school assembled immediately in the dining hall and make sure everyone gets a drink and some toast straight away."

With that, the headmaster turned away from Peter, strode through the French windows and was gone. The headmaster's wife, recognizing the urgency, quickly fetched her bicycle from the garden shed and gave it to Peter.

"Don't you worry, Culham, I'm sure everything will be fine, " she said in a cheerful tone, but deep down she, like her husband, was deeply disturbed by the news.

Peter cycled like a man possessed back down the drive to Langtons and arrived panting at the chapel just as Mr. Gray was gathering the stragglers from the run together.

"The head is on his way, sir, and says to assemble everyone in the dining room. He says to give everyone a drink and toast."

The boys heard Peter's message and moved towards the dining room. Mr. Gray hurried the last few runners in the same direction and before long the whole school was together. The boys helped themselves to cold drinks and the senior boy on each table was soon toasting bread for his group. The headmaster arrived shortly after, conferred with Mr. Gray, and then announced.

"Boys, you've probably gathered that Pearson is missing, we think somewhere on the route of the run. Culham saw him last as the path went down towards the sea from the Priest's Way. I gather that there was a dense sea mist for a short time, so he could easily have become disoriented. Because of this, there is no point in searching beyond there, as he is unlikely to have doubled back. What we're going to do is organize a search party right now, backtracking over the second half of the cross-country course. We'll do it by everyone keeping in a straight line, half of you either side of the course. If you keep two yards apart, we should be able to search fifty yards either side of the course. This should be adequate to find him. As there are no other masters available today, I will take one flank and Mr. Gray the other. Everyone will move forward, searching slowly and carefully, keeping the line, unless of course, you find him. Any questions? Right finish your drink and we'll meet at the orchard gate immediately."

Drinks were gulped down and any remaining pieces of toast taken with them as the boys streamed out of the dining hall. Within minutes the boys were organized into a long line either side of the cross-country route. The worried group of boys headed along the familiar track towards the Priest's Way. As they reached the ancient trail, the boys stopped momentarily as the headmaster shouted from the end of the line.

"Right boys," he shouted, "from here on is the most likely place to find him. Remember, he may be have fallen and be on the ground, so look carefully in any long grass. Of we go."

The line moved forward like a platoon of soldiers on cautious offensive. It descended gradually towards the lower path near the sea. There was no sign of Colin Pearson as the line moved in unison, ever forward. After about ten minutes, the track stopped going down and set off either right or left.

"Right boys," shouted the headmaster once again, "We now swing round to the right, half of you on the far side of the path and the others this side with me. Let's go."

The line, with almost military precision, swung in a big arc to the right with the path at its centre. After another ten minutes of walking, the boys reached the point where the path headed inland again to rejoin the Priest's Way. Once again the line swung right and gently uphill. Another ten minutes later, the line met the Priest's Way and stopped.

"Culham, are you absolutely sure that you were still with Pearson when you left the Priest's Way?" said Mr. Gray, labouring a little after the climb up.

"I'm almost sure he tripped between here and the where the route turns left onto the lower path nearer the sea."

Mr. Gray was going to question the use of the word 'almost' but thought better of it in view of Peter's obvious distress.

"So we must have missed him. Everyone turn round, and then take just one extra step sideways. This way we'll cover more ground on the way back. Culham, one more thing, can you try to tell me the point where you hit the sea fog?"

"I'll try," Peter replied, although he was now getting a little confused and worried that he was remembering things clearly.

The search party turned round and retraced its steps. They were now covering a wider expanse of ground. In doing so, the land was more uneven, particularly towards the ends of the line. As they turned once more, this time to the left, Peter struggled to speak.

"I'm sorry, sir," he said to Mr. Gray, "I was running flat out so can't be sure, but I think I hit the fog about here."

"Thank you, Culham, that's helpful. Boys," he shouted, "now is the time to search really well. It's possible that Pearson got lost from here on."

With that exhortation, the line continued, slowly and methodically, with every boy now primed with the prospect of finding the injured runner. They arrived, once again, at the point where the route turned left and the runners would have headed uphill and eventually back to the school. The headmaster called a stop. He spoke quietly to Mr. Gray and then addressed the boys.

"The fog or sea mist, now thankfully gone, was apparently in this area. It's possible that Pearson missed this turn and carried on. The track gets a little tricky from here, as many of you know. This means we're going to reorganize a little. I will take just the senior boys with me and the rest of you will head back to school with Mr. Gray. But remember the search is not over. Those turning left here and going back to school must still search very carefully for Pearson. He could be anywhere. Right, time for the groups to split. All senior boys with me."

With that, the headmaster organized the group of eleven senior boys, Peter included, into a line across the path and set off. They were walking more slowly as the path was less clear and the ground a lot more rugged than before. There were loose stones, some small rocks and tree roots crossing the path. It would be easy to trip on this path, especially if running. Still there was no sign of Pearson. The boys were cautious about their own footing, as well as searching thoroughly either side of the indistinct path. After another ten minutes of searching, the group came to the steep, short, rocky descent to the familiar Dancing Ledge. The group stopped, because to continue would involve a scramble. It was the headmaster, his extra height giving him the advantage, who was the first to spot something in the pool below.

"I want you all to stay right here," he said, clearly alarmed by what he had seen, "I am going down to the pool."

Before he clambered down to Dancing Ledge, he gave one more command.

"I want all of you to sit down, just where you are and wait for me to come back."

He knew that if the boys sat down, they would be unable to see the pool. This would spare them any sight of what he feared most. He had seen something floating and quite still. He clambered down the rocks, still a little slippery from the earlier sea mist. He soon reached the pool and waded in to what he could now see all too clearly was a boy, head down and motionless. As he reached Pearson, the movement of the water caused a deep crimson stain to spread from the boy's head. He turned him over and one look told him that he was staring at death. There was no point in trying to revive him. He was holding in his arms the dead body of one of his best boys. Pearson's life had been lost to freak weather. It was he, the headmaster, who'd agreed the cross-country race should go ahead on this particular day. It was the 24th June 1957. Colin Pearson would have been thirteen years old, his adolescent life about to begin.

The boys, waiting at the top of the scramble down to Dancing Ledge, were sent back to school with clear instructions to send for an ambulance. The ambulance could get no further than the track from the school to the Priest's Way. The crew then used a stretcher to carry Pearson back from the pool and took his body away for examination. The headmaster called all the boys together in the chapel early that evening and told them the grim news. He explained that no one was to blame. It was the result of a cruel freak of nature. Prayers were said and Peter was asked if he knew Colin's favourite hymn. Peter, although overwhelmed by the events of the last few hours, was able to suggest 'Fight the good fight'. The boys, many with tears in their eyes, tried to sing, but most could do little than mouth the words as the organ played the stirring tune.

For Peter, it was the worst birthday he could imagine. The euphoria of winning the race had been thoroughly eclipsed by the loss of his close friend.

Peter was unable to eat properly for days, just picking at his food. His mind constantly went back to the time in the race when the two parted. Why did he leave his friend? Should he have stayed with him when he twisted his ankle? Did Colin really insist he went on alone? Colin said he would catch him up, or did he? These thoughts and many more raced through Peter's mind for days. He could hardly sleep. The headmaster's wife spent time with Peter. She patiently tried to explain to Peter the natural process of grieving. She described a circle, the circle of friendship between Peter and Colin, which would always be there. But then she added another circle outside, which she said would be new experiences in Peter's life. Things that could not involve Colin, because he was no longer with us. She tried to explain that these new life experiences, all in the future and over time, would give hope to Peter and help him cope with his great loss.

It was on the last day of term that Colin's funeral took place. The end of term service at Langtons took place at the same time and the boys stood for one minute in silent memory. Peter never forgot Colin. Peter thought of him every day for the rest of his life.

CHAPTER 12
ILLNESS

David was enjoying his final year at the local primary school in Witchford. Compared with other boys at the school, he was not a natural soccer player. He often suffered the indignity of being last choice when the boys picked the teams in the playground pick-up games. He tried hard, but had no great expectation of ever playing in the school team. One day, to his amazement and utter joy he was selected to play for the school's first team. For the first and only time, he relished the moment he pulled on the team shirt in the bright, quartered colours of green and purple. His performance was, as expected, modest, but at least he had played in the team. It was most likely the teacher's attitude to inclusion rather than his ability, but David never forgot the moment he wore that first team shirt. It was to be one of many, but never again in the game of soccer.

Rugby was more David's game. Every weekend, he would go with a friend from the village into Ely to learn the game with the junior section of the local club. The coaching started with small-sided teams in a restricted area and over time built up to tag rugby over half a pitch. Then came simplified tackling, introductions to scrums, lineouts, rucking and mauling. David, being tall for his age, became a specialized lineout jumper. He just loved the hurly-burly of the game, where the delicate footwork of soccer was less important. By the age of eleven, David had become the club's outstanding player and frequently won the man-of-the-match award. He enjoyed every moment of his rugby and looked forward to the weekends immensely. He could now compete in a game that suited his physique and temperament. For David, every match was the nearest thing to heaven.

One Friday, David felt a little off colour and came home from school feeling lethargic. His mother, Maggie, dosed him with mild aspirin and he went to bed much earlier than normal, not even wanting much to eat. When Sunday came and David showed no interest in going to the rugby club, his mother knew that something was wrong and planned to take him to the doctor first thing on Monday morning. Overnight, David showed all the symptoms of flu. He had a sore throat, a headache, his muscles ached and he'd been sick early on Monday morning. His mother, with her nursing training, decided against taking him to the surgery and requested a home visit. Dr. Taylor, a man known for his direct approach but excellent diagnostic skills, agreed that it was most likely to be flu. He insisted that David had complete bed rest for at least a week. The doctor, just before he left the Clarke household, took Maggie to one side.

"There is another possibility for young David, but being a fit lad, I'm not unduly worried. However if he gets worse in any way, I want you to ring me, day or night. Is that clear?"

The next morning, David awoke to find he was unable to move his legs and he was struggling to breathe. Maggie phoned for an ambulance and then Dr. Taylor. He reassured her that she was doing the right thing and would meet them at the hospital. True to his word, Dr. Taylor met Maggie at the emergency room and accompanied them both into a nearby cubicle.

"I'm sorry, Mrs. Clarke," began Dr. Taylor, "I had my doubts, but it was too early to be sure. The symptoms David are now showing suggest something much more serious and a throat swab and a blood test will confirm the worst."

He then rushed off to insist that a blood sample was taken immediately and analysed for antibodies. When he returned, the emergency staff had started to treat David, concentrating on his breathing, and setting up a variety of tubes and bags to get vital antibiotics into his body. David's breathing was still labored and Dr. Taylor, intervening once again, took the registrar to one side.

"I am positive we have a case of poliomyelitis here and with his breathing so labored, I am concerned that his respiratory muscles are involved. It is even possible that his diaphragm is paralysed. Have you ever seen a case of polio like this?"

The registrar admitted that he'd only seen the mildest of cases, never someone with such breathing difficulties.

"I've seen this twice before and he needs to be in tank ventilator immediately. You need to get him transferred to Cambridge as soon as possible. Addenbrooke's is the nearest place with a tank ventilator and the lungs of that young lad will fail without it. Do you understand my concern?"

The registrar nodded his agreement and immediately organized the transfer to Addenbrooke's. At Addenbrooke's, he was immediately placed in an airtight chamber in the form of a large metal tube. Only David's head protruded from this ghastly piece of apparatus, known to most people as an iron lung. At the other end of the ventilator, a motor moved a diaphragm and this changed the pressure inside the metal tube, forcing air in and out of David's lungs. It was two days later that the throat swab and blood test results confirmed David did have polio. There were two other iron lungs, side by side in the small ward. David was at first too weak to make himself heard above the constant hissing of the three machines, but within a week had gained enough strength to be able to chat to the other two boys in the ward. He learned that their experiences had been similar, none of them knowing how long they were likely to be in the infernal contraptions surrounding them. The nurses were kind, positive and cheerful, but they couldn't predict the future for the three incarcerated boys. They would just have to wait.

At the end of David's first week in the iron lung, one of the other boys, Thomas, was released from his metallic captivity and allowed to leave the ward. David was horrified to see that Thomas's left leg dragged on the floor as he was helped out of the ward by two orderlies. His own legs, which had been paralyzed on the day he was taken to hospital, now seemed to be much better. Within the iron lung, David could move his legs a little, but found them twisted into a strange position, something he found painful and alarming. Was this to be the end of his rugby? Was he going to be a cripple for life? Was he ever going to get out of this horrendous machine? He asked these questions and many more, but never received even a half satisfactory answer. He felt the medical staff were being honest; they simply didn't know.

At the end of the next week, Gareth, in the other iron lung, also left the ward. He was put straight into a wheelchair, so David couldn't see whether he could walk unaided. The two, iron lungs, either side of David, now lay empty and menacing. The motor keeping David alive continued to pulsate its ever-present rhythm. Every hiss of the motor was one more breath for David. Every movement of the diaphragm at David's feet gave him a few more seconds of life. One more stroke of the piston; one more moment of life. For hours at a time, David would fixate on the machine keeping him from certain death. This much he knew. At other times, David could forget the machine entirely and concentrate on other things, his mother, his father, his family, his friends. He even dared to think about his rugby; the thought of never playing again was especially upsetting.

During his time in the iron lung, David's dreams were vivid and often frightening. He saw himself getting older, unable to move unaided. In a kaleidoscope of illusions, he was totally paralyzed, running freely outside in the fresh air, and swimming in the broads; a whole mixture of images, some dark, some pleasant, a few exciting. The nurses assured him it was quite normal to dream in this way. They said it was probably the many drugs he was taking, stimulating his imagination. David wished he could make sense of it all, but mostly he just wanted to be well.

David suffered his eleventh birthday entrapped in his iron lung. By now it had become part of his being, a part of his life. He was troubled by the fact that no one could tell him how long he was to be entombed in this carapace of steel. Was it to be days, weeks or even years? Every three days, the doctors would come and make slight changes to the pressure changes in the fiendish device, but otherwise nothing changed. His parents and younger brother all came to see him on his birthday, bringing a selection of birthday and get well cards. His greatest wish was for a new pair of rugby boots, but his parents said to wait until he was better. They promised a pair for the beginning of the next rugby season, when, as they tactfully put it, his feet may have grown to a new size. David was unconvinced and the decision reinforced his fear for the future. Instead, David was given a three-piece fishing rod as his birthday present. He was excited at the prospect of his dad or grandfather taking him to lure the elusive fish from the hidden depths of the river. Under normal circumstances, it was something he could enjoy before the end of the summer. This, above all, gave him hope. Perhaps he would be freed from the snare that kept him so trapped. He just longed to be released from the shackles of the rhythmically hissing machine. He dreamt of the day he could be sitting at the side of the Great Ouse. His new rod in hand, his legs stretched out in the sun as he patiently watched the float bobbing in the moving stream. Was it a dream or reality? Would his life ever be so tranquil?

His mother showed him his birthday cards one by one. They were carefully propped up on a nearby windowsill so he could see them after they had left. He recognized almost all the names on the cards. Distant cousins and aunts were often familiar names, but rarely seen. There was one, a birthday card, sent by someone who meant nothing to him. The message, in a flowing style of writing, was simple. 'Best wishes for June 24th' was all it said. It was unsigned, adding to the mystery. David asked his mother about it and she appeared equally perplexed. As David looked at her, he noticed an enigmatic smile, or perhaps a slight frown, but she kept her thoughts to herself. Her response struck David as strangely curious, but he felt unable to pursue the matter further. David was sure that if she had anything to add, she would do so, but only when the time was right.

Another week went by, with David continuing to be imprisoned in his gruesome iron lung. At the end of the week, two doctors, accompanied by four younger medical students, gathered around him. They talked to David openly and in hushed tones to each other. They asked about his legs, they adjusted the motor driving the pressure changes in the ventilator. They watched. They waited. David sensed something quite different in the way the iron lung was behaving. He slowly felt the pressure changes over his body becoming less and less. Yet he was still breathing. At first a little hesitantly, but slowly he was taking control. Over a few minutes, perhaps ten, he could tell that the machine was becoming sluggish. Then it stopped. The sound he'd heard every moment for three tedious weeks had ceased. It was silent. The silence shocked him into taking a deep breath, then another and on and on. He was breathing by himself. The doctors still waited. They still watched. David could see them visibly relax. They seemed pleased. Then, as one, the great clamps holding the infernal machine together were released. It was open. He was almost free. But not quite. The doctors were fussing over his legs. They prodded and pushed. They felt and they bent. They made notes and they spoke to each other using words, which meant nothing to David.

They called a nurse, who came in with an orderly. Words were whispered. Decisions made and then the doctors all left. David's parents both came in with smiles on their faces. David sat up for the first time in three weeks. It was a struggle and he needed help. He looked down to see his legs, little more than skin and bones, the muscles badly wasted. As a precaution he was lifted gently into a wheelchair. As he left the ward he looked back at the machine that had saved his life. It didn't seem as horrendous when he was leaving it behind, but he would never forget the perpetual hiss of its motor as it breathed life into his struggling lungs.

David could not go straight home. He was taken immediately to the physiotherapy department on the ground floor where an attractive young lady explained what rehabilitation was needed. She was slim and athletic, with her blond hair tied in a ponytail. She introduced herself as Julia and explained she'd recently been trained but had some experience of polio. It had been of special interest during her clinical training. She gave David a series of exercises to strengthen his lungs, but her main concern was the limited movement in his legs. She explained that the lack of mobility was in part caused by localized damage to some of David's nerves. It was also caused by the way his muscles had wasted when in the iron lung. She was positive yet retained a level of honesty. She didn't believe in raising hopes unrealistically. David, although an optimistic child by nature, appreciated her sincerity. The first thing Julia did was to remove David's leg braces – those awful reminders of his disease. He was given them just in case they were ever needed, but David resolved there and then that they did little but reflect the past. He considered keeping them as a memento, but that would undermine his resolve to look forward, not back. It showed David's determination when he returned his braces to Julia and asked never to see them again.

She told David that with the exercises they would do together, his legs would soon grow stronger again. She also said that the limited flexion of his leg joints was likely to take longer and may never recover entirely. David had seen boys his age in leg braces and feared the worst. He suspected he might never play rugby again and shared these uneasy thoughts with Julia. She could make no promises, but told him about a very new procedure, yet to be fully evaluated. She wanted to see if it would help in his recovery. It was experimental, but earlier trials on adults had looked promising. David's parents readily gave permission for her to try this novel approach. David was the very first young person to test this new form of treatment. It involved strapping David's legs into a primitive machine that allowed movement but always resisted the movement at a controlled speed. The machine could be adjusted to fit either side of David's knees, or his ankles or his hips. At first David could move his joints very little, but both he and Julia persevered. Over several weeks they could see a remarkable change in the range of movement and the strength of all his leg muscles. By the end of the summer, David was able to walk, although he couldn't straighten his left foot fully. Running was virtually impossible, but David was grateful that he could walk unaided. He soon found that although his left ankle remained stiff, he could do everything except run any faster than a slow trot. As David left the hospital, Julia kissed him goodbye. He couldn't hide a tear of gratitude. He wanted to hug this divine creature who had restored his limbs and his confidence, but she was gone.

He was desperate to get back to his rugby and depressed by the prospect of never again playing the game he loved. It was his grandfather who suggested he might try refereeing, as this was something he could do at a more leisurely pace. David was excited by the prospect and volunteered to referee some of the practice games at his old club. He took to it well and loved the way he was involved again. It was then that his grandfather recommended he should sit the basic referee exam to become qualified. It involved reading and re-reading the book on the laws of the game, a chore that David actually enjoyed. In spite of his young age, David passed the written test. Arrangements were then made for him to be watched by an assessor while he controlled a proper match. His old club at Ely made all the arrangements and David, although making the odd mistake, was considered easily good enough to be awarded the Cambridge Referees Association basic award. It didn't compare with playing the game, but it gave David a new and fulfilling goal. There were times, when locked in that pulsating metal coffin, that David had felt any purpose in life slowly ebbing away.

He now decided that refereeing a rugby match was only to be the start. The experience had taught him fortitude, perseverance and above all hope. This meant he had a new resolve to achieve considerably more. The direction was as yet uncertain. For David, this uncertainty was to be a stimulus. For the first time in his life, he felt a developing fire in his belly. He was determined to fan the flames of tenacity. The setback of his illness, would serve him well.

CHAPTER 13
CATHEDRAL

David was the only one from Witchford Primary School to win a scholarship to the prestigious Ely Cathedral School. The honey-coloured buildings were in the shadow of the magnificent Ely Cathedral and the Ely scholars were the backbone of the Cathedral choir. David was excited, yet apprehensive when he first walked through the imposing gates of the school. He was expecting to know no one and was relieved when a familiar face from his old rugby team was seen sitting just a few seats away. He was in the mysteriously named lower 4B, a class of eager, but unsettled boys like himself. He found that the boys in the other class, lower 4A, had already been taught Latin, mostly in the junior school attached to the Cathedral. David's first history lesson explained all about the origins of the school, going back over 400 years, when founded by King Henry VIII. The school uniform was a dark blue blazer with a badge showing the coat of arms of the Cathedral, three gold crowns on a red background. David could hardly believe the extent of the school buildings and grounds. He was shown the rugby fields, the tennis courts and even an outdoor swimming pool.

Every morning there was an assembly for the whole school in College Hall, a building that was originally the refectory for the monks. The boys sat on wooden benches facing a raised area on which sat the masters of the school. In front of the masters was a row of thirteen chairs, six either side of the imposing headmaster, the Rev Dr. Wilfred Jackson, or 'Big Willy' as the boys nicknamed him. The twelve most senior boys in the school, the monitors, sat in the other chairs. These boys were the heads and deputy heads of the school houses, four of which were boarding houses and the other two dayboy houses.

Around College Hall were mahogany honour boards, listing in gold lettering all the former students who had gained scholarships to Oxford and Cambridge colleges. David looked at these with mild interest, wondering if his name might one day grace these hallowed boards. At the very back of College Hall were some badly defaced statues, set in a large alcove. It was said that Oliver Cromwell had defaced these statues during the Civil War and that College Hall had been used as a stable for his horses.

David was allocated to one of the dayboy houses, named Orford after one of the former bishops. Membership of houses was mainly used for sporting contests and each boy wore a special tie to depict their house. David's was dark blue with gold stripes. David was worried that the slight limp, left over from his polio, would prevent him from representing his house. Once the news was out that he was a qualified referee, David found himself in big demand to referee house rugby matches. At first one of the masters would watch him, but it wasn't long before he was trusted to referee the matches alone. He still missed playing the game, but gained huge satisfaction from controlling the boys under his charge. Some boys might have been cautious in penalizing friends for breaking the laws of the game, but David showed no bias or favour and would deal with any transgressions suitably.

In spite of David's physical limitation, he enjoyed most aspects of school life. He particularly took to English and Maths, but struggled with Latin, hating the rote learning of conjugations and declensions. It was in David's third year at Ely Cathedral School that everything changed. The school was five minutes walk from the River Ouse and during the summer holidays, David had spent many a happy hour fishing from the pontoons of the school's boathouse. In term time, the boathouse was a hive of activity, with the senior boys rowing on the long stretch of river reaching majestically into the surrounding, tranquil countryside. In the summer of David's third year, he was introduced to the sport of rowing, a sport he had only previously seen from afar. The poor flexibility of his ankle was no handicap in rowing and he was excited by the prospect of trying something totally new. His introduction to rowing was initially using what was called a 'tub pair'. This was a heavy, clinker built, wooden boat, with two fixed seats, not unlike the sort of craft you might have seen on a public boating lake. It was so heavy, that these boats were usually left in the water between outings. This meant that after rain, the first job was to bale out the accumulated water. One of the school's coaching team, always a master, would sit in an uncomfortable wooden seat facing the two rowers. He would steer and teach the boys the basics of rowing – legs, body, arms in a continuous cycle. It was hard in these wide, heavy, uncomfortable boats, but over time the boys learned to cope with difficult water conditions. Over the summer term, David and other novices learned to use their whole body to pull the oar through the water in the most efficient way. The following year, boys progressed to rowing in a four-oared boat. It was still a wooden, clinker built boat, but unlike the tub pairs, these boats had sliding seats. As the boys became more skilled and they learned to balance the boat, it started to move through the water faster and faster. David had now found a sport he could enjoy fully and not be limited by the after effects of his polio. He loved the rhythmic movement of the crew as they moved in near perfect synchrony within the boat. They learned to catch the water as a single unit, to push hard through the water and to drop their hands to remove the blade before sliding to the front to repeat the cycle. They would adjust the pressure on their feet and the level of their hands to balance the boat, to rotate their inner hand to make sure that the blade hit the water at exactly the right angle and to keep perfect time with the stroke. There were times when David was cold and wet; times when he was exhausted from the demands of the outing; times when his hands blistered from the constant chafing from the wooden handle; yet throughout he knew that this was his sport, and would become his love, and his passion.

David matured to become bigger and stronger. His size and strength soon made him a key member of the crew. The next year the boys progressed to rowing an eight-oared boat, made of very thin wood. It was a much lighter boat, slimmer in outline, faster, but more difficult to balance. David loved to feel the rush of water under the boat as it sped along the surface of the river. He was in his element.

David was selected for the Colts VIII and represented the school at various regattas in the summer term. They won medals at schools' events at Hereford and Newark. David, for the first time in his life, started to enjoy the feeling of testing his own body against others of his own age. The training had been hard, but the excitement of winning made it all worthwhile.

In the spring of 1960, David saw a short article in the Ely Gazette referring to the possibility of applying for a place in a cultural exchange to the USSR. He applied but was rejected on the grounds that the tour was restricted to people who had no plans for higher education. However some weeks later, David received a letter inviting him to re-apply. Evidently applications had been few and so the County of Cambridgeshire was prepared to broaden the field of applicants. David duly applied, was interviewed, and accepted onto the trip, which was during the summer holidays. The visit to the USSR was the first time David had been abroad. It was with great excitement that he boarded the train at St. Pancras station to start the journey across France, Germany, Poland and eventually to the heart of Russia in Moscow.

This was to be an experience that would awaken his love of adventure.

Browsing in the famous GUM departmental store on Red Square, David felt a slight nudge followed by "Have you any money?" in a strong Russian accent. His immediate reaction was to answer "No", because the currency exchange on entering the country had been thorough and exacting. Then he remembered a five-pound note in a back pocket and pulled it out, only to find that the questioner had disappeared. Five minutes later he was back and whispered "Don't show the money; meet me in the toilet".

A few minutes later David was 35 roubles richer, some five times the current exchange rate! After a hurried, stilted and uneasy conversation, they agreed to meet later that night, planning to sell any of his spare clothing.

David confided in a fellow student and they arranged to go together, if nothing else, for moral support. David arranged to meet his contact at midnight in nearby Gorky Park. They cautiously left their hotel wearing several layers of clothing, planning to sell everything they could manage without.

The air of expectancy and anticipation was electric as the two friends walked from Park Kultury Metro station through poorly lit streets towards the rendezvous. Nothing happened at first and then out of the shadows came the contact, slowly, slyly and constantly checking in every direction. Clothes were stripped off, handed over and exchanged for a small fortune in roubles.

The two boys strolled back to the hotel, totally unaware of the serious consequences of their action, but buoyed up by cascades of adrenaline, coupled with sheer naivety.

The next morning, realism hit them hard; not so much the concerns of criminal action, but simply the large amount of surplus cash now in their possession. They just had to find a way to spend this embarrassing and potentially dangerous newfound wealth. They travelled everywhere by taxi, ate caviar and drank champagne. In restaurants they devoured the most expensive dishes, even resorting to the local delicacy of bear steaks.

After three weeks in Russia, they left the country with numerous, costly souvenirs and when the currency exchange was complete, had apparently spent no more than £30. As the steamer headed into the Baltic from Leningrad, it was an incredible relief to know they were outside the three-mile international boundary and free from Russian control.

David picked up a paper from the purser's office and with help, translated the front-page headline. "Students arrested in Moscow for possession of foreign clothing." David broke into a mild, guilty sweat.

By the time David reached the lower sixth year at school, his growth spurt had resulted in the height and physique of a young man. He was as big and strong as boys at least a year older and was promoted to row in the school first VIII. The boys he now rowed with were much older, so he was moved from the powerhouse of the boat to the number three position, near the bow. The training became severe and David was out on the water for four days a week; on Wednesday and Saturday afternoons and after school on Monday and Thursday. Each outing was at least two hours in length and involved demanding schedules of rowing at different speeds, distances and intensities. David would get home after these training sessions totally exhausted, with little energy to devote to his studies. But the rewards made it all worthwhile. The crew developed the rhythm of catch, drive and recovery – the timeless cadence, which is rarely found on grass or ballroom. They were now a solid, cohesive unit, with the boat surging forward as eight oars struck the water in faultless unison. The crew performed well in the long distance Head of the River Races. The crew won the schools division at Ely Head of the River, and came third to Radley and Eton Colleges on the tideway in London, over the same course as the Boat Race. Following this success, David was awarded his rowing colours. It meant he could now wear the resplendent white blazer, trimmed with blue braid and with the school badge and crossed rowing oars on the left breast pocket. Every July, Ely Cathedral School's first VIII went to Henley Royal Regatta. They rowed in the Princess Elizabeth Cup, an event for schools and colleges from around the world. Henley was very much the highlight of the rowing calendar and one of the main social events of the year. It was host to thousands of spectators along the bankside and was rowed on a dead straight course of almost a mile and a half. The men would sport their rowing club blazers and the ladies would look elegant in the latest summer fashion. Crews would come from around the world to compete and the prestige of rowing at Henley was considered the highlight of any rower's personal ambition. The regatta lasted for four days, with only the winning crews progressing to the next day. Ely Cathedral School had always booked rooms at the Angel Hotel in Henley and this year was no exception. David had read about Henley for years and even had a clipping in his scrapbook of two crews competing there. He had now been rowing for four years and had put in numerous hard miles on the River Ouse, not to mention the additional, arduous training with weights and running. It had been a huge commitment, but to go to Henley would make it all worthwhile. To add to David's excitement, he would be seventeen years of age, just before the regatta started.

Two weeks before Henley, at the end of one particularly exhausting training session, the captain of the crew came up to David and took him to one side.

"David," he said, "have your folks booked accommodation at Henley for the regatta?"

"I doubt it," David replied, "They will both be working during Henley week so I will just be there with the crew."

"Well that's the problem," said the captain, "the coach has decided to move things around a bit. Purnell is to be promoted to the first VIII in your place and from now on you will now be rowing in the second VIII."

David was devastated. His ambition to row at Henley was dashed in a conversation lasting less than a minute. He failed to appreciate fully what had just been said. He was numbed by the thought, the disgrace, and the consequence. For years his sole aim in rowing had been to race on the magnificent and iconic stretch of water at Henley. This worthy goal, this personal and honourable aspiration was now in tatters. He was overwhelmed with shock and couldn't find words to express his loss, his grief, his feeling of utter dejection. He took the bus back to Witchford in a state of semi-paralysis; unable to function beyond the most basic movements required to reach his home. He dropped his bag in the hallway, slumped down at the dining table and sat staring at the meal his mother had prepared. He knew that he had no option but to tell his parents the awful news and did so quietly, hesitantly and tearfully. Then came the floodgates. He wept, openly and uncontrollably. It was hard for his parents to see this boy, this young man, in such a state. They did the best thing. They waited. After several minutes, David stopped crying, blew his nose, wiped his face and silently ate the now cold meal.

David's parents were desperate to hug him, to console him in any way, to support him, but they took their time. It was for the best. David needed to find his own way through his disappointment.

Later that night, as David was going to bed, his father stopped him for a moment. This was the man who had seen first hand the horrors of war in Burma, so David always listened to him, even if he didn't always agree.

"David," he said, "what I am going to say will be of little help to you right now, but perhaps in time you will understand. The real measure of the man is not that you appear, by your standards, to have failed, but how you respond. You have choices. You can be miserable, bitter, resentful and seek recrimination. Alternatively you can accept the situation as it is and use this disappointment to better yourself in some way. Not easy, especially right now. It's your choice. Now get yourself off to bed, young man."

David lay in bed that night and thought back to what had been said to him at the boathouse. It all seemed to hinge on whether his parents had booked to stay at Henley for the week. David knew deep down they could never afford such extravagance and part of him wished that they could. It might have meant that things could have played out so differently. Life was cruel, but the one thing his parents had taught him over the years was that regret is a wasted emotion. Never did he feel it more keenly than now. After a wretched night, wallowing in self-pity, David awoke with his father's words still fresh in his mind. "It's your choice," he had said. It was hard, and David struggled to choose. The overwhelming news of yesterday failed to lift his spirits, especially today. It was David's seventeenth birthday, the 24th June.

The first VIII, now without David, went to Henley Royal Regatta that year and was knocked out on the second day. David joined the second VIII and won three regattas at Marlow, Bewdley and Newark. It was the best set of results the second VIII had ever achieved and David was pleased to be part of it. Yet, he still had to learn to live with the disappointment of not rowing at Henley. He thought for some time about his father's wise words, but found acceptance to be a huge challenge. He hoped that time would heal, but for now the wound was still deep.

CHAPTER 14
DOWNTHORPE

Peter started at Downthorpe in September 1957. The school, set in the rolling Quantock Hills to the west of Bridgewater, was originally part of the Franciscan community at nearby Downthorpe Abbey.

The school buildings were austere and forbidding. They looked particularly so as Peter arrived on an overcast day, with the nearby hills hidden in the mist. Peter, having survived five years at Langtons, thought he knew what to expect of his new school. With few exceptions, the staff were all monks, steeped in the Franciscan tradition. The air of Catholicism exuded from the very walls of the school. The doctrine started with prayers at breakfast, and continued with a formal assembly, composed of hymns, prayers and school notices. Mass was observed every Sunday and failure to attend was considered sinful. A few boys thrived in such an environment and happily accepted the spiritual routine as one of comfort. A few rejected it entirely and dismissed the whole ethos as intolerable, just waiting to escape its confines or becoming militant. The majority, Peter included, travelled a middle road of benign acceptance. They found a balance between the companionship of close friends and the rigours of questionable learning, seasoned regularly with harsh levels of discipline.

With the exception of science, art and music lessons, the boys would remain in one room throughout the day. The classroom became their cell with a rare escape for exercise or food. The monks, in their robes, would wander from room to room looking like scarab beetles searching for scraps of food.

Peter soon made friends, mainly boys from the same dormitory. He still couldn't erase from his mind his close friend, Colin, who died at Langtons. Every evening, Peter, along with other boys would kneel in silent prayer. He never failed to include Colin's soul in his prayers. He believed strongly it was the least he could do.

At Downthorpe, punishments were common for a range of misdemeanors, mostly trite such as not raising one's cap to a master. The most common punishment was what was called a 'penal drill'. It involved cleaning the school for an hour after lessons had finished for the day. Mostly the drill required the boys to empty rubbish bins, but sometimes the boys were given filthy tasks such as cleaning out drains. The worst part of the penal drill was that it could be given by the prefects and even traded for personal chores such as cleaning their shoes, clothes or studies. It was typical of boarding schools that a hierarchy existed, but exclusively for the benefit of the senior boys.

Other punishments at Downthorpe included detentions and running. Detentions were only for poor academic work and took place every Wednesday evening, supervised by either a prefect or one of the monks. The running was given as an alternative punishment to the penal drill. This punishment developed in most boys a deep hatred of running. A group would assemble after school, wearing only shorts and a singlet, whatever the weather. The set punishment course was about five miles long and went from the school up the lanes into the Quantock hills. A senior prefect would check off the names of the miscreants from his clipboard and then set them off. The board would then be attached, with great care, to a spring clip on the back of his bicycle. The prefect would then return to his room for a cup of tea and after about twenty minutes would set off in pursuit. Any laggards would receive discouraging threats of being made to repeat the run. These were usually empty threats. No prefect would want to repeat the exercise, but no boy could be sure. At the furthest point in the run, the prefect would wait with his bicycle, stub out his cigarette, and laboriously tick off the names of the offenders. As the boys turned and headed for home, the prefect would cycle past, taking great delight in slapping each one on the back of the head as he sped by. The prefect would be re-acquainted with his tea and toast long before the fastest runner was even half way home. The punishment run was always at five-o-clock on a Thursday. In the summer this was almost tolerable, but once the clocks went back in October, the dark evenings and poorly lit lanes created extra hazards for the runners. There was also the additional incentive of returning to school before the start of the evening meal. The food itself was of little interest, but a youngster who had not eaten since noon would be desperate for any form of sustenance. As latecomers had nothing but leftovers, it meant the punishment of running became a serious race. It seemed fairly random whether the boys would receive a penal drill or a run as punishment, but they suspected that if the weather were bad, the run would be chosen.

Cross-country running was also used at Downthorpe as a form of exercise, especially for those boys incapable of catching or kicking a ball. In Peter's first year the cross-country runs were no different from the punishment runs, organized in exactly the same way. Then in Peter's second year at Downthorpe, a new member of staff, Nick Yates, joined the school. Mr. Yates had a real interest and love of running. Peter had enjoyed his running at Langtons and soon became one of the youngest, but keenest, members of the newly formed cross-country club. Nick Yates was an experienced runner, who had competed for his county in cross-country and on the track. He introduced training methods unheard of at Downthorpe. Members of the running club learned new terms and new techniques. These included fartlek, interval training, tempo runs and hill repetitions. They were hard, intensive sessions, but Nick Yates was able to adjust them to every boy's ability. Most importantly, he made them fun and the boys soon progressed to become outstanding athletes. For the first time in its long history, Downthorpe School became a force in cross-country running and Peter loved being part of the team.

During every school holiday, Peter would return to Hadleigh Hall to spend time with his mother and stepfather, Viscount Culham. He enjoyed these times, particularly wandering alone around the Hadleigh estate. In the summer, he would volunteer to be the scorer at Hadleigh Cricket Club and watched the game keenly. On one day, towards the end of the summer holidays following his second year at Downthorpe, Peter detected a change at Hadleigh Hall. There seemed to be a sense of urgency about life, with household items being moved, stacked and packed. Peter asked his mother, what was happening, fearing that the Hall was to be sold or closed for some reason. Celia sat Peter down and explained as best she could.

"We were about to tell you, Peter, but nothing had been confirmed until today. Your father has been appointed as Governor-General of Rhodesia. It means that we will be moving there within the next few weeks. I'm sorry to break the news to you like this, but we honestly didn't know until today and I didn't want to worry you unduly."

"But mummy, what about my school, " said Peter in alarm, "will I have to leave Downthorpe?"

"Absolutely not, Peter. Arrangements have been made and you will be able to stay at Downthorpe until you go to University. You will always be able to come to visit us in the holidays, just as you do now. The only difference will be the long journey to Rhodesia, but I am sure you will be able to manage that. In fact it could be quite exciting. It is a five year appointment and after that things will soon be back to normal here."

Peter was stunned at the news, but was relieved that the unusual activity at Hadleigh Hall was now clear. He had never been to Africa, so was excited by the prospect. He looked forward immensely to visiting a country so different from his own. It was a land of wide-open spaces, of huge skies and a variety of wild animals. How could a young boy not be excited? Most of all, he was able to continue his studies and his beloved running at Downthorpe. Peter's life had changing again and it was changing him.

Back at Downthorpe, life was to change in a most unpleasant way. One of the masters, Father John as he was known, would teach small groups of boys in his own flat attached to the school. This was fairly normal at Downthorpe, because the small groups meant that a large classroom was available for other classes. Peter, now aged fourteen and with a shock of blonde hair, would sit in the flat with five other boys as Father John introduced them to the basics of philosophy. As the class was dismissed, Father John asked Peter to stay behind. He said that there were matters he needed to discuss.

"I've been concerned about your level of concentration in my class, Culham, and I'm thinking of putting you in detention."

Peter accepted that sometimes his mind had wandered. He was worried about his parents over in Rhodesia. He particularly missed talking to his mother, something he did often when she was in this country. For Peter, the prospect of a detention had a more worrying outcome; he would miss one of his running sessions with Mr. Yates, something he looked forward to immensely.

"Alternatively, Culham, we could deal with it differently," said Father John, interrupting Peter's thoughts.

"Just you bend over that chair, Culham and wait for me."

Peter had never been beaten before. He knew that at Downthorpe it was used occasionally to deal with certain serious offences such as staying out late. He also knew that it could hurt. He was terrified of the prospect, especially as he could hardly see why he deserved such punishment. A minute later Father John returned to find Peter bending over and gripping the chair handles tightly. The anticipation was excruciating.

"Stay bent over and put your hands behind your back," commanded Father John.

Peter did as he was told as Father John spread what seemed like some type of cream on Peter's hands. Peter was mystified. Why was Father John doing this? Was he going to hit my hands and the cream would lessen the pain?

"Stay bent over and looking forward Peter. Just rub your hands gently together."

Father John unfastened his dark robes and undid his trousers. It was then that Peter felt Father John's enlarged organ slide between his own slippery fingers. Peter froze with shock, now realizing exactly what was happening.

"No, Peter, keep your hands cupped and a little firmer," demanded Father John.

Peter was incapable of thought, action or any lucid response. He just wanted it all to finish. Father John suddenly laid his hands on Peter's head as he mumbled something totally incoherent. With a final gasp, Father John climaxed into the poor boy's hands and collapsed on his knees as if in prayer. Peter daren't move. He was trembling, totally devoid of understanding. After less than a minute, Peter just heard the word 'Amen' and Father John rose from his knees.

"Now Peter, go and wash your hands in the bathroom."

Peter did as he was told, still in a semi-hypnotic state and quite unable to believe what had just happened. On his return, Father John was totally composed and handed Peter a bowl of ice cream.

"I know you boys all like ice cream," he said, "take your time."

So this was the repulsive payoff, thought Peter. You get a disgusting bowl of ice cream so Father John can have his hateful way. Peter ate the ice cream contemptuously, not enjoying a single mouthful.

"Peter, you can go now, but you realize that this little business has to remain a total secret. It wouldn't do for something like this to prejudice the important work you father is doing in Rhodesia, now would it?"

Peter was silent. He left Father John's flat concerned and upset. Above all, Peter's overriding emotion was simple. He wanted revenge. Peter was prepared to wait until the right moment.

It was several weeks later that Father John asked Peter to stay behind again after the philosophy lesson in his flat.

"How are your parents getting on in Rhodesia," asked Father John. Peter knew he was trapped. He knew how damaging things could be to a newly appointed Governor-General if the wrong thing was said. Peter also realized that it would be one person's word against another and no one would believe him.

"You like ice cream don't you Peter," said Father John, once they were alone.

"Yes sir," Peter replied as he turned towards the chair.

" No not this time, Peter," came the disturbing response from Father John.

"Just sit on the chair facing me."

Peter had no option but to do as the loathsome creature demanded. Father John once again unfastened his robe and unzipped his trousers to expose his engorged and fully erect member. He took Peter's hands and placed them either side of his repulsive organ.

"Right, Peter, I think we will start with a little kissing. Just place your lovely lips on the end."

Peter, now terrified into submission, did as he was told.

"Lovely Peter, now a little gentle sucking."

Peter was utterly revolted, but had little option.

"Good, Peter. Very good."

At this Father John placed his hands on Peter's head as he had done before.

"Now Peter, deeper, suck deeper. Oh beautiful. Oh Peter, lovely, lovely"

At this ghastly moment, Peter felt an acrid taste in his mouth and Father John sighed in quiet ecstasy. Peter grabbed a nearby tissue and spat out while Father John slipped to his knees. Peter watched as the pathetic and vile specimen of humanity stayed on his knees for a full minute. With a whispered 'Amen', Father John rose, and, as before, sent Peter to the bathroom. When Peter returned, he was, once again, given a bowl of ice cream. It was the last thing that Peter wanted; he just needed to get away from this odious man. Peter grabbed the bowl, rushed to the bathroom and spooned the ice cream into his mouth. He spat each mouthful straight back into the toilet, trying his best to rid himself of the revulsion he had just experienced. Every time that Peter spat he swore an oath that one day he would get his revenge.

A month later, Peter was, once again invited to stay behind after the lesson with Father John. Peter was ready and gave a good reason to leave with the others.

"I just wanted to chat about your parents," said the abhorrent teacher.

Peter dared not risk any shame to become attached, by inference, to his parents. He had little choice but to stay behind and suffer the perversions of this detestable man.

"Peter, it wouldn't do if your parents got to hear of what you have been doing with me, now would it? Most especially if it were made public?"

Peter remained silent,

"I thought so, Peter, now turn to face that chair."

Peter automatically put his hands behind his back.

"No, Peter, not this time. Just put your hands on the back of the chair and leave them there. I do like a cooperative young boy."

Peter obeyed, unwillingly. The prospect of his parents suffering was too much for Peter to contemplate. Peter' trousers and underpants were pulled down roughly, leaving his feet trapped in the crumpled clothing.

"There, Peter, it wasn't too bad was it?"

Peter was horrified to feel the monk caress his buttocks, skillfully rubbing cream into him.

"What are you doing to me?" Peter cried in alarm as the rubbing became more intense and more intimate.

"Just shut up you little runt," was the abrupt reply, and with that Father John slipped himself inside Peter.

Peter could have lashed out, but was disabled by the quite unbelievable experience he was suffering. The pain was intolerable, but Peter gripped his teeth and refused to cry out. Father John placed his hands on Peter's head and with one last agonizing thrust, and a guttural scream, discharged himself into him. Peter was in agony. Knowing that it was over, he turned to see the repulsive monk on his knees. Peter pulled up his trousers and still in considerable pain, walked toward the door. As Peter fled from the room, the last word he heard was 'Amen'.

Peter knew that if he went to see matron, the whole incident would be out in the open. Any investigation would be Peter's word against a member of staff. He could never win. Not only that, but his parents would get involved and he would have to leave Downthorpe. He swore that this would never happen again, whatever it took.

Peter hardly slept that night, his physical and mental discomfort keeping him awake. He thought of nothing but retribution, but how? In spite of his persistent soreness, he finally fell asleep. Even the few hours of sleep were troubled by a nightmare of frightening proportions. He was locked in an airless room with a group of hooded monks, some in prayer and others holding him down. He managed to escape but as he tried to run, his legs were heavy and he could hardly move them. He awoke in a cold, fearful sweat, the sheets damp and clammy. As he turned he, once again, felt sore. The soreness of sodomy.

Peter didn't turn up for the cross-country club session that week. He mentioned to one of the other runners that he felt a little off colour and to tell Mr. Yates he would be back soon. After four days, Peter went running by himself and began to feel a little better. His discomfort had eased a little and he hated to miss his running training. He went back to the regular session the next day and took part as best he could. He was still feeling sore, but was desperate to be back with the club. It was important to him after what had happened. It represented normality, something he craved. At the end of the session, Nick Yates took him to one side.

"Peter, you don't seem to be yourself today. Are you OK?"

"Sorry, sir, just a little sore."

"I thought as much, you seem to have lost a bit of your usual confidence and your running style isn't as fluid as normal."

"I could have been overdoing it, sir. I went on a long cycle ride and seem to be suffering"

Nick Yates had run in a number of marathons and had often experienced soreness on the inside of his upper legs.

"I've got just the thing for that, Peter. I'm pretty sure I have some in my office. Come over when you've changed."

Later that afternoon Peter went to Nick Yates's untidy office to find him behind a pile of books.

"Hi, Peter, good to see you. You know earlier that I thought you had lost a bit of confidence. It seemed to me a little more than that. You didn't mix with the others like you normally do. You seemed a bit withdrawn, morose even. Are you sure you're OK?"

Peter tried to change the subject without appearing too rude.

"I've just come about my soreness, Sir. You said you might have something."

"Oh right. Yes. Now where an earth could I have put it."

Nick Yates rummaged around on the shelves behind him and then looked in a filing cabinet.

"No. Can't find it. Hang on, it could be in my training bag."

With that, Nick moved towards his bag, which had been thrown by the door. In doing so, he brushed past Peter, who recoiled visibly from his touch.

"Hey, steady on, Peter. It's OK."

At that, Peter slumped in a chair and looked bewildered, almost vacant.

"Look Peter," Nick said, "this may not be the time, but if you need to talk about anything, feel free. It doesn't have to be me, but you know I will listen and you can be assured of my confidentiality."

"Thanks," was all that Peter could manage.

Nick Yates paused for a moment and then opened his bag, turning to search for the Sudafed cream.

"Here you go," he said, "just the thing. This stuff is used by cyclists and runners when they get sore and works wonders. Use it liberally and you'll be fixed up in no time."

Peter thanked him and promised to see him at the next session in three days time.

"And no long-distance cycling," Nick shouted as Peter left the room.

Three days later, Peter turned up for the running training and seemed more like his old self. The soreness had improved, but more importantly so had Peter's resolve. As the session finished and the boys were jogging back to school, Nick Yates waited until Peter was alone and casually commented that he seemed to be almost back to normal.

"Thank you sir, yes the cream was a great help."

Nick Yates was happy to leave it at that, but then Peter surprised him.

"I've thought about things, sir and I would like to talk."

"Come to my office, just as soon as you've changed. There is no time like the present."

Nick then called all the boys together when they reached the changing rooms.

"In a circle, boys, shoulders touching." This was the way they always finished a session, with Nick Yates part of the circle.

"Great session, boys. Plenty of excellent quality there and I loved the way that many of you are looking more relaxed in the shoulders. Those intervals were hard, but when it comes to the next race, you will find it very worthwhile. Now get away with you and have a good evening."

With that the boys and master all ran to the centre of the circle and slapped their right hands together in perfect unison before heading off. Peter showered, perhaps a little more discreetly than normal, and made his way to Nick Yates's office. Mr. Yates already had a cup of tea waiting for Peter and placed it in front of him. He moved his chair so they were both on the same side of the desk and sat down.

"Peter, lets start by repeating what I said earlier. Unless I have your permission, anything that is said between us stays that way. Now in your own time, tell me what's troubling you."

Peter took a deep breath. He knew this wouldn't be easy, but with Nick Yates he felt a little more comfortable. Peter thought it best to come straight out with it and say what had to be said.

"One of the masters has been taking advantage of me, sir."

""Taking advantage?"

"Yes sir, he makes sure that I am alone with him and then he performs crude acts on me. It's really horrible."

Nick Yates was visibly shocked. His features took on a determined look of deep concentration.

"I see."

"The problem is, sir, that I only stay because he threatens me. He says he will let my parents know and that would cause them distress. Dad may even lose his job and it would be unbearable."

"I see."

"Do you believe me, sir? If you didn't believe me, I just don't know what I'd do."

Mr. Yates sat still for a moment, thought and then, turning to Peter, said,

"Of course I believe you, Peter, let's get that straight from the start. It takes a lot of guts to talk to anyone about this horrible business, especially involving a master. Be assured, Peter, I trust you."

"Thank you, sir."

"Now the thing is, Peter, what to do about it. Whoever this scum is, and at this stage you don't have to give me a name, I will support you. I will do my best to get him away from this school before any more damage is done. But we have a problem, Peter. In a situation like this it's always one word against another. What we need, Peter, is corroboration. We need to find out if this is happening to other boys. Not an easy task, because I am sure, like you, it's too difficult a subject to talk about. Even if you did give me a name, it may not help just now. What you need to do is a little detective work. You need to talk to other boys about him; boys of your age and perhaps a little younger. See if anyone else will open up. See if what he's doing is widespread. Then if you do find that he's molesting other boys, find out if any one of them would be prepared to talk about it. Some may not. Like you, the rotten brute may have some sort of hold on them. But if two or three of you would agree to testify to what he is doing, then that should be enough. Corroboration, Peter, it's all about corroboration. Peter, I'm dreadfully sorry this has happened. It must be absolutely horrendous for you. Rest assured, I am determined to do something about it. You find other lads he has abused and leave the rest to me. Peter, do you have any questions?"

"No, sir."

"Right, then we have a plan. Best of luck."

Nick Yates stood up and almost stretched out to shake Peter's hand, but thought better of it. He was annoyed that a simple gesture of support like this was inappropriate right now. He was looking forward to a level of normality.

Over the next few weeks, Peter slowly and cautiously spent his free time talking with a number of boys. He broached the subject with sensitivity, often just chatting about other masters, but eventually bringing Father John into the conversation. In almost every case, he found that Father John was either totally disliked or his reputation was questionable. The boys would often make negative comments such as 'that bastard should be locked up' or 'the guy's rotten, he shouldn't be left around boys'. The trouble was that Peter couldn't get anything specific. He was getting downhearted, as remarks seemed nothing more than hearsay. Then came the breakthrough. He noticed two boys a year younger than himself who seemed to be upset and keeping away from others. He talked to them, casually at first and then more specifically about his own experiences. This was what both these boys needed, someone who had shared their experiences and soon they were talking openly. Peter was horrified that they had suffered the same abuse, possibly worse because they were younger. He patiently explained that there was someone on the staff who could help them, but he needed written evidence. Over time the boys, with much reluctance, agreed. They wrote down their experiences in as much detail as they could. It all took time and considerable bravery on the part of each of them, but they were by now convinced that this was the only way.

Peter handed the incriminating documents to Nick Yates, who read them with increasing horror.

"Are you happy to leave these with me," he said.

Peter trusted him to deal with things in the best possible way, and answered "Yes, sir. I hope it'll stop this vile man from what he's doing. There may be more boys affected, but this is all I could get on him for now."

"It should be enough, Peter, but you must be prepared for some rather horrible interviews with the headmaster."

"Yes, sir. I told the others the same."

Two days later, the headmaster and one of the school governors interviewed Peter and the two younger boys. It was a harrowing experience for them all and one of the boys broke down under the stress of the detail he was forced to describe.

Nothing was said for several days and then a notice went up on the school board. It read 'Due to ill health, Father John will not be teaching any of his classes for the rest of the term'. Peter and the other two boys were delighted and the general feeling in the school was one of relief.

One month later, at the end of year school assembly, the headmaster traditionally gave thanks to those members of staff who were leaving. Following mass, he stood up and paid tribute to the deputy head, who was retiring, to the French assistante who was going back to France and to Father John. After he thanked the deputy head, a popular man who had been with the school for 32 years, the school erupted with appreciative clapping. After he thanked the French assistante, who had only been at the school a year, there was another round of enthusiastic clapping. Following his brief thanks for the ten years that Father John had been at the school, there was absolute silence. Nick Yates couldn't help a wry smile and Peter couldn't help but notice.

Peter looked forward to the summer holidays knowing that justice could never fully be achieved, but it was a start. The day might yet come to gain revenge for the mental and physical hurt caused by the repugnant Father John. Peter was prepared to wait for that day.

CHAPTER 15
EIGHTEENTH

On the day Peter finished his A levels, he said goodbye to his friends at Downthorpe, to Nick Yates, his running mentor, and headed home to Hadleigh Hall. He had sat through three weeks of examinations and it was a great relief to put them behind him for the summer. He left a school that had given him great satisfaction from his running and misery during the dark moments of his abuse. His mother and Viscount Culham, who knew nothing of these things, had returned from Rhodesia for a short break. They used the time away from diplomatic service to plan his eighteenth birthday party.

The weekend was organised in its entirety by his parents, with Peter being offered little input to the festivities. In some respects, Peter accepted this, especially since his mind had been focused on exams for so long. In other respects, Peter objected to his lack of involvement. He was not initially consulted over the guest list. Almost as an afterthought he was asked to invite a couple of friends from school. Peter was to be eighteen, on the threshold of manhood and was a little resentful of his parents' control. When the weekend of celebration arrived, Peter resolved to put these issues to one side. He was determined to have a good time. He was ready to move on.

Friday 22nd June was a glorious summer day with not a cloud in the sky. The Hadleigh Cricket Club pitch was immaculate, well suited to the special game that had been arranged. Viscount Culham had used his influence to assemble an impressive touring MCC team, which consisted of three current England players and the rest from the local County squads. The Hadleigh team had been strengthened for the occasion by former England players, past their best, but still useful with bat and ball. Peter played for the Hadleigh team and although his contribution was limited to a three-over spell of bowling and arriving at the crease late in the innings, he held his own in the distinguished company. The single-innings match was played with skill and verve on both sides and the result was a two-wicket win for the MCC. Celebrations went on well into the night, with most of the players staying overnight at Hadleigh Hall. The players left the next morning after a splendid breakfast and, once gone, preparations began in earnest for the evening party.

Outside caterers were brought in to cook and organize the food, some of which was stored in huge refrigerators in the old stables. Viscount Culham took personal responsibility to oversee the bar arrangements, paying particular attention to the choice of wines and spirits. His time at University had included a useful spell as vintner for his College. At University, he was supposed to be studying the ancient Greeks, but learned considerably more about wine. He had, with some foresight, laid down a selection of fine wines at Hadleigh, including some Gevrey Chambertin and Sancerre. Single malt whisky was also one of Neil Culham's interests and he generously made a case of his Mortlach Rare Old Speyside available for the celebration. The guests were mainly the great and the good of Shropshire, with a few high-ranking diplomats and other friends and colleagues of both Celia and Neil Culham.

The Long Gallery was laid out for the food and the adjacent Ballroom for the dancing. A jazz quartet provided the music; jazz being a genre that both Celia and Neil especially enjoyed. Peter half expected the guests to be announced by name as they entered the ballroom and was thankful that this particular embarrassment was avoided. The men wore dinner jackets and the ladies looked resplendent in their ball gowns. Peter found the majority of them a little mature for his tastes, especially as a number of the middle-aged ladies insisted on dancing with him. Peter himself, although he would have preferred to party with all his friends from Downthorpe, resolved to make the best of it. He had grown into a tall and handsome young man, with chiseled features, which suited him. Although he felt his parents were controlling all aspects the weekend unnecessarily, he did his best to accept the situation. He appreciated that it was done with the best of intentions and he had little ground for complaint. Hadleigh Hall itself had been lit from the outside with a large array of spotlights and looked very impressive. It was a memorable evening, although Peter wasn't sure that it was really for his benefit or those of his parents.

The next day, after mass in the little church that sat between the Hall and the cricket pitch, a smaller number of guests prepared for Sunday lunch. As they gathered outside for pre-lunch drinks, an unusual noise was heard from the East. It was the sound of rotor blades from a helicopter and it soon landed with care on the outfield of the cricket pitch. Peter half expected a minor royal to emerge, but Neil Culham turned to him and said simply,

"Peter, time for your first lesson!"

Peter was thrilled. He had gained his private pilots' licence as part of his CCF training at Downthorpe and had always hoped that one day he'd have the chance to fly a helicopter. The half hour lesson was a great success and Peter was totally captivated by the experience. Little was he to know then, the dramatic consequence of his 18th birthday present.

Many of the guests over the weekend gave him presents, but two stood out for quite different reasons. One was a beautiful brass microscope in a walnut box. Clearly not new, but in excellent working order and made by the master craftsmen of R and J Beck. It had three separate eyepieces to give different optical magnification and came with a selection of slides. There was no gift tag with it, so Peter asked his mother who had so kindly given him such a splendid present. His mother was a little evasive and said, with a degree of mystery, that all will be revealed in the morning. The other was even more mysterious. It was a long-playing record by Tony Sheridan entitled 'My Bonnie', issued on the Polydor label. The band listed on the back was credited as The Beat Boys, but the name meant nothing to Peter. The record intrigued Peter and he resolved to ask his mother about it in the morning.

Monday morning duly arrived, with a few overnight guests leaving after breakfast. The caterers had returned to remove anything left over from the party and a whole army of cleaners descended on the hall to return it to normal. Peter was slow to surface that morning, although his intrigue over the two mysterious presents made sure he appeared for morning coffee. He found Celia and Neil in the Drawing Room and joined them for a pot of strong Arabic coffee, something he missed when away from home.

"Good morning, Peter," said his mother, looking a little uneasy.

"Thanks for a great weekend, it was very special," Peter replied, "especially the helicopter lesson."

Neil smiled but said nothing.

"Neil and I have been wanting to talk to you for a little while," said his mother, "but we have never really found the right moment. We think that this is it."

Peter put his coffee cup down carefully and turned to face them both.

"The microscope you were given yesterday, originally belonged to my former husband, Willard Boulton. It has been in my possession for over ten years and I've kept it all this time, thinking that one day you should have it for yourself. He was a doctor and I assume that the microscope would have been part of his training or indeed his work abroad. I didn't consider it appropriate at the time, because you were only six years old, but I can now tell you that Willard was killed in action in Korea. He was working with the Canadian Army. In fact, although we lived in Britain, he was originally Canadian."

Celia stopped speaking and indicated to Neil, who poured her another coffee from the silver coffee pot on the table next to him. Peter was stunned into silence, but then regained his composure.

"I do remember him," said Peter. "He told me he needed to go away, but I thought over the years that you'd fallen out of love for each other and he'd found someone else."

"No," said Celia quietly, "that was never the case. I think you may not have remembered correctly. You were only six, but I told you then that he had died. He worked with the British Army as a medical officer and was transferred to join the Canadians in the Korean War. He was killed in the defence of Kapyong Valley, along with a number of other Canadian soldiers."

"So where is he buried?' Peter enquired, desperately wanting more details.

"I'm afraid I could never find out. Details were very scant and the front line moved backwards and forward all the time. Perhaps one day you might be able to find out for yourself. I'm sorry, Peter, I just wish I could tell you more."

Peter sat in thought, struggling to remember the man he saw so rarely when he was so much younger.

"Peter, as the three of us are together, there is one other thing, I think you ought to know."

Peter looked up, still contemplating the news about the death of Willard.

"Peter, although Willard and I were married when he died, you were conceived some time before that."

"I know that, Mum. I've seen your marriage certificate and it was clear that I was born a few months before you were married to my biological father."

"That's exactly right, Peter." She paused, took a deep breath and then added, " Peter, I just need to tell you that Willard may not, in fact be your biological father."

"What do you mean?' Peter said with renewed interest.

"When we were together, we had no plans for children at that stage in our lives. During the war, Willard was finishing his training so was not called up immediately for active service. Towards the end of the war, he was conscripted and joined the Army Medical Corps. He served in Germany and saw some things so revolting he could never talk about them. During the early part of our time together, he was not the only man in my life. I had other boyfriends, some more serious than others. It is difficult for you to understand, but the war years made everything more intense somehow. Things happened with greater spontaneity than normal. I make no excuses, Peter. It was just the way things were, or perhaps I should be more honest and say it was my way. When I became pregnant with you, it was a total shock and as I said earlier, totally unexpected. It was then that Willard and I decided to get married."

"So what you are saying is that Willard may not be my true father?'

"Peter, all I can say is that it is a possibility. My heartfelt feeling is that Willard was your father, but I feel this is the time to be totally honest with you."

Peter frowned and sat motionless for a while, reflecting at length what he had just heard. He then got up, strode across the room and kissed his mother full on the lips.

"What the heck, Mum, that was eighteen years ago and everything's changed."

Celia smiled, a mixture of relief and joy. Relief that what had been said was over and joy that her only son had shown such understanding.

"Peter, there is one other thing; not as dramatic as what has just been said, but still important. Neil and I have been considering your future with us. We wondered if you would consider formalizing our family relationship. Neil would like to adopt you and make you his heir. It's nothing too special at the moment, but in years to come it will make a difference. As you know, Neil has been like a true father to you for the last ten years and…"

Viscount Culham interrupted and looked straight at Peter.

"Peter," he said, "I know it hasn't been easy for you over the last few years. With your mother and I now living abroad, it makes it doubly difficult. I have tried to make you welcome to Hadleigh Hall and I have enjoyed our time together. I think it would be marvelous if you became a Culham in every sense of the word. Please feel free to think about it and let us know your thoughts."

Peter promised to do so, although he was inclined to say yes there and then. He had never expected to become part of the Culham dynasty, so was shocked yet excited at the implications. He did need to think carefully about what had been just said. Along with the benefits of his future inheritance, he would incur huge responsibilities. He lay awake most of the night, going over and over in his mind what had been suggested and what it all could mean. As the dawn light stole across Hadleigh Park, he had made up his mind. After breakfast he took Neil to one side, thanked him for his offer and said,

"You've made me a wonderful offer and I fully appreciate what you are suggesting. I realize that in due time the responsibilities and challenges will be enormous. However, I'm more than willing to face these and would love to see the Culham family name continue here at Hadleigh. My only reservation is one of timing. As you know I was set on reading either medicine or engineering at University. Strangely the gift of the microscope has become a sort of portent for me. It has made me commit to medicine and the whole notion of studying it is suddenly very exciting. It's as though it has been something I wanted to do all along, but never quite realized until yesterday. Can you understand that, Neil, or am I being melodramatic?"

"Not in the slightest, Peter. It's great to have a passion for something, even if it's come rather out of the blue."

"So you would support me going to medical school for five or six years, even though I couldn't possibly be involved in Hadleigh during this time."

"But of course. Although I plan to be in Rhodesia for a while, my post is only temporary. To be honest with you, Peter, things are moving so fast in that country that I could be kicked out pretty soon. Then I'll be back and managing Hadleigh as before. When you have qualified and settled, then we can discuss the future of the place in more detail. Your own studies are far more important for now. Other things can wait."

Peter's concerns abated and the prospect one day of taking on Hadleigh Hall was quite electrifying. He was confident that the challenge was something he could tackle. He just needed time to learn all the skills to achieve it. This was all in the long-distant future. For now he would concentrate on University and all it offered. Before that he decided there were two things he needed to do. One was to find Willard's grave. The other was to investigate more the mysterious gift of the long-playing record. Of the two, Willard's grave was the most pressing.

Over one dramatic weekend, Peter had learned things about his past and made critical decisions about his future. It was weekend that would stay in his memory forever.

CHAPTER 16
MISSION

Peter was not starting at medical school until September, so he could now plan the rest of the summer. The reminder of his father's death had hit hard and he felt a strange yearning to find his final resting place. It would mean travelling to a part of the world that had until recently been off limits, but this added to the excitement of his mission. Although he had no need, he sought the blessing of his mother and she showed interest without enthusiasm. The money he'd been given for his birthday was more than sufficient to cover his airfare to Seoul. He'd saved enough over the years to cover any additional expenses he might need during his proposed trip. Peter took a charter flight out of Gatwick for Korea. Charter flights had only recently been introduced as an alternative to the main airline carriers. He was intrigued to see how the charter process would work. Peter was required to join a notional club before he could use the charter flight. From a choice of three, he chose the Yorkshire Ornithological Association and duly paid his one-pound membership. This amused Peter as he had never been to Yorkshire and wasn't that interested in birds.

The plane was completely full; mainly students keen to experience the fascination of South East Asia. There were a few Koreans, returning home for the first time since the war and three Indian families, loaded down with presents for home. It was a motley group of 68 young people that boarded the Douglas DC6, with most having never flown before. Rucksacks and battered bags were dumped unceremoniously into the sparse overhead lockers. The eager passengers settled into the narrow and uncomfortable seats, quickly establishing friends, at least for the next 24 hours of the flight. As the four propellers wound up to full speed on the tarmac, the whole plane shook alarmingly. It trundled along the runway, slowly gathering sufficient momentum to defy gravity. The miracle of flight was like a giant bird heading into the overcast skies over South East England.

The first stop was Ankara in Turkey, where there wasn't even the opportunity to stretch cramped legs. The passengers were denied the option of leaving the plane, as it was nothing more than a refueling stop. The dated craft, almost as old as Peter, took off once again, heading further east, this time to Delhi. The three Indian families disembarked in Delhi, to be replaced by more students, all clearly sampling the hippy trail. Their long, lank hair, bright clothing, beads and faint smell of marihuana added an air of mystery to the final leg of the flight to Seoul. After so many hours in the air, most people had lost interest in flying, but when the co-pilot announced their imminent arrival, the air of expectancy was palpable. The plane drew to a halt, early in the morning, to the steamy, oppressive atmosphere of the Asian summer. Peter was relieved this first stage of his mission was now thankfully over. The passengers walked unsteadily down the plane's steps. They tested their legs gingerly after such a long time folded like hermit crabs in the limited space of each seat.

Peter was able to clear customs quickly as he had no luggage in the hold. He made his way into the dazzling sunlight of a country he'd rarely considered until the day after his birthday, just two weeks before. He bought a cheap map at a small bookstore on the airport concourse and sat down to study it. His mouth was dry after the flight and was pleased to see the nearby coffee bar sold fresh orange juice from a strange-looking machine that squeezed the individual oranges, one after another.

He saw that Kapyong was directly to the east of Seoul. It seemed to be in a mountainous, sparsely populated area of the country. His map could tell him little else. With the help of staff at the airport information office, he took a local bus to the centre of town. Other airline passengers, those who couldn't afford taxis, were all crammed into an ancient vehicle with only three rows of seats. Peter was the first on the bus, but was happy to give up his seat to a very attractive Korean girl of about his own age. She smiled and thanked him in perfect English, which encouraged Peter to ask her for onward directions to Kapyong. The girl, whose name was Mi Sun, was studying English at Seoul University. She was on her way back from New York, where she'd been taking an intensive English course as part of her studies. They happily talked all the way into the town centre, the conversation distracting Peter from the fatigue of travel. As they arrived, Mi Sun admitted she lived close to Kapyong and would show him the best way to get there. Peter was intrigued she hadn't admitted to living there earlier in their conversation, but assumed she was finding out more about him before committing to any further involvement. The two young people soon found a bus going to Kapyong and settled down together in adjacent seats. The prospect of spending time with Mi Sun was something Peter was looking forward to immensely. He took every opportunity to talk to this delightful lady about her country and the region of Kapyong, but tactfully avoided any mention of the war. The bus journey was hot, airless and uncomfortable, but Peter hardly noticed it in the presence of this dark-haired beauty. When Mi Sun asked where he was staying, Peter had to admit he'd made no particular plans. He welcomed her advice and she recommended a small teahouse just outside her village. After a journey of several hours, the two of them left the bus to be refreshed by the light breeze of the early evening. It was then, almost as an afterthought, that Mi Sun asked Peter why he was travelling to that part of the world. Peter explained cautiously that it was a long story, but Mi Sun seemed genuinely interested. Peter then took the initiative and invited her to join him for dinner, not really knowing where they could eat. She explained the opportunities were limited, but agreed to meet him at his teahouse at seven that evening.

The teahouse was a simple affair, with two rooms above what appeared to be a stable. The family lived in one room and guests in the other, all sleeping on simple futons on the floor. It was clean and Peter was the only guest, so he threw his rucksack on the floor and stretched out on a futon to relieve aching muscled from the cramped conditions of the journey.

He awoke two hours later, still fully dressed, to find it was now dark. It took a moment to realize where he was and as his eyes adjusted to the dark, he could just make out a small, rather scruffy child staring at him. He stretched, took a torch from his rucksack and looked at his watch. It was seven thirty. He scrambled to his feet, annoyed with himself that he had overslept and already ruined his date with Mi Sun. He rushed outside to find Mi Sun sitting peacefully on a wooden bench in the garden. She looked heavenly in the clear moonlight and had changed from her travelling clothes to wear a modern styling of the traditional hanbok dress. Peter was captivated and couldn't help but take a deep breath of appreciation. He felt himself blushing at the sudden strength of feelings towards her. She smiled, accepted his apologies, and suggested that he took a shower before they went for dinner. Peter then realized what a sight he must have looked. His hair was uncombed; his face unshaved; his teeth uncleaned; his clothes rumpled from two days of travel and he probably smelt foul. He gladly accepted her suggestion and ran inside to find a shower. The lady running the teahouse showed him the shower, which was outside and hardly even tepid. It was a joy to feel the cool water trickling over his body and he was tempted to stay there and enjoy the moment. Peter had always found a shower the best way to revive the spirits, especially after a hot and long day. The prospect of an evening with Mi Sun brought him to his senses and as he toweled himself down with a renewed sense of anticipation. He pulled on fresh clothes, shaved rapidly with the now cold water, combed his hair, and presented himself afresh to Mi Sun, waiting patiently in the garden.

"I must apologize," she said, on seeing Peter, "but tonight is a religious festival and there is nowhere open to eat. To make amends, I have brought us a small picnic. I do hope you will not be too disappointed."

Peter was far from disappointed and was excited by the prospect of trying some local food, especially in the company of such an attractive woman.

"We can eat here, or if you wish walk to my favourite spot overlooking the river. It's not too far."

Peter would have walked any distance to be with Mi Sun that evening and soon the two of them had strolled the short distance through the woods to a small knoll overlooking the River Kapyong. It was an enchanting setting and Mi Sun's preparation was superb. She first laid out a blanket on the grass and took a small bottle from the heavily laden basket.

"Please spread this on your face, arms and legs. It is to avoid the terrors of the night insects," she said with a smile. Peter took her advice, but noticed that she didn't follow his lead.

"Aren't you using it?" he said, surprised that she seemed to find it unnecessary.

"We local people add it to our bath water and do not seem to be troubled. You foreign people will need all the help you can get. The insects at night, especially out in the open, are worse than mosquitoes."

Peter knew full well from his annual visits to Rhodesia that night insects can be incredibly annoying and was relieved that Mi Sun had cared for him in this way.

The basket was opened and Mi Sun revealed, one by one, a fascinating selection of dishes, each wrapped either in fruit leaves or, less romantically, in tin foil. Peter was delighted as she explained the contents of each dish. First there was bulgogi, which was marinated beef, barbequed to perfection and wrapped in vine leaves. In an instant, Peter's senses were stimulated by the soft, delicate smell of the sauce as the vine leaves were parted. It was more than sufficient to appreciate the skill and endeavour of the person who had prepared this delight. A person, Peter was sure sat beside him at this magical moment. Fermented vegetables called kimchi followed the bulgogi. Peter wasn't so sure about this particular delicacy as his taste buds had been conditioned to school meals and simple home cooking. Mi Sun placed the kimchi on delicate china plates and couldn't help but laugh out loud watching Peter's efforts with the chopsticks. Peter struggled as best he could and was soon able to manage a small amount without losing most of it to gravity. He was relieved that Mi Sun gave him a beautifully painted bowl with matching spoon to eat the sundubu-jjigae with bibimbap. This was a soft tofu stew and mixed rice. The final course of the meal was a sweet confection of sweet syrupy pancakes, called hoeddeok.

Peter lay back on the blanket, savouring the palette of tastes he had just experienced. To him it was nothing less than a medley that suggested the comfort of a whisky after a hard day on the fells with the joyous clink of goblets filled with celebratory champagne. With his hands clasped behind his head, Peter watched as a few remaining streaks of crimson and violet shot the sky to the east. The rising moon soon cast its embryonic glow over the valley. Mi Sun packed everything away in the basket and temptingly lay down beside him.

"Do you have nights like this in England?" she asked out of genuine curiosity.

"Very rarely," Peter answered truthfully, " and never after such a wonderful meal and with such a beautiful girl."

The two lay there, neither wishing to speak and spoil the magical spell that seemed to embrace them. They couldn't fail to be mesmerized by the night sky, now in its full starlit glory.

Peter edged his hand closer to Mi Sun's and cautiously placed his little finger on Mi Sun's. At first there was no response but then to Peter's delight, she entwined her finger in his. The two of them, lay still, linked together by the barest of touch. Peter had never felt quite like this before and found the moment both peaceful and exhilarating. He was captivated by Mi Sun's charm but he felt unable to express himself further. His mind went back to the reason for his visit and wondered if his father had moments like this. Then this flight of fancy gave way to the present. He felt Mi Sun gently unwind their fingers, stand up, smooth out her hanbok, and almost in a whisper say,

"We should go."

With great reluctance, Peter followed her lead. He folded the blanket, took the basket from her, smiled and strolled alongside this exotically captivating woman. Peter stopped for a moment, and took one last, lingering look at the place they had shared together. Mi Sun also stopped and as they turned and walked back to the village, it seemed perfectly natural that when their hands touched, their fingers should once again intertwine. Neither spoke, each one thinking their own private thoughts; thoughts that if they had shared, could almost have been as one.

The next day, Peter struggled to know how much he should involve Mi Sun in his search for his father's grave. He was worried that memories of the Korean War would be raw in the minds of local people, yet he needed help. In the end he decided to raise the subject directly with Mi Sun. At first, she was reluctant to discuss the past. She patiently explained to Peter that although she was only a child, the war had been devastating for her family. She had lost close relatives to the brutality of the hostilities in the area and found difficulty in talking about such torrid times. Peter understood and was content to let the subject drop, not wishing to cause Mi Sun any further distress. The wounds of the past, if not healed, should remain untouched.

Peter was unsure how to proceed because he was still desperate to find evidence of his father's death. Mi Sun suggested he talk to the local mayor, someone she knew could be helpful and would in all likelihood be very knowledgeable about the recent conflict. Mi Sun offered to act as a translator for Peter. They met and the three of them sat in the shade, sipping coffee as the difficult subject was broached.

The mayor was obliging, but uncertain how he could best help Peter. He explained that the nature of the warfare made it extremely difficult to recover remains of the fallen and to conduct burials. The front line was constantly changing and the rugged nature of the area made such things challenging. It was a harsh climate and above all there was the ever-present danger from unexploded bombs and booby traps. He explained that of the 516 soldiers killed in the Kapyong Valley offensive, only 378 were buried, the rest having no recorded place of rest. Peter was disappointed, but accepted that in times of war this was inevitable. Then the mayor surprised Peter by telling him of a recently opened Memorial Cemetery at the nearby city of Busan.

"I am told that over 2000 soldiers from the Korean War are buried there. That may be your best hope."

Peter was inspired by the news and made arrangements to take a bus to Busan later that day. It was with a heavy heart that he said goodbye to Mi Sun. They stood together at the bus stop, remembering the gentle touch from the night before – the tentative linking of their fingers in the moonlight. As the bus arrived, Peter bent to kiss Mi Sun. As they drew together, Mi Sun placed an upturned finger between their lips and said quietly,

"To the future."

Peter, sad that his intended kiss had been averted, was still encouraged by her words. As he climbed aboard the bus, he turned to back, wanting once more to see her smiling face and to repeat "To the future." But she had gone.

The journey to Busan took less than two hours and was as uneventful as it was hot and clammy. Once again the bus was filled with locals and their various items of luggage. Peter studied with interest the loads that people were carrying, most perched precariously on their knees. He decided that the woven plastic bags, raffia boxes and cages must be full of produce to sell in the markets of the larger town. He wondered if Mi Sun's family bought and sold in the same way, but his deeper thoughts were for Mi Sun alone.

The bus arrived in the heat of mid afternoon. In spite of Peter's dehydrated and sweat stained state, he used the rest of the day to pursue his personal mission. He was lucky to find a shopkeeper, who, for the price of a bottle of water, would direct him to the Memorial Cemetery. It was in the outskirts of the town, but Peter was determined. He trudged wearily, but with purpose, along the dusty highway in the direction he'd been given. The blocks of concrete flats in the city soon gave way to small brick bungalows, most with tiny gardens planted with a variety of vegetables. Then further on, the buildings were little more than wooden and corrugated iron shacks, some housing a thin goat resting in the shade. The road itself deteriorated from tarmac to a pot-holed sandy track, but up ahead Peter could make out some large gates set in a low stone wall. As he reached the gates, a sign in Korean and English told him he had reached his destination. The sign read "United Nations Memorial Cemetery of Korea". Two booths were outside, one selling flowers and the other offering cold drinks. These he ignored and pushed open the gate to find a small sentry box just inside. The creaking of the gate had clearly woken the sole occupant. This unshaven man, hastily put on his official cap, and stood to attention.

Peter showed his father's name to the guardian of the gate, who by now was fully awake and noticeably more animated. The guard recorded the name in a dog-eared book. His official duties over, he waved Peter into the cemetery. Peter walked on see an orderly vista of graves, each with slate coloured gravestones set slightly above the ground. Between each gravestone was either a small, beautifully maintained box tree hedge or a shrub, most commonly a red rose. Peter was overawed by the size, symmetry and sheer beauty of the place. Each nation was marked with its national flag, so it was easy for Peter to make his way to the Canadian section. On his way to the Canadian graves, he was surprised to see the burial places of the dead from nations such Turkey and Norway. Peter was ashamed to be unaware that these countries were involved in the Korean War. Eventually he stood, with head bowed, facing the graves of the Canadians who had lost their lives in the conflict. After a short prayer, he moved from gravestone to gravestone, searching with anticipation for the name of his father. He checked and double checked, but could find no grave marked with the name he so longed to see. He walked solemnly to the British section to repeat the process, knowing that his father was seconded to the Canadian detachment from the British Army. Peter suffered the same fruitless search. At the centre of the cemetery was a brown marble wall with all the names of the fallen etched in gold. In the British section he found two members of the Royal Army Corps, but neither was the one he was so desperate to find. The Canadian section on the wall, with the few names on it, was the same. Peter was disappointed, but was mature enough to accept that in times of war, things rarely happened in a logical fashion. He'd already been warned that many bodies were never recovered, but still he could only hope.

At this moment, the guardian of the gate came rushing over to Peter and started stabbing at his watch, indicating that something was to happen quite soon. It took them both a little time to make each other understood, but after much gesticulation, Peter realized there was to be a flag ceremony at precisely six-o-clock. Peter walked with indecent haste back to the gate and was fortunate to find for sale a bunch of arum lilies. These were the very flowers that had adorned the lichgate for his mother's wedding. He went back inside to stand alone at respectful attention. The flag ceremony was observed nightly by the tribute guard of the 53rd division of the Korean Army.

It was a short, poignant ceremony and Peter felt honoured to be part of such an emotional occasion. Before it finished, the sergeant at arms, seeing Peter there with his bunch of lilies, marched up to him. He indicated that Peter should place the lilies on the grave to the unknown warrior. Peter was moved by the invitation and walked over to the spot, tearfully bending on one knee to place the lilies in position. The flags of the nations involved in the conflict were then raised and the ceremony ended with a lone bugler playing a short, haunting lament. The soldiers marched away and Peter stood in silence. The grave of the unknown warrior could be that of his father.

CHAPTER 17
MUSIC

Back home in Hadleigh Hall, Peter had most of September to occupy before starting at University. His disappointing experience in Korea had not daunted his enthusiasm for adventure and meeting Mi Sun had lifted his spirits, just when it was needed most. In quiet moments, there was still something leaving Peter perplexed. At first, he couldn't bring it to mind, but one day as he was sorting out a few items to take up to Cambridge, he remembered. It was the strange, long-playing record he'd been given for his birthday last June. He'd planned to ask his mother about it, but with the revelation about his father and the offer from Neil to be his heir, he had quite forgotten. Over dinner that evening he raised the subject with Celia.

"You know for my birthday, I was given Dad's antique microscope. Well if you recall, I was also given a long-playing record, something called 'My Bonnie' featuring Tony Sheridan. I found it this morning and it means very little to me. Who was it from?"

"I've no idea," replied his mother truthfully. "I seem to remember it came by post a few days before your birthday. It was addressed to you. I put it with the others, so we could see you opening all your presents together."

"You make me sound like a six year old," Peter retorted, but was smiling as he spoke.

"I'm sorry. Perhaps I shouldn't have done that. Force of habit I guess. Have you played it yet?"

"Yes, I did, on the gramophone upstairs. It seemed to be some sort of recording of various bands, all rock and roll. Some were good and some pretty rough. I had the impression that most of the recordings were made live, perhaps in a club or dance hall. Only two of the tracks seemed to have the clarity of a studio recording."

"Peter, I'm as mystified as you. Could it just be a friend, perhaps from school or something?"

"I've no idea, but I doubt it. I'm sure after almost three months they would have mentioned it by now."

At this point Neil added to the conversation.

"Treat the mystery with respect, Peter. Things like this can lead you in strange directions and it would be a shame not to know more about it. Why don't you at least check with your friends?"

Peter was unsure. Was it really worth following up, or was it just another unimportant event, which had little significance? For now it could just lie unanswered. He had other things to occupy his mind and anyway the reading list from Cambridge had just arrived. This, he knew, should be his immediate priority.

Peter somehow felt drawn to this record, still lying beside the old gramophone upstairs. He took the back stairs and looked again at the LP cover. There was nothing there to explain its origin or who had sent it him. The cover listed little more than the usual information about the composers and the performers, with the singer Tony Sheridan as the main artist. Peter held the edges of the record sleeve up to let the vinyl LP slip out. As he did so, he was surprised to find a thin envelope drop to the floor. It was addressed to him. He ripped it open and unfolded a single page of writing paper.

"Dear Peter," it read, "there is something special about the band playing with Tony Sheridan on this record. If you have the time, you could do far worse than investigate further. It may be a wild goose chase, but the Odyssey was never undertaken from an armchair. I cannot join you on this adventure, but it could be the first of many, bringing you acclaim and hopefully joy. I wish you well."

Peter was more than intrigued. He was enthralled. How could he resist an invitation like this? But from whom? Peter decided he would keep this astonishing find to himself. One thing was certain, Peter would act. This time he looked at the record sleeve with much more care and made a note of two important things. Tony Sheridan had been playing at the Top Ten Club and the Top Ten Club was in Hamburg.

Peter knew he had little time as the University term started in about three weeks, but he was determined to start what the letter described as an Odyssey. He was attracted to the idea of taking a boat journey from Harwich to the Hook of Holland and onward by train. It seemed a more glamorous route than travelling the whole way by train, but time was against him. He eventually settled on the more mundane route by taking a train from St Pancras, changing in Brussels and continuing to Hamburg. It was strange, but Peter had rarely travelled by train. Although the journey was long, he found it absorbing. He loved the hustle and bustle of the stations, the variety of languages of the staff and passengers and the gentle motion of the train as it made its way northeast.

Peter arrived at Hamburg Hauptbahnhof late in the evening and found a rather run-down hotel near the station. The room had a linoleum floor, a single bed and a cracked washbasin in one corner. Storage was limited to a few coat hooks and a bedside cabinet of an ancient vintage. Peter took the precaution of taping his passport behind the mottled mirror and found a small bathroom at the end of the corridor. He waited a while for the occupant to emerge, a rather florid, middle-aged gentleman with a vast stomach barely covered by his bath towel. Peter rinsed the scum from the bath and took a tepid shower from the flexible pipe attached to the bath taps. After so long at boarding school, he was quite used to questionable levels of hygiene.

Returning to his room, Peter finished the last of his sandwiches brought from home and settled down for the night. As he drew the curtains, he found that his room overlooked the railway goods yard. He needed to decide whether fresh air or noise was the preferred company for the night. He chose fresh air, but found the window was stuck solid. At least the shunting of the rolling stock throughout the night wouldn't disturb him.

He lay in bed, using his torch to study a map book of Hamburg he'd bought at the station. Very soon it dropped from his grasp as he fell into a dreamless sleep.

Breakfast was not a feature of this third rate hotel, so after another tepid shower, Peter walked half a block to a lively cafe and was revived by a strong coffee and croissant. Peter took out a small hard-backed book and made some notes, trying to plan how best to use his time in Hamburg. The limited information on the LP said that the record was made at Hamburg's Friedrich Ebert Halle, but Peter decided this was likely to be a recording studio. It would be too long a shot to find Tony Sheridan and his band there. He thought a far better option was to find the Top Ten Club. It wasn't listed in the telephone directory, but Peter showed the name to a number of young people at the caf and at the third attempt was lucky to find someone who could give a street name. Map in hand, Peter strode off, seemingly heading towards the docks. Along the way he asked a number of people for directions showing the street name and noted that they seemed intrigued, almost alarmed by his request. His starting point, the area around the railway station, was far from pleasant, but as he approached the streets around the docks the general appearance worsened. The buildings were poorly maintained, often derelict and the area was strewn with unsavoury litter.

There were few people about at this time of day and Peter was approached twice by women offering themselves for a few marks an hour. He soon realized he was in the red light district of the city, a novel experience for him. He resolved to move quickly and hopefully avoid any further offers. In the distance, Peter could now see the massive cranes of the docks and decided if time allowed he would take a closer look later. Finally he reached Reeperbahn 136, and found a disheveled building hemmed in either side by what looked like a warehouse and a less than glamorous coffee bar, the Flamingo. It was clearly the right place, with dull neon lights signaling 'Top Ten Club' above the heavy metal doors. The main doors were locked, but Peter found a smaller door to one side and pushed it open. It took time for Peter's eyes to adjust to the dull interior, but soon was able to make out a medley of tables and chairs with a small dance floor and a raised stage at the back of the hall. As he made his way cautiously into the room, suddenly a blaze of lights momentarily blinded him. Peter stopped dead.

"Hallo," was the only word spoken from within the gloom, but the voice seemed friendly enough and Peter, recovering from the glare, replied in the more formal "Guten tag."

"Where you from?" the unseen voice replied, "You sound foreign."

Peter, having said he was English, apologized for walking in without an invitation. The voice then materialized to become a middle-aged man with a goatee beard and long hair tied up in a ponytail.

"No problem," he said, "I was just about to set up for a sound check when you disturbed me. The name's Kurt"

Peter explained that he had heard the LP 'My Bonnie' by Tony Sheridan, but was interested in the other band on the record called the Beat Boys.

"Why you interested in the Beat Boys?" Kurt asked, "you from Liverpool?"

"No," Peter replied, "someone just sort of suggested I caught up with them."

"Strange," said Kurt, "there have been one or two enquiries recently. You're not the first. The thing is they seem a bit elusive. Seem to do the rounds of the clubs here in Hamburg and then suddenly disappear back to Liverpool. It's difficult to keep up with them. One thing I can tell you is that they're no longer the Beat Boys. Changed their name a few months ago to the Beatles."

"So they haven't been playing here for some time?" Peter enquired, disappointed that he seemed to have drawn a blank.

"I've been out of town for a while, so it's possible that they played here while I was away, but I don't think so. Tell you what. If you want to track them down, you need to talk to Astrid."

"Whose Astrid?" asked Peter, hopeful that this would give him a new lead.

"She's a local photographer. Always hanging around with the Beat Boys. She's the one who gave them all the crazy haircuts. Crazy but distinctive. Her boyfriend, Stuart, is one of the band. I say is, but the line-up is always chopping and changing, he may be out by now. Who knows?"

"And where can I find this Astrid?' Peter asked, keen to pursue his personal mission.

"She's here most nights, but I'm pretty sure I have her address. Hold on a minute and I'll take a look in my office."

With that, Kurt strolled to the side and behind the stage, indicating for Peter to follow. They went into a small, disorganized office with shelves stacked with what looked like programmes or leaflets and tables strewn with record sleeves. The walls were plastered with posters of a variety of groups, none of which meant anything to Peter. Kurt hunted in the drawers of one of the tables and eventually pulled out a grubby loose-leaf file.

"I am sure that Astrid gave me a receipt for some photographs of the club I commissioned from her, but it was over a year ago."

Kurt flicked through the file and eventually found what he needed.

"There it is. I knew I had it somewhere. He took the receipt from the file and gave it to Peter.

"You can have it. I don't keep records for more than a year. In fact I sometimes wonder why I bother at all."

Peter looked at the receipt and saw the name Astrid Kirchherr, with an address and phone number.

"Perfect," said Peter, "this could be a great help."

"No problem, " said Kurt, smiling, "Now make sure you come back to the club tonight. You can buy me a drink."

Peter shook his hand, promised he would be back and headed back out to the fresh air blowing inland from the nearby sea. His plan to visit the docks could wait, as he was keen to meet Astrid.

He looked up her street name on his map, but was disappointed to find it was on the other side of town. Although Peter was unfamiliar with the German telephone system, he thought ringing Astrid was worth trying first. Peter enjoyed another coffee, but mainly to get some change for the phone call. He was now ready and went to the small booth at the back of the coffee bar to use the public phone. He was put through immediately and Astrid answered. Peter asked if she spoke English and very soon they were in animated conversation about the Beatles and their nights playing at both the Kaiserkeller and Top Ten nightclubs.

"Look," said Astrid, "instead of chatting on the phone, why don't you come to the Top Ten tonight? I'll be with my fianc e, Stuart Sutcliffe, who was once in the band, and he'll tell you anything you want."

"That will be perfect," Peter replied, "what time?"

"Oh, about eleven. I'll be the one with the camera."

She rang off and Peter now had a long day ahead of him. He resolved to see the docks and perhaps a little more of the town. He strolled in the direction of the cranes and soon found himself in a bustling port. He saw huge cargo boats with freight being loaded and unloaded from the numerous docks. As he watched, he could see the way everything was being organized into a highly efficient operation, with each component of the process connecting smoothly with the next. Peter marveled at such industry and wondered if the great docks of Britain such as Tilbury and Liverpool operated as efficiently.

Peter spent the rest of the day seeing as much of Hamburg as he could. He walked miles, starting with the nearby Landungsbrucken or water station and then visiting St Michael's Church, the Rathaus, and finishing at the Speicherstadt. This was a complex of warehouses, which housed numerous cafes and restaurants. Peter suddenly realized he was hungry, not having eaten since his breakfast croissant. He soon found a cozy caf , the Keese, where he enjoyed a meal of rouladen and sauerkraut. As he ate, he remembered the last time he had eaten abroad. How could he forget the view overlooking the River Kapyong and the beautiful girl by his side? So different from this dismal September evening. The sky darkened, and he made his way back to the Reeperbahn. He still had plenty of time, so enjoyed a pleasant, if lonely, couple of local beers. On reflection, Peter wasn't really sure why he was here. A mysterious note from an unknown person had prompted this visit, but none of it really made sense. Why should he, a person with fairly conventional musical tastes, be getting information on an unknown band in a foreign country? Peter was suddenly struck by the stupidity of the whole trip. He was inclined to dismiss what he was doing as just fanciful. He might just as well find out what he could from Astrid and Stuart and head home. He was no nearer to understanding his motives for being here, when a local bell tolled eleven-o-clock. In a strange way, Peter felt buoyed by his complete lack of comprehension. He headed down the road to the Top Ten, avoiding the tired looking women waiting for custom, now far more numerous than earlier in the day.

The main door to the Top Ten Club was now open and Peter pushed inside to be greeted by a pulsating beat. The fug and stale smell from cigarette smoke filled every corner of the club. He bought a drink and settled down near the bar in a place overlooking most of the club. People were in groups, mainly around tables, with no more than half a dozen on the dance floor. The music boomed from the four massive loudspeakers either side of the stage. Members of a four-piece band were on stage, setting up their equipment. Peter watched in fascination as the drummer at the back adjusted and re-adjusted his drums until he was happy with the spacing of his kit. A thin, rather scruffy person on bass guitar was tuning his strings and using a small electronic device to achieve the right balance. The rhythm guitarist was wearing a dark brown leather jacket and strumming a few chords, holding the neck of the guitar close to his ears so he could pick up the tone above the wall of sound around him. At the centre of the stage was a rather good looking, fair-haired, young man sitting on a high stool and changing the height of his microphone. Clearly dissatisfied with the one microphone, he pulled another one over from the edge of the stage and set this one up a little away from the stool and at a height that would suit him better when standing.

Just then, Kurt, who Peter had met earlier in the day, walked by. Seeing Peter, he stopped dead and grabbed him by the arm.

"Did you contact Astrid?" he asked, looking concerned.

"I did," Peter replied, "I've arranged to meet her here tonight."

"Come with me to my office, straight away," Kurt insisted and led Peter firmly by his elbow to the room behind the stage.

"Sit down for a moment. I've just heard some terrible news," Kurt blurted out. "Stuart Sutcliffe, Astrid's fiancé, died this afternoon. I don't know the full details, but it seems he had some sort of brain haemorrhage. Evidently Astrid drove him to hospital and he died before he got there. Terrible business. I'm in shock, but Astrid must be feeling terrible. That's all I know."

Peter sat numb for a time, and then turning to Kurt, said, "Is there anything we can do? It must be awful for Astrid."

"It's just too early to know anything yet. Give me your hotel phone number and I'll let you know as things develop. I'm sorry, Peter, but I need to talk to others who may know Astrid."

With that Kurt left the room, leaving Peter dazed by the news. Once again, he tried to justify to himself the whole purpose of this crazy mission. What on earth was a rational person like him doing in a back street nightclub in a foreign city just weeks away from starting his University course? He had books to read, clothes to buy, plans to make. It made no sense, but here he was and Peter resolved there and then to finish his strange quest as best he could. He now had no leads except Astrid and she would be totally absorbed with Stuart's unexpected death. Peter left Kurt's office and went back to his seat at the bar. The band, who introduced themselves as the Jets, were now playing their first number. It was a wild rock and roll song, with the words inaudible against the volume of the guitars from the speakers. The live music seemed to energize the club and the dance floor was soon full of people enjoying the heavy, dynamic rhythm.

Peter watched for a while and then found that after the recent news his confusion was best served by sleep. He headed out into the still night, enjoying the fresher air compared with the smoky atmosphere inside. He made his way back to the hotel deep in thought. The girls on each corner were tempting, but at every proposition, his mind returned to Mi Sun. The hotel was as unwelcoming as he remembered it from that morning. As he made his way up the stairs to his room, he could hear the muffled sounds of unknown voices from behind closed doors. He wondered if the girls from the street were entertaining behind these same closed doors.

Peter lay for a while thinking on the events of the night. It took time, but eventually he slept. There was an inviting knock on his door in the early hours, but Peter was dead to the world and it was ignored. After his morning shower, still as tepid as before, he returned to the same café he'd found the day before. While enjoying his coffee and croissants, he tried to evaluate his current situation. He'd only been in Hamburg for one full day and he seemed to have covered more ground that he could have expected. But it had taken him nowhere. He was no nearer to hearing or seeing the Beat Boys, or Beatles as they may now be called. If the band had gone back to Liverpool, then perhaps that was the place to find them.

Once again his thoughts returned to Cambridge and his medical degree. Surely this must take precedence? He had to make a decision. He did, resolving to let this spontaneous quest remain dormant and to get home to move on with other aspects of his life. He returned to the hotel, packed and went to the grimy front desk to pay his bill. As he did, the manager passed him a note. Dated that morning, the note said simply, 'If it is still your wish, please ring Astrid', followed by a phone number. Peter was surprised and puzzled by the note. Surely Astrid would have other more important things on her mind than speaking to him, especially right now, hours after Stuart's death. Peter was uncertain how to react. In the end his intuition led him to make that call. Astrid clearly had her reasons and the only way to find out was to ring. He left the hotel, made his way to a public call box, and using the last of his small change phoned Astrid. After a few rings, she replied and sounded, unsurprisingly, tired and a little frail. Peter said how sorry he was to hear the sad news and Astrid thanked him for his concern. Peter asked how she was and, predictably, she said she was coping but only just. Astrid faltered but then recovered to invite Peter over.

"I have found some things you may find of interest," she said. "I'm sure Stuart…" she paused, took a deep breath, and then went on, "….would like you to have them. If it's convenient, this morning would be as good a time as any. I have things I need to do this afternoon."

Peter was astonished by the request and took a moment to respond.

"Of course, I'll come over straight away."

"Good, I'll see you soon," and with that he phone went dead.

Peter's first reaction was one of utter amazement. How could Astrid think of him at a time like this? From what Kurt had said, Stuart must have died literally in her arms on the way to the hospital. The thought was both shocking and bewildering. Peter's mind was a jumble of unconnected thoughts as he called a taxi to take him to Astrid's home. He'd kept her invoice and was able to show it to the taxi driver, who nodded in recognition before heading across the river.

Peter arrived at Astrid's home, a tall, terraced, townhouse in a quiet street, and tentatively knocked on the door. He could hear light feet descend some stairs and then the door opened.

A blonde, attractive woman, a few years older than Peter stood in the doorway. Her makeup was smudged as if she had been crying and she seemed to be wearing little more than a white housecoat or dressing gown.

"You must be Peter," she said, "come in."

"Are you quite sure this is a OK?" Peter asked, rather concerned that he was intruding.

"No. I wanted to see you," and with that she led the way upstairs to a sitting room, lit only by a single table lamp. Astrid then turned to Peter and fell into his arms, quietly sobbing. Peter, although unused to displays of affection, found it quite natural to respond by hugging Astrid closely. The two of them stood locked in a stationary embrace. Peter was a little shocked by what was happening, but couldn't bring himself to release his grip on Astrid. After a while, her breathing became more shallow and regular and then, releasing her grip on Peter, she broke away and said.

"I'm sorry Peter, but you're the first person I've seen since yesterday and I just needed that hug."

Peter smiled and said nothing.

"Strangely," she said, " you remind me so much of Stuart and when I heard you speak, it was just too much. You probably didn't know, but Stuart was from England. I'll get us some coffee. With that Astrid left the room and Peter took a seat by the shuttered window. As Peter looked around the room, he noticed quite a number of paintings, both on the walls and stacked haphazardly on the floor. Astrid returned with two cups of steaming coffee and put one down beside Peter. He went to stand up, but she waved him down again.

"These paintings are all Stuart's. I've no idea what to do with them all, but I suppose someone might like them."

"So none of them are yours?"

"No, I stick to photography, Stuart was the talented one."

There was a minute of silence between them as they sipped their coffee, then Astrid spoke again.

"I guess you're wondering why I asked you over," she said, "it's something I found in Stuart's studio upstairs."

Peter was intrigued and looked at Astrid with renewed interest.

"I found some tapes from when Stuart was in the band with the others. They are a bit of a mixture, but also include some demo discs, both from Stuart's time in the band and more recently from after he left. I want you to have them Peter."

"But Astrid, why me?" Peter interjected, "Sadly I never knew Stuart."

"No, but I happen to believe in coincidences. Only yesterday morning, you phoned me and we had a great chat about the early days of the Beat Boys and the Beatles. You just seemed interested in their music and so you seemed the obvious person to have them."

Peter was amazed but excited by this turn of events. Perhaps his mission had not been a complete waste after all.

"That's very kind of you, Astrid, but are you quite sure?"

"Peter, just take them. It's one less thing for me to worry about."

With that she disappeared upstairs to return a little later with a shoebox, its lid sealed with tape. Peter finished his coffee, stood up, and took the box from her.

"It's really awfully kind of you. Once again, are you quite sure?"

"Just take it and go, Peter, before I change my mind," and with that she led Peter downstairs to the front door. At the door Peter turned to thank her again. Astrid took the box from him, put it carefully on the stairs and once again flung her arms round him. They hugged and as Astrid lifted her head towards Peter, their spontaneous kiss seemed perfectly natural. Astrid was the first to break away, picked up the box from the stairs, gave Peter a quick kiss on the cheek and opened the door. Peter walked away, looked back, but the door was closed.

Peter returned to Hadleigh Hall immediately. There was no reason to stay abroad a moment longer. He told his mother and Neil about most of his adventures in Hamburg, carefully omitting details of the hotel.

"And this was all based on a note you found from someone who gave you an LP record? What's more, a person unknown," said his mother.

"Strange isn't it mum, how we are sometimes driven to do something different, unusual, perhaps even a little reckless."

Celia decided that perhaps enough had been said, especially in view of her confession to Peter the day after his birthday. Neil diverted the conversation skillfully by adding,

"I think its great to follow the less chartered sea sometime. What was that poem by Robert Frost, 'I took the road less travelled by, and that has made all the difference? Anyway Peter, what do you propose to do with these tapes and demo discs? Any plans?"

"To be frank, I haven't given it a lot of thought. I've been concentrating on getting ready for Uni'."

"Well if it's any help, Peter, I know one or two people connected with the music industry. Perhaps they could tell you what to do with it all. It's a shame to let them just sit in that box of yours."

"Thanks, Neil, I'd really appreciate that. I'll give you the stuff later today when I've had a chance to go through it all myself."

It was over a week later that Neil came back to Peter with some news.

"My contacts have recommended someone up in Liverpool, some sort of impresario, who may be prepared to look over the contents of your precious box. Do you want me to send him the stuff?"

"Why not. I've sort of lost interest and anyway I start at Cambridge in just over a week. I'm sure I'll have more than enough on my plate then."

It was exactly two weeks later that Peter received a letter postmarked Liverpool. It simply read, 'Received with thanks assorted tapes and demo discs originally belonging to Stuart Sutcliffe, deceased. I enclose a cheque for £200 for the contents to include £100 for your expenses in obtaining them.'

The letter and cheque were both signed by Brian Epstein.

The record 'Love Me Do' came out on October 4th that same year and it was the Beatles' first worldwide hit.

By then, Peter was hard at work studying anatomy and physiology and had little time to notice any record in the hit parade. In moments of relaxation, he occasionally thought about Astrid Kirchherr and wondered if she still hugged strangers.

CHAPTER 18
SPA

David's 18th birthday was not a big cause for celebration in the Clarke household. It was seen as just another birthday, with the 21st being the real 'coming of age'. The birthday was enhanced by the news that David had won an open scholarship to Pembroke College, Cambridge to read geography. His birthday presents were all things he would need at college, mainly clothes and books. David could easily have travelled to Cambridge from Witchford on a daily basis, but his scholarship meant he could live in the college for free. David was excited to be moving somewhere new, knowing that it would be easy to come home to see the family at any time. He received birthday cards from family and friends and these included one mysterious, unsigned card. The note inside read:

"Dear David,
The grid references 279755, 372499 and 268328,344932 may be of interest to you. If you have the time, you could do far worse than investigate further. It may be a wild goose chase, but the Odyssey was never undertaken from an armchair. I cannot join you on this adventure, but it could be the first of many, bringing you acclaim and hopefully joy. I wish you well."

David was totally mystified by this note and even more by the grid references; they meant absolutely nothing to him. Over breakfast, he showed his parents and they were equally perplexed.

"It's all very strange," said his mother, "are you going to do anything about it?'

"Well, I've nothing specifically planned for next week and it may be my last opportunity to follow up a mystery like this before college."

"But you don't even know where these place actually are, assuming they exist in the first place," said his father.

"You're right, dad, the first thing to do is to locate these grid references and then I shall make a decision."

David, still intrigued, finished his breakfast and took the bus into Ely. His plan was to use the local library for information and then, if necessary, buy maps from the bookshop in town. The bus journey followed the familiar route he had used for seven years. It seemed strange to be returning to the town centre and not heading down towards the Cathedral and school. The librarian was helpful, but all the maps in the library covered the immediate area of the east of England. The grid references he'd been sent were very different from the local area. David headed up the High Street to Moran's bookshop, which dealt in a range of antiquarian and second hand books. He was not very optimistic, but hoped that old Mr. Moran could help.

David showed the grid references to Mr. Moran, a man with placid face and a mop of white hair. He struggled to his feet from the comfortable chair next to a small gas fire, adjusting his spectacles as he spoke.

"You youngsters are always coming up with challenging questions. But that's what books are for, to give you answers. What you need is one of those OS maps that cover the whole country and from that we should be able to work out roughly the area you are talking about. Just give me a minute will you. I had some stuff come in yesterday and I haven't had time to sort it. You may just be lucky."

With that he went into a room behind the shop, calling out as he disappeared, "If anyone comes in, give me a shout will you."

David promised to do so and went immediately to the geography and geology section, hidden away behind one of the numerous, high shelves. He picked out a rather musty book on the Geology of England by Connybeare and Phillips and dated 1822, appreciating the leather bound, marbled cover as much as the contents.

"Hello. Is anyone there?" sang an amiable, feminine voice from the main part of the shop. David stopped reading and walked back to the shop counter, appearing rather suddenly from behind the shelves.

"Gosh you gave me a shock, creeping up like that," said the owner of the voice, a petite, striking young lady, who David thought he recognized.

"Sorry, I was hidden amongst the shelves. Mr. Moran asked me to call him if anyone came in. Haven't I seen you before?" said David. "You look vaguely familiar."

"I'm not sure if that is a compliment, " she replied, "but anyway, the name's Laura."

"David, temporary shopkeeper, at your service."

Laura smiled, curtsied mockingly and then added, "Perhaps the temporary shopkeeper shouldn't frighten the customers."

David smiled and called out, but there was no reply. He called again without success.

"Do you think he's OK?" said Laura.

"I guess I'd better go and see," David replied, "he was looking for something for me."

David made his way, with some hesitation, behind the counter and into a much gloomier area behind the shop. As his eyes adjusted, he saw with horror Mr. Moran sprawled over a low couch at he back of the room. David ran over and tried to move him into a more comfortable position. Mr. Moran was a dead weight and it was difficult to get him upright. David then noticed that his face had dropped to one side and he seemed to be dribbling. David was alarmed, felt for a pulse on his wrist and thought he could detect some sign of a heartbeat, but he wasn't sure. David shouted for help and the girl in the shop appeared, slightly breathless. When she saw the state of Mr. Moran, she knew straight away that it was serious.

"You stay with him," she said, "I'll phone for an ambulance."

"Use the phone on the desk," David shouted as she ran out.

He wasn't sure what to do next so made Mr. Moran as comfortable as possible. He was relieved to see he was breathing, even if rather rapidly and without any rhythm. Propping Mr. Moran up as best he could, David fetched some water from a tap in the nearby kitchen. He put the glass to Mr. Moran's lips and he slurped it noisily, with most of the water going down his shirt. One arm then moved and gripped David tightly, but the other arm seemed to hang lifelessly. Mr. Moran tried to say something, but the words came out as a sort of random burble. David tried to reassure Mr. Moran, although he was feeling far from confident in himself. The girl he met in the shop rushed back in, saying

"There's an ambulance coming. It shouldn't be long."

Kneeling next to Mr. Moran, she took his hand, looked directly in his eyes and said gently,

"Don't worry, Mr. Moran, help is on its way. You'll soon be in good hands."

She stayed there, kneeling beside him and still quite content to look directly at the stricken man. David watched silently with growing admiration, but his thoughts were interrupted by a voice from the front of the shop.

"Anyone there?" sounded a strident voice.

"In here, at the back," David shouted, turning away from Mr. Moran. Two uniformed men came in; both dressed in the black uniform of St John's Ambulance Service.

One knelt down beside Laura and held Mr. Moran's wrist.

"What seems to be the problem," he said, to no one in particular.

"We found him unable to move. He just dribbles water and only one arm seems to be working. Also his speech is slurred," David replied.

"That's a great help," then turning to his colleague and speaking quite softly, "looks like a classic stroke. Get the stretcher, Chris, and we'll take him in the van as quickly as possible. If you two could stay for a moment, that would be a great help. It's quite difficult manoeuvering a stretcher in this small space and we may need you."

The stretcher was quickly brought in and the two men from St John's skillfully strapped Mr. Moran onto the taut canvas. The four of them slowly and carefully carried him to the ambulance outside and he was whisked away to the nearby Princess of Wales Hospital. As soon as the ambulance left, both David and Laura went back into the shop and almost collapsed against the counter.

"That was rather unexpected," said David, "I hope the poor guy will be all right."

"I hope so too," said Laura, "to be honest without us being here, it could have been far worse."

"I need some water, can I get you some?"

David went back into the kitchen at the back and brought out two glasses of water. As they sipped their drinks, David said,

"I'm a little unhappy just leaving the shop like this. Any suggestions?"

"Why don't we try to find some keys and lock up? There's little else we can do right now."

The two searched the shop and found a set of keys near the till. They locked up, changed the sign on the door to 'Closed'. They were about to push them back through the door, when Laura said,

"If he lives above the shop, this could be his only set. Shouldn't we deliver them to him personally?"

"Good idea. We don't both have to go, though I'd love you to join me."

"I really ought to get back to work, they'll be wondering what's happened to me."

"Where is work?" David enquired.

"I work in the library, just down the road. It's only a holiday job, but helps pay the bills."

"That's strange," David added, "I was in the library earlier and didn't see you."

"No you won't. I work in the back office, mainly cataloguing and stuff."

"I shall make a point of coming in to ask for something really strange and perhaps I might catch you."

"Why not," Laura replied with a mischievous smile, squeezed David's arm, and trotted off in the direction of the High Street.

The next morning, David took the bus once more into Ely and headed straight to the Princess of Wales Hospital. He asked at reception where Mr. Moran's ward would be, and the receptionist asked whether he was a relative. David's immediate reaction was to tell the truth. Then he realized the hospital policy might be only to admit relatives and he quickly answered,

"Yes, his nephew."

"Then you can go to join his niece. She's in the family room just outside ward C."

With that, David, now reddening a little from his white lie, saw a sign to ward C and headed rapidly in that direction. As he opened the door to the family room, David was pleasantly surprised to see that Mr. Moran's niece was, in fact, Laura.

"Ah, my sister, My Moran's niece," laughed David as he sat down, "Have you seen him yet?"

"The doctor's in with him now, it shouldn't be long."

The two of them started to relive what had happened the day before, sharing the intimacies of the moment. The door opened and a young man in a white coat came in.

"You two waiting to see Kenneth Moran?"

This was the first time that either of them had heard the name Kenneth and it took a moment to react. Laura was the first to speak,

"How is he?"

"He's not in bad shape considering what he's been through. It will take a week or two for him to get back some of his faculties. Hopefully with some speech therapy and physiotherapy, we should see some real improvements in time. He'll be with us for at least a week and then we'll get him transferred to a rehabilitation unit in Cambridge. You can both go into see him now, but please don't stay too long, I don't want him overtired."

With that the doctor strode out of the room and disappeared. Laura and David opened the door to the ward and found Mr. Moran in the second bed on the left hand side. He was propped up with pillows, looking tired but managed a weak smile.

"Hello," said David brightly, "Do you remember me?"

Mr. Moran tried to speak. His words were faint and a little slurred, but David and Laura could just make out what he was saying.

"You were in my shop," he said to David, "asking about a map. Am I right?"

"Spot on," David replied, "you went in the back to look for it and that's when you had your little turn."

"I'm afraid I remember little of that, but it seems that you two helped me to the ambulance. And you, young lady, do I know you?"

"I came into the shop when you were in the back, so you wouldn't have seen me at first," Laura replied.

"We locked up the shop and have brought you the keys," added David, "I hope that's all right."

"Of course it is. Most thoughtful, most thoughtful."

"Is there anything else we can do for you, Mr. Moran, I understand that you will be here for a few days?" enquired Laura.

Mr. Moran thought for a while and then answered,

"Well there is one thing that's worrying me. You see I have a cat in the house. She's pretty independent, but will needing feeding while I'm here. Do you know anyone who could help or she could be taken to a cattery for a few days?

"Leave it to us," Laura said cheerfully, and without a moment's hesitation added, "We'll sort it out between us."

David wondered how, or even if, Laura had thought this through. His thoughts were interrupted by Mr. Moran whispering.

"That would be wonderful. Such a load off my mind."

"Now the doctor said we were not to stay too long, so we will leave you in peace. If you let us have a key to the back door, then we'll look after your cat for you and let you know how things are."

"You're most kind. I'm afraid I'll have to ask you to remove the back door key from the ring, as my hands don't seem to be working so well just now. It's the large brass one."

With that, David and Laura said their farewells and promised to report back soon.

As they made their way out of the ward, David suggested coffee and Laura accepted willingly. They headed for the small cafeteria in the hospital and soon sat at a small table with two steaming mugs of coffee in front of them.

"Good of you to offer to look after the cat," David said with a smile.

"I seem to recall that the offer was for both of us to look after it," Laura added, "Is that a problem?"

"No. Well sort of, yes, to be honest," David answered, "You see, I was planning to go away for a few days. Is there any chance…"

"Leave it to me," laughed Laura, "I quite fancy looking after a cat for a few days."

David was relieved. Cats were not really his thing anyway and it would mean he had an excellent reason to see Laura again. The two of them chatted amiably while they enjoyed their coffee. They agreed to meet again, here at the hospital in a week's time and as they parted, David bent to give Laura a kiss. She responded, not fully on the lips, more a brush of cheeks, but they both felt comfortable and relaxed. David wanted the next week to go quickly. He somehow felt that Laura was someone special and hoped she felt the same.

Later that day, David took the bus to Cambridge. He bought a map in Waterstones of Snowdonia and the Conwy Valley, the very map that fitted the grid references. He also enquired after train times to North Wales. He'd some difficulty in justifying the trip to his parents, but they recognized that sometimes things are done without rhyme or reason. They were as intrigued as him over his little expedition and looked forward to hearing more on his return.

The next day, David travelled by train from Cambridge to Conwy in North Wales, followed by a local service to the tiny station of Tal-y-cafn on the east bank of the River Conwy, as it made its way south from the sea. The grid reference was located on the other side of the river, but fortunately one of the few roads crossing the river led directly from the station. David noted that there was a small pub in the village. He'd brought with him a small tent, but was comforted that food and drink would be available that evening, if needed.

As he crossed the river, the road took him close to an old hotel, which had clearly seen better times. Even from the outside, the place looked faded and tired. The size of the hotel suggested that it must at one time have seen plenty of business. Nowadays its good times were clearly over. Just before the hotel was a marked footpath, following the western bank of the river and David followed this as his reading of the map said he still needed to head south. After about a mile, he passed the remnants of an old dock, which he was surprised to see was marked on his map. The path then turned away from the river and he could now see a minor road ahead of him. Before he came to the road, there was another feature marked on his map, an ancient Roman Fort, called Canovium. The feature on the map was clear, but there was no sign of the fort, apart from a few stones, set in the ground at irregular intervals. The exact location of the grid references put him somewhere between the ancient fort and the road. Apart from a couple of old farm buildings, there was little else to be seen. David felt slightly uneasy about straying off the path into private land so walked to the farmhouse by the side of the road.

He knocked on the door of the farmhouse, to be answered by the howling of dogs. Following stern words from within, the dogs were silenced and the door opened by a middle-aged woman, dressed in working clothes, covered by a worn apron.

"I'm sorry to trouble you," said David, "but I was hoping to look around here and just wanted your permission to… "

"What do you mean 'look around'?" interrupted the woman, suspiciously,

"Are you from the council or something."

"No, not at all, to be honest I am not sure…"

Just then the whimpering of the dogs from inside the house, made conversation difficult and the woman softened a little as David realized that it would be difficult to explain why he was here.

"You'd better come in," she said, "the dogs will quieten down once they get to know you."

With that, she ushered David into a small kitchen and sat him down. The two border collies circled David, sniffed him approvingly and slunk off to another room.

"I was just having a cup of tea, would you like one?"

"Please, that would be most kind."

The woman poured him a cup from a large pot that looked as though it was always on the go. She wiped her hands on her apron and sat down.

"Now what were you saying about looking around?" she said.

"It's a long story," David started, "but to be brief someone gave me a map reference, which is near here and thought I should investigate. To be honest, I don't know why or even what I am looking for, but…"

"So why don't you ask the person who gave you the information?" the women interrupted.

"Well, it's not that simple, you see I don't even know the name of the person."

"It all seems mighty strange to me," she added, but I don't see any harm in you looking around. We've nothing to hide here. In fact if you find anything, my husband and I would be more than interested. We've only been here for six months and are just finding our feet so to speak. As long as you talk to my husband when he comes in and don't leave any gates open, that should be fine."

"And when do expect him home?"

"Oh, anytime after 5.00. Depends on what he's up to."

"Well, thanks for the tea. I'll just have a look around and report back later."

David went back outside and wandered around the farmyard rather aimlessly. He started to wonder why he was investing in this little enterprise, especially armed with so little information. Once more he checked the map references, trying to locate the exact spot with more precision. He found that going over to the farmhouse had taken him a little away from where the coordinates crossed. He should have been nearer to the site of the Roman fort. As he approached the remnants of the fort, he noticed a gully between two large rocks and David wondered if this might be of importance. The gully was filled with rubbish, a combination of old builders' rubble and bits of long-abandoned farmyard equipment. On closer inspection, the gully seemed to lead downwards into the ground. The orientation of the rocks seemed to suggest that the gully could open out into something larger, but clearly underground. Over the years it was clear that farmers had used this as an unofficial landfill site and access at the moment was impossible. David resolved to investigate this further, especially as it corresponded fairly accurately with the map references on his birthday card. He continued to walk around the area to see if there was anything else of interest. David knew full well that map references could never be more precise than a square of about 100 yards on each side. Nothing else seemed to be of interest and David kept coming back to the rubbish-filled gully as his best hope. Before he knew it, the afternoon sun began to fade and he hoped by now the farmer would have returned. David made his way back to the farmhouse, a welcoming light now on in the kitchen. As he went into the yard, the dogs started up again and an old tractor turned towards the gate. David opened the gate, waved the tractor inside and shut it firmly. A burly man, with ruddy cheeks and a wild mop of blond hair jumped down from the tractor.

"Thanks," he called, "can I help you?"

"Please," David replied, "I spoke to your wife earlier and she suggested I had a word with you."

"What about? We're not selling any meat at the moment, it's too early."

"No, I've got some interest in your land."

"Well, we're not planning on selling, if that's what you mean. It's all green belt and any building is prohibited anyway."

"No, you've got it wrong, I wonder if I could come in and try to explain?"

The farmer shrugged and invited David in to the house. They introduced themselves properly and David learned that his hosts were Dai and Meg Morgan. They had only moved from Anglesey about six months ago, and the farm was a mixture of diary and arable land. Over another cup of tea, David tried, once again, to explain his strange quest, realizing that none of it made much sense.

"So let me get this clear," said the farmer, "you want to move all that rubble on the back field by the old fort, just in case there's something there of interest."

"I suppose that's about it," said David unconvincingly, "and to be totally honest I have no idea what could be there – or nothing. It's just a stupid hunch, based on very little."

"Well, if you want to spend your time shifting a load of rubbish, which has probably been there for decades, you're welcome as far as I'm concerned. Just so long as it all goes back afterwards, then there's no harm done. I've got no animals in that field at the moment, so there should be no damage, but just you make sure that it's left as it was when you've finished."

"That's a promise," said David, somewhat encouraged by the farmer's practical approach.

"And when do you plan to start this excavation of yours?"

"Tomorrow, if that's alright with you."

"So where do you plan to spend the night? I saw no car in the drive."

"If you don't mind, could I camp over by the old fort? I have a tent and sleeping bag, that should do me."

"Not a problem, but you'll need some food. Have you bought a stove or anything?"

"No, I'm planning to eat in the pub in the village. That should see me through."

At this point, Meg turned to the two men and insisted that David join them for breakfast the next morning.

"Seven-o-clock sharp," she said, "bacon and two eggs should set you up for a day of hard labour."

121

David took this as a dismissal, thanked them both again and went back to the field to set up his tent. He chose a spot facing the gulley, hoping that sleeping like this could be a good omen for the next day. Once having set up his tent, there was little more for David to do that day. Having read for a while, he retraced his steps along the footpath and headed back to the village and the pub, The Bodnant Arms. From outside, he could hear the congenial chatter of others enjoying a drink in the warmth of the pub. He pushed open the door and as he went in heads turned his way and all conversation stopped. There was an eerie, awkward silence as David walked to the bar on the far side of the pub.

"Oh, he's alright," came a low voice from the corner. David turned to see Dai Morgan sitting with friends around an open, coal fire.

"He's staying at my place. Just visiting."

With that, the tension lifted and soon the conversation returned to normal. At first David couldn't work out what was different about the place. He settled down by himself in a quiet seat and then it dawned on him. Everyone was speaking in Welsh. He was a foreigner in this little enclave of traditional North Wales. Dai Morgan's interjection had made all the difference. It made David realize that his assumptions about the similarity of people throughout Britain were sometimes misplaced. He enjoyed a couple of pints of a beer called Sheep Dip from the local Black Cloak Brewery, finding the taste far better than the name. The pub served a limited range of snacks and David found the homemade steak and ale pie with chips just perfect. A pretty girl with the most kissable lips he had ever seen served his meal. His immediate thoughts went to the lone tent in the field and how he would enjoy her company, but any such thoughts were quickly replaced by a much stronger image – that of Laura.

David slept fitfully, worrying that he might miss the seven-o-clock breakfast deadline. He need not have worried as the noise of the dogs at 06.30 gave him plenty of time to dress and appear at the farmhouse kitchen as invited. The bacon and eggs were washed down with plenty of tea and followed by a great pile of toast and marmalade. He asked to borrow a pair of gloves and was given a battered pair of leather gauntlets, ideal for the job in hand.

After giving his thanks once more, David set to the task of moving the rubbish from the gulley. It was a hot day, even this early, and he soon needed to take off his sweat-soaked shirt. Now stripped to the waist, he was more comfortable and worked on with renewed energy. The variety of rubbish was surprisingly extensive. There was everything from regular builders' rubble, piles of small rocks and stones, lumps of indistinguishable metal and some old farming implements, which must have come from the last century. As David worked, he slowly opened up more of the gully. At first the gap between the rocks was quite narrow and David had little space to move as he brought the detritus out. He worked solidly and enthusiastically, but still unsure of the purpose of his efforts. After a time, his ankle, the result of his polio, became painful and he needed to rest. While resting, he reflected on what he had been through over the last ten years. He was grateful he was even able to apply himself to any physical task, let alone this harsh labour. As the afternoon wore on, David started to tire and he realized he'd eaten nothing since breakfast, such had been his industry. After another short break and downing the last of his water, he soldiered on. He'd cleared most of the rubbish and found the rocks were now getting bigger. By a process of leverage and twisting the rocks, he was able to move most of them, although it was becoming increasing difficult. He then he came across a larger group of rocks and, despite trying his best, they were immoveable. David was frustrated having reached so far into the gully but could see no immediate solution. He needed some sort of help. It then struck him that Dai's tractor and some sort of chain or grappling hook was the answer. He found Dai back in the farmhouse, described what he's done so far, and asked whether he could use his tractor.

"You're pretty determined," Dai said when David explained his predicament. "It's getting late now, but if we start first thing in the morning, I can spare you an hour or two, but that's my limit. Too much to do at this time of year."

David had no option but to abandon his task for the night, but enjoyed another homemade pie at the Bodnant Arms, this time washing it down with another local ale, Grumpy Jack, from the Great Orme Brewery.

Early the next morning after another wonderful breakfast cooked by Meg, he and Dai hitched up the tractor to a winch and drove the short distance to the gulley. David showed Dai the progress he'd made and Dai was impressed with his industry, yet still uncertain about his reasons. The two of them quickly hitched a strong chain to the first of the large rocks and engaged the full force of the tractor's massive gearing. Slowly but surely the large rocks were moved one by one, revealing an opening into a dark cave. David looked into the gloomy interior and estimated it to be at least 15 yards deep and two yards from the floor to the roof. He fetched his head torch from his tent and was surprised that the cave was far from natural in appearance. It had clearly been fashioned to create a large, box-like, rectangular space. It was a substantial underground room and the walls and ceiling seemed to be covered in plaster with most of it still intact. Dai was waiting outside with the tractor, but David said nothing, wanting to investigate properly before describing his find.

"I'll have a good look and let you know later," David said, privately being keen to look for himself before sharing anything with others. Dai was sorry he had to leave to get on with his work on the farm. He invited David to join them for dinner, adding, "I'll expect a full report tonight, young man" before he drove off.

Once Dai had gone, David returned enthusiastically to the task ahead of him. Closer inspection revealed that the room had one dominant feature in one corner. It looked like an ancient basin set in the wall. David cleared the vegetation from around it and found that it was indeed some sort of stone bowl, with what looked like a primitive drain beneath it. David assumed that at one time water would have flowed into it, but there was no evidence of this now. Or was there? David was worried about damaging what could have been an artefact of some interest, but his curiosity overcame his caution. Using the heavy metal spike and lump hammer, borrowed from Dai earlier, David chipped away around the wall above the bowl. He had no idea what to expect, but was hoping some sort of inlet would appear to feed the bowl. After removing small chunks of mortar, piece by piece, the full depth of the bowl could now be seen. David guessed that any inlet would be about a foot above the bowl, so he excavated this area a little deeper. He thought he detected a trickle of water, and as one last piece of masonry was removed, the trickle became a spurt and the spurt became a flow. The water quickly filled the bowl and overflowed on to the drain below. The drain couldn't cope with the regular flow of water and soon the floor of the room started to flood. David attacked the drain with his bare hands, ripping out any plants, sediment and accumulated deposit that covered it. His efforts were successful and soon the water was flowing sweetly from the wall, into the stone bowl and over its rim into the drain. Where it went from there, David had no idea, but at least the floor of the room was now draining and David was no longer standing in water.

David's head torch could only give a limited view of the room, just enough to see the main features. As the water drained, he could now make out on the floor a number of small bricks laid on their side in a herringbone pattern. David's knowledge of construction was limited, but he recalled seeing something similar in the floor of a Roman villa he had once visited at Chedworth in the Cotswolds.

As David explored the room further, he noticed that the far wall, the one furthest from the entrance, was not plastered like the others. It was made up of cut stone blocks that seemed to be cemented together. The overall shape of the blocks resembled a low doorway and once again David's curiosity was immense. He was loath at first to interfere with something that may be of important architectural interest. He finally took the view that this may be his one and only chance. With great care he removed the highest of the stone blocks. As the block came loose, David was overwhelmed by a strong smell coming from beyond the wall. It reminded him strongly of formaldehyde, the chemical used to preserve the animals he had dissected at school. At first David retched on the smell, but as it spread throughout the room he found he could cope with it better. With the top block removed, he only had a very limited range to shine his torch, certainly insufficient to see the floor of whatever was beyond. David made up his mind to carry on and, scraping away at the concrete binding the stone blocks, he removed them one by one.

David eventually just managed to squeeze through the small doorway into the space beyond. He was utterly flabbergasted, because there, lit only by the weakening light of his torch, was as even larger room. The room resembled a church with stone benches about two feet high surrounding a central well. It was about 20 yards square, with a stone seating area cut into all the walls. The amazing thing was the floor, which, although filthy with accumulated grime, looked to be of interest. David fetched some water form the first room and cleaned a small patch of the floor. It seemed to be a made up of small tiles and what looked like pieces of marble or coloured glass. David's mind went back to Chedworth and then he realized, he was staring at a mosaic, most probably Roman. It all started to make sense. The ancient Roman fort as shown on his map, would in later years, have a villa on the same site. This could be part of it. As David moved to the centre of the room, he then found the most exciting discovery of all. The well in the centre of the room was not as he expected. It was only about two feet deep and there were terracotta pipes running in and out. A steady stream of water flowed in from one of the pipes and out from another. But this was no ordinary water. David had by now become accustomed to the strange smell, but as he stood above the pool, he realized that it was in fact a faint smell of sulphur. This made no sense, having just found pure water in the other room. It was only when David was closer to the pool of water that the truth dawned. At first he saw a fine mist above the water, then on closer inspection, David realized it was actually condensation, rising, almost invisibly from the water below. He bent down to touch it and was amazed to find the water was surprisingly hot. He had found one of the more rare geological features in Britain - a hot spring. The room could even be a Roman bath, centuries old and as far as he was aware totally undiscovered.

David now realized that if he was right, the implications were enormous. He also appreciated that he was getting way out of his depth. Roman history was not a subject he knew much about and this discovery needed professional investigation. He was desperate to tell Dai of his discovery, but just before his torchlight dimmed and gave out, he saw on one wall a magnificent relief of a sun with a human face. In the darkness he made his way with considerable caution out of the inner room, through the low door he had made in the wall, and into the first room. He touched the cool water flowing into the ancient basin, just to confirm that he wasn't dreaming, and finally stepped back into the sunlight.

That evening, sharing a lamb stew with Dai and Meg, David could hardly contain himself.

"Well, David, what've you got to report," asked Dai, "Was there anything in that underground cave? A few bats no doubt."

David took a deep breath and trying to remain calm, said,

"Actually Dai, it looks as though I might have stumbled on something rather special."

"Well go on lad, we're all ears, aren't we love?" Meg just smiled and offered David more stew.

"That cave, as you call it Dai, is actually quite a spacious room and from what I could see had been constructed with great care. I found on one wall what looked like an ancient basin. I then hacked away at the wall above the basin and to my surprise seemed to release a sort of flow pipe into the basin. Very soon there was a steady flow of water over the basin and into a sort of drain below it. I was in the room for some considerable time and the flow didn't stop. I think I must have hit an ancient spring or possibly a drain of some type. The thing is, Dai, from what I could see, the water was absolutely pure, so I doubt if it was a drain."

"Well if you're right, David, and it is a natural spring, then it would be brilliant for us. We have no way of getting water to that part of the farm without transporting it or piping it some considerable distance. Well done."

"There is rather more to my report, Dai, something even more amazing than a natural spring."

Meg sat down, clasped her hands in front of her, and looking at David directly, said, "Well go on. You're making me nervous."

David continued as if recounting a mystery story to his small audience.

"In the far wall, there was something that looked rather odd. The other walls in the room looked as though they were constructed of some sort of mortar. Yet in just one place the wall was made of stone blocks, cemented together. It was about the shape of a low door, so with a lot of effort, I removed most of the blocks."

"Go on," said Meg, "I don't think I can stand more suspense."

"The room beyond the blocked up door is even bigger than the first. I would guess about 20 yards square."

"Full of gold, I hope," Dai interjected.

"Well, possibly worthy of gold, if not the real thing. You see I think that the inner room was an ancient Roman bathhouse. To my untrained eye, it seemed to have the sort of features that I would expect in a bathhouse, seats and pipes and such. But I am now coming to the killer."

"Killer, what do you mean?"

"Sorry, schoolboy slang. In the centre of this room was bubbling into a sort of central well, more water. But not just cold water as in the outer room, this water was hot, really hot, just like a bath."

"You mean on our farm, you have found a source of hot water, just bubbling up from the ground? Like you see in other countries like New Zealand and Iceland? I don't believable it."

"That's exactly how I felt when I first saw it. It's quite unbelievable."

Dai and Meg sat for a while without moving and then Meg stood up.

"I'm going to fetch the apple crumble from the kitchen and when I get back I want you both to tell me I've not been dreaming."

She returned a minute later with a dish filled with a glistening, brown-coated crumble and a jug of custard.

"Well," she said, "did I really hear something a moment ago about hot and cold water pouring out of the ground on the back field?"

"You did," David answered, "and I am sorry if I've complicated your lives a little, but there it is."

"How do you mean, complicated our lives?" asked Dai.

"Well, I've had a bit of time to think through the implications of our find. But before I go on, I must reassure you both, that I plan to do absolutely nothing without your full permission. You see if this is a genuine hot water spring, especially if the Romans knew about it, then this must be a major historical and geological find. I know of only one other place in Britain, which has a hot spring, associated with a Roman bath and that is in the City of Bath itself. There may be others, but I am not familiar with them. You could be sitting on something incredibly important concerning our history and the very nature of the local rocks, which no one knew anything about."

"You mean scientists and historians may want to come and examine all this and possibly dig around some more?"

"Dai, you are perfectly at liberty to tell no one. You could tap off the water to use for your cattle. You could even pipe the hot water to your house and use it for heating and washing. It really is your choice. I may be totally wrong, but if this really is the only thermal spring outside of Bath, then it's of national significance. I don't want to overdramatize this, Dai, but it could be the find of the century."

"I'll tell you what, David, why don't we make a few more enquiries, subtle like, and then we can make a decision later on? How does that sound?"

"That's fine by me, Dai. There's a sort of compromise you might want to consider. Assuming this is all I think it is and the archeologists want to have a good look around, then you could specify a limit on it; say one month a year. That way you'll maintain your privacy and be able to get on with your farming around it."

"I think it's time for this crumble, before it goes cold," Meg added, "Let's drop the whole thing for now and give each other time to think."

Dai took David to the pub that night and they met up with Dai's usual crowd in the back bar of the Bodnant Arms. David excused himself for a while and made a phone call to Laura.

"Hi David," she said, "How are things going in deepest Wales?

"Pretty well, thanks, Laura. I've located the map references I told you about and still working on it. Actually I wonder if you could do me a big favour?"

"Fire away, unless it means coming to Wales. I've got an extra shift at the library this week."

"No, it's just a bit of information I need. You know the Roman baths in Bath, well could you find out if there are any other hot springs like those anywhere else in Britain. I'm just doing some background research before I go to Uni."

"Of course I can, but can't it wait until you get home?"

"I would rather like to know soon, if it's no trouble."

"Leave it to me, and by the way, I'm fine," she added a little sarcastically.

"I'm sorry. I should have asked. And how's Mr. Moran?"

"I saw him today and he seems a lot better. His speech is slowly coming back and he's starting to get a bit of mobility on his weaker side. It will take time, but the doctors reckon he'll make a full recovery."

"Great. I must go, but I'll ring you back at the same time tomorrow."

David returned to the back bar to find Dai in deep conversation with one of the others in the group.

"You mean that there was a pool near the river that seemed warmer than the others?" Dai confirmed.

"Oh yes," said the farm worker sitting next to Dai. "My grandfather used to bathe there before it all got washed away in the great flood of 1902. Back in those days it was more of a natural lido, just this side of the docks. No one knew how the water kept warm, but it did, year after year. It was strange because it was just that one pool, nowhere else."

"When you say warmer than the others, how warm do you mean?" said Dai, the pitch of his voice revealing a note of excitement.

"Oh, not hot, just took the chill off the normal temperature. Strange thing was, it happened all year round. I was told that people would come for miles, just to bathe in that lido."

David couldn't help but interrupt, "Have you any proof of this warm pool," he said.

"Well that's what I was told and I have no reason to doubt it," retorted the farm worker, a little offended. "In fact I do have some proof, young lad. If you was to go to the Royal Hotel, just across the bridge there, you'll find in there some old prints or photos of the lido. That's my proof."

Both David and Dai realized that enough had been said and the conversation fortunately moved on to other topics such as farming and how Wrexham Town Football Club were performing this year.

David refused a lift home that evening, wanting to check out the pictures at the Crown Hotel. The hotel receptionist, thinking David was to one of the hotel's very few guests, greeted him warmly.

"I wonder if I could have look at any historical pictures or photos that show the old lido near the river?" said David hopefully.

"I'm sorry, sir, but we had the public rooms refurbished last year and those pictures were taken down."

Just then the night manager walked by and, overhearing the conversation, was more helpful.

"I believe they were stored in the basement, just to the side of the door to the lower car park. Daniel, why don't you take our guest down there? I will hold the fort up here."

Daniel was pleased to have a change from his duty at the front desk and rapidly agreed. He took David down a back staircase and using a master key, showed him the place the night manager had mentioned. There, stacked against the wall were six picture frames. With the exception of one, they were all old photographs, clearly taken in earlier Victorian times. David was amazed to see clear black and white prints of people bathing in a swimming pool with the river in the background. There was a print of people arriving by horse and carriage and even one of small boats, sailing and tied up at the old docks. It was enough for David. He now had evidence that there must have been some sort of pool or simple lido down near the old docks well over a hundred years before. One of the pictures was a watercolour, rather stylized to show swimmers, boats and carriages. It was a perfect, if not accurate representation of this period and David took it back with him to the hotel reception.

"Any chance of me borrowing this?" David asked hopefully. "I could photograph it and bring it back tomorrow."

"Oh keep it," came the unexpected reply, "we were about to throw all that stuff out anyway."

David was starting to like these generous people.

The next day, David took Dai and Meg to the site. They took with them a small portable generator and some heavy-duty lights. Meg and Dai were amazed by what they could now see. The inner room with the hot spring was like something they'd never seen before and they were astounded. Dai was enough of an engineer to see how the hot water in the central well could be diverted using a simple sluice gate to flood the rest of the room and make it a large bath. When David showed them the mosaic floor and the image of the sun with the human face, they started to appreciate the sheer majesty of the room. For a time they were speechless, but then all three broke out into a spontaneous hug of joy. This was incredible and as Meg eventually said,

"Just to think this was sitting under our land for all those years. Quite remarkable."

After Dai and Meg left, David spent a little time gently cleaning some of the mosaic floor, but was conscious of the fact that it needed professional restoration, not the meddling of an amateur like himself. The other thing he did was to record the temperature of the water in what they now called the bathhouse. He had borrowed a clinical thermometer from Meg and was intrigued to find that the temperature was a constant 42 degrees centigrade, well above body temperature. He kept checking for a few hours and it never varied. Now the rooms were well lit, David was able to take a number of photographs. David's own camera was a simple Brownie 127, and it took reasonable black and white pictures, which David used occasionally to record family events such as holidays. He used this to take as many photos as he could, although he was limited by only having one reel of film. Luckily David's dad was a keen photographer. He had generously lent David his Nikon F camera, only produced a few years earlier, and David unpacked it carefully from its protective case. He was disappointed to find that there were only 10 prints available on the roll of film in the camera, so he selected his shots with great care. Finally he bricked the inner room back up as best he could. When back in the outer room,

David took the thermos flask he had cleaned in Meg's kitchen with boiling water and filled it with the cold water flowing into the ancient basin. He then went outside and barricaded the entrance to the outer room with some of the rocks and rubble he had previously removed.

He could hardly wait to ring Laura that evening and arrived at the pub just after it opened.

"Hi Laura, how are you?" were David's first words when she answered.

"I'm fine, and you?"

"All the better for speaking to you"

"Ah, how noble. So do you want to know what I found out today?"

"Of course, and before I forget, thanks for your help."

"As you said the hot spring at Bath is the most famous and I think it's largely because it's associated with the Roman baths there. But there are others."

For a moment David was concerned. Perhaps there were hot springs all over the place and the one here was nothing special.

"There are a fair few other hot springs in a number of places in England, particularly in Derbyshire and Worcestershire. But the interesting thing is that they vary in temperature enormously. The ones in Somerset are the hottest at over 40 degrees, then there's one at Droitwich at 35 degrees, the one at Buxton is 27 degrees, but all the rest are a lot cooler. The thing is, David, that true geothermal springs are defined as those above body temperature. That really only leaves the ones at Bath and possibly the one at Droitwich"

"Any in Wales?"

"Hang on, let me check my list."

"Yes, there is one in South Wales, the Taff Wells Thermal Spring."

David's heart sank. The one he'd found was not the only one in Wales.

"But it is relatively cool at less than 19 degrees."

"Does it mention any Roman settlement?"

"Just let me check my notes. No, it's just a small building, no mention of Romans."

"Laura, that's brilliant. You've been a great help."

"So what's this all about, David. Aren't you going to share with me, or is my homework going to be kept a secret?"

"A secret for now, but when I get back, I promise to share everything. You'll be the first to know."

"Is that a promise?"

"I promise, sealed with a kiss."

"I'll look forward to that."

David smiled and unbeknown to him, Laura had also.

David shared the latest information with Dai and Meg. They now knew that under their land they had what seemed to be the only true geothermal spring in Wales. It was as hot if not hotter than the ones in and around Bath. Like Bath, it seemed to be associated with some sort of Roman settlement. David thought it was wise to leave Dai and Meg to consider their options and told them that he was leaving the next day for Snowdonia.

The mysterious birthday message had spoken of an Odyssey, an adventure. So far, David's visit to North Wales had been both.

CHAPTER 19
CAVERN

David used local buses to reach the little village of Blaenau Ffestiniog. The adrenaline, which had been keeping him going for the last few days, was no longer coursing through his veins and he suddenly felt quite tired. He was desperate for a hot shower and shave, so stayed overnight in a bunkhouse in the village, sharing a dormitory with a group of four climbers from Sheffield. They were good company, if a little boisterous after a few drinks in the local pub. David slept well, in spite of the snoring and nighttime trips to the toilet from his new companions.

The next day, refreshed and armed with little more than his map, he walked to the point indicated by the grid references on his birthday card. It was a dismal morning, with the squally weather showing no signs of easing. Once again, David wondered why he was following this less than glamorous quest. He was buoyed up by the incredible outcome from the map reference near Conwy. It was clear form the surrounding countryside he was in an area populated by old slate quarries. The map even indicated them, with names such as Llechwedd, Gleddfa Ganol and Maen-Offen. The path he took led just beyond Maen-Offen and to the best of his ability this was the spot marked by the coordinates. He sat down out of the wind, trying his best to avoid the perpetual drizzle. The landscape was barren and grey, made worse by the drab weather. He'd bought a sandwich and three welsh cakes back in Blaenau Ffestiniog and wished he had a hot drink. The flask he usually carried still held the precious water from the Roman cave and David was not going to sacrifice that, even for a hot drink. The rain now fell relentlessly and David searched for a better shelter. He spotted a place that looked hopeful; it seemed just a little bit darker than the usual grey of the slate spoils around him. David moved the 30 yards to this spot. He noticed the darker colour was caused be a deep fissure in the surrounding rock. There was a slight overhang, giving him more shelter than before. Moving the short distance was the right decision as he now found himself far better protected from the miserable weather. As he sat eating his final welsh cake, David noticed that the overhang above him was a large slab of slate, set into the sides like the lintel of a door. Closer inspection showed that the slab of slate seemed to run deeper than the pile of slate pieces of his backrest. Out of interest, David cleared the vegetation from the wall he was sitting against, only to find that the slate pieces were in fact interlocking. It reminded him of the dry stonewalling he had seen in the Lake District, yet there was little evidence of it anywhere else. This was quarrying country and stone walls were to keep animals in one place. David was intrigued and with a feeling of d j vu, he methodically removed the slate pieces one at a time.

As had happened a few days earlier, there was a clear space behind the wall. This time it did not open up into a cave or room, but a narrow passage, just wide enough for a man, bent double, to move forward. David had no torch with him, so he could only crawl along the passage for about ten yards before it was too dark to see further. David assumed he had stumbled upon an old mine working and he knew that any change in level could prove fatal. He returned to the daylight and, checking his map, found that he was as near to the coordinates as was possible. The unknown sender of his birthday card had guided him to this very spot. Without light, there was nothing more that he could do. David rebuilt the wall and marked the spot by making a small cairn out of small pieces of slate. He then headed back to Blaenau, cold, wet and intrigued.

He was in good time to buy some batteries for his torch; making sure this time he had spares, and a pair of strong gloves. If this were an old slate mine, then David realized he would need a rope. He found there was a bus to Betws-y-Coed, one of the climbing centres in the area, but was now starting to worry about the cost of his trip. He had already spent longer away than planned and his budget was limited, especially as he was to start at University in three weeks time. He decided to wait and see if the climbing party back at the bunkhouse could lend him a rope for a day. David now bought some rice, eggs, bread, tinned tomatoes and half a pound of minced beef from the small store in the village. He was no cook, but was confident that with these simple ingredients, he could manage to produce something reasonably edible that evening.

He was cooking his modest meal when the climbing party from Sheffield returned. They were all soaked to the skin, but in good spirits as they had climbed a difficult route that day. David overheard them using strange names like Will-o-the-Wisp and Suicide Wall and decided that for the moment he would stick to safer sports like rowing. Over a pint in the Bryn Arms that evening, David found the climbing group had planned a walk the next day, so wouldn't need their ropes. They agreed to lend him a rope for the day and were interested to know why he wanted it. David was a little evasive at first, but then as the third pint took effect became more open about his discovery. The boys in the climbing group said it was most likely an old mine working and cautioned David about the dangers of a novice exploring underground.

"Tell you what," said Martin, who seemed to be the spokesman for the group, "why don't we abandon our planned walk and come with you. We have quite a lot of caving experience between us and it sounds fun."

David was worried that he could be leading his newfound friends on a wild goose chase, but with amazing good humour, they responded positively.

"Ah, what the heck. If there's nothing there then we can bale out and start our planned walk a little late. We've got our caving kit with us, so we could go prepared for a bit of underground stuff."

The next day after a hearty breakfast of David's favourite eggy bread, the five set off back up the track and David soon identified the cairn he'd built the day before. Between them, it took little time to remove the wall of slate and they squeezed into the narrow passage, with David leading the way. The passage descended slowly, before separating into two further passages, one considerably larger than the other. The group split, agreed to explore further and to meet back at the junction in ten minutes. A solid wall of concrete blocked the larger of the two passages, after a distance of only 20 yards. This passage seemed to be the main one for the mineshaft and the other, a subsidiary one, was probably of little interest to the miners. When the group reformed, they all agreed that the main passage had been blocked off quite deliberately, most likely to seal the mine as the slate was worked out. The smaller, subsidiary passage finished when the roof dropped to within inches of a pool of water.

"It looks like this is the end of the exploration and the beginning of our walk," said one of the climbing group.

"Pity," David responded, "I'd such high hopes."

"Could be a duck," said Martin.

"A duck, what's a duck?" David asked.

"It's just a small sump."

David was none the wiser, but then one of the others chipped in.

"I don't mind giving it a go. I can feel under the slate roof here, just above the water, and it only seems to be a foot across. Trouble is I'll get mighty wet tackling it."

"Ah, come on. We're not made of sugar! Let's have a crack at it."

David was amazed to see that the group seemed to have in their rucksacks a whole variety of kit for underground exploration. They each had a wetsuit, a small towel and flashlights that seemed to work underwater. They were all packed in waterproof bags, so if necessary they could also keep their outdoor clothes dry, even underwater. Jimmy, who'd offered to go in first, soon changed into his wetsuit and slipped on a climbing harness. The plan was that he would try to go under the low slate roof above the water and would signal with a two tugs on the rope if all seemed well on the other side. With a cheery "See you," Jimmy slid into the pool and disappeared under the slate roof. A moment or two later came the reassuring tugs on the rope and it was decided that David would go next. He didn't have a wet suit, so stripped down to his underpants, his clothes following him in one of the waterproof bags. It was with considerable hesitation that he slipped into the pool and the freezing water at first took his breath away. He stood there for a moment, regaining his composure, before ducking down under the roof and pushing off to follow the rope. He was surprised how quickly he surfaced and was relieved to see Jimmy's smiling face on the other side. David borrowed a towel from Jimmy and redressed while the others followed through the small sump. The passageway then led steeply downhill and it was clear that no miner had dug this particular tunnel. The walls were uneven and the slate soon gave way to more solid rock, rather like the exposed rock on the surface of Snowdonia itself. The five men made their way forward cautiously. They could only move at the speed allowed by the light from their head torches. It was slow progress, but exciting because they were all in unexplored territory. The lead man suddenly stopped and they realized that ahead of them was a sheer drop. The three ropes they had with them were only 100 feet in length each, so they tested the depth ahead before making any further decision. Tying a loose rock to the end of a rope, they lowered it gently over the side. It snagged after about 25 feet, but once it was unhooked, they found the rock rested at a depth of about 50 feet. Martin volunteered to go first this time and Jimmy attached the rope to his harness ready for the abseil into the unknown. David was now getting seriously concerned. He had never abseiled, but far more importantly, he had no idea how he was to get back up the steep rock face.

"Not a problem," said Martin. "We fix up a jumar for you and you just sort of winch yourself up."

"But I've never been climbing, let alone try something like that," David said with a slight tremor in his voice.

"Don't worry, David. I saw you stripped off and you looked strong enough to me. Anyway, one of us will go first on the way back. We'll ascend first and if you can't make it, we'll just haul you up, although it will be pretty undignified."

David said nothing more, his concern now transferred to the present, which was to attempt his first abseil. David could see that the rope had been securely belayed to a rock post a few feet behind them, but he was still very apprehensive about walking backwards down a rock face.

"The first two steps are the worst," said Jimmy, "then you might even enjoy it."

David was unconvinced, but was at least prepared to try. As he'd brought the four of them down here in the first place, he wasn't going to back off now. David's 'polio ankle', as he called it, was sore from walking and crawling on the uneven ground, but the exhilaration of the moment helped dull the pain.

After about ten minutes, all five of them were at the base of the rock face and could now reevaluate their situation. The area they were now in was no more than ten yards square and apart from the rope left dangling behind, there only appeared to be one exit. It was another passageway; probably formed over the years by an underground stream and all agreed it was worth investigation. It was now Harry, the smallest member of the group, who took the lead. As before, a rope was attached to his harness and Harry headed into the claustrophobic darkness. The others waited until the telltale two tugs on the rope said all was well. David was the next to go into the tunnel, followed by Jimmy, Martin and Colin, the last of the party. As each one reached the end of the tunnel, Harry, who had gone in first, told them to switch off their head torches and just sit down. This strange behavior was unsettling, but soon Colin was through and the five intrepid explorers were sitting in the dark, wondering what was to happen next. It was then that Harry spoke up.

"On the count of three, put your torches on and look up," he instructed.   "Ready, one, two, three."

Five faces looked up simultaneously and five young men were utterly amazed. They were in a huge cavern, at least the size of a detached house. As their torches, moved around, their amazement turned into breath-taking awe. The cavern was a multi-coloured palette of red, orange and green hues, with huge stalactites and stalagmites of every description. It was like being in a huge colourful cathedral. It was an underground Gaudi. No one spoke for a full minute such was the impact of the cavern. Then Colin spoke.

"It's not possible. I've studied the geology of this area and these come from limestone, not the volcanic rocks of Snowdonia. It's a freak."

"Freak or not we've all seen it and as sure as anything for the first time."

"It's just unbelievable," David added, "what are we going to do?"

"Well no one will believe us without photographic proof," said Martin, "We'd better come back better prepared."

David wasn't keen on the idea of another three more freezing swims, but realized this was the only option. The five of them, after one last look at the phenomenal sight around them, made their way back up the narrow passage. They soon reached the point where they all needed to climb the sheer wall. David was instructed in the use of the jumar and after two others had gone first, he worked his way slowly up the rope. He started well but tired as he reached the top. The others encouraged him and with one last heave, hauled himself onto the ledge above. The others followed and soon they were back at the first obstacle, the sump with its slab of slate just above the water level. They were surprised to find that the water level had dropped and now there was a good ten inches between the top of the water and the slate. It meant coping with the sump would be easier, because they could all now keep their mouths and noses above water. It also brought serious concerns. If water levels could vary so quickly, then it could easily flood. They all took note, hoping that in any return trip would not be threatened by changing water levels. All five of them were now back outside the tunnel and grateful of the warming sun to relieve the chill of the sump. Partly in exhilaration of their find and partly to warm their cold muscles, the group broke into a jog. It continued all the way back to the bunkhouse, where a hot shower restored aching bodies to a degree of normality.

The next day, the clouds looked full of rain, slightly worrying for an underground adventure. The group pooled together what photographic equipment they could find. David contributed his two cameras and two of the boys had a camera each. Luckily one of them had a flash attachment, but, in spite of that, they all bought the most powerful torches to be found in the village. They returned to the start of the mineshaft, excited by the prospect of being able to photograph the wondrous, and previously unseen, depths below. When they came to the sump, there was some concern that the water level was now right up to the height of the slate roof. They prayed that the recent heavy rain would not make matters worse. They all made good progress, with David now enjoying the abseil, though still wishing he had a wetsuit like the others. Once again, when they saw the array of pastel hues in the cavern, with its range of shapes and limestone sculptures, its beauty silenced them. Martin brought them all back to earth with his concerns about water levels and they busied themselves taking as many pictures as they could. The most impressive structure of all was a huge array of stalactites, resembling a magnificent church organ. They all agreed that they had never seen anything like it anywhere in the world. Once all the camera rolls of film were finished, they reluctantly headed back. The climb up the sheer wall went without incident. David now making better progress as his technique with the jumar improved. They headed toward the sump, to be met by the cavers' worst nightmare. It was the horrendous sound of falling rack and it was right ahead of them. David felt the worm of fear turn in his stomach. In a nauseating fraction of a second, his mouth went dry and his throat closed. In spite of the cold of the underground tunnel, sweat broke out from his head to his feet. The five momentarily froze, not knowing which way to turn. As they stood there, a cloud of black and grey dust came cascading towards them, choking each one as it rolled past.

It seemed as though forever, but the choking dust eventually settled and the five could then see their desperate state. Ahead the path was completely blocked. Fearing another fall, the five desperately started to move the rock fall, grasping each piece of slate with their bare hands to move the obstruction ahead. They worked tirelessly for about 30 minutes and with a shout of sheer joy, Martin said he could see the other side. In spite of mounting fatigue, they renewed their efforts and managed to clear a space big enough for them all to squeeze through. When they'd all made it through the rock fall, they stopped momentarily, totally exhausted. David took one look back and was about to follow the others out, when he noticed something strange. The light from his head torch picked up an unusual glistening on top of the fallen rock. He stopped momentarily, his curiosity momentarily stronger than his need to get out of this increasingly dangerous subterranean dungeon.

"Come on David. We still have the sump to get through," he heard from well ahead. But David was determined. He grabbed the glistening rock, about the size of his clenched hand, rammed it in his rucksack and half stumbled after the others. He soon caught up to find Colin waiting for him by the sump.

"The water level's rising fast. You'll have to dive right under the slate roof now, as it's well underwater. We should just make it. No time to strip off this time. Just go."

David did as he was told without hesitation. He surfaced on the other side, all his clothes thoroughly soaked. The five soon emerged into the fresh air. It was still raining heavily and they all agreed they had probably had a lucky escape. Their final task was to rebuild the slate wall at the tunnel entrance. By the time they'd finished, it looked perfectly natural. No random walker would ever find it.

That night in the Bryn Arms, the five explorers were all in great spirits. They had found something truly remarkable and were debating what to do about their discovery. After much light-hearted discussion, Martin proposed that David should take the lead.

"After all," he said, "David found the spot. All we did was lead him underground. It was David's commitment to the project and his enthusiasm that made us do it."

The others all agreed and David promised to do his best. He would seek advice from the best sources he could find and report back. Harry and Colin happily took the rolls of film out of their cameras and gave them to David.

"Hey one last thing before we turn in for the night," said Martin, "we haven't got a name for the cavern"

Over one more pint, a number of names were suggested, some bizarre, and some plain stupid.

"How about 'The Cathedral of Colour'?" David eventually proposed.

The others all agreed it was perfect. They all shook hands solemnly on their chosen name. That night, as they slept in their bunks, five young men dreamed vividly of 'The Cathedral of Colour'.

After exchanging addresses and telephone numbers with his new friends, David took the long journey back to the flat lands of Cambridgeshire.

As he sat in the train, he reflected on the last few days. He could hardly believe that in the space of less than a week he had made two major discoveries. He had yet to start life at University, but he now knew with some certainty, that a life of adventure and exploration was something he wanted with a passion. That and Laura.

It was with some trepidation that he returned to the chemist in Ely who had been entrusted with developing his photographs. The black and white prints of the Roman bath near Tal-y-cafn were reasonable, but the slides taken with his dad's camera were superb. There were only ten in total, but the main features of the underground bathhouse were quite distinct. The photos of the cavern near Blaenau Ffestiniog suffered from the low light conditions, but in many of the photos the vivid colours could be seen. The incredible features, especially the stalactite organ, were very clear. Overall David was pleased with them and was confident that he had enough evidence to convince the most vociferous doubter. He first showed them to Laura, who was almost as excited as David.

"What are you going to do with them?" she asked.

"I thought I might show them to the Professor of Geology, particularly the cavern, when I go up next week. He would give me some idea of the basis of the features, especially the presence of limestone in that particular rock structure."

Laura agreed, although she thought a historian might understand the Roman bath better.

"Let's see," said David, "there's no hurry."

One week later David settled in his room at Pembroke College, one of the older colleges, founded in 1347. The first few days were filled with the boisterous activities of 'freshers week' and David had little time to do much else. He joined the Pembroke College Boat Club and looked forward to rowing again. As things settled into more of a routine, he made an appointment to see the Professor of Geology, a Dr. Ernst Young. Prof. Young was a thin, scrawny man of an indeterminate age. He wore a grey suit, which had clearly seen better days. Although he wore a University tie, it was loosely tied, giving him a careworn look. His steel-rimmed glasses, constantly dropping to the end of his rather beak-like nose, accentuated his disheveled appearance. David also detected a faint German accent, but one that had no doubt lessened during his time in the ivory towers of Cambridge. Prof. Young was surprised that a first year student, especially one who was not his tutee, was keen to meet him. As David explained why he was there and showed him the print photographs, his original disinterest changed markedly. He questioned David carefully and methodically. He even repeated a number of questions to make sure David was consistent with his answers. At the end of the meeting, David detected a level of friendliness that was not there earlier.

"Would you mind if I showed a colleague of mine these pictures?" Prof. Young eventually enquired.

"Of course not," David replied.

"Give me a week and I'll be in touch," the professor promised.

True to his word, some five days later, Professor Young invited David to his rooms. The meeting was more cordial than the first one and David noted that Prof. Young was now calling him by his first name.

This indicated a level of rapport, which was totally unexpected. The professor came quickly to the point and invited David to present his findings at the University Geological Society.

"I haven't arranged the programme for this term and would be more than happy for you to be our speaker. No more than half an hour, followed by questions. Could you manage that?"

David hesitated, as the request was totally unexpected, but happily agreed. What had he to loose after all? He could do little more than tell the society what had happened and all about it. David's only concern was to explain how he came to be investigating at that particular place. He hoped this enigmatic question wouldn't arise.

The Geological Society met in the main geology lecture theatre at 7.30pm on the first Wednesday of each month. David arrived early and was relieved to find a technician was available to put his precious slides in the carousel and allow him to run through his talk. The technician also showed David how to work the epidiascope, a cumbersome piece of equipment that projected his photographs.

People started arriving at 7.00pm and David was surprised that red and white wine was offered. The assembled company was a mixture of staff and students from most of the colleges. David was slightly nervous before his presentation and hoped his anxiety wouldn't be too obvious. He turned down the attractive option of wine, before excusing himself to go to the toilet. As he stood there, adjusting his tie, he took the view that he was only telling a simple story, without any scientific background. There was no good reason to worry unduly. At 7.30pm prompt, everyone moved into the auditorium and after brief announcements about the society, he was introduced. David spoke clearly about the experience, acknowledged the contribution of his friends from Sheffield and explained each photograph, as they were projected on the screen. There was a murmur of interest within the hall, which put David at his ease. Then David switched on the carousel to show the slides. As the first slide came up on the screen, the audience went silent. They were amazed at what they were seeing. Even though the photographs had only been taken in torchlight, the projection onto a big screen, seemed to give them all more depth. The features of the cavern stood out, almost as if they were there. As David switched off the projector and invited questions, the room went from hushed awe to a hubbub of interest and the questions came fast and furious. The factual questions about the trip were easy to answer as David simply reported what had happened. Then came a couple of technical questions about the geomorphology of the area and David's interpretation of what he had seen. He was asked about the context of the predominant Cambrian and Ordovician sedimentation. David had no answer, and was saved from embarrassment by Prof. Young explaining that Mr. Clarke was only a first year student, yet even to attend a single lecture on geomorphology. The professor went on to say that he hoped in time, David would be able to explain his findings in some detail. The meeting finished with David being given enthusiastic applause and all but Prof. Young left the room.

"David," he said, "one of your questions asked about any other experience you had of subterranean exploration and I noticed you were a little reticent in your answer"

"I didn't think it relevant to geology, sir, but a few days earlier I'd found an underground spring, both hot and cold, possibly associated with a Roman settlement."

"Not relevant, young man, not relevant. Water is the essence of geology; tell all. Better still; let's go somewhere cosier. I suggest the Cambridge Arms. See you in the library bar in 30 minutes. Bring any photos you have."

Little did David appreciate that the library bar at the Cambridge Arms meant so much to his parents in years gone by.

When Prof. Young arrived, he brought with him a colleague from the history department.

"This is Dr. Deane. He's a Reader in Ancient History, with particular interest in the Roman period. I took the liberty of inviting him to join us in view of what you told me after your talk."

Dr. Deane was younger that Prof Young and dressed in a tracksuit and trainers. He was slim, athletic and had a natural tanned face, which David guessed was the result of a summer spent outdoors.

"Excuse the casual dress, Ernst," he said, "but you caught me just after I came home from a game of squash. Five minutes later and I would've been in the shower. Your invitation sounds tempting, Ernst. Tell me more."

"This is David Clarke, Hugh, just joined as here. He has an interesting story to tell."

With that David went into as much detail as he could, making sure that he was suitably vague about the precise location.

"Extraordinary," was Dr. Deane's reaction to David's account. "Quite extraordinary. Do you have any evidence?"

David produced the photos and the slides, which Dr. Deane examined closely.

"There are two things here that I found most interesting. The mosaic of course, but the sun image is truly exceptional. I have only seen one anything like it and that's at the Temple to Sulis Minerva at Bath. So David, let me get this straight. You found this by removing a large volume of rubble and stone?"

"Yes, it took me about two days, and I needed help with the farmer's tractor for the bigger rocks."

"And the time you spent in there was just two days?"

"Yes, the first day was basically finding it and then I went back to take the photographs."

"Unbelievable. This has just got to be properly excavated. You may have come across a most remarkable find. Perhaps not on the same scale as Bath, but a Roman bath nonetheless. Are you absolutely sure about the thermal spring?"

"Well as I told you, I measured the temperature over a few hours and it remained constant at 42 degrees centigrade."

"Quite remarkable. We need to organize a proper archeological expedition for this. It sounds quite exceptional."

"Before we get too involved, there is something you both need to know. The land belongs to a local farmer and his livelihood depends on being able to farm all his land all of the time. I suggested to him that a proper dig might be feasible for perhaps a short period every year. I suggested a period such as a month."

"I see. Sorry, I got a little carried away," said Dr. Deane. "We certainly must respect the wishes of the landowner, although I am sure English Heritage may take a different view. I'll tell you what David, leave me to make contact. I'll even go over to North Wales and meet the farmer. I'm sure we can come to some sort of appropriate access, even if only for a short time. Why can't we get all our students put their precious summer vacation to good use like this?"

Prof. Young interrupted Hugh's line of thought.

"Tell me Hugh, you weren't at the Geological Society seminar this evening were you? No matter," he continued "but you missed the other find from our young friend."

"Do tell," Dr. Deane responded, "this gets more interesting by the minute"

David then summarized what he had found in the cave in Snowdonia, with Dr. Deane just as fascinated, especially when he saw the photographs.

"This is more your field than mine, Ernst. I stop at Roman history not geomorphology. I leave the boring stuff to you. I've just had a thought though. Why don't we invite young David here to give an illustrated paper at the joint meeting of the Royal Geographical Society and the Royal Historical Society? You know, Ernst, the first joint meeting, the one to be held over Christmas. We could help him get some basic facts behind him, both historical and geological. It could be brilliant. How about it?

Prof Young thought for a moment and then agreed. He was cautious at first, but soon he was convinced.

"Perfect, the abstract will have to be in by early next week, but we can do that. David perhaps you could make a draft and discuss it with me by Friday?"

David was a little overwhelmed by the speed at which things seemed to be moving, but happily agreed. The three of them parted. One to his shower, one to his late dinner, and David, who by now had missed his evening meal, to his room to draft his very first abstract. David sat and wondered how he could possibly summarize all his discoveries into 300 words. He then suddenly remembered the other piece of evidence he'd collected. He couldn't believe how he'd overlooked the water from the pipe that flowed into the ancient basin. He went to his rucksack, lying forgotten in a corner of his room, and pulled out his old thermos flask. It was still securely sealed and thankfully undamaged. As he pulled the precious flask out of his rucksack, he noticed another grubby object at the bottom. Then it all came back to him. The rock fall, the glistening piece of stone; the one he grabbed as they all escaped. He looked at it again, turning it over and over in his hands. In the light of his room it did seem to be even brighter than he remembered. He realized that it was most probably 'fools gold', but after his recent experiences he saw no harm in having it examined by experts. He was prepared to look stupid if it turned out to be nothing of interest.

The next day, David took the two items, the water and the rock, back to show Prof. Young. He was busy with other things, but directed David to the analytical lab in the geology department. He handed the two objects over to a technician, who promised to look when he could fit it into his busy schedule. A week later, David found a note in his pigeonhole in the porter's lodge at Pembroke College. It asked him to come to see Prof. Young as soon as possible. After his morning lecture, David went to Prof. Young's study to be greeted warmly.

"David, please sit down and let's get straight to the point. Are you absolutely sure that the water you sent for analysis came from the cave you described so well at the recent seminar?"

"Absolutely, I washed out the flask thoroughly in boiling water before I collected the water from the cave. I didn't have any way of collecting any of the hot water but as I told you before, I did note its temperature."

"It's the cold water, I am interested in, because the lab have run a full content analysis. I won't bore you with the details, but the fluoride and magnesium content are virtually the same as Buxton water and even better than the purity of Malvern water, two of the popular brands. It's almost as pure as distilled water, so your farmer in North Wales could have the basis for a commercial success. Now to your rock. What did you think it was David?"

"To be honest, I had no idea. It was just that even in the dim light of the cave, it seemed to glisten. It was clearly a bit different from other rocks in the fall."

"It is very different. My analytical staff did some initial analysis, which looked promising, but then carefully split the rock along its central axis. What they found was quite remarkable. They found a totally intact nugget of gold."

"Gold. You mean that piece of rock had a lump of gold in it."

"Absolutely and what's more the remaining rock is high grade ore, which could easily yield more gold after the correct treatment. I'll be honest with you, David, I have rarely come across this phenomenon. It will need highly specialized input to get the best out of it. Would you be happy for me to organize it, or would you rather take it on yourself?"

"To be frank, I wouldn't know where to start. Is it something you could do for me?"

"It would be a pleasure, but I cannot promise just when. Why don't we focus on your presentation at the RGS?"

"The RGS?"

"Sorry, yes, the Royal Geographical Society meeting. I heard this morning that your abstract has been accepted, so you need to get down to planning your presentation. I will expect a draft in two weeks and then with Dr. Deane's help we can polish it together. Can I make a suggestion? Keep the gold issue under your hat and finish the presentation by revealing it. You may have to do a bit of research into the history of local mining, but I can assure you now that North Wales was known for copper and even gold. There is a seam known as the Dolgellau belt, so you may have stumbled on an outcrop from that."

"Just one other thing, sir, will it have any value?"

"It certainly will, but I cannot give you a figure. Welsh gold seems to have a premium value. It was used for Princess Margaret's wedding ring a couple of years ago. It's a sort of tradition for the royals to use Welsh gold. You could be a lucky boy."

With that news ringing in his ears, David was dismissed and went to his afternoon lectures, potentially a much richer man.

The joint meeting of the Royal Geographical and Royal Historical Societies was held at the headquarters of the Royal Geographical Society's London headquarters next to the Albert Hall. It was held on December 22nd and was the last and major event of the year.

As David sat in the oak-paneled main lecture theatre, he marveled at the historical significance of the place. In this very room had stood the legendary characters of exploration. These included Charles Darwin, Dr. David Livingstone, Ernest Shackleton and Robert Scott. Only a few years earlier Sir Edmund Hillary had captivated his audience with his account of the conquest of Everest.

When his time came, David was nervous and excited in equal amounts. His rehearsal with Dr. Deane and Prof. Young had gone well, so he felt suitably prepared. He had a tendency to talk to the ceiling, so Dr. Deane had taught him to pick on someone in the audience and focus on that person alone. It seemed to work and after a slightly hesitant start, David soon started to relax. He handled the five questions from the audience well and all too soon his time was up. He received polite applause and walked from the podium relieved that the ordeal was over. It was then that he felt the sweat running from his armpits and was relieved he was wearing a suit to hide his discomfort. It was then he saw, on the far side of the room, his Sheffield friends, Harry, Colin, Martin and Jimmy. The five of them retired to the Prince Albert down the road and talked climbing, caving and walking until the pub closed.

Christmas at the Clarke household was a joyous, family affair, but for David the best part by far was the time he spent with Laura. She was fascinated by all his stories about Cambridge and David was just as interested to know all about her experiences at Bristol University, particularly her social life. He admitted to a degree of jealousy when Laura told him about her new friends. David's feelings for Laura were steadily growing and he hoped she felt the same.

It was when David went back to Cambridge for the Lent term that he received two unexpected letters. One envelope was marked the Royal Geographical Society and the other the Birmingham Assay Office. He opened the one from the Royal Geographical Society first. It read:

Dear Mr. Clarke,

It is with great pleasure I inform you of the award of the Society's Bronze Medallion. This award is in the Young Researcher category. It is in recognition of your discovery of a Roman bathhouse and subterranean "Cathedral of Colour", both in North Wales.

I would welcome a note to indicate your acceptance of this award and then arrangements will be made for your investiture.

With kind regards

James Guthrie

Secretary to the Royal Geographical Society

David was flabbergasted and could hardly contain his excitement. He was about to rush out to tell friends on his staircase, but then remembered the other, unopened letter. He ripped it open and read

Dear Mr. Clarke,

The Birmingham Assay office is pleased to inform you that the sample of Welsh gold and gold ore is combined to weigh 4.8 troy ounces. This, for information, is more than sufficient to make at least five (5) wedding rings of substantial quality. I am authorized to offer you the current market value for the gold presently in our possession, which is £1400.

If it is your wish, we could engage a jeweler of repute to fashion a number of rings to use all or part of the gold.

I await your instructions with interest.

Yours sincerely

Karl Levins

Senior Analyst

David planned to celebrate his award and good fortune with friends and members of staff in the geology department. He showed the letters to Prof. Young, and it was the one from the Royal Geography Society that interested him the most. He congratulated David, told him that he was worthy of such a prestigious award and happily announced it to all in the department. He considered the other letter to be a private contract and counseled David to think carefully about its implications. After consulting the market prices in his copy of The Times, he thought it a fair offer, but warned David that agreeing to the price meant he lost control. David had already decided most of the money should be shared with his four friends from Sheffield. He also wanted some form of memento from his time in North Wales and eventually decided to have two rings made from the gold and to sell the rest. He was assured that the rings could be adjusted to fit any size of finger. This decision was driven by his growing affection for Laura. Time alone could turn his dream into reality. By the end of the Lent term, David had a received two beautiful gold rings and a money order for £1100, the residual cash from the sale of the gold. He sent a substantial cheque to each of his friends from Sheffield and turned his attention to the end of year exams.

Little did David know the Welsh gold he had found was to be used in years to come to make the wedding rings for several of the royal family.

CHAPTER 20
COLOURS

As David was settling into his first year in Cambridge at Pembroke College, Peter was becoming used to pre-clinical studies across the city at Downing College. Peter found the work hard, spending a long time memorizing the details of anatomy and physiology for his part 1 examination. He still found time to train hard at his cross-country running. He used it as a pleasant, if arduous, respite from his medical studies. At the beginning of Peter's second year, the University hired a specialist athletics coach who took particular interest in the cross-country squad. Peter soon found that the Hare and Hounds Club, the name given to the cross-country club at Cambridge, was the best way to gain the experience needed to improve his overall performance. Much of the training was similar to his experiences at Downthorpe, but the intensity was always greater. Sunday morning was the worst session. The squad would assemble about five miles from Cambridge in the woods of the Scraptoft estate. This was chosen because it was the only place for miles that had a hill of any significance. It was not a big hill, but there were numerous, steep trails up and down of about 200 yards in length. After a lengthy warm-up, the students would race each other up the steep slope, almost collapsing with exhaustion at the top of the hill. Then it was a gentle jog down another of the trails, a sharp turn uphill and another sprint to the top. This continued for a minimum of six hill runs, with the runners' legs screaming for a rest. Recovery would be a long run around the base of the hill, before the whole set of sprints would be repeated. This was the point when many of the squad would be ready to quit, but the coach would call for one more set. He would note in his little red book the students who could respond to the torture once more. Few enjoyed these sessions, but they all knew the end result was each one of them would be fitter and stronger. These things would be needed for the grueling cross-country season ahead.

In Peter's first year, he worked his way steadily up the ranks of the runners. Eventually he was selected for the University second team. He was convinced that with more hard work and the right sort of training he could make the first team. He could even, with luck, be awarded the coveted blue. This would mean being selected for the Oxford versus Cambridge race, held every year at Roehampton in March. Peter's dream was realized a year later, in 1964. The team was announced and his name placed on the board in the pavilion at the main athletics training ground. He was overjoyed, especially as he knew his medical studies would complicate his life from now on. Cambridge had few teaching hospitals and he would probably have to transfer to one of the London hospitals for most of his clinical training.

The team had stayed overnight in London, courtesy of the parents of one of the runners. It was a spacious house with ample spare rooms, each team member sharing with one other. They dined well the night before the race, enjoying a small steak and a big bowl of pasta. Alcohol was not allowed; that could wait until after the race.

The day of the race was dull and dreary and it felt as though the cold easterly wind was blowing directly from the steppes of Russia. The sixteen runners lined up at the start of the five-mile course. It included the traditional elements of cross-country races; flat fast land, hills, a ploughed field and a five-bar gate. Peter struggled over the initial stages, taking time to get used to the cold, but soon got into his stride, overtaking the runners in front steadily, but deliberately slowly. He knew that pace judgment was critical. At the four-mile marker, he was comfortably placed, with the expected team members ahead of him. It was difficult to judge the overall positions, because the Oxford runners were intermingled with the Cambridge team. The final 400 yards included a five-bar gate, which slowed up the runners and most lost their rhythm as they climbed over it. Peter decided to risk all and attempt a gate vault, knowing that it would be faster, but he could easily slip and fall. As he approached the gate he focused on the third bar down. This was where he'd place his hand as he swung his body over, with all the weight on his stomach. An Oxford runner was a fraction in front as he came to the gate. Peter was utterly determined and kicked hard, swinging his legs, tight together, over the gate. He landed slightly askew on the other side, but quickly regained his balance. Peter sprinted the last few yards, not daring to look back at the Oxford runner who was alongside him at the gate.

It took a little while to calculate the result, with only the first six from each team to count. An Oxford runner had won the race, but Cambridge had managed a better aggregate, especially as they had managed second and third places. Peter finished in ninth place, well ahead of the last Cambridge runner to count. The long-anticipated result was eventually announced; Cambridge had won by just two points and the celebrations went on late into the night. This time alcohol, mainly in the form of champagne, was not only allowed, but also thoroughly enjoyed.

*   *   *   *   *

David's sporting experience at Cambridge was equally demanding. In his first year he joined the College Boat Club and, based on his experience at King's Ely, was chosen for the College first squad. The crew rowed well and in the Lent Bumps, Pembroke College bumped the crews ahead on every day. The reward for this achievement was for each member of the crew to be presented with his rowing blade. It was a somewhat cumbersome prize, but David managed to find a place for it in the garage at home in Witchford.

In David's second year, he put his name forward to join the University Boat Club. Trials were held in early September and he was selected to join the squad of 24 rowers who would eventually row in the Cambridge first and second boats. The arduous training involved a 6.30am start, six days a week, rowing for up to two hours on the River Cam or for longer stretches on the Great Ouse at Ely. In addition, David had to endure four sessions of land training every week. These were held in the gym at the University sports centre and involved a frightening amount of weight lifting and high intensity sprints. David was excused the sprints because of his 'polio ankle', but compensated by his incredible performances with the heavy weights. A student in the engineering department had designed a novel rowing machine. It was based on a large piston, with the rowing handle being attached to the end of the plunger. It was a fearsome piece of engineering and allowed a direct comparison between the squad members. David was not the best, but he was one of the top performers and hoped his results would be enough to be chosen for one of the University boats. When the final selection was made, David was delighted to be selected for the Goldie boat, the University second boat.

The race against Oxford's second crew, called Isis, was held during the Easter vacation. The week before the race, both first and second boats spent the week down in London, training over the same course as the race itself. The crews stayed in houses lent to them by former students. It was a rather sombre week, two outings every day, and concentrating hard on the advice of the finishing coach, brought in especially for the final stages of preparation. All the food was controlled, with large amounts of carbohydrate and protein for every meal. Evenings were spent together, either watching television or playing endless games of cards. No one was allowed out of the house at night. It had the feel of a spiritual retreat, to finish not in religious ecstasy, but in a grueling four-mile race from Putney to Mortlake.

Rather like Peter's experience of cross-country, the day was overcast and uninteresting. The prevailing wind gave a slight preference to one boat and the Cambridge crew was unfortunate to lose the toss. This put them at a slight disadvantage, but they had prepared for this and adjusted their tactics accordingly. They now knew they had to go off fast and try to keep their position as the wind benefitted Oxford later in the race. David, sitting in the centre of the boat, was the last to take off his light blue tracksuit top. He passed it down the boat to the official holding the eight steady on the stake boat in the middle of the river. The whole crew had practised starts well over a hundred times, but David was still visibly tense and could feel his stomach muscles contracting uncontrollably. Both coxes dropped their hands, the umpire's red flag descended, and they were off. The Cambridge crew were slightly rushed over the first few strokes, but soon settled into a solid rhythm. They were rowing at a slightly higher rate than the Oxford crew, but knew this was essential to force the lead they needed. The cox was shouting the timing, and exhorted the crew to push themselves hard at every stroke. After 30 seconds, the cox changed to a different style. He was looking towards the Oxford crew and called out "I have stroke!"

The whole of the Cambridge crew knew what this meant and redoubled their efforts. Their own cox was now level with the stroke man in the Oxford boat, meaning they had gained about six feet. The Cambridge cox was now screaming encouragement and timing, interspersed with another number. "I have seven. I have six...." As they heard these numbers go down, the Cambridge crew settled into a much steadier pace. They relaxed during the recovery phase of the stroke and started to row as a single unit. As they shot Hammersmith Bridge, there appeared for the first time to be clear water between the two crews, but Cambridge knew that the big test was to come. The next stage of the race gave Oxford a great advantage as the river swung round to the left. Oxford would be on the inside of the bend and it was worth all the ground they had gained so far. Slowly and predictably the bend started to favour Oxford. The Cambridge crew could hear the Oxford cox calling that he was gaining on Cambridge. Slowly, irrevocably, the Oxford crew came alongside. Then the bend was over and both crews were back on equal terms. The Cambridge rowers were supremely confident that their relaxed rowing over the last two minutes would pay dividends. At the bandstand, the crews were neck and neck and it stayed like that as they shot under Barnes Railway Bridge. Both crews knew that they had about two minutes to row to the finish and every sinew in every person strained to keep the power on the blade as it was driven through the water. The Cambridge cox called for 20 strokes. It meant that each member of the crew would put in every ounce of effort for just 20 strokes, hoping to break the will of the opposition. The effect was formidable. Cambridge gained six feet in just 20 strokes.

"I have seven, I have seven," screamed the Cambridge cox, making sure he turned to face Oxford as he repeated the chant. Cambridge now steadied themselves again, concentrating on the all-important style and rhythm to let the boat run smoothly between each stroke. The effect was impressive and they continued to make gains on the Oxford boat. They crossed the finishing line half a length up and splashed the water with their hands in jubilation. The traditional three cheers followed and both crews turned to make their way to the boathouse. For David, nothing could be as memorable as this glorious experience. He was exhausted but ecstatic. Unbeknown to David, Laura was waiting near the boathouse. She kept out of sight until the boat had been put away and the cox had been unceremoniously dumped in the river. The whole crew hugged each other in a tight celebratory circle. David then turned away to see Laura standing in the crowd. He almost cried with delight and this time the only hug was with her.

At the beginning of David's final year, he decided to apply, once again, for the blue boat – the Cambridge University first VIII, which would compete in the main University boat race. His weight training and diet meant that David had put on almost two stone of solid muscle since the previous rowing season. He considered himself more than ready for the challenges ahead.

Training for the six months before the race was as intensive as ever. The coaches had dreamed up even more horrendous fitness and land training activities than the previous year. It was a tough year, especially as it was the year of David's finals, but he was more determined than ever to row at the highest level the University could offer. The crew was finally selected after a training camp during the Christmas vacation. David was delighted to be chosen to sit in the five seat in the blue boat. His ambition was about to be achieved, to row for Cambridge first crew in the boat race. Once the crews were settled, the intensity of training increased more and David was usually too tired to socialize. Laura understood and accepted that it would only be for a few more weeks. The Easter vacation, with the boat race behind them, would be a wonderful opportunity to make up for lost ground in their relationship.

With just two weeks to go before the boat race, David started to suffer unexpected fatigue and pains in some of his joints. At first he put this down to the intensity of training. Other members of the crew were exhausted by the regular outings, but the coaches knew how to give adequate rest periods to overcome this. With David it was different. He then found himself unusually out of breath. This was at a time when all his training should have left him at the peak of fitness. Reluctantly David went to see the college doctor, who, being fully aware of his sporting pedigree, was surprised at the sudden turn of events. It was only when she reviewed his previous medical history that his childhood polio came to light. She sent him for a series of tests at Papworth Hospital and he was called back for the results two days later. He went to the main entrance and was directed to the outpatients department to be met by Professor Julius Montgomery, a world expert on virology. He looked serious and David had a feeling of impending doom.

"Mr. Clarke, I'm afraid the news is not good. The tests we have undertaken, particularly the blood tests, reveal that you have an unusual condition we call post-polio syndrome. It's exhibited as fatigue, muscle weakness, joint pain and breathing difficulties; all symptoms I understand you are suffering from right now. Am I right?"

David could only agree with the Professor's observations and remained silent.

"It is a rare consequence of your earlier bout of polio, but it can happen."

"But why after all this time and why now?" David asked in desperation.

"We don't know fully, but we believe it's the result of gradual deterioration of nerve cells in the spinal cord that were damaged by the polio virus. This is why it has taken so long to appear."

David was devastated, but managed to ask one more question.

"Is it something I will get over?"

"Absolutely, but not immediately. Normally the symptoms you show would take much, much longer to appear. What I mean by that is the time scale for all your symptoms seems to have been condensed into a couple of weeks. Normally it could take years."

"But why?" David asked.

"I would put it down to your incredible level of fitness. I think this has been going on for some time, but the symptoms have been delayed until right now. Some underlying infection could have triggered the sudden change. We just don't know."

"So what must I do right now?"

"Complete rest for two months, then see how it goes. I would imagine you'll feel much better by then and you'll be able to build up your strength and fitness very slowly after that."

David left the hospital in a daze. He couldn't argue with the diagnosis, but refused to accept he wouldn't be in the race of his life in ten days time. His whole life ambition ruined by an invisible virus that he'd struggled so hard to overcome. He knew he had little option and went straight round to the

College of the boat club's president. When he broke the news, there was sympathy and concern. At this late stage, one of the key members of the crew was lost and they would need to draft in a member of the Goldie crew. This was unsettling at the best of times, but ten days before the race it was overwhelming. David could do nothing more and felt it best to leave the president alone to make his plans. David had no plans. He felt thoroughly wretched, distraught and verging on a state of depression. He had experienced profound setbacks in his life before - his polio and losing his seat in the boat to row at Henley. He knew he had a variety of options, one being to hide all evidence of his new situation. But there was no hiding place. He phoned Laura and broke down on the phone, totally unable to control his desperate state.

"I'm coming to see you," she said.

"Thanks," was David's muted reply.

Laura arrived early the next evening and David met her at the station. The subdued couple walked hand in hand to David's small flat and, almost in silence, prepared a simple meal together. As they sat down to eat, Laura turned directly to David and said two words, "Talk, David."

It was only then that the full impact of David's situation came to the surface. For the first time he spoke openly of the hurt, the pain, the utter frustration of being so close to achieving his sporting ambition. He told Laura of the time it had happened to him at school when he was dropped from the crew just before the chance to row at Henley. Laura listened. David reached the point when his grief became uncontrollable and he wept openly. Laura took him in her arms and let the floods of pent up emotion wave over her. It took time, but then the tears stopped and David now relaxed. The worst was over. Laura led him by the hand to the bedroom and they made love tenderly and gently. David was at peace.

The biggest event of the sporting social calendar was the Colours Dinner. It was traditionally held on the evening of the Oxford versus Cambridge athletics meeting and was a grand, black tie affair with the students wearing their club blazers. The rugby club was the noisiest group in spite of having a poor season. The hockey club, who had won their first match against Oxford for many years, closely matched their revelry. The athletics club members were rather morose, having that very day lost closely to Oxford. The boat club was buoyant, as both crews had won their respective boat races. The president of the boat club invited David to attend in spite of having to withdraw from the race at the last moment. David was reluctant. He was sure it would bring back memories of one of the most miserable days of his life. At the last minute, he accepted. He realized it was time to face up to his devils. There was no better time than alongside the people he had bonded with so closely over the last year. He initially felt slightly distant from the students of both crews who would today receive their blues. As the evening wore on and the alcohol took effect, he visibly relaxed.

David watched as members of the Hare and Hounds Club, the cross-country club, stood up to receive their full blues. One in particular caught his eye; the tall, blond student with piercing blue eyes. David had read in the programme that he was the only medical student in the team and David was well aware that the workload of medics was way above most students. David had great respect for a medical student such as this, who could combine intense studies with the highest level of sport.

His name was Peter Culham.

The president of the boat club stood up to award full blues to the first crew. This was honour that David by rights should have been receiving. David tried to blot out the moment back in March when the doctor had told him the devastating news. He sat there in quiet reflection as the familiar names were read out. Then the half blues were awarded to the Blondie crew, the crew that David had been part of the previous year. Finally the president made one last unexpected announcement.

"Lords, ladies and gentlemen. Tonight the colours committee has agreed unanimously to break with tradition. As you are all aware blues are only awarded to students who compete against Oxford. Tonight we will make an exception. As you are all aware, David Clarke was only ten days away from representing Cambridge in the boat race, before he fell ill. It is my pleasure to award an honorary full blue to David Clarke. This award is given, not just because of the unfortunate circumstances, but also to represent the exemplary contribution that David gave to the boat club over the last two years."

The applause was deafening and David had to be pushed to his feet by others around him. In a semi-hypnotic state, he walked unsteadily to the rostrum. When the colour diploma was put into his hand, David finally recognized the implication of his award. In spite of everything that had happened, he was now the proud recipient of a full blue from Cambridge. Life was good.

Across the room another student was watching with interest. He had heard about David. He had great respect for someone who had suffered from the debilitating condition of polio, yet had fought back to represent Cambridge at rowing, known to be the toughest sport on campus.

The name of the student watching David with admiration was Peter Culham.

The celebrations finished at two-o-clock in the morning with David being pushed out of a taxi near his room in a semi-comatose state. The next morning, with a sore head, he first phoned Laura and then his parents.

CHAPTER 21
POEM

David's 21st birthday on June 24th was a quiet, but pleasant occasion at his home in Witchford. Close family and a few University friends crowded into the small family house. Everyone had a relaxed time, made special by the welcome from David's parents. There wasn't room for everyone to sit down, so his mother organised a running buffet and people were happy to spill out into the small garden. To David's surprise some champagne appeared and his dad proposed a toast to David's future. By early evening, all but the family had drifted away and David and his brother, Iain, happily helped clear up the dishes and glasses. When all was back to normal, David's mother arranged a light meal of an omelette and anything leftover from the party. As the light faded, David's mother took David alone into the garden. They sat together on a low wall out of sight of the others. She took a deep breath and announced in hushed tones.

"David, I think the time has come for you to be told about your birth."

David looked at her, an inquisitive frown on his face.

"I re-married your dad a couple of years after you were born. I had a loving relationship with someone during the war. You were the consequence of the affair, but things didn't work out. Dad, quite understandably, divorced me when he came home from Burma."

David paused for a moment, uncertain of his own reaction.

"You said re-marry?"

"Yes, after some time we got back together and re-married. It was several years later that Iain was born."

"I see, well I think I see. I don't really know what to say."

"David, I don't think you should say anything right now. Give this news some thought and please come and talk to me some more when you're ready. There is just one thing, David. Your dad, Bill, doesn't know I planned to tell you."

With that she grabbed David by the hand and the two walked quietly and thoughtfully back through the French doors into the house.

David took a little time to accept what he'd been told on the evening of his birthday. He wanted to ask questions but was too concerned that the relationship with his dad could be damaged. He shared his thoughts with Laura, who asked him what he planned to do.

"I think the simple answer, Laura, is nothing. I have always respected and loved my dad, and I would be horrified if anything changed that. I think it may be best to do absolutely nothing, at least for now."

Laura agreed and gave David a loving kiss of acceptance and approval.

David had a number of presents and cards for his 21st from family and friends. He was very grateful and made every effort to thank people personally or write a note of appreciation. There was one present that David found incredibly strange. The giver hadn't included a card, or any indication of their name.

The present was a book of poetry, specifically those of William Blake.

The inscription on the flyleaf, in a hand that was vaguely familiar to David, read,

Dear David,

There is something amiss about this book of poetry and I recommend you seek it. I would love to join you on this second quest, but time and distance prevent it. You have proved yourself before and I have every confidence in you. I wish you well.

It was the expression 'I wish you well' that David read a second time. He had seen it before, but couldn't quite place it in context.

The book meant little to David, but it was a rather fine volume, bound in some sort of leather. David knew the man to ask was Mr. Moran from the bookshop in town. It was time to pay him a visit.

The next time David was in Ely, he took the book to Mr. Moran's bookshop. It was a delight to see the old man again and David was pleased he seemed so much better. He still had limited use of one arm, but managed very well in the shop, in spite of his slight handicap. Mr. Moran looked carefully at the volume of William Blake's poems.

"It is quite a fine specimen, David," he said at last. "The morocco binding is quite superb and it is undoubtedly a first edition. I wouldn't put a huge value on it, but it is undoubtedly worth several hundred pounds."

This, to David, was a huge value, but he remained silent.

"There are a few pencil marks in the margins of some pages, but that is most probably because the book was used for studies of some type. If you could establish the provenance of these margin notes, that could possibly increase the value significantly."

David explained that it was a gift and he had no idea of its history.

"There is one thing," added Mr. Moran, "you must have noticed that one page is defaced. It is the poem 'Garden of Love' on page 63. Here it is. Look."

David took the book and saw that page 63 was folded inwards, right across the end of the poem. As he straightened it out the words "There must be more" had been written in a bold hand, underneath the last verse, the writing matching that of the flyleaf.

"Strange," said David, "I have no explanation, but it would be fascinating to find out what it means."

"Before you go, David, I have a little gift for you. A little thank you for your help when I had my stroke."

With that, Mr. Moran pulled a large, wrapped packet from under the counter and presented it to him.

"No need to unwrap it now, David. It's an old atlas. I'd heard that you'd landed a job with the Ordinance Survey and I thought that this old atlas may be of interest."

David was surprised on two counts. Firstly that Mr. Moran had somehow been told of his new job and secondly the gift itself.

"You're very kind, Mr. Moran. I really appreciate the thought and I know I'll enjoy every moment of studying it."

"Oh and I have something for your kind friend Laura. Do you still see her? If so, please ask her to call in."

"I'm sure that can be arranged," said David with a wry smile, "leave it to me."

"Oh and one other thing, David. I'd be honoured if you called me Ken. Mr. Moran seems so formal after what we've been through together."

"Certainly, Ken and thank you again."

When David told Laura about meeting up with Ken Moran, she promised to drop in to see him as soon as possible. Her gift turned out to be a first edition of 'The Variation of Animals and Plants under Domestication' by Charles Darwin, Volume 1. She was amazed Ken Moran had chosen a book that related so closely to her degree in Natural Sciences and thanked him profusely.

David, for the second time in his life, was totally mystified by a present from a complete stranger. His adventures in North Wales were a direct result of his 18th birthday card and he couldn't resist the chance to see if this inscription led him anywhere interesting. His new job, based in Southampton, gave him little uninterrupted time to research the works of William Blake, so he had no choice but be patient. Laura was now working for English Heritage, using her skills to explore the natural history of trees and gardens in the main estates of East Anglia. She and David would try to spend most weekends together, but it meant a lot of travelling. They enjoyed their time together immensely, but realized that if there were to be a future together, they would need to save for a deposit on a house. One opportunity to revisit Blake's poem came in the winter of 1966, when David was sent on an assignment to Cambridge. He was to stay for a few days while he spoke to some cartographers based in his old department.

He made an appointment to see the Professor of English, who by chance was associated with his old college, Pembroke.

On a drab Monday morning in March, he went through the familiar gates, had a pleasant chat with the porter, a character he knew well, and found his way to Professor Shapiro's study. The study was larger than most and David assumed it was to accommodate the vast array of books on the floor to ceiling shelves. Prof. Shapiro was far from the archetype professor in appearance. He was of an indeterminate age, dressed in a smart three-piece suit, black-rimmed glasses and had a fashionable haircut. At first sight, one would take him for a lawyer or even a manager of a large departmental store. Prof Shapiro welcomed him and they talked briefly about the time David had spent at the University.

"I understand you have a problem," the learned professor enquired.

"It's a strange one really," David replied, "my question doesn't really have a solid foundation, more of a strange hunch really."

"Hmm," commented Prof. Shapiro, "luckily I'm no scientist, so hunches are a part of my armoury. Tell me more."

"Well, I'm investigating a poem by William Blake, 'The Garden of Love'."

"Ah yes, I think I know it. 'I went to the Garden of Love, and saw what I never had seen.' Is that the one?"

"Yes. You see it only has three verses. I was wondering, is there any chance that Blake wrote any more?"

"Most unlikely. I must confess that I am not really a Blake scholar. My field is more the 17th century. Now ask me about Milton and I could help you. There's been a huge amount of scholarship around

Blake and I'm sure any additional verses would have turned up over the years. Why do you think there may be more verses anyway?"

"As I said earlier, it's just a strange hunch."

"Well if you want to pursue it further, your best bet would be to contact the Blake Society. Their members have a detailed collection of material on Blake. If anyone were to know, it would be them. I'm sure I can find the address of the society's secretary. It's probably at home somewhere."

"Thank you, Professor, that would be most helpful," said David, a little disappointed, but hopeful that the Blake Society would be more forthcoming.

After a few final words about expectations for the boat club over the next year, David made to leave. Prof. Shapiro promised that the Blake Society contact would follow soon.

That evening, he took Laura to a folk club they used to enjoy when they had weekends together in Cambridge. The club was in a room above the Black Horse pub just off Gonville Place and was popular with students and locals alike. The guest group was from Liverpool, under the name of Scouse Harmony. They were on tour prior to the Cambridge Folk Festival and sang a mixture of sea shanties, ballads and protest songs. Towards the end of the evening, they started a haunting melody and David could hardly believe it when they sang the first verse. It was 'The Garden of Love', the very poem that David was relentlessly pursuing. The third verse of the song, beautifully arranged by the band, finished with the lines:

'and priests in black gowns, were walking their rounds,

and binding with briars, my joys and desires.'

Then the words stopped, with a final chord spelling the end of the song. David's heart sank, for he genuinely thought that there might have been more and the conundrum would be solved. Clearly there was more to be achieved and he had every intention of achieving it.

The secretary of the Blake Society, a Dr. Gregory, lived in Marylebone Village in the north west of London, a short walk from Marylebone Station. David arranged to meet him early one evening and took a half-day off work to get there in good time. He took the train from Southampton Central to London Victoria and decided to walk the 45-minute journey to the secretary's house. The streetlights were coming on all over London as he strolled through unfamiliar streets, crossing Wigmore Street to reach his destination at 46 Harley Street. He gained the distinct impression that most of the houses were private rooms of medical consultants, so was not surprised when number 46 displayed the brass plates of several surgeons. One other plate simply stated 'The Blake Society' and David rang the brass bell. He was welcomed through an electronic answerphone with instructions to push open the door and to take the stairs to the second floor. A buzzer sounded from inside and David followed the instructions, surprised by the weight of the door. He reached the second floor, composed himself and knocked on the first of the two doors at this level. It opened and a young lady answered. She was dressed in a loose flowing robe, which David took to resemble something from the Middle East. She was dark, with flowing black hair and a handsome, striking face. It was difficult to see her shape under the robe, but she held herself in the confident way you would expect of someone with a figure to match.

"Do come in," she said with a smile, "I've been expecting you."

"I've come to meet Dr. Gregory," said David.

"And you've met her," said the young lady, "I do hope I don't disappoint."

David faltered for a moment, his expectations differing from the young lady in front of him.

"Far from it," said David trying to sound convincing, but quite sure that his surprised face must have given it away.

"Anyway," said Dr. Gregory, gesturing David to come in, "I prefer to be called Susan. Can I offer you a drink?"

David was unsure whether he was being offered a hot drink or something alcoholic, but it was made clear when she said, "I'm having a gin and tonic, will you join me?"

David, slightly taken back by this unexpected turn of events, agreed. The two sat down on the only seat in the room, a two-seated sofa, made deep with soft cushions. David explained his mission to Susan, who seemed intrigued but mystified. She thought it rather strange that a young man with no particular background in the life or times of Blake should wish to follow such an odd pursuit. She explained to David that Blake was a complex character, quite a rebel in his time, and had for some time been opposed to organized religion. She went on to say that towards the end of his life, he was reported to have recovered his faith.

"It is theoretically possible," she said, after pouring them both another gin and tonic, "that he could have re-written some of his earlier work to reflect this shift in his view. Somehow I doubt it, because there is no evidence for it. But as I say, it is a theoretical possibility."

David then asked about the location of manuscripts and papers belonging to Blake.

"The Blake Society ran out of space, so the important works are now stored in the British Library. We have a few items here, mainly material which is in the public domain, but also some fine examples of his handwriting."

"Would it be possible to see these?" David enquired.

"Of course," she said and stood up a little unsteadily, before pouring herself another gin and tonic.

David refused the offer of another alcoholic drink, insisting that he was only given tonic water. When he tasted it, David was convinced it was the same as before. If anything, he thought it was stronger, but said nothing. Susan walked into a different room and after five minutes came back with a spring-back file containing a number of plastic sleeves. David couldn't help but notice that her robe was now open from the neck to between her breasts. The momentary glimpse of her dark skin was tantalizing. She slumped down next to David on the sofa and, moving a little close to him, started to show him the contents of the file. In it were a number of letters, bills and receipts from William Blake. Towards the back of the file was a manuscript with the original of the poem 'Love's Secret'. It had some corrections and notes in the margin and was signed and dated 1789. Susan, putting her hand on David's arm, started to read the last verse aloud.

"Soon after she had gone from me,

A traveller came by,

Silently, invisibly:

He took her with a sigh"

Are you that traveller, David?" she said, without taking her hand away.

David said nothing, not sure of his own thoughts at that moment. Susan lay back for a moment, and then struggled to her feet.

"I have something else for you," she said, "give me a moment"

Susan went into a different room and David sat, feeling slightly light-headed after the pleasant but intoxicating drinks.

"David, I'm in here," came Susan's voice, now slightly slurred. "Come and see what I have for you"

David hesitated, took another look at the manuscript and then walked across the room to the open door. In the half-light, David saw Susan, naked apart from a pair of exotic silk briefs. She was lying on her back across a double bed with her eyes closed. Her left hand was on her breast, gently caressing her nipple and her right hand was lying sensually inside her briefs.

"Christ," he said under his breath. He stood for a moment, unable to move. He was confused, yet aroused by the pleasure on offer. He stood a moment longer. She lay there, silent, inviting, willing him to press his lips to every part of her. He bent over and gently pulled the sheet over Susan's enticing body. He kissed her gently on the forehead and walked slowly away, looking back for one last look, almost in disbelief. He picked up the manuscript, closed the file and pushed it, well out of sight, behind one of the cushions on the sofa. As he left the flat, he closed the door as noiselessly as possible and headed back down the stairs to the fresher air outside. It was only then that he noticed the erratic nature of his breathing. He was honest enough to question whether he'd made the right decision up there. He remembered the line from the poem, now in his hand. Deep down in his inner consciousness, he knew it was for the best and 'soon after she was gone from me.'

Early the next morning, soon after the doors opened at the British Library, David requested access to the Blake's archives. The receptionist on the main lending desk would only admit recognized scholars to the archive material. Luckily David's old student card from Cambridge seemed to be sufficient. An archivist took him to a lower ground floor, somewhere beneath the tracks of Euston Station. David could occasionally catch the rumble of a train far overhead. The numerous room contained row upon row of brown boxes, labeled and indexed and all stacked on shelves that slid in and out easily to the touch. She showed him the boxes of material dedicated to Blake.

"I'm not sure what you're looking for, but good luck. There is some sort of order in those boxes, but I'm afraid it's a bit patchy. If you do come across anything that you want to handle, then please use the gloves at the end of each stack."

With that she walked away, leaving David wondering why he was spending time on this seemingly fruitless task. His mind went back to his 18th birthday card and where that had led him. Mysteriously, he now shared the feeling of his unknown giver that something was not quite right with The Garden of Love. He remembered the phrase used was 'something amiss'. So what could be missing? David relished the challenge. It was the only incentive he needed.

David worked his way through the numerous boxes devoted to Blake. There was a huge amount of information, but nothing seemed to be relevant to his personal quest. Most of the material was contemporary essays and comments and criticisms of his work. He noted that during the 18th century, Blake was criticized by the established church for his extreme views and this seemed to fit in with comments made last evening by Dr. Gregory. The thought of Susan Gregory made David smile and shudder at the same time. He contemplated what could have been.

Eventually, David was pleased to find a copy of the very poem he was seeking. It was unsigned and undated, so the first thing he did was to compare the hand writing with the signed poem he had temporarily 'borrowed' from Susan, There was little doubt it was the same hand. At last he was looking at either the original, or at worst a copy of Blake's poem The Garden of Love. By now David could recite the whole poem and the copy he now had in his gloved hand was the same as in his own book of poetry. Just three verses of four lines each. Nothing added, nothing missing. There seemed to be nothing amiss. David put the manuscript to one side and continued his search. Thoroughly and carefully, he waded through all the remaining boxes. Towards the end, he found a further copy of The Garden of Love, clearly in the same hand, still unsigned, but this time dated. The date surprised David, because it was 1826, barely one year before Blake's death. There was something slightly strange about this version of the poem. David compared the two versions, putting them side-by-side on a nearby, well-lit desk. He pored over the two versions and apart from the date could see little difference. If anything the dated version was in a slightly more varied hand, but it was clearly that of Blake. David put this slight difference down to the fact that Blake was now in his late 60s and perhaps his hand movements were less controlled. David was rapidly coming to the conclusion that his search was coming to an end.

Then he noticed it. The paper on the later, dated copy was slightly thicker. On closer inspection, David saw that it was not a single sheet of paper, but a double sheet, but sealed together as one. He was unable to separate the two sheets as either time or intent had bonded them together. Against the advice of the archivist, David took off his gloves for a better examination. Yes, it was clearly two sheets fused as one, occasionally seen in the pages of antiquarian books. But there was something else. There seemed to be a very slight difference in the central part of the manuscript. It was as if a further piece of paper was enveloped between the two bonded sheets. David was by now both fascinated and challenged. Was there something in this manuscript? Something that had been there for over 140 years? Something that was intended to remain hidden? David was desperate to know the truth. He was well aware this document was not his to examine beyond the scrutiny of his own eyes. Already he had probably gone too far by taking off his gloves to explore the precious artefact. David couldn't resist. He had come this far in his search and he wasn't prepared to give the final explanation to anyone else.

He put everything away, marked the box by leaving his pen on top and left the library. He strode briskly along the Euston Road until he found a chemist. There he asked the helpful assistant for something to remove hard skin. She suggested a number of products, but David knew exactly what he needed. Eventually the assistant suggested the very thing.

"If you're very careful, you could use a fine lancet to remove the skin."

"Perfect," said David, paid and rushed back to the British Library.

It was unfortunate that at the lending desk, he was faced with the same receptionist as before. She was surprised to see him again, but made no comment. In her job she came across all sorts of what she called 'scholarly types'. The same archivist was called to escort him, once again to the lower ground floor. She was more talkative and commented that she thought he'd finished for the day.

"Just a final check for my research," David said, keeping his response just to the honest side of the truth. "I should be through by lunchtime."

He waited until he heard the sound of her steps disappear up the stairs and then set to work. He retrieved the manuscript from the box he'd marked and laid it out on the nearby desk. He had noted before that there was one corner where the two sheets of paper were very slightly separated. It was this corner that he worked on initially with his scalpel. It took far longer than he thought, but slowly the two sheets separated and in time he could look with satisfaction at his handiwork. He was right, there was another smaller sheet between the two outer ones, but it was not as he expected. On close examination, he recognized a very thin sheet of absorbent paper. It had the texture of blotting paper, but much thinner. He tentatively turned it over. To his utter astonishment he could now see, not clearly, but without question, eight distinct lines of writing. Not just eight lines but separated in to two blocks of four lines each. They just had to be two more verses. The writing was faint, but just about readable, even in the artificial light of the depths of the Library. David held his breath in amazement as he leant over to read the script. Could this really be what was amiss? It was then that David's hopes were utterly dashed. The writing was in some foreign hand. It looked like Arabic, but David couldn't be sure. How could he get this far by himself and then have to share the joy of his discovery with someone else? It was devastating. The dream was crushed. The moment was lost. But was it? David's analytical mind started to explore the options. Could he share this incredible finding with someone he trusted and still claim the honour due? But who? He knew no one to turn to in his hour of need. Clearly he could find someone to translate the verses, hidden for so long. It would mean all his efforts, the long line of investigation, would finally be the privilege of someone else. Was there another way?

David sat back in the chair deep in thought. As he did, the polished surface of the table reflected the electric light from above. His mind wandered as he considered his next move. He stretched out his legs to avoid stiffness and as he did, he accidentally kicked a table leg. The reflection of the bulb swung on the shaking surface of the table. It was his moment of recognition. Of course, reflection! The polished table is reflecting the bulb. It is acting as a mirror. The writing is not Arabic at all. It's a mirror image formed by blotting the surface of the original ink script. David could hardly contain himself as he bent over the eight lines, but it was hopeless. He needed a mirror to translate the words. Leaving everything as it was on the table, he laid some old, rather turgid reports on top and headed back outside. He ran back to the chemist and bought a hand mirror and a cheap magnifying glass.

"So I can see my hard skin more easily," he stuttered, a little flustered as it was the same assistant he'd seen earlier.

He jogged back to the British Library, not wanting to be too out of breath when he arrived for the third time that day. This time both the receptionist and the archivist were different so he had less to explain, but his knowledge of the underground rooms must have appeared strange. At last he was back at the place of his earlier labours and, importantly, alone. First he took the magnifying glass to enlarge the writing and then the hand mirror. It was just as he had presumed. He could now make out the words on the blotting paper. With utmost care he copied them down.

God's grace returned to that place
Brought hope through a child so small
The structures of sin rotted and hid
And love replenished the gall

The flowers returned to the green
And children now played on the sward
I went back to the Garden of Love
With peace and joy its reward

He had it. He really had it. The 'something amiss' was in front of him. But who would believe him? A few words from a blotter were unlikely to be accepted by a critical public.

He looked at the words again. They seemed to suggest that Blake had changed the original poem to reflect his renewed faith. This could be so incredibly important to students of Blake. Now he held the missing verses in his hand, could he find further evidence? There was only one thing to do. He went through the files in the boxes once more. This time he was quicker because in the process of the original search he had started to sort items into similar categories. He now had receipts and bills in one box. He had letters between publishers and printers in another box and diary notes and letters to various women in another. He put everything referring to paintings to one side and was left with a number of unfinished poems with margin notes. Then he found it. An exact copy of the two verses he had found on the blotting paper. It had meant nothing before, because it was separated from the main poem and without a title. Now it all came together, he had his proof. He took the two sheets of paper, upstairs, first remembering to put on the gloves and asked if he could make 10 copies. The complete poem was now in his hands. He had his evidence.

The Garden of Love
BY WILLIAM BLAKE

I went to the Garden of Love,
And saw what I never had seen:
A Chapel was built in the midst,
Where I used to play on the green.

And the gates of this Chapel were shut,

And Thou shalt not. writ over the door;
So I turn'd to the Garden of Love,
That so many sweet flowers bore.

And I saw it was filled with graves,
And tombstones where flowers should be:
And Priests in black gowns, were walking their rounds,
And binding with briars, my joys & desires.

God's grace returned to that place
Brought hope through a child so small
The structures of sin rotted and hid
And love replenished the gall

The flowers returned to the green
And children now played on the sward
I went back to the Garden of Love
With peace and joy its reward

David, for the last time, returned to his subterranean lair; the place of promise and ultimate success. He carefully tidied all the boxes away. David was overjoyed that all his efforts had been worthwhile. He was strangely content. He wasn't sure who to entrust with his discovery, but decided the wisest choice would be Prof Shapiro back at Cambridge. It was another two weeks before he was back in East Anglia and it was difficult to contain his excitement, even from Laura. First he needed confirmation from a Blake authority and had no wish to return to the salacious Susan Gregory. Prof Shapiro would know the right people and David was not to be disappointed. Prof Shapiro could hardly believe the trail that David had followed to reach his goal, but knew from repute that David had the ability and the honesty. He quickly spoke to a number of people in the higher echelons of the Royal Society of Arts. When the evidence was studied and the handwriting compared, the provenance was agreed. David's finding was considered ground-breaking. It was not just the two extra verses, but the significance of them to acknowledge Blake's acceptance of the Christian faith he had questioned for so long.

David was invited to present his findings at the Annual Meeting of the Royal Society and his paper was published in the Journal a month later. David was amazed and honoured to be awarded the Shipton Medal for original research, named after the founder of the Society. It was bestowed by the President, Sir John Tanner at the annual meeting the following year in June 1966.

Laura and David spent the weekend together at West Wycombe, the venue for the meeting that year. They thought it was a strange place, but the Royal Society for Arts owned the whole village, having saved it for the nation years before. Following the meeting, David surprised Laura by taking her into

London, where they celebrated the occasion in a cosy hotel just off the Euston Road. David thought this was a suitable choice after the time he spent there hunting for the poem. This was not the only surprise, because over the evening meal, David gave Laura a rather special present. It was the second volume of the same book that Kenneth Moran had given her namely, 'The Variation of Animals and Plants under Domestication' by Charles Darwin, Volume 2. Laura was delighted as this completed a most valuable and fascinating collection. She was even more delighted when she was also presented with a much smaller present in the form of an engagement ring. It was a single sapphire surrounded by very small diamonds. Laura couldn't have been happier and when she accepted David's offer of marriage, he was equally elated. The date was June 24th, exactly one year after his 21st birthday. They planned to get married in two years time, when between them they could save enough for a deposit on a house. Finding Blake's lost verses had been an experience of a lifetime and taught him to value a leap into the unknown. David still wondered who his mysterious guide could be. Would he ever know?

CHAPTER 22
OXYGEN

Peter was coming to the end of his medical studies by 1968 and had established himself as a competent clinician. He was appointed as a registrar at University College Hospital in London, where he worked in a number of roles including emergency medicine. He had a particular interest in mountain medicine and had already been on three high altitude trips to the Himalaya and Andes. He was especially interested in oxygen therapy as a treatment for people suffering from altitude sickness. He was the first to note that high altitude sickness had many of the characteristics of pneumonia, but with rather subtle differences. Their lungs were functioning well; it was just that they were suffering from low levels of oxygen. The solution in most cases was to descend rapidly and those that couldn't usually died. This was not his only line of enquiry because he had studied the flu pandemic of 1918 and read with care some detailed reports that had never been published. He found that the conventional symptoms of pneumonia were rarely present in many of these cases. He also noted that people living in higher altitudes, such as the Himalaya and Ethiopia, were affected far less than would have been expected. Peter wondered if there was any link between people who had naturally higher levels of oxygen in their blood and survival from certain viruses such as flu. Few people were thinking this way at the time, but he persisted. He started to move in the rarefied circles of medicine, which allowed his original thoughts to be considered properly.

Peter suggested a revolutionary theory. He argued that placing people suffering in this way on a respirator alone was pointless. He believed that the solution was supplementary oxygen. He took his proposals to the Royal Society of Medicine's annual conference on high altitude medicine at their June meeting.

The Royal Society of Medicine has its headquarters at Number 1, Wimpole Street and was the world's foremost provider of postgraduate medical education. Peter loved to delve into its extensive library, housed on the second floor of the vast building. There he could study the Society's wide range of journals to his heart's content. He prepared his presentation as best he could and delivered his talk on June 24th, his 24th birthday. The audience was generally responsive; although one person was antagonistic and considered that his theories were totally misplaced. That person, dressed in an ostentatious black bow tie, as though in part evening dress, was known to be critical of anything that was revolutionary. Peter found the criticism disappointing, but resolved to prove him wrong if the opportunity arose.

For the previous few months, Peter had been working on a device, which would measure levels of blood oxygen directly. This was key to his research because it meant that he could measure oxygen levels without the need to take samples back to the laboratory. He had a friend, Tony Barnicott, who worked at the hospital's biomedical department and the two of them would often discuss Peter's ideas for measuring blood oxygen. Peter would often meet Tony at The Grapes pub off Cadogan Street. The Grapes was a dark, fairly dingy pub, but had a reasonable variety of real ales, and a guest bitter that the two friends would always like to sample. Students from London University filled the pub most evenings, but Peter and Tony could usually find a quiet seat in the back bar after work. Peter explained to Tony that infrared light is absorbed differently by the amount of oxygen in the blood and he needed a device that could differentiate between levels. Between them, they came up with a light sensitive device, which seemed to give promising results. Back at the laboratory, the two worked on the system and eventually perfected the technique. They did it by fine-tuning the sensor against a measurement of blood oxygen by old-fashioned and more conventional means, such as blood analysis. The trials showed that it was very accurate and especially exciting as their device was highly portable. The two young men demonstrated their technique at their first opportunity, the Physiological Society meeting in Edinburgh. They gave it the name pulse oximetry and following the meeting, found a manufacturer who was willing to produce and market their device. The final machine had a small probe that could be attached to either the finger or earlobe and seemed to be equally satisfactory on either place. At last Peter had something he could take to the mountains to test his theory in practice.

A month later, a serious flu outbreak occurred in Mongolia and Peter was soon fully involved in a clinical trial to support his theory. It was hard work in a desperately uncomfortable environment. Peter travelled through remote yet majestic landscapes to get to the worst of the outbreak. The Mongolian steppes were about as inaccessible as any traveller would choose; yet Peter loved the seclusion and the proximity to the natural world. He travelled using an old Landrover he had managed to hire in Ulan Bator. It was crucial that the flu outbreak was contained within a region away from Ulan Bator. Once the flu made its way into the capital, with its extensive population, it would be devastating. Peter, using his new device, was able to isolate those people with low blood oxygen and allow others to continue their normal activities. It seemed to be working well and the epidemic was well controlled. The problem was that the people with the low oxygen levels were most likely to suffer badly, even die. There was no effective treatment, so Peter was determined to find a way to increase their oxygen supply. There was no perfect answer, but Peter devised a simple system for getting more air into the worst patients by increasing the air pressure above normal. The first way he tried was to pump air into a large chamber, sealed around the patient's head. This was highly successful, even if labour intensive. He taught the family members of the patient to take turns in keeping pumping the air. Every household had leather bellows, used to start their kitchen fires, and they were ideal for the task. Peter saved many lives during that time in Mongolia and was treated royally by the local leaders.

Months later, when he returned to London, he developed his method further by replacing the Mongolian fire bellows with an electric pump. Many other applications followed, including helping people who stopped breathing momentarily while asleep. He even combined his method of continuous air pressure with higher oxygen levels. Before long, people with an unpleasant condition called multiple sclerosis seemed to benefit.

Peter's reputation as an inventive clinician grew. He was eventually recognised for his ground-breaking work in medicine by being invited to the annual dinner of the Royal College of Physicians. The dinner was not held as usual at the headquarters of the Royal College as it was being refurbished that year. The venue was moved to the nearby Guildhall in the City of London. The dinner was held in a room that dated from medieval times and Peter was astonished to find himself in such grand surroundings. The ceiling of this magnificent hall was painted with numerous banners and shields. They told the story of the Livery Companies, organisations which meant very little to Peter. The master of ceremonies reminded the Members and Fellows that this was one of the few buildings in the City of London that escaped the Great Fire of London and more recently the Blitz. After a sumptuous dinner with a different fine wine for each course, the awards ceremony took place. The introduction was bland and lengthy and Peter, unaccustomed to wine in such quantity, was starting to feel sleepy. His senses were rapidly restored when he heard some reference to his work on oxygen measurement and continuous air pressure. He was to receive the award of the Holter Prize, presented to an exceptional young clinician, in recognition of his outstanding work in the field of respiratory dynamics. Peter was elated and just managed, with a lot of encouragement from those around him to stand to receive his award. It was a beautiful medal engraved with the College's coat of arms and housed in an equally glamorous silk-lined box. Peter suddenly realised he was expected to say something. The best he could manage after all the wine was to utter his thanks and particularly to his co-workers, naming Tony Barnicott by name.

It was a wonderful evening and as the dinner finished, one of the staff from the Lancet suggested they continue the evening at a nightclub. Peter was a little concerned about the cost, but was assured by his new host that all expenses would be covered. They soon found themselves outside Ronnie Scott's Jazz Club in Frith Street, Soho. They were ushered in and sat down at a table for four in a dark, smoky, but atmospheric part of the club. The main act was not expected until about midnight and turned out to be the illustrious Miles Davis, who performed a set to promote his latest album. Peter was having the time of his life. As the alcohol took over, he was hardly aware that the legendary Thelonius Monk, one of the greatest jazz musicians of all time, had followed Miles Davis. As Thelonius Monk finished, Peter made his excuses because his bladder was calling him into action. On the way back, Peter brushed past a young lady, nearly spilling her drink. He turned to apologise and could not believe what he saw.

"Mi Sun?" he said, "I don't believe it's you"

"Peter," she cried, "I never thought to see you again, what are you doing here in London? I thought you were based in Shropshire."

The effect on Peter was both euphoric and sobering and he was absolutely delighted to see her.

"Look," said Mi Sun, "I finish my shift here at three am, can we meet tomorrow?"

Peter was ecstatic and agreed instantly.

"Where, what time?" he said.

"One-o-clock, for lunch, right outside here." Then she kissed him briefly and rushed off.

Peter went back to his table and try as he might, he couldn't see her in the surrounding darkness and haze of smoke. He thanked his hosts, left the club and went back to his hotel. He was walking on air. Sleep was essential for Peter after such a night, but luckily he remembered to request a wake up call from the hotel receptionist.

"What time did you say, sir? Did I hear you right? 10-o-clock."

"That will be quite early enough," Peter replied dreamily, visions of Mi Sun fighting with his prevailing fatigue.

Peter arrived early the next day and as he waited outside Ronnie Scott's, he recalled with pleasure the time he'd spent with Mi Sun in Korea. He hoped, beyond hope, that she felt something for him and couldn't wait to catch up on all the news. Then she was there. Linking her arm in his, they headed for a little restaurant, which Peter had already booked. It was French, smart and intimate. Peter learned that she was in London on a one-year student visa, studying English at the School of Oriental and African Studies. Her work at Ronnie Scott's helped pay the rent, something she found challenging compared with costs in Korea. They both gently probed into each other's private lives, trying to establish if either had any current romantic involvements. They were like old acquaintances at the lunch table, exchanging details of their lives since they first met. The lunch started as friends, but by the end of the meal they had agreed to see each other regularly. Soon they were lovers. Both knew it was right and before long could think of little else but each other.

Peter took Mi Sun to Hadleigh Hall to meet his parents and they warmed to her. They were pleased to see Peter so happy and saw no reason for Peter and Mi Sun not to be the eventual heirs of the Hadleigh Estate.

Things were moving quickly for the pair, but time has a nasty habit of being unpredictable. For the moment, the time they had was focussed happily on each other. For now, these were euphoric, halcyon days.

CHAPTER 23
REVENGE

Following his time spent in London, Peter returned to Cambridge to work in intensive medicine at Papworth Hospital. It was a happy time for both Mi Sun and Peter as it gave time to plan their future together. Mi Sun had her student visa extended for another three years and they planned to get married long before it came to an end. Peter's work involved him in a range of medical specialties and it was cardiac surgery that he found most interesting. As he developed his surgical skills, he was increasingly given more responsibility. Eventually he was entrusted to assist with complex cardiac procedures, but always under the direct guidance of more experienced surgeons.

Late one night, a patient was admitted who had apparently suffered a massive heart attack and needed emergency treatment. It would involve breaking through the rib cage and performing open-heart surgery. Peter had worked with a team before on this complicated and dangerous operation, but had never taken the lead. He never expected to, as years of training would be required before he'd ever be allowed to have total responsibility for this difficult procedure. He knew that Mr. Weiner, the most experienced cardiac surgeon at Papworth, would lead that evening. Peter looked forward to being a junior member of the surgical team. He recognized he had much to learn and Mr. Weiner was the ideal man to teach him.

The patient was being prepared for surgery in a small room alongside the operating theatre. The cannula was in his arm and a mask was being placed over his face ready for surgery. The anaesthetist handed Peter the patient notes and Peter glanced casually at the name. It read Rev. John Warnes. Peter was horrified. This was the name of the odious creature who had assaulted him all those years ago at Downthorpe. He looked at the address on the forms. It read 'Catholic Chaplain of Queens' College, Silver St., Cambridge'. The truth dawned. This revolting specimen of humanity had managed to find a position at Cambridge. No doubt so that he could perpetuate his evil ways on other poor innocents. But he had to be sure. He turned to the others in the room and tried in a casual manner to say,

"Know anything about this patient?"

"Not really," came the vague answer from no one in particular, "I believe he's only been here for a short time. Was a schoolteacher, I believe, somewhere down south."

That was all Peter needed. He felt physically sick at the prospect of operating on a man he hated so intensely. Peter knew he had no option but to withdraw from the surgical team, whatever the cost to his professional reputation. He strode outside to talk to Mr. Weiner and found him checking the cameras used to record every movement of the operation. A teaching hospital like Papworth made recordings of elaborate surgery to show students the most up-to-date procedures. Mr. Weiner was pleased with the arrangements and went to scrub up before starting the operation.

"Mr. Weiner," said Peter, "I need to speak to you."

"Of course, Peter, how can I help?"

The screaming from a wall-mounted telephone instantly drowned out the surgeon's voice. This meant only one thing. There must be a serious emergency down in the A and E department. Peter was the first to pick up the phone.

"Major trauma coming in from a serious rail crash. Multiple injuries expected," came the disembodied voice from the phone.

"I'll go," Peter offered, glad of the opportunity to avoid operating on the loathsome Rev. Warnes.

"No, best I go," said the senior surgeon. "This'll be your chance to prove yourself. I'll get back as soon as I can." With that brusque comment, he left the room and disappeared down to A & E.

Peter was horrified at the turn of events. He was now left as the only cardiologist, a trainee at that, to deal with such an intricate procedure. More importantly, this particular patient was known to him and known under the vilest of circumstances. He had no choice. The patient was already sedated. It was his personal responsibility to complete the job to his best ability.

Peter steadied himself and considered the task ahead with little enthusiasm. He made a deep vertical cut in the sternum to expose the heart. He then pulled the pericardium away from the heart to give him direct access to the source of the trouble. He could tell from the notes that it would be a demanding operation, most likely requiring a triple bypass to clear the major arterial blockages. It was rigorous and tiring work. It required a level of concentration that was difficult for any surgeon, let alone someone operating on his own for the very first time. As he came to a critical phase in the work, when the vessels were being reconnected, the memories of Downthorpe came flooding back. He looked up momentarily at the positions of the cameras and moved slightly to his right. This small movement obscured the image shown on the only camera trained directly on his hands. He knew it would be his chance to slit the vessel with no video record. The outcome would be fatal. Peter's only regret was that Father John would feel no pain. He deserved to die in intense agony. He warranted nothing less for his crimes against Peter and many others. The blood would surge through the severed vessel. Attempts would be made to stem the cascade of blood, but nothing could be done. In seconds he'd be dead. Never again would he torment the souls of the innocent. Peter gripped his scalpel in readiness. Retribution would be his and he was prepared. He made one, last, minor adjustment to obscure from the camera this ultimate act of revenge. Others were looking elsewhere. Slowly and deliberately, he lowered the deadly weapon towards his lethal goal. Then, almost imperceptibly, came a brief moment of calm; a small voice of tranquility; the fragmented moment of reason; the fundamental teaching of the Christ of his youth. Could he forgive? Peter had seconds to decide. His thoughts contested his deep-seated desire for revenge with the basis of his medical oath - to do no harm. As he carefully placed the dagger of death in the chosen place, he was overcome with thoughts of a deep renewal, of a promise, to strive for good, to reject the evil act.

Peter relaxed his grip on the steel blade and sutured the final vessel in its rightful place. It was over.

Minutes later, Mr. Weiner returned from the mayhem below.

"Everything's under control down there," he said. "Well done, Peter. Take a break and I'll finish this one off. Great job. We'll look at the tapes together tomorrow. Get yourself home, you look absolutely shattered."

Peter thanked him and left. He would normally see his patient the next day, but he chose not to.

Peter had been given the perfect opportunity for revenge. He could never forget the evil of that man. Peter felt he'd somehow moved along the difficult and overgrown path of forgiveness. He was unsure how far.

CHAPTER 24
ISLAND

Peter and Mi Sun's engagement was announced in The Times in early 1970. Soon after, Peter received another mysterious note, sent apparently from Sussex. It was written in the same hand as the note he had received on his 18th birthday. It was unsigned and read:

Dear Peter,

Congratulations on your engagement.

Can I encourage you to go west from the Outer Hebrides to seek the Island of St Brendan. There is a discovery awaiting you. Try 57.49.

Once again, I wish I could join you on your quest, but such things are not possible. I wish you well.

It was the phrase 'I wish you well' that resonated with Peter. He remembered with clarity that the same words were at the end of the note he found with the long-playing record. It was the 18th birthday gift that started Peter on his first quest all those years ago. Peter reflected on the excitement of his time in Hamburg. It had all happened because of a comparable, unsigned message. This made it difficult to resist the prospect of something similar, although little of the message meant sense. Peter searched through his parents' copy of the Encyclopedia Brittanica and found an entry under St Brendan of Clovert. It appeared that this venerable saint lived from 484-577AD and was known, among other things, as the Navigator. St. Brendan travelled widely using a fairly crude form of boat, starting in Ireland and reaching Scotland, the Isle of Man and the Outer Hebrides. By the ninth century, a document in Latin, Navigatio Sancti Brendani Abbatis, had been produced, which detailed one of his most famous voyages in the Atlantic Ocean. The voyage was dated 512-530 and reputedly included up to 16 monks with him on this incredible voyage. Peter managed to find a translated version of this epic trip. The more he read, the more he appreciated it was most probably legend not fact. In the way the Scandinavians had their sagas, so too did the Irish have their legendary poetry and this was no exception. The tale told of sea monsters, landing on islands that turned out to be turtles and other fanciful peculiarities of his voyage. The main feature of the epic journey was the search for St Brendan's Isle, a blessed island covered with lavish vegetation. Peter understood it was essentially an allegory for the Garden of Eden. As the voyage was supposed to be in the Atlantic Ocean, some scholars have proposed that Southern Ireland, the Canaries, Madeira or even the Azores were possible venues for St Brendan and his clerical crew. There had even been talk that St Brendan was the first European to sail to North America. Unlikely though this was, Peter was fascinated to find that recently, the explorer, Tim Severin had built a leather-clad boat, as described in Navigatio and sailed it across the Atlantic.

Peter's researches into St Brendan were fascinating, but failed to discover anything new. He then turned back to the note and wondered again what the numbers 57.49 meant. Was it a time, a date, some reference to a manuscript? Peter wondered in vain.

As Peter's studies had become more intense, he had less time for his cross-country running. He had managed, however, to continue his other hobby, his flying. In some way, this was necessary, because Peter needed to fly at least 12 hours every year to retain his licence. While at Cambridge, this had never been a problem because he joined the University Air Squadron. There he had plenty of opportunity to fly chipmunks and other training aircraft. Flying was an expensive hobby, but his parents encouraged him and helped to fund it. It was especially useful when he went to see them in Rhodesia, because travel out there by light plane was often the best option. The fun of Peter's very first flying lesson in a helicopter, on his 18th birthday, was never forgotten. He was desperate to do more and indulged in a number of lessons at the Blackbushe Airport in Camberley. He was hooked, and over the last three years had passed all his examinations to become a fully qualified helicopter pilot. Peter loved the freedom that flying a helicopter gave him and wished he had more time to enjoy this extravagant, yet satisfying hobby. Peter would occasionally fly from near Cambridge, where he was working, to Hadleigh Hall. He sometimes took Mi Sun with him, although she was far from keen on the experience. He would finish work quite late on a Friday evening, head down to the airfield and, after safety checks on the Gazelle SA 340, would arrive at Hadleigh some two hours later. It had been on a recent trip to Hadleigh, when Peter was flying solo to celebrate his mother's birthday that the mysterious number 57.49 came into focus.

He was flying just south of Wolverhampton, when the air traffic control informed him to head west on 52.36. Of course, how could he be so stupid? The four digit number he was struggling with for so long was a map reference! It was a latitude reading! How could he, of all people, with his flying experience, not recognize it as such? Peter landed the helicopter with great skill on the outfield of the cricket field next to Hadleigh Hall. He first joined his parents in the main drawing room to congratulate his mother on her forthcoming birthday. After a celebratory drink, he went to his flight bag to find his precious map book. This would answer the question he was so desperate to solve. He was encouraged to find that the latitude of 57.49 went through the Outer Hebrides as mentioned in the unsigned note. It suggested going west, and this took a direct line to the St. Kilda archipelago, the most westerly part of Scotland.

Peter found this utterly intriguing and resolved to investigate further any connection with St Brendan. His investigations led him nowhere as he could find little more than he'd discovered before. The whole legend of St Brendan was shrouded in mystery and it appeared that there was no solid information on the elusive St Brendan's Isle.

Peter decided he would make one attempt to follow the latitude reading from the unsigned note. It meant first hiring a light plane, a single engine Bellanca, from Glasgow and then flying to Stornoway on the Isle of Lewis. It was Peter's first flight in this particular plane, so he wisely took the precaution of hiring an instructor for this leg of the journey. His instructor, Tony Griffiths, was a broad Glaswegian, who took the view that breakfast should be in the form of strong brown liquid. He wore a Second World War flying jacket, which, by its patina, Peter took to be genuine. Tony spent the short trip regaling Peter about his wartime experiences. They seemed to involve flying specialist Norwegian forces from eastern Scotland to the Norwegian fiords in a variety of seaplanes. In spite of Tony's continued consumption of whisky, they arrived safely at Stornoway and Tony was impressed with Peter's handling of the unfamiliar craft. Peter explained he was on a strange and possibly foolhardy mission to fly directly west and Tony, who had little better to do, volunteered to come along for the ride. This pleased Peter immensely. Although he was happy being alone, he knew the trip would be more fun with Tony alongside. All he had to do was keep Tony away from Scotland's greatest export during the flight.

The two of them filed a flight plan that would take them southwest from Stornoway until they hit the line of latitude 57.49 and then directly west. They were unable to provide a destination, so filed it as an exploratory trip looking for a pod of whales. They indicated that the flight would be finishing back at either Stornoway or even Hirta, the largest island in St Kilda. Peter and Tony called the local weather stations before leaving and tried to establish wind speed and direction in the North Atlantic. It appeared variable, which could cause them problems once they were out of range of the Hebridean beacons. They filled the little plane's fuel tanks to capacity and both did the routine pre-flight checks. The cloud level was at about 3000 feet, so they were confident that flying beneath the clouds should give them good visibility for the flight.

Take–off was smooth and uneventful with Peter taking the controls and Tony keeping a watchful eye. They immediately picked up the land-based beacons and headed on their planned course towards St Kilda, Tony reached into his flight bag and pulled out his usual sustenance.

"You joining me?" he asked, knowing full well the answer. Peter just smiled.

"We're here to look for an invisible island. At least one of us needs 20-20 vision," said Peter. This time it was Tony's turn to smile.

The outline of St Kilda was soon seen ahead and Peter dropped to 2000 feet to get a better view of this remote archipelago. They could see the smaller island of Soay to the west and as they flew over the highest point of Hirta, the beacons gave them the latitude they needed. Peter banked sharply to the right and flew in the intended westerly direction for the first time. Peter was at first surprised that they still had land-based navigation. Tony explained that Hirta had a small army base and beacons would be necessary to monitor all flight activity in the region. They now headed due west and within 50 miles had lost all signals from beacons. From now on the route would be plotted by dead reckoning. Peter was grateful he had Tony on board to check and cross check the limited information they were using from air speed and the gyroscope. As they continued west, the two of them scanned the ocean for anything that might be of interest.

"Peter," said Tony, "I've just checked fuel burn and I reckon we are close to our PNR."

"Was that from Stornoway or Hirta?" Peter enquired.

"From Stornoway, there's no guarantee of a landing at Hirta. I told you it's an army base not a bloody civilian strip. Anyway, it may not have escaped your notice, Peter, but I live in Glasgow. I know it may seem strange to you, but I have a family to feed, not be on a mystery tour of the Western Isles."

"Sorry," said Peter, "you're right. We'll turn in five."

"OK and no more."

Peter dropped the nose of the aircraft a little and the two of them scanned the ocean for any island or rocky outcrop.

"There's a bit of sea cloud to the left, about one mile. Seems odd out here just by itself. Worth a look?" said Tony, still more concerned about heading back.

"Why not," said Peter with slightly more enthusiasm, "what's to lose."

"Nothing but empty fuel tanks," came the rather terse reply.

Peter steered left to the sea cloud. It seemed to hang in the air like a ball of cotton wool above the surface of the sea. The feature was illogical, as all other clouds in the area were at least 3000 feet above sea level. As they came closer, Tony thought he saw the outline of land beneath the cloud, but he wasn't sure. Peter put the nose down and leveled off at 500 feet to get a better look. He circled the cloud trying desperately to see if there was anything beneath it. From the northern side they could both see what seemed to be surf. This surely was an indication of some form of landmass, if only a rocky outcrop in an otherwise flat and uninspiring ocean. Peter flew past one more time, circling the strange rock in a different direction.

"It doesn't make sense," said Tony. "A lump of rock couldn't create a cloud like that. There's got to be some physical reason for it."

"Let's at least try to get a fix on its position and get home, " said Peter, "seeing this thing has delayed as too much already."

"Jees," Tony replied, a note of concern in his voice, "the fuel has just gone critical. Head back right now, Peter, otherwise we'll be swimming."

Peter banked the plane hard and headed due east. He knew that with luck they could make Hirta, the largest island in St Kilda. Stornoway was now out of the question. Within half an hour they picked up the St Kilda beacon and thanked their lucky stars that the army, for whatever reason, still had a base there. They tried to make contact with the ground control at St Kilda but none of the normal frequencies were responding. There was little for it but to land without permission. All they could do was hope there was a half decent runway. Peter skillfully brought the little plane into wind and headed towards the military masts he could see to the east of the island. Tony took over the controls as they dropped steadily towards the uncertain terrain. There seemed to be a track across a big field and Tony took the view that this may be the only option. As the nose dipped down, the two of them were horrified to see sheep scattering in all directions. The landing was hard, a little bumpy, but safe. Greatly relieved, Tony brought the plane to a standstill and the engine died.

"Aren't you going to taxi up to those buildings back there," said Peter.

"It's a great idea," Tony replied, sarcastically, "but this plane doesn't run on fresh air. We're right out of fuel"

With considerable relief, the two pilots climbed out of the small cabin and walked over to one of the few scattered buildings. It was labeled the 'Puff Inn'. Pushing the door open, they were greeted by two steaming cups of coffee, pushed into their hands by a uniformed military policeman.

"I always offer coffee before arresting people," he said smiling, "it's my way of checking if they're armed."

Tony was keen to get home, although Peter was rather enjoying the unusual hospitality provided by the military personnel on Hirta. They refueled, moved the sheep that by now had returned to the so-called runway and set off northeast. Thirty minutes later, they had landed at Stornoway and Peter treated Tony to some excellent local oysters, followed by the best fish and chips in the town. Over the meal, they discussed the strange sight they'd both seen in the ocean. They both agreed that the small island had, at least for the time they were there, a permanent cloud or mist hanging above it. Neither of them could be exactly sure of its size, but they thought it was roughly circular and at most a mile in diameter. It certainly was on no map. They had no clear idea of the features of this particular island. It could have been nothing more than a low-lying rocky outcrop. It was the permanent cloud, something more substantial than sea mist that intrigued them most. At last Tony made a most unlikely suggestion.

"Peter," he said, "the only time I've seen something like that was in much warmer places. You can get a permanent or semi-permanent cloud above a rainforest. Of course by definition, you would need substantial plant life, usually trees, for it to work. The canopy of the trees or jungle creates just the right environment for the cloud or mist to form and it will result in a regular supply of fresh water for the area. I've seen it in Borneo and Belize. I believe the nearest one to these shores is in La Gomera, one of the Canary Islands, but I've never been there."

"Do you really think that's possible?" said Peter, starting to get seriously interested in the prospect.

"Frankly, not really, but it's all I can think of, however far fetched."

Peter thought for a minute, then added,

"Of course the gulf stream splits about where we were into the Iceland and the Scottish sections. Is it possible that the it gives enough warmth to generate some plant life out there?"

"Very unlikely. That area would be pretty inhospitable for most of the year. A few hardy plants, perhaps, but unlikely to be sufficient to create a cloud forest. I think we are barking up the wrong tree. Anyway, my good friend, I shall bid you farewell as my flight back to Glasgow leaves in half an hour."

Peter thanked Tony for all his help and went with him back to the small airport just over two miles east of the town. They shook hands and Tony wished Peter good luck in his quest, fairly certain it was far from over. Peter took a room in a nearby bed and breakfast overnight. He was exhausted, lay on top of his bed and the next thing he heard was the swish of the shower in the bathroom next door. Over a hearty Scottish breakfast, which included porridge, Lorne sausage and white pudding, Peter decided on his next move. He'd made up his mind whatever the cost. He just had to get back to that place in the ocean and have another look. He realized that a light airplane was not the answer and the best option would be a boat or helicopter. It took a day or two to make all the arrangements, but finally it all seemed to come together well. He was to take a scheduled flight back to St Kilda and to hire a helicopter from there. There were only two helicopters on this remote island. One was for search and rescue, operated by the military. The other was really a back-up machine in case of emergencies when the other one was in action. It took some time to obtain approval to use it, but the island economy was stretched and the income would be useful. He was told he would need to have a test flight with one of the regular pilots, at his own expense, but Peter, by now, was determined. The next day after he arrived at Village Bay on Hirta, he was again greeted with coffee and mock arrest. Apart from the military unit at the tracking station, the only other permanent resident was the island warden. Peter spent the night in the military base, sharing the standard dormitory accommodation with the six other soldiers on site. The Puff Inn was officially off-limits to visitors, but Peter was made welcome, as was the island warden, Robbie Stirling. Robbie was a hard man, with the ruddy face to be expected from a life spent outdoors. He dressed in a fleece and waterproof cagoule, the outdoor clothing needed for this remote, windswept island. Robbie had a cheerful disposition and was thoroughly committed to his work on the island.

It was a long night, but Peter enjoyed the company, especially learning about Robbie's work on the island. It mainly involved managing the Soay sheep, the very ones that Peter's plane had nearly run over when they landed here the first time. It was clear from the conversation with Robbie, that his knowledge of the local flora and fauna was prodigious. When Peter told him of his mission to find St Brendan's Isle and the mysterious place they had found in the western ocean, Robbie asked to join Peter in his quest. Peter was sure he'd be an excellent companion, so they agreed to meet the day after next. Peter's training session with the resident instructor went well. It took time to adjust to the Whirlwind chopper, but Peter was soon in complete control and enjoying every minute of the flight. Both were confident that to fly it solo was possible, although not recommended, and Peter was granted permission to pilot it alone the next day.

At the break of dawn, Peter and Robbie went through the final safety checks. Robbie had brought with him some powerful binoculars a notebook and warm clothing. He knew the local climate better than anyone. They took off heading directly west and were soon out of range of the land-based beacons. Robbie had listened that morning to the shipping and weather reports for the area and this was fed into their dead reckoning calculations as best they could. Peter knew the range for the Whirlwind was just over 300 miles. Both accepted that at 150 miles out they would have to turn back, whatever the outcome. It was at this point of no return that the cloud above the ocean was spotted to the right. Peter confirmed excitedly it was exactly as he'd seen it before. He manoeuvred the chopper until it was just to one side of the cloud. It was now in a position where he thought he could see, once again, the outline of waves breaking. He slowly took it down, yard-by-yard, fearful that any cliffs or hill would be obscured until too late. At the point when the altimeter was reading just 200 feet, far too low in poor visibility, the cloud suddenly cleared and the two of them could see something quite remarkable.

The ground below them was flat, just inland from a rocky beach. As they looked inland it rose to form a perfectly conical hill, covered in dense vegetation, including numerous trees. Peter landed the chopper gently on the flat land and, with considerable relief, switched off the engine.

It was a revelation. Robbie was ecstatic and could barely believe what he saw. He was eager to be out examining the plants he could see all around. Peter likewise could hardly believe the view from this small beach. Here, in the wild Atlantic was an island that looked so perfect, it just couldn't be true. He quickly did his post-flight checks, secured the helicopter, and joined Robbie who was already out of the cabin and on his knees looking at the soil and plants around him. Robbie was jumping around for joy, taking photographs and filling his notebook with lists of Latin names. Peter just took in the scenery, soaking in the sights around him. The two walked with increasing interest up the hill behind them. As they did, the vegetation became thicker until they were soon in the dense wood near the top.

"This is mainly a form of laurel," said Robbie knowledgeably, "It's quite rare in this part, but is often the basis of a cloud forest. I'm sure this would be the reason for the permanent cloud above this island. What's more the cloud will precipitate, keeping the whole area damp. It's bound to produce fresh water and there're likely to be streams to the lower levels. It's quite remarkable."

"What's this stuff growing all over the trees?" said Peter, pulling some short tufts off the lower branches.

"That will be some form of moss and lichen, further evidence of permanent damp conditions. Look at the wax myrtle and ferns as well. There are several different varieties, not like the limited ones we have at home."

Robbie took more photographs and then carefully removed some leaves from a variety of plants and put them in his bag. They headed in the opposite direction down the hill and came across a range of shrubs, which Robbie was able to identify as tree heath and hawk's beard. They found a stream coming down the hill and followed it the half mile to the beach. Alongside the stream was a bigger range of plants. Many were in flower and, although exotic in appearance, seemed much more like the summer annuals usually bought in a garden centre on the mainland. The air was pungent with the smell of wild garlic but punctuated with the far more attractive fragrances of honeysuckle, jasmine and lavender. This place was a botanist's haven and Peter was delighted that Robbie had asked to join him. Slowly they headed back around the island towards the point where the helicopter was standing. Its metallic hulk looked incongruous amongst this perfection of nature. It was a discordant invasion of this flawless Eden.

Halfway back they spotted what looked like a small building made of stone. It was covered in ivy and other vines but with a little effort they were able to strip these away. The building was almost circular, a single room and just tall enough for the two of them to stand up inside. There was little to be seen inside the room apart from a stone seated area all around the inner wall. There was a small hole in the roof, which they assumed was to let smoke out when the occupants had a fire. Their eyes became accustomed to the dark inside the room and Peter spotted one stone that seemed to have some writing on it. He cleaned the lichen that was covering the stone and was amazed to see the two words 'Brendani Abbatis' carved deep into the soft sandstone. Above the name was an even more interesting relic. It was clearly an early form of Irish cross, easily distinguished by the cross and circle.

"We've done it," he shouted with joy, "we've found the Isle of St Brendan, and just as the legend says, it's just like heaven. Thank God for medieval graffiti."

Robbie was more intrigued than excited. His botanical mind was working overtime on the luxuriant range of plants he had seen. Peter grabbed him by the hand, shaking it vigorously.

"Just wait 'till you report this lot to the authorities. No one will believe it."

"They will have to when I show all the plants I've collected and the photos I've taken," said Robbie.

"Have you got enough?" Peter said, "I'm starting to think more like a pilot than an explorer and we should be getting back."

"It's your call, Peter. I could stay here all night."

"Don't forget we're flying the reserve chopper for the air sea rescue and we don't want to set off an alarm back at the base."

The two made their way begrudgingly back to the helicopter and started the engines for the return journey. They were almost silent on the way back, each absorbed in what they had seen. As they hit the St Kilda beacon, they needed to adjust the direction somewhat before finding Hirta.

"Just shows you," said Peter, "how navigating without a beacon can be a bit hit and miss. Wind direction must have shifted since we left, throwing my dead reckoning well off."

"Would that have added many miles to our journey?" enquired Robbie, a little concerned about the state of the fuel.

"A little," Peter replied, looking down to see the red fuel light winking at him menacingly.

Peter brought the helicopter in to land skillfully. He thought is best not to tell Robbie the true position of the fuel. Zero is not a good word to use when you're in the air.

That evening, Peter and Robbie recounted their experiences to an unbelieving audience at the Puff Inn. Peter was glad Robbie could corroborate his find, otherwise no one would have believed him. He could hardly wait to have the photographs developed and show the wider world the Isle of St Brendan.

The following day, nursing a slight hangover, Peter took the one scheduled flight back to Glasgow. He thanked the soldiers at the tracking base for their hospitality, promised to keep in touch with Robbie and looked forward to telling Mi Sun of his adventures. The photographs came out well and Peter made sure a copy of them all went to Robbie on St Kilda. They showed most of the island's detail, especially the small house or cell they now started to call it. Cell seemed appropriate as the resting place of Brendan the Navigator. A month later, Peter received a detailed letter from Robbie. It read:

Dear Peter,

Sorry this took so long, but I had to send away for some books on the flowers and plants of the Canary Islands. I've done the best I can to identify the specimens we brought back from 'our isle'. I know you like to call it St Brendan's Isle, which is fine by me and in some ways the information I have could help. As you'll recall, I was of the opinion that the island we saw was populated by a 'cloud forest' of the sort seen in La Gomera. It appears that the plants I collected were almost identical to those of the Garajonay cloud forest in La Gomera. I remember you telling me that the legend of St Brendan's voyage may have included the Canaries, so what we saw may have been some sort of interplay between the two places. I would not like to speculate on how this could have come about. The bottom line is that you have found an unknown island with a unique biosphere for this distance north. I have attached a full list of the plants I collected or observed. There is no doubt in my mind that this should be reported at the highest level. It really is quite a find. Do keep me informed

With kind regards

Robbie

Peter studied the attached list, but the names of the plants meant nothing to him. Over time, he decided on a plan of action. First he would seek further professional advice about the plants. If that looked promising, then he would inform the Ordinance Survey of the island and leave them to decide its ownership and whether or not it should be included as British territory. Beyond that he was unsure.

One thing was for certain, that unsigned birthday note had resulted in something very special. Something of which Peter could be very proud, although pride was a trait that Peter rarely displayed. It was the endeavor that excited him not the outcome. His belief that something amazing could happen was the ideal basis for taking that initial leap into the unknown. The birthday note had called it a quest. Sometimes weird or unusual choices have to be made, irrespective of how they may seem.

The reply Peter received from Kew Gardens corroborated everything Robbie had said. The experts there confirmed that most of the plants and flowers could only exist in the cloud forest ecological system. The given latitude perplexed them and they asked for further verification. If true, they were of the opinion that this was a most important find and should be published at once. Peter's correspondence with the Ordinance Survey was with a Mr. David Clarke, a name vaguely familiar to Peter. The mapping agency showed a degree of interest and gave Peter naming rights. They promised to consider the possibility of including the island on future editions of the Scottish Western Isles but regretted that without a full survey, this would only be an appendix to the existing maps. Peter was not too surprised. He accepted that cartographers had a formal process and the information he and Robbie could provide was limited. An aerial photograph would have been invaluable, but this was impossible with an island covered permanently in cloud. Finally, Peter contacted the Royal Geographical Society, well aware that they had extensive knowledge of the scientific boundaries of places. They appeared interested in what he claimed to have seen and invited him to London to share his findings with a panel of Fellows. He managed to arrange for Robbie to travel down from St Kilda to join him.

The meeting was intense, direct and confrontational. It was held in the boardroom of the Society, the panel seated on one side of a huge oak desk. Peter wondered who else had reported their adventures in this very place. Could the likes of Ross, Franklin and Shackleton have sat here pleading for funds to support their expeditions? Peter and Robbie found that a disbelieving panel was questioning them as though they were on trial. It was an uncomfortable hour for the two young men as they faced a barrage of questions. The factual ones were easy to answer, but the panel seemed to find the basis for the original search rather eccentric. The meeting came to a halt and Peter and Robbie were invited to take tea in the members' room, while the panel came to a verdict. It was a long wait, but eventually the chairman returned and invited Peter and Robbie to return to the boardroom. The chairman, Lord Ingleborough, leaned forward.

"Gentlemen," he said, "the panel find your report extra-ordinarily fantastical. The basis for you trying to find an island implied in a 9th century document of dubious provenance is not for us to judge. We take the view that this is immaterial compared with your thorough and remarkable observations. It is recognized from what you say, that this island would be very difficult to locate again and a certain amount of luck was afforded to you on both occasions. Nonetheless, we believe you and congratulate you for your fascinating discovery. We invite you both to present your findings to the members of this society and look forward immensely to constructive academic criticism of your observations. Well done."

It was over. They had passed the test. The celebrations began with Peter treating Robbie to a meal at the Savoy Grill. It was the least he could do.

The summer meeting of the Royal Geographical Society was a great success. All the serious national newspapers ran the story, using some of he photographs taken on the island by Peter and Robbie. The headlines varied but most used Peter's choice of name for the island, 'St Brendan's Isle'. He was content, especially as they were published on his birthday, June 24th.

CHAPTER 25
MARRIAGES

David was the first of the two boys to get married, but only by a matter of months. He married Laura in the small parish church of St Andrew's, Witchford. The bells of the 13th century tower rang with utmost clarity and in joyous celebration over the local countryside. Laura and her mother had decorated the church with local summer flowers. They had cleverly created a palette of wild flowers including columbine, cornflower, cow parsley and meadow cranesbill. All the flowers came from the fields around the village, giving the wedding a local flavour. They gave the church a beautiful, yet understated effect, appreciated by all the guests.

Laura looked stunning in a simple, white wedding dress. She carried a small posy of wild flowers, which matched the arrangements in the church. Laura had three bridesmaids, all close friends and they looked lovely in bright summery dresses. David and his best man, brother Iain, had hired dark morning suits from a dress hire shop in Cambridge. They were both suitably nervous as they waited for the bride; David anxiously waiting for his bride and Iain concerned about his speech. The couple's finances limited the number of guests, but they managed to include close family and a few of their best friends. Local people, who knew the couple, but could not be invited to the reception, came to the church service to be part of the celebration. Some would have known David since he first moved to the area and they sat at the back so they would not be confused with the official wedding party. Laura or David would, at the very least, have been on nodding terms with them all. There was, however, one person that neither of them knew. He sat a little apart, almost hidden from view by a pillar supporting the church's medieval roof. He appeared tall, middle-aged and wearing a dark overcoat.

As Laura arrived at the church door, on the arm of her father, she stopped momentarily. Her eye caught sight of a beautiful golden Labrador, its lead attached to a hook on the church wall. She couldn't resist bending to stroke its head. The dog's mournful eyes looked up at her as it sat patiently waiting for its owner to return. Laura smiled, straightened her wedding dress and walked confidently into the church. A good friend of David's gave a solo performance of the Trumpet Voluntary by Purcell as Laura walked up the aisle. There was some initial concern because the organist had not been briefed on the couple's choice of hymns. Fortunately he had the music for 'Angel voices, ever singing', 'Love divine, all loves excelling' and 'Let all the world in every corner sing' in his personal collection, so all was well.

It was a simple and informal service; a perfect way to start their life together. The exchange of rings brought back memories of the time David had spent underground in North Wales, but nothing could dampen the joy of the day. During the signing of the register, which took place in the vestry, the man in the dark overcoat disappeared. His dog went with him.

After the service, everyone walked to the village hall where David and Laura's parents had prepared a wonderful cold buffet. The traditional speeches were well received, including Iain telling some rather dubious stories of David's supposed activities at University. David and Laura, the new Mr. and Mrs. Clarke, decided to change out of their wedding clothes as the guests were finishing the meal. On their return, they were surprised to find everyone lined up to wish them farewell. It was not their intention to leave just then; they had planned to mingle for some time. Together they made their first married decision and left the reception earlier than expected. Everyone seemed so relaxed and it seemed the right thing to do. They still had a long journey to their new home in Southampton, so they let the celebration continue without them.

As the new couple opened the front door of their rented flat, the first thing they noticed was the smell of gas. It took no more than two hours for the gas board to identify the problem, but it meant that all gas supply to the flat had to be disconnected. David and Laura laughed when the confetti from one of their suitcases spilled over right in front of the gas fitter. If it was to be a cold night, he had no reason to worry.

They went on honeymoon just under a week later, enjoying a low-cost package holiday to the Costa Brava. They both relaxed on the beach and swam daily in the calm sea. They even found time to explore part of the Spanish coast by train, content in each other's company. They looked forward excitedly to many happy years together.

*   *   *   *   *

Peter's marriage to Mi Sun was a far more lavish affair. The service was held in the Church of Our Lady the Virgin, in the grounds of Hadleigh Hall. The lych-gate, leading into the churchyard was festooned with arum lilies. They'd been chosen by the same florist that Peter's mother had employed to decorate the church when she married Neil. Inside the church, the flower arrangements were opulent and characterized by magnificent sprays of strawberry blush roses on every available surface.

Mi Sun chose to wear a beautiful, silk, light purple hanbok, which was embroidered in pink. She looked stunning, with her dark features and hair complementing the traditional Korean wedding dress. She carried a bouquet of arum lilies, successfully connecting her wedding with that of Peter's parents. Mi Sun had no relatives of her own in Britain, but unbeknown to her, Neil had arranged to fly her parents over for the occasion. Mi Sun was overcome when she saw them and the wedding ran a little late while Mi Sun recovered from her surprise. Mi Sun's parents had been delayed in travelling from Seoul, but they arrived just in time for Mi Sun's father to be able to walk his daughter down the aisle. It was the happiest start to a wedding that Mi Sun could have imagined.

Peter and his best man, Robbie Stirling, wore grey morning suits, both with very fancy gold-coloured waistcoats. The wedding followed the traditional Catholic service starting with the nuptial mass and finishing with Holy Communion. Over 150 people came to the wedding; a few were Peter and Mi Sun's friends, but by far the majority were associates of Neil and Celia, particularly from the diplomatic corps. A wedding ceremony of this size meant that many people were strangers to each other. None more so than the tall, middle aged man in the dark overcoat, who left straight after the ceremony and was last seen climbing into a taxi at the bottom of the drive.

The wedding breakfast was held up at the main house, Hadleigh Hall, with all 150 guests seated at tables of eight in the long gallery. The four-course meal started with fresh lobster and smoked salmon on a bed of summer salad. Then Mi Sun's Korean heritage was celebrated with a kimchi. This dish, spiced with garlic, ginger and shrimp paste, was served in delicate bowls. It was eaten either with chopsticks or for the less adventurous a small spoon and fork. Peter had particularly asked for this delicacy to be included, because it was part of the very first meal he had shared with Mi Sun. The main course was more traditional, a fillet mignon served with asparagus. The dessert was a Hadleigh variation of Eton mess, with a reduction of summer fruits. A different fine wine, chosen with care by the sommelier to complement the individual flavours, accompanied each course. Over coffee, port and brandy, Robbie gave an amusing speech about their trip to find St Brendan's Isle and the party went on well into the evening before guests started to drift away.

Peter and Mi Sun spent their wedding night at Hadleigh Hall before setting off the next day for two weeks at the Carana Beach hotel in the Seychelles.

The future Viscount Culham now had a gorgeous wife and together they had every reason to look forward to a time of true contentment.

CHAPTER 26
PAINTING

A few weeks after David's wedding, he received a package. It was a domino set, in a box inlaid with walnut. When Laura and he were alone that evening they looked at the box and its contents together. They tipped the dominos out of the box and found underneath a postcard. It seemed to be taken from a photograph of a painting. The painting meant nothing to David, although the message on the back did, but only because the handwriting was familiar. It read:

Dear David and Laura,
Many congratulations on your wedding. I hope you will enjoy using these tiles.
Your recent missions have been a great success and you may find the search for this painting equally exciting.
I only wish I could join you, but circumstances prevent.
I wish you well.

Once again, it was that phrase 'I wish you well' that David recognized and couldn't fail to ignore. As always the message was unsigned. Closer inspection of the dominos surprised them both. They turned each tile over so they were face down and then each picked seven tiles at random. The double six was the usual way to start the game, but if neither of them had it, then another double would be used. Try as they might, neither of them could find a tile with a double on it. Not sure what to do next, they turned over all the tiles until they were now facing up. It was then they realized that this was no ordinary game of dominoes. There seemed to be no repetition at all. Each tile was individual and had one, two or three spots on each half of each tile. They had never seen a game like this and were utterly confused. Clearly the tiles couldn't be used for the conventional game of dominos. There must be another meaning. They also found stuck on the bottom of the box, a series of paper tiles in a single line. It served to confuse them more.
"I think we may need advice over this one," said David, "any suggestions?"
"I think it's time for bed," was the only answer that Laura gave.
David and Laura settled on a plan. First they would try to obtain some information about the photograph of the painting. If that proved intriguing, as they were confident it would, then they would spend more time with the strange domino set. The painting seemed to be of a young man wearing

white shirt and with a fur coat draped over his left shoulder. The man had long dark hair and a black cap perched on the back of his head. The photograph was in black and white, so it was not possible to tell the colours in detail.

The next time that David was up in London on business, he took the photograph to the National Gallery. David was asked to leave his enquiry at the front desk, with the promise that someone would make contact with him in due course. David was unhappy about this casual arrangement and wrote a note, asking for it to be delivered to the right person immediately. In the note, David mentioned his discoveries of the Blake poetry and the North Wales thermal baths. As anticipated, the result was electric. David was escorted to the office of the Director and was offered a drink. David accepted tea and then showed the Director his postcard. The Director took one look at it and excused himself. He returned moments later with the Gallery's head archivist.

"Mr. Clarke did us the honour of showing me this postcard," he said to the person who had just joined them. "I think I know what it is, but I need confirmation."

The head archivist, a Mr. Potter, looked at it with care. It was as if he were handling a precious object.

"I think you know this painting, sir," he said.

"I was fairly confident, but just needed confirmation."

"Mr. Clarke, would you mind telling me how you came by this postcard?"

"Of course," David answered, "it was sent to me by a friend."

"And can you tell me where this friend came by the photograph?"

"Sorry, no. It was rather out of the blue."

"Hmm, well I think we can both confirm that this friend of yours has managed to photograph a most interesting painting. It is a portrait of a young man, as you can see. It is by Raphael, a most striking and valuable portrait. There is the suggestion that it is in fact a self-portrait. But the most interesting fact is nothing to do with the painter or the painting."

"And that is," said David, now very much engaged with the way the discussion was heading.

"The fact is, it is missing."

"Missing, do you mean stolen?"

"Well in a manner of speaking, yes. I think my colleague will correct me if my memory fails, but this painting was originally on display in Poland. As I recall, it was the Czartoryski Museum. As the Nazis advanced through Poland, the Raphael was moved, I think by Prince Augustyn Czartoryski himself. The plan was to hide this painting and several others from the Nazis. I believe he hid the paintings at a private home in the town of Sieniawa. Unfortunately the Nazis found them and took the Raphael originally to Krakow and later to Berlin to be part of Hitler's personal museum. Mr. Potter, will you take up the story from there as I cannot recall the detail?"

"Certainly sir. Our understanding is that a senior Nazi called Hans Frank took the Raphael to Wawel Castle in Krakow in January 1945. This is the last place that anyone saw the painting. A month later, in advance of the Russian offensive, Hans Frank reputedly took the painting to his own villa in Newhaus am Schliersee. He was arrested there in May 1945, but the Raphael was not among those paintings recovered there. That's where the trail went cold, because Hans Frank was hanged for war crimes and he never revealed the Raphael's true location."

"Wow, what a story. So no one has any idea where it is?"

"There have been various rumours, with the likely location being somewhere in Germany. The truth is no one really knows."

"So what about this postcard?"

"Well back in the 1940s it was quite common to make a postcard out of a photograph. People would take a photo and it would be printed as a postcard, so that it could be posted without using an envelope. Apart from anything, postage in those days was cheaper for a postcard, so it made sense. Of course that doesn't tell us where the photo was taken, but the most likely answer is when the Raphael was on display at the Czartoryski Museum. Perhaps your friend will be able to tell you."

"Perhaps," said David.

"Well thank you for showing us a most interesting artefact. It is the first time I have seen a photo on a postcard of this Raphael, so I recommend that you investigate further."

"I may well do just that," said David, with a wry smile.

That evening David told Laura all about the information he had gathered at the National Gallery. Laura was fascinated and keen to help.

"I've been thinking," she said, "is it possible that the tiles in the domino set are some form of code? If we could crack the code, then it might give us a clue to the other tiles stuck on the bottom of the box. Somehow, I think there is some form of relationship between the two. Let's face it; the only tiles that are stuck down in any sort of order are the ones on the bottom of the box. All the others are loose and could have dropped out of the box in any random way."

"You're right, let's get started later. There's still one thing I'm struggling with. Why does the person who's sending me these challenges have to make things difficult? It was the same with the North Wales grid references; they meant nothing to me at first."

"And the Blake poem. Although to be fair the mystery writer did say there was something amiss, but didn't tell you what." Laura chimed in.

"My only explanation is that it is was a sort of preliminary challenge. Just to see if there was any interest, without any form of commitment. I guess some people simply wouldn't bother to follow up any of the leads."

"Yes, but you did and thank God you chose to persevere. It's made each enterprise very special."

"So you think I should pursue this next challenge in the same way?"

"Oh don't be silly, David. Of course you should, and I'm here to help you now."

After dinner that evening, the box of tiles was emptied on to the small table they had in the kitchen. They moved them around in a haphazard way looking for clues. There were a total of 36 tiles, each with a different configuration of spots. Some had one spot, some two, some three and a few with four spots. At first they put all the ones with one spot together and then the same with the tiles with two, three and four spots. Then Laura had a brainwave.

"Just noticed, David, the total number of tiles is 36. That's the sum of the number of letters in the alphabet plus numbers one to nine plus zero. Could it be that each tile represents just that?"

"Sure, that makes sense, but it doesn't tell us which one is which."

They could both see that the single spot tiles made a natural progression as if the spots were going around a clock face, but little more than that.

"Look," said David, "the ones with two spots, all have one spot in the same place and then follow a sequence like the ones with one spot."

"So it looks like some form of continuous system, the one spot tiles leading on to the two spot tiles and so on."

"OK, so following on from what you said about the meaning of the 36 tiles, lets start by assigning the simplest one spot tiles the letter A and as the spot moves, give it a different letter."

After considerable trial and error, the two of them arranged the tiles into a logical sequence, assigning each tile a letter and the last ten a number.

"Now for the real test, lets look at the tiles on the bottom of the box and see if it spells anything out."

It took a long time, but eventually they found that the tiles stuck to the box did seem to produce some sort of message. It read: '14BODENSTRASSEMEERSBURG'

"It must be an address," said Laura, "Straase means Street in German, so presumably it's 14 Bodensee Street in the town or village of Meersburg."

David looked in his World Atlas and found Meersburg was a small town on the German side of Lake Constance or Bodensee as the Germans called it. After some discussion about the merits of such a strange quest, it was decided that David would go to Meersburg himself. He had a small amount of leave owing from his job with the Ordinance Survey, but Laura had yet to accrue much holiday entitlement. Apart from that, the cost was a little above their current budget, so it was decided that only one of them would go. Flying would be too expensive and David decided that travelling by train would be too complicated. He decided to drive, accepting that it would take the best part of a week to get there and back. He booked a week's leave the following month and made preparation for a short trip.

David was travelling on instinct more than logic. His heart was ruling his head, but coupled with a huge amount of optimism. Before he went, David arranged to meet a military historian based at the Imperial War Museum. The meeting was difficult, as David didn't want to explain too much about his mission. He enquired in general about the loss of paintings during the Nazi occupation of countries such as Poland and France. It would appear that paintings were mainly stolen from galleries and from private collections. This was especially the case if Jews owned the paintings. He double-checked by letter with Mr. Potter at the National Portrait Gallery and was intrigued to find that the Rafael was indeed owned by a Jewish family and only on temporary loan to the Czartoryski Museum.

The military historian at the Imperial War Museum also told David about rumours that were circulating during and just after the war. Apparently a number of the paintings were to be moved for safekeeping as the allies advanced. There were rumours of a train loaded with paintings and other works of art ostensibly taken from Stuttgart to Munich. En route the carriages were disconnected and redirected onto a minor branch line towards the Swiss border. There were numerous tunnels in that part of southern Germany and the stories suggested that the train was stopped in one of these tunnels. Both ends of the tunnel were bricked up and the staff on the train, mainly Polish, were all killed. No one has ever discovered the whereabouts of this tunnel and its carriages and its very existence is still speculative. For David, these rumours just added to the intrigue, especially as the small town of Meersburg was right on the German/Swiss border.

David took three days to drive to Meersburg. He took his car across on the Dover to Calais ferry and drove through northern France, crossing the border into Germany at Strasbourg. He then headed south to Freiburg before turning east on the minor roads until he came to the northern shore of Lake Constance. His overnight stops were in the simple bed and breakfast accommodation he managed to find near the smaller towns along the route. It was a tiring drive and he was pleased to arrive in Meersburg at the end of the third day.

Meersburg was a pretty town, full of old world charm and quite reminiscent of the Swiss towns on the other side of the lake. Having found a small hotel for the night, David, in spite of his fatigue, couldn't help but try to find number 14, Bodenstrasse. It was not easy as it was a small street, hidden away in the medieval quarter of the town. It was a very ordinary-looking house in a small terrace, dating, David guessed, from the early 19th century. It appeared to be empty and clearly in a state of disuse for some time. The paint on all the window frames was fading and peeling and there was no evidence of people living there. David was disappointed, having come so far, and wondered, yet again, if his trip had been a complete waste of time and money. He was slightly encouraged by the fact that both houses either side were occupied, with one of them being a small boarding house. It was getting late, so David headed back to his hotel. After his journey he suddenly felt hungry and was fortunate to find a small caf still open at this late hour. After a satisfying meal of highly spiced German sausage with chips, he returned to his hotel and settled down for the night. As he lay in bed, he thought through the options to gain access to number 14, but fell asleep long before reaching any conclusions. Early the next morning, David enjoyed a typical German breakfast of strong coffee, a variety of bread rolls, cheese, salami and honey. By 9.00am he had made his way back to Bodenstrasse, armed now with a slip of paper on which he had written the name Gaarder and the address of 14, Bodenstrasse. He hoped that the name and address would convince anyone he was legitimately seeking a person by that fictitious name. He enquired at number 16, the terraced house on the left hand side of number 14. Fortunately the young couple there could speak a little English and tried to be helpful. They had only lived in the area for six months, so could tell him nothing of value. He then went into the boarding house on the right hand side of the terrace. Instead of asking for information about number 14, he decided, on the spur of the moment, to request a room. David made it clear, with some difficulty, that he wanted a room on the top floor. He claimed that he was hoping for a view of the lake. The owner, Frau Hiron, took him up to an attic room and with a little imagination, the lake could be seen through gaps in the roofs of the surrounding buildings. David said this was fine and asked how much the room cost. David fully expected to have to pay rent for a minimum of a month and was surprised to be shown a list of options with room prices for one night, a week and a month. He took a room for that night, cancelled his accommodation at the hotel and brought his suitcase with all his belongings to the bare attic room.

The room was reasonably clean, had a washbasin, a small double bed, a rug, an old wardrobe and a bedside light. The bedside light, which had a deep maroon shade, gave the room a light red hue. The window was the only other source of light. The curtains at the windows were also a deep maroon colour and when drawn at night created a room with a distinctive, rather shadowy, almost threatening, mood. It was clear this room was designed not for reading, but for more adventurous nighttime activities. There was one other room across the hall in the attic. David opened the door to find it was filled to the brim with old furniture and racks of somewhat bizarre clothing.

David went back downstairs and casually asked Frau Hiron, a rather flamboyant women of indeterminate age, about the house next door. Her English was surprisingly good and she told David the house had been unoccupied since the end of the war. She believed it had once belonged to a German gentleman who had been 'misplaced' during the war, never to return. David thought it diplomatic not to pursue her understanding of the word 'misplaced' and changed the subject to other things.

David had by now concocted a rather loose plan. He had every intention of breaking into number 14 and decided the only route was to be through the loft. He knew that it was quite common for the loft areas to be separated by nothing more than a low wall. Builders had no reason to divide houses above the top floor as they were rarely used apart from storage. There was little point in spending money on walls if they were not needed to support the roofs. He needed to find a way to reach the loft space. David was disappointed that there was no trap door into the loft from his room, but had noticed that there was one in the other room in the attic. This could provide the access he needed. Once his plan was made, David had little else to do until night-time, so he decided to enjoy the day by taking a steamboat on picturesque Lake Constance. It was a pleasant trip across the lake to the larger town of Konstanz. There he bought a torch, a lump hammer, a boiler suit and a small crowbar, thinking he may have to use some force at some stage to get into number 14. He took the precaution of buying these items at different shops, yet wondered if he might be over-reacting to the prospect of an arrest for his planned mission. By the time David returned from his trip and had his evening meal, it was dark.

On his return to the boarding house, he was surprised to find that the place was much livelier than before. There appeared to be a number of young women wandering around, and dressed in either revealing clothing or in little more than bathrobes. It was only when Frau Hiron offered him a choice of ladies that David realized he had stumbled upon a brothel. David declined her offer and made it clear that he had no wish to be disturbed. She assured him he had no need to worry; he had the only occupied room in the attic.

David waited until after midnight. He went to the bathroom, which was one level down and listened carefully. The noises coming from the other rooms at this level indicated varying levels of sexual activity. David was pleased that the occupants would have their minds on other things. It meant he was less likely to be disturbed. He then returned to his own room and prepared himself for his night-time adventure. He pulled the boiler suit over his clothes, took his tools and, having checked the passage outside was clear, crossed into the other attic room. Moving the clothes rails to one side, he tried to pull a table directly under the trap door to the loft. At first the heavy table scraped on the floor and David was concerned he would be making too much noise. He then lifted the table from one end, a little at a time, repeating the process from the other end. It worked and he managed to position it just where it was needed. He climbed on the table and found that even then he couldn't quite reach the trap door. He placed a chair on the table and this gave him just enough height to force the trap door open. As it opened, years of accumulated dust and debris poured out of the loft, almost causing David to choke as it swept over him. Fortunately the debris was not heavy and as it swirled around him he managed to suck in enough clean air to breathe without coughing. Whatever was going on below him, he didn't want a coughing fit to cause any investigation at this late hour.

With great care, David climbed up into the loft. He took his torch from a deep pocket and took a good look around. There were no boards in the loft, just exposed rafters. To his relief, David could now see he'd guessed right about the walls separating the houses. They were only about a two feet above the floor and would make movement between the two houses relatively easy. Cautiously he walked along the rafters to the wall that divided this house from number 14. He had the roof beams to give him support, but still took extra care not to lose his balance. A slip here onto the floor below could have been disastrous. He climbed over the low wall to find that the loft of number 14 had been used for storing a large number of wooden boxes. Using his crowbar, David managed to prise off the lids of two boxes. He peered inside and saw what seemed to be military uniforms. He took one out and saw the tunic had the distinctive double lightening motif of the SS on the collar. Other uniforms seemed to be of high rank because of the extra insignias and medal ribbons. These finds gave David renewed optimism that he had found the right place. It was now a question of searching the building for the ultimate prize – the Raphael. The door out of the attic room was locked so David used the crowbar to rip the lock from its mounts. With the tools he had bought it was an easy job, but David was still concerned about the noise he was making. This meant it took longer than planned, but he was soon out at the top of the stairwell. The design of the house was the same as next door where he had been staying, so it took David little time to become oriented. He made his way downstairs, looking in every room at each level. They were mostly full of furniture and personal effects. He checked in each wardrobe, only to find them empty apart from the odd piece of dusty clothing.

Eventually he made his way to the ground floor, which had a kitchen, a living room and a room that looked like a study of some sort. David tried to think where anyone would hide a painting or similar things of value. He checked everywhere, but could find nothing of note. There were open fireplaces in most rooms, but David noticed that there didn't seem to be any storage area for coal. He thought back to when he was young and remembered that a common storage place for coal was a cellar. He daren't go outside, even at this time of night, but assumed there was an entrance to the cellar from either the front or the back. Coal merchants would have delivered the coal directly to the cellar from the outside. It would have been the owners of the house, or their maids, who would have brought the coal up from inside. He could find no entrance to the cellar from the either of the ground floor rooms. He was now getting desperate as time was running out. David worked out that the coal delivery was likely to be at the front of the house, so he returned to that side. He looked again under the kitchen sink, flashing his torch from side to side in the dark. Then he noticed something odd. There did not appear to be any connection between the kitchen taps and the main pipe coming in from the ground. He checked again. Yes, he was sure. The sink unit had been installed but not connected properly. It suggested that the sink was there to hide something, as it certainly couldn't be used in its present state. He cautiously, and as noiselessly as possible, prised the sink unit away from the wall. It took some effort as it was sealed well against the wall. Whoever fitted this clearly wanted it to look authentic from the outside, but must have seen no good reason to connect the taps. Or perhaps, David thought, they were just in a hurry. Once the sink was taken from the wall, David could now see that the wall hidden behind it was constructed differently. It was not made of the stone blocks like most of the house, but more conventional bricks and mortar. This just might be the entrance to the cellar and encouraged David to renew his efforts to find out.

He took time to remove the first layer of bricks, as he needed to chisel out the cement. After that it was easier and, although he was concerned about the noise his hammer was making, he had little choice. It took him about half an hour of strenuous effort to clear a hole sufficiently large to squeeze through. From what he could see, the other side of the wall did have steps beyond and he hoped these would lead into a cellar. The cellar steps were slightly damp and uneven, so David trod cautiously. As he raked his torchlight from side to side, he soon made out a small number of slim wooden boxes, stacked on top of pallets and well away from the damp walls of the cellar. This, David thought, is the most likely way of storing pictures. He counted them and there were 13 individual boxes. Most were small, about two feet square and David realized that it would be impossible to remove them all. David knew that the Rafael portrait was slightly larger than this, its actual size being 22 inches by 28 inches. Assuming it was framed and allowing for packing, David appreciated that if the Raphael was in this small collection, it was likely to be in the largest box. He was loath to open any of the boxes for fear of damaging the contents. He looked at his watch and saw that by now dawn would be breaking and the nocturnal activities of number 12 would be coming to an end. He took the largest box and as an afterthought grabbed one of the smaller ones. He squeezed back through the hole from under the sink, like a rat with a stolen treat, and went back upstairs.

Once he was back in the attic room, the task of getting up into the loft space was much more difficult than getting down. He managed it by piling three of the large wooden boxes on top of each other, creating enough height to push himself through the trap door to the loft. Taking his precious treasure, he went back over the low wall to the next house and down into the attic. Finally he checked the landing outside the room to see if it was clear and slipped back into his own room. Locking and bolting his bedroom door, David then started to work on the boxes he had taken from number 14. He soon realized he didn't have the right tools to open these boxes. He needed something narrow and strong to get the lids off the boxes.

He could hardly sleep with anticipation, but had little option than to wait until the shops opened the next morning. He was the first down for breakfast and his excitement made eating difficult. At last nine-o-clock arrived and he walked rapidly into town to find an ironmongers. The small town had a distinct shopping area and he was soon rewarded by finding an ironmonger, just one street away from the main square. He bought a screwdriver and a pair of strong pincers. These, he thought, should be all he needed to open the boxes.

As he arrived back at the so-called boarding house, Frau Hiron challenged him. She made it clear his room was needed and he'd only paid for one night. David rapidly negotiated a rate for one hour. The owner seemed unsurprised at this request and smiled to David, assuming he had a personal assignation to enjoy. She was right, but David's assignation was not of a sexual nature. His assignation was with two potentially valuable paintings. David carefully lifted the lid off the smaller box, using the pincers and screwdriver he'd just bought. As he'd hoped, it was a framed painting, a portrait of a young woman. The painting or the artist meant nothing to David, but he was somehow confident it could be of some considerable value. The larger box was potentially the bigger prize. He worked with considerable care on the nails that secured the lid, slowly working the screwdriver and the pincers until each nail had been removed. He then lifted the lid to reveal the exact image he'd seen on the photograph sent to him. Even in the dim light of his room, David was astonished at the vibrancy of the colours and the amazing detail in the painting. The photograph could never do justice to this incredible work of art. David could almost feel the effort and joy that the artist had put into the painting. It was a true masterpiece. David almost punched the air with excitement; such was his feeling of elation at having these two paintings safely in his hands.

He soon came down to earth with the realization he now had to find a way to pass through two countries with these stolen items. The custom posts in France and Germany had been fairly straight forward on his journey here, but he had no illusions that things could be different travelling back. He replaced the lids on the two boxes, packed the smaller painting into his suitcase and went downstairs. There he paid his bill, shrugged his shoulders at the extortionate rate for the extra hour and went to leave the building.

The owner of the brothel stopped him in his tracks saying,

"Your package Herr Clarke. Is it something special?"

David was flustered for a moment and felt the blood rising in his cheeks.

"But of course, it is for my wife – a present from Meersburg."

"I hope she enjoys it as much as you have enjoyed the last hour, Herr Clarke," she replied with a wicked grin.

David decided not to reply and made his way as quickly as he could to his car. He put both packages in the boot of the car and covered them with a grey blanket. He then took a short wave radio from a hidden compartment in his boot and placed it in his suitcase. Before he left Meersburg, he bought a pack of 200 cigarettes and a small and rather cheap bottle of perfume. These he also put in his suitcase.

The drive back though Germany was uneventful in itself, although David's mind was in a whirl over what he had discovered. He kept going back to the conversations he'd had with the Director of the National Gallery. Could he really have in his boot a long lost original painting by the famous Raphael or was it all a cruel hoax?

At the border with France, David duly showed his passport and without any bidding held the cigarettes and perfume at arms length out of the car window. He was waved on his way by a rather disinterested border guard. He probably looked at the age of the car before deciding this person was unlikely to be a major smuggler. David stayed overnight at a farmhouse offering bed and breakfast in France before his onward journey took him to the ferry port at Calais. The two and a half hour ferry crossing was calm, which could hardly be said for David's nerves. He drove off the ferry, parked in the assigned bay for cars and stood by the car with his suitcase. A British customs officer sauntered over and asked him if he had anything to declare. Expecting the usual negative response, the customs officer asked David to open his car boot.

"Yes I have," added David hurriedly. "I have 200 cigarettes, a bottle of perfume and my short wave radio."

David opened his suitcase, now on the bonnet of the car, revealing its contents. The officer lifted the perfume and cigarettes out of the way and looked more closely at the short wave radio.

"These required duty to be paid up to three years ago, but that stupid practice was abandoned then. Didn't anyone tell you?"

"No," said David, "I thought they still had to be declared."

"You're well out of date. Put it away and get on with your journey. You'll know next time."

With that, David put his suitcase away, got back in his car and drove off. His little diversion had worked. He was much happier now to be safely back in England with two old people in the boot, even if only portraits.

His arrival home to Southampton was met with minor celebration. Laura could hardly believe the saga when retold. She laughed when she said she didn't normally go to bed with common housebreakers.

It was over two weeks before David had another reason to travel to London. He arranged to meet the Director of the National Gallery and requested that an authority on Raphael be present at the meeting. It was planned for 11.00am and David arrived with his two packages thirty minutes early. While waiting, he wandered around the gallery, heading directly to the paintings in the High Renaissance period. The collection was impressive, with eight paintings by Raphael. Interesting there was also one entitled A Portrait of a Young Man, but it was considered to be by an imitator of Raphael. David wondered if he had the real thing.

The meeting was held in the Gallery's Trustees' Room. It was used for a number of small functions, but particularly to discuss the prospect of purchasing new pictures. There was a large, well-lit easel so the trustees could see the paintings on show. David was joined by the director of the Gallery, by Mr. Potter, the head archivist, and Professor Oliver, who was introduced as a world authority on Raphael. David was invited to place his find on the easel and the three men gathered round. The amazement of the three men was palpable. They found it quite incredible that they were looking at a portrait that had been lost for 25 years. Not just any portrait, but by one of the Old Masters of the early 16th century. All three confirmed that it was most likely to be the original, but all agreed that it needed scientific analysis to confirm its authenticity. Prof. Oliver offered to arrange this as soon as possible. David was congratulated and to celebrate a bottle of champagne and four flutes were brought into the room. They drank to David and his success and it was only then that they turned their attention to the other package. Once again the package was opened and the painting placed on the easel for examination. There were gasps from the three experts as they each recognized the painting and its importance.

"It's got to be," said one.

"None other," said another.

Finally David heard a name mentioned.

"It really is the lost Klimt."

"I never thought I would see The Portrait of Trude Steiner again. It is quite incredible."

At this point David felt able to interrupt the three experts and ask questions.

"Please tell me about this painting," he said, "it's clearly known to you."

"Absolutely," replied the director of the National Gallery, "like the Raphael, it was stolen by the Nazis during the second world war. Gustav Klimt painted it in Vienna, where he was living at he time. It is the daughter of Jenny Steiner, a Jewish art collector. It was sold at auction in 1941, strangely to another Jewish family. The Nazis acquired it for their collection and it has never been seen since. That is not until today. It is a most important piece. It was painted about the turn of the century and before Klimt started to experiment with gold colour."

"So," said David, "assuming scientific analysis proves these to be the true originals, who exactly has ownership of them."

"That's a difficult one," answered Mr. Potter, the head archivist. "The Raphael should logically be returned to the Czartoryski Museum in Poland. The Klimt would be a different matter because it was stolen from an individual. We would have to establish if any members of the family are still alive and return it to them. Not an easy job, and it could take time. Nevertheless something that would need to carried out before there could be any claim to it. At the moment, David, I guess you are technically the owner, because they are both in your possession. However I would prefer to take the view that you are simply a custodian until its true owner can be traced."

It was agreed that both paintings would be left with Prof. Oliver to arrange the scientific tests and that Mr. Potter would initiate the search for the owner of the Klimt. David was warned that these actions would take time.

Two months later, David was invited to return to the National Gallery. He and Laura took a day's leave from work and they both arrived at the Gallery just before the appointed hour of 1.00pm. They were led up to the Trustees' Room once more and were surprised to see that six men and four women were seated around the oak table. The Director introduced them as the Trustees of the National Gallery. Laura was also introduced to Prof. Oliver and Mr. Potter, who were seated with the Trustees. The table was littered with the remnants of a light lunch. David and Laura were asked if they had eaten and when they said no, two further lunches were brought in for them.

The Gallery Director took the chair and invited Prof. Oliver to speak. He firstly discussed the Raphael. He stood and explained that full scientific investigations had taken place. All the forensic evidence had been positive, with carbon dating and paint analysis all being consistent with a date in the early

1500s. He explained that his opinion coupled with forensic analysis was insufficient. He had invited the former Director of the Czartoryski Museum, now retired, to come to London. He had corroborated every fact. In addition, he had consulted with the Raphael Institute at the University of Florence. In summary every consultation had been in agreement. This was The Portrait of a Young Man last seen in public at the Czartoryski Museum. Prof. Oliver then handed to David a legal document, a Certificate of Authenticity. Those around the table broke into spontaneous, if muted applause. David was slightly embarrassed, but thanked Prof. Oliver and his team for everything he had done. The Chairman of the Trustees then spoke.

"Under normal circumstances," he said, "it would be the will of the Trustees to make an offer for this exceptional painting. However in this case, we all agree that the painting should be returned forthwith to the Czartoryski Museum. I am assuming, Mr. Clarke that this would be your wish?"

"Of course," David replied, "that is exactly what I expected to happen.

"Good," added the Chairman of Trustees, "then I can reveal that we have already been in preliminary discussions with the current director of the museum, a Dr. Jakovlevicz. He has confirmed that once the painting is returned to his care, in its current condition, he will authorize a reward of 300,000 Czech koruna to the finder, to you, David."

David was amazed and was unable to comprehend what was being offered.

"To help you, David, that is equivalent to about £10,000, sufficient for you to buy a very pleasant house."

Laura sat there in disbelief.

"And now, David, after that rather exciting news, can we turn to the Klimt?"

"Of course, sir," David replied, still stunned by his good fortune.

The chairman then turned to Mr. Potter and asked him to speak.

"Thank you, Chairman. As you know, David, it was agreed that I should lead the investigation into the provenance of the Klimt. It was not an easy task as the Nazis had covered their tracks rather well. However in summary, we were able to trace the Klimt as far as its final owner. As we said earlier Jenny Steiner sold it at auction in 1941 to a Herr Levins, a successful Jew living in Heidelberg, The Nazis stole it from him, on the premise that he owed unpaid taxes. That was the last time it was seen until a few weeks ago. We tried to trace the Levins family, but sadly the whole family was murdered in the Holocaust. The majority perished at Auschwitz, but one side of the family went to Belsen. We were able to trace these family members because one of the very first people to arrive at Belsen when it was liberated, a Canadian doctor, kept accurate records of the surviving inmates and what subsequently happened to them. We were able to contact him and he informed us that this side of the Levins family had died from complications of starvation and pneumonia. So there is no member of the family that is traceable. We think it is reasonable to assume that the ownership of the Klimt rightly belongs to David, assuming of course that he came by it legitimately."

David made no comment. The Chairman of the Gallery Trustees then spoke.

"Thank you Mr. Potter. Irrespective of the legitimacy of obtaining the painting, we are of the opinion that the ownership currently rests with Mr. Clarke. It was last held by what is now an illegal organization; therefore it is unlikely to be contested, especially after such a length of time. Mr. Clarke, the trustees are prepared to offer a substantial sum for the Klimt, but under certain conditions."

David and Laura leaned forward in their seats, hardly believing what was being proposed.

"The Klimt is a valuable addition to our current collection, particularly as it relates to some of his early work, several years before his so called 'golden period'. The amount of our offer is £50,000, but as I said there are two conditions. The first is that all the money should go towards a memorial or some such suitable project that will remember the Jewish dead during the holocaust. Our view is that the painting was stolen from a family that perished in the holocaust and it is fitting that it should result in something of that nature. Our second condition is that you should never reveal the manner by which you found the painting, or should I say paintings. You are of course free to consider this offer, but we would hope that a decision could be made in less than one week."

There was silence in the room. David and Laura were both stunned, yet in some way relieved. They had already discussed the options that may be open to them if the paintings turned out to be genuine. Neither of them wanted to benefit substantially from the find; the adventure and the outcome was enough. The proposal from the Chairman of the Trustees seemed to give them an opportunity to do something really special and something of which they could both be proud. They thanked everyone involved and promised to let them know as soon as possible. They had both learned from a young age that if difficult decisions have to be made, then it is always best to buy time.

On the train home to Southampton, the two discussed the options open to them. In truth, they both knew that the conditions of the offer were fair and made life much simpler. It meant that the responsibility of ownership would be lifted from them and David's night-time activities in Meersburg could be kept quiet. They both debated the moral dilemma of knowing about the other paintings, still hidden at 14, Bodenstrasse. They considered the compromise of not revealing how David had acquired the paintings, but at some stage in the future telling the authorities in Meersburg of the secret hoard in the cellar of a terraced hose in the town. They decided to sleep on the offer and make up their minds when more refreshed. It had been a long, exciting and tiring day, hardly ideal for such a momentous decision.

The following day, David received a telegram from the National Gallery. It read, simply:

"The trustees considered their offer after you left. Should you be prepared to accept it, they would take pleasure in having a copy of both paintings, produced by a professional artist, for you to keep as a memento."

The telegram made little difference to their decision. It was to accept.

David and Mr. Potter corresponded at length, following his investigations. Mr. Potter suggested that David was in touch with the Canadian doctor who had been in Belsen. He thought this person might have views on the style of a suitable memorial. Over several months, the two men wrote to each other regularly. They soon established a professional, yet friendly rapport. The doctor's first hand experience of Belsen helped enormously in planning the memorial. This was especially so as he could send David a sketch of the site as it was in 1945. It turned out that the doctor had always planned to return to Belsen and had been trying for some time to raise funds in Canada for a suitable memorial. The offer from the National Gallery would make his dream come true and he and David decided to become partners in the project. He even offered to share his proposal for the memorial. Between them, and with the assistance of an architect and landscape designer, a suitable memorial was designed. It was a simple granite wall in the form of a low rectangular shape. The wall surrounded a mound to represent the mass graves of so many innocent people. The inscription on the wall said in English, German, Hebrew and Yiddish, 'A memorial to the many who died in this place. Their memories will live on for ever'.

The National Gallery, as promised, funded the project and it was officially dedicated in April 1971. David was invited to the dedication ceremony. It also gave him the opportunity to meet the Canadian doctor who had helped so much with the design and positioning of the memorial. The time they spent together was brief, but it gave David the chance to tell him about the quest to find the paintings, especially how it had all started with the strange, unsigned note.

It was a moving occasion with representatives from many groups of Jewish survivors from Belsen. David followed behind the line of all those who were there. He felt humbled by the simple act of placing a stone on the wall. David placed one of the tiles on the wall; one of the tiles that had been the start of this momentous odyssey. The Canadian doctor asked David for one of the tiles. He also placed it on the wall, choosing a spot next to the one put there by David.

On the way back to Britain, David reflected on a journey that had taken from him from a box of tiles to a moving ceremony in Belsen. It was quite hard to absorb what had happened in such a short period of time. He had learned to trust his own instincts, but more importantly to trust the instincts and support of Laura. It was enough.

CHAPTER 27
TRAIN

On Peter's 28th birthday, he received a present of a model railway engine. The model was unusual because of its size. Peter, when he was younger, had a Hornby OO model railway. This one, however, was twice the size of his own, but was beautifully made in high-quality painted tinplate. The writing on the base of the engine told him it was made by the Marklin Company, but little else. The name meant nothing to Peter. He was familiar with names such as Airfix, Triang and Hornby but little else.

As had happened before, the enclosed birthday card was unsigned. The note on the card read:

Dear Peter,

Many happy returns.

The enclosed model is one from a substantial set of important historical significance.

If you have the time, I encourage you to seek the rest. The location is as before in Germany, but this time in the Eastern part. It can be found in the city of Magdeburg. Use Caesar's code letter 'P', your own initial, to establish the exact location.

Sadly I cannot join you on this quest. I wish you well.

On a separate piece of paper was the string of letters 'hzqqslfdyzcoqwzye'.

As before, when Peter was invited to find the Isle of St Brendan, it was the phrase 'I wish you well' that meant so much to him. This, without question, established its authenticity and also its intrigue. The quest to find St Brendan's Isle was so exciting and resulted in such an honour for Peter that he couldn't possibly resist this latest challenge. He discussed it with Mi Sun and they both agreed that it was something he should embrace fully. But there was a problem. The code to find the exact location meant absolutely nothing to him. The next time the two of them went back to Hadleigh Hall, they consulted The Encyclopedia Britannica, but it was no help. Then Peter recalled that one of his friends in the running club at University had a hobby that involved code breaking. He had even formed a society by the same name. Luckily, Peter had kept his address after all this time and was able to contact him. After a week, Peter received the following letter:

Dear Peter,

It was good to hear from you after so long.

Great to hear about your marriage and your medical work.

The so-called 'Caesar code' is one of the easiest to unlock. It is simply a transposition of the letters of the alphabet by a number of places. The sender can either give you a number or a starting letter. The simplest way is to write the alphabet out in a line and then re-write the alphabet again in the same way. Place the second line beneath the first and then move the bottom line to either the key letter or the number of places indicated. Then the letter in the lower line will convert to a letter in the top line.

Give it a try and if it doesn't work then let me know. You shouldn't have any trouble.

Trust you are still running. We were a great team in our day!

Yours sincerely

Gareth

That evening Peter and Mi Sun followed Gareth's instructions. It worked well and Peter now had the decoded message in front of him. It read: wolfhausnordfront. Peter assumed that it referred to an address and was looking forward immensely to the investigation.

Peter's busy hospital schedule gave him only four days leave in the next month. He arranged with a colleague to exchange shifts and this gave him an extra day. He took the train from Liverpool Street Station to Brussels and then onwards via Cologne and Hanover. The last section of the journey was the most difficult, as it took him across the border into East Germany. At the border he was thoroughly searched and the interior of the train carriage was taken apart. Peter wasn't sure what the guards were looking for, but they were surprisingly thorough in their investigation. The cushions on all seats were taken out and every possible hiding place was searched. Peter filled in a currency form, which he assumed would be double-checked on departure. The purpose of his visit was stated as 'to meet a fellow research scientist at Magdeburg University'. Peter was able to supply a name from an article he'd read in an obscure medical journal and just prayed it wasn't checked.

He'd been travelling for almost 24 hours when he finally arrived at the city, tired and grimy from the journey. He'd read about the damage the RAF bombers had inflicted on Magdeburg and was surprised to see so much rebuilding in the city. He immediately took a taxi to the Nordfront area of town, a suburb that had been badly damaged during the war, destroying most of the original Grunderzeit buildings. He found a small hotel and his first requirement was sleep, having been awake for most of the lengthy trip. First thing the next morning, Peter took a brisk walk along the River Elbe. This gave him an appetite and after a brief shower, he looked forward to breakfast in the hotel. He was disappointed to find no breakfast was served there, but the swarthy man at the front desk recommended a caf just around the corner. He went in, requested a standard breakfast, and sat down with his back to the wall. An elderly man, clearly overheard his English accent, stood up, and faced Peter. He looked at him, uttered the words "Verdammter Amerikaner" and left. The owner of the hotel came over with his coffee and said "Please sir, take no notice. He is one of the old guard. He's either complaining about the American involvement in the war or the way they gave so much to the Russians. It's difficult to know. Please enjoy your breakfast."

Peter took this as a warning to be careful in a city with such a recent history and, for many, an unacceptable occupation by the Russians.

As he ate his breakfast of rye bread, cheese and strong coffee, Peter noticed a group of young people come into the caf and sit at the next table. Peter had a poor command of German, but the students seemed prepared to speak English and Peter asked them if they knew of the Wolfhaus.

"Of course," one of them said, "everyone knows of the Wolfhaus."

"I'm sorry," said Peter, This is my first visit, is it famous?"

"Not famous," came the reply, "infamous."

"And why is it infamous?" Peter persisted.

The circle of students grew a little tighter around Peter as if to share a terrible secret.

"It was the Nazi headquarters during the war, at least in this area. Reichsmarschall Goering was a frequent visitor. A number of people who went into that building never came out. It had an appalling reputation. We try to forget."

"And what is it used for now?" Peter enquired, suddenly engaged by the direction of the discussion.

"It's now part of the University. Something to do with the sports department. It's well guarded. You often see the top athletes go in there, although to our knowledge there are no training facilities."

"Could it be some sort of laboratory, for testing athletes and the like?" Peter asked, wondering why it had to be guarded.

"Best not to ask too closely, but most of us suspect that the athletes have special nutrition there including drugs."

Peter decided he'd asked enough and thanked the group for their information. He finished his breakfast and strolled towards the Nordfront deep in thought. Peter could find no connection between a sports laboratory, a former Nazi HQ and a train set. Peter, inquisitive as ever, had every intention of satisfying his curiosity. He quickly made the decision to find a way into the Wolfhaus, whatever it took. He was reasonably convinced that his medical knowledge would be a reasonable basis for a discussion if the Wolfhaus was being used as an exercise-testing laboratory. He could but try. By the time he'd walked the few blocks to the Wolfhaus, his confidence was growing. Peter planned to say he was a research worker studying sports training in Eastern Germany. He hoped a bit of flattery might at least get him into the building. On his arrival at the Wolfhaus, he saw the distinctive sign 'Department of Sports Sciences'. He was met by a security guard, who took him to an anteroom just inside the building. Peter tried to explain his fictional reason for being there. It was apparent that the guard had either no authority or insufficient English to admit him further. Peter was left in this room for fifteen minutes, his hopes draining by the minute. Eventually another person appeared and asked Peter his business. Peter explained that people in the West were amazed how successful the East Germans were in certain sports and he was travelling the country visiting Universities to learn of their success. He said he had been recommended to come to the University of Magdeburg, because it was recognized as a centre of excellence. Peter explained that he had a special interest in high altitude medicine and was keen to find out if the East Germans used altitude training in their preparation for top athletes. This seemed to be an acceptable explanation for the member of staff who'd been sent to interview him and he was issued with an official visitors' badge. Peter's host now introduced himself as Dr. Reinhart and offered to give Peter a brief tour of the facilities. As Peter suspected, it was a series of research laboratories, focusing on athletic training. There were a number of electronic treadmills and other machinery to test athletes. The few who were exercising were attached to machines recording all sorts of physiological responses. Peter had never seen such an array of monitoring equipment outside of an emergency room in a hospital. Dr. Reinhart explained that here at Magdeburg they concentrated exclusively on field athletes, javelin and discus throwers, shot putters, and a few high jumpers. The benefits of high altitude training were far less in this breed of athlete, where raw power was far more important. Over coffee, Peter broached the subject of the history of the building by asking how long the facility had been open.

"You will have to ask our Director," came the reply from Dr. Reinhart, "he is the only person who was here when the department was first opened, soon after the end of the war."

Peter decided not to pursue his enquiries about the building any further with Dr. Reinhart. He detected that there was far more to the training of these athletes than he was being shown. He tried one more approach, more from clinical interest than any other.

"What special dietary or nutritional programmes do your athletes follow?" Peter asked, suspecting full well that these athletes were on drugs to improve their strength and power.

"We have developed a world-leading regime of dietary supplements, concentrating on the optimum balance of vitamins and minerals. Each athlete has a personal programme, based on his or her dietary requirement."

It was clear to Peter that there was to be no admission of drug use and this was exactly what he expected.

"Our Director is away today, but if you want to know about the history of the department, then please call again tomorrow. If you give me the address of your hotel, I can let you know his movements."

Peter took this as a dismissal. He thanked his host and left, none the wiser for his efforts. Peter was unsure what he should now do. He'd managed to get into the Wolfhaus, but found out nothing. There was little else to do than wait and see of the Director would meet him the next day. He was far from confident it would happen, but tried his best to remain positive. Meanwhile Peter happily spent the little time he had left in Magdeburg to look around the city. It was clear from everything he read and saw that the RAF had virtually obliterated the city. He understood it was part of Britain's plan to concentrate bombing on centres of oil production, Magdeburg being one of them. Peter visited the newly restored cathedral and, once again, strolled along the banks of the Elbe. It was noticeable that the communist era had cast a dull grey blanket over the city, robbing it of the vitality seen in the west.

When Peter arrived back at his hotel, he was intrigued to find a message from the Director of the Department of Sports Sciences. It was an invitation for Peter to join him for dinner at his home that evening. It was signed Prof. Hermann Block. A phone number was attached to the note and Peter rang it immediately to confirm the time and place. He arranged for a taxi to pick him up from the hotel at six-o-clock that evening. The drive to the Director's home surprised Peter. He fully expected it to be within the confines of the city walls, but the taxi drove into the surrounding countryside for several miles. It turned down a dark and quiet country lane, which soon became a dirt track. The taxi turned through large iron gates, along a tree-lined driveway and up to the door of an impressive house. As Peter left the taxi, he could see that the house had a tired look about it, with ivy dominating the walls and the windowsills clearly in need of paint.

He was greeted by the Professor Block, taken into a small study, and offered schnapps. Prof. Block was well built and had the look of a former athlete, who'd lost the muscle tone of earlier years. He had short grey hair and a rugged face that clearly spent a long time outdoors. His eyes were small and piercing. They were the sort that gave nothing away, yet made anyone looking at them slightly uncomfortable.

They talked at first about general matters such as the difference between the east and the west, about the success of the East German field athletes and about countries that they had visited. Hermann had clearly travelled extensively with the East German team, yet Peter sensed he had little opportunity to see the countries beyond the hotel or the athletics track. After two more schnapps, Peter was taken to another room where dinner was served. It was a basic meal of little more than stew, coarse rye bread and stewed apples. The meal was served by a woman of a similar age to the Director, but she was not introduced. Peter assumed it was the Director's wife, but nothing in their relationship gave any clue to the situation. The conversation over the meal continued about aspects of sports science. The Director gave away few details of his work and Peter just managing to answer intelligently about his own interests as if he were a sports scientist himself. Over another schnapps, the Director then asked Peter why he was interested in the history of the Department. Peter guessed that the detail of his visit had already been relayed back to the Director. He thought quickly, suddenly realizing he could be sitting in the presence of a former Nazi. Prof. Block could easily be of the right age and Peter imagined him as a younger man wearing the dreaded black uniform.

Peter had concocted a story, but was not convinced it would be sufficient to convince this resolute character. He decided to roll the dice and see which way they fell.

"A friend of my father was attached to the 9th US Army when they occupied Magdeburg towards the end of the year. He told me about the devastation here. They found out about the Wolfhaus being the regional HQ of the SS during the war. They also knew that Reichsmarschall Goering was a frequent visitor, in spite of being the commander of the Luftwaffe. Although hardly relevant to the war effort, the other thing they knew was that Goering was a fanatical collector of model railways."

Hermann Block seemed to stiffen slightly at the mention of the model railway, but kept his blue, piercing, unblinking eyes on Peter.

"Go on," he said as he poured another schnapps.

"There was an unsubstantiated rumour that Goering kept at least part of his model railway at the Wolfhaus. It was supposedly quite a large collection, so it might have been just a small part. Sufficient perhaps to keep him amused on his visits."

"You said an unsubstantiated rumour."

"So I believe, but possibly based on the odd item that the Americans may have stolen."

"You mean some of the model railway?"

"Either that, but more likely a contemporary photo. The friend of my father's was here at the time. He once showed me a photo of a German model railway. It could theoretically have been the one he saw here in Magdeburg. I don't know.

"But why your interest? I thought that you were a doctor, with interests in altitude medicine."

"That's true, Hermann, but from a young age I've been fascinated by model railways."

"Tell me more."

"I have a Hornby OO. Manufactured in England, just outside Liverpool."

Peter was worried that Hermann might delve into his knowledge of model railways further. The truth was that Pater had lost interest in his train set at about the age of seven.

"I'm not familiar with such a model, over here we tend to use the O gauge track, usually made by the Marklin Company."

Peter wondered if his eyes had given away his increased interest. This was the very same manufacturer of the engine he'd been sent for his birthday. He tried to remain calm. Hermann broke the momentary silence.

"Would you like to see a Marklin set?"

"But of course," Peter replied, "do you have one here?"

It was then that the numerous glasses of schnapps seemed to take effect and Hermann became more talkative.

"My late father had a huge train set, possibly one of the biggest in Germany. During the war it was broken up into somewhat smaller sets, although even then it was very impressive. He kept a few specimens at the Wolfhaus, which would be where your American contact might have seen them. The majority of the engines, rolling stock and track came here to his private house."

"You mean this was your father's house?"

"Of course. When he was alive it was in much better condition. He was a wealthy man with great influence. Sadly under the communist regime, it has fallen into neglect. On my salary I am unable to keep it in good repair, but consider myself fortunate to be able to live here still. So many homes of this size have been requisitioned by the state for communal living. Anyway, enough of my problems. Come, I will show you."

With that, Prof Block struggled to his feet and walked, a little unsteadily out of the room. Peter followed and was led through a dimly lit passage to a door at the end. This door opened to some stairs, which led down to a cellar. Hermann switched on the lights to reveal a model railway track measuring some four yards by three yards at the very least. Peter was amazed. He saw straight away that it was the same style as the one he had at home, but the layout was extensive. It had a number of interlinking tracks, bridges, cuttings, stations, model buildings and all the paraphernalia associated with a model railway. It was a magnificent layout.

"I assume from your reaction, that you are impressed," said Hermann.

"It is by far the grandest model railway I have ever seen," said Peter, "your father must have been a great collector."

"Oh he was, and you are seeing only a small part of it. The rest I have stored in boxes, at least twice as much as this. I did not have my father's abiding interest in this particular hobby. My sport came first."

For Peter the dice so far were rolling in his direction and he thought it worth pursuing.

"The remaining part of the model railway. Do you have any plans?"

"Over the years, I have given it much thought. Circumstances are such that no time seemed right to take any particular action. Life under the communists makes things difficult, but now I am prepared to sell the remaining parts of the railway. Not on the open market, there are reasons why this would not be appropriate. But to a private buyer, perhaps well away from Germany, may be a possibility. I would like to keep the layout you see in front of you as a memento, but the rest can go. Would you like to see the other parts?"

Peter was amazed at such an offer. He and Hermann then spent well over two hours opening and examining eight tea chests, filled with the most incredible variety of model railway items. There were boxes filled with tracks, 20 volt controllers, numerous engines, carriages, rolling stock and hundred of other smaller items. Each item was carefully double wrapped in paper and had the musty smell associated with age and lack of use. Yet the condition, to Peter's untutored eye, looked perfect.

Peter could barely believe that he had been told about this collection, let alone allowed to see it.

"So," said Peter, "are you telling me that all these have all been wrapped just like this since the end of the war?"

"They have, only you, my wife and I know of their existence."

"So what are your plans for them, especially now that you've shown them to me?"

"As I said earlier, I would be happy for them to have a new home. The historical situation is a little complex, but through you, Peter, there may be a solution."

"Through me?" Peter asked.

"Yes. I need a little time but I believe that between us arrangements can be made."

"Arrangements. What do you mean?"

"Peter, why don't you stay here the night. I can make satisfactory arrangements overnight."

"Hermann, it's a kind offer, but I am not sure where this is all going."

"Peter, I know we have only just met, but you will have to trust me."

Peter was uncertain, especially as the house seemed mildly threatening, let alone his host.

"Why not," he said, thinking he had very little to lose. He had come a long way. He had found a complete railway, matching the single engine he owned. He was so close to completing this strange and still uncertain mission.

"That would be very kind, Hermann. Are you sure it's no trouble?"

"Let's drink to a successful outcome," was Hermann's reply.

Peter spent a restless night in a small guest room. It had an air of unlived and uncertainty. The single bed was hard and cold and Peter struggled to relate to his situation. Here he was in a remote part of Eastern Germany, a guest of someone he hardly knew, yet someone who had hinted at parting with a most magnificent model train set. It was not until the small hours that Peter eventually fell asleep. Just before he did, he heard movement from nearby. Someone was clearly awake as late as him.

There was a knock on Peter's bedroom door and he awoke with a start. He opened the door to find a tray laid out with an embroidered napkin, a mug of hot chocolate, some rye toast and what looked like home made plum jam. He ate in his room, washed in the cold water from the basin in his room and went downstairs.

"Ah, Peter, " said Hermann, "arrangements have been made. First I need you to read this document. I apologize for any clumsy English, but I sat up late last night composing it as best I could."

Peter was handed an official looking document. It had been typed using an old machine, which was uncovered in the corner of the room.

It read:

Memorandum of Understanding

This document is to agree that Dr. Peter Culham will act as sole agent to undertake the following:

Establish a relationship between the towns of Magdeburg and Coventry (from now on to be called 'twinning').

This twinning will honour those who died or were made homeless during the air raids on the two cities during the Second World War.

The twinning will be seen as a peace initiative between the two countries and will take the form of lasting reparation.

Dr. Culham will undertake to establish a permanent memorial in or near Coventry Cathedral, a building damaged badly by the Luftwaffe.

Prof. Block will undertake to establish a permanent memorial in or near Magdeburg Cathedral, a building damaged badly by the Royal Air Force.

Funding will come from the sale of a model railway, loaned to Dr. Culham for that purpose. The income will be divided equally between the two cities.

Signed……………………….Dr. Peter Culham

Signed……………………….Prof Hermann Block

Witnessed……………………………..and …………………………….

Dated……………………..

It took Peter a little while to appreciate the significance of the document in front of him. He read it a second time without saying a word. He then looked up from the paper he held in his hand.

"Hermann, this is most extraordinary. Can I ask why you are so moved to decide on this 'arrangement' to quote your words from last night?"

"It was not an easy decision. I have been thinking for some time to make such an arrangement. I did not know until last night how this could be achieved. Your arrival and interest in model railways was the opportunity I needed. I hope you will find the railway of some value. Sadly in this country these things are just not possible. There is too much state control and corruption over everything we do. If you are willing to follow my plan, then I believe some good can come out of the horrors of the past. The choice, Peter, is yours."

"I have to be straight with you, Hermann, this is totally unexpected. I can give you my word that I'll try my utmost to fulfill your request. But you haven't explained the detail. How will I get the boxes home to England?"

"I was up late last night making the arrangements. A van will arrive here very soon and take the boxes to the border. You will be issued with special documents to ensure safe transit out of Eastern Germany and into the West. From there it will be up to you. You will share the driving of the van with one of my most trusted employees. He will come with you to England and once you have unloaded your precious cargo, he will return with the van empty. When I say empty, it may be sensible to load it with items of little consequence to reduce suspicion. I will leave that decision to you. Does all this sound reasonable?"

"It does, Hermann, as long as we can cross the borders of France and Britain without incident."

"By midday, I will have in my hands the required import/export documents. There may be some modest duty payable. My suggestion is that you pay that as you cross the border and reclaim it from the sale of the railway. If there are no more questions for now, I suggest that we go to my department to get this document witnessed and await the paper work. Do you have any questions, Peter?"

"To be honest, Hermann, I am slightly overwhelmed by this turn of events. Matters appear to be moving so quickly and I seem to be losing control of them."

"Don't worry, Peter. Just as soon as we have the boxes safely loaded, you will be back in control. It will then become your mission, not mine."

Peter was surprised how quickly things then seemed to fall into place. He was impressed by Hermann's efficiency. Peter wondered how he had such influence in a country known for its inefficiency. The van arrived and the eight tea chests were loaded with great care. Peter and Hermann followed the van back the few miles to Magdeburg and together they went into the department. Two junior members of Hermann's were summoned to witness the signing of the memorandum. They sat opposite Hermann and Peter and the documents were folded so the typing could not be seen. Hermann made it clear that their only function was to witness the signatures as having taken place. He gave the first copy to Peter who duly signed it and his signature was witnessed. Then Hermann took up the pen and leant over the sheet of paper. As he signed, he suddenly let out an oath and the words 'Dummes Gerinnsel – stupid clot', as much to himself as anyone. He demanded that one of the witnesses brought him some tippex and carefully brushed over his signature. He then resigned his name and had it witnessed. The second copy was signed and witnessed without incident. The first copy was placed in a brown envelope and handed to Peter. The second copy was folded and placed in Hermann's briefcase.

"Good," said Hermann, "all is well."

He produced two glasses, the inevitable schnapps, and they both made a solemn toast to the success of their enterprise. Peter was still a little stunned but was pleased that everything so far was not only going to plan but exceeded his expectations. He still had concerns over the model railway as to its worth, but was content to let things unfold in their natural order. As he kept reminding himself, what did he have to loose. Peter was introduced to his co-driver, who appeared thoroughly briefed, and the pair set off on the lengthy journey home.

Peter's new colleague was called Pieter Dortmund and was keen to practise his English. As they crossed the borders into West Germany and France, the paperwork seemed to be sufficient. They stopped to eat and to sleep at small hotels, with Pieter insisting that he slept in the van. It was clear he'd been given very clear instructions and Peter could hardly argue. Three days later, they arrived at Calais and caught a ferry some four hours later. As things had gone so well so far, Peter thought it best to tell the customs officer about the goods, still secure in the tea chests. He explained that the trains were for an exhibition at a national model railway show in York later in the year and he was just the courier. He was asked where in York the exhibition was to be held. Fortunately, Peter had been at a medical conferenced there. They had used the conference suite at the racecourse, so Peter explained that the model railway exhibition was held between race meetings. When asked to assess the value of the goods, Peter explained that they were old and probably worth no more than £200. He also said that they were to be returned to Magdeburg after the exhibition, so would not be staying in Britain. The customs official went away to consult with his manager. Peter and Pieter spent an anxious 15 minutes waiting for his return. It was decided that a fee of £20 was chargeable. Peter handed over the cash and waited for a receipt. None was forthcoming and after a short standoff, Peter formed the distinct impression that the best strategy was to leave. A grateful customs officer, no doubt £20 richer, waved them off.

Peter and Mi Sun's small house in Cambridge was too small to store eight tea chests, so he drove straight to Hadleigh Hall in Shropshire. They were unloaded and stored in a locked garage on the edge of the Hadleigh estate. It was an ideal location until Peter could find a way of selling the models. Pieter stayed the night and Peter left him to return the van, after giving him a first rate English breakfast.

It was later that day that Peter took another look at the Memorandum of Understanding. He decided that until he sold the train set, then the notion of any sort of war memorial would be impossible. He imagined that the City of Coventry would have little objection to the plan, even if it were to be a modest affair, perhaps something like a plaque. Even that required money, so the key was the sale. As he looked again at the document, he was reminded of the strange business of the signature. It was unusual for someone like Hermann, someone who must sign things all the time, to make as error like that. He noticed that the signature that had been tippexed out was a fraction longer than Prof. Block's final signature. Perhaps that was the problem. Perhaps he had inadvertently doubled a letter or something. Even that didn't seem to ring true. He tried to lift the tippex off with the nail of his index finger but it had no effect. Peter thought of other options and then had a brainwave. The people to ask were his colleagues in medical illustrations at the hospital. He was sure they dealt with adjusting illustrations as part of their work. He would ask them.

On Peter's return to Cambridge, one of the first things he did was to seek out the medical illustrations department at the hospital. The people there assured him that it shouldn't be a problem and they would tackle it that afternoon. Peter was welcome to come back then if he wished. Peter adjusted his clinic so he returned at 3.00pm. The staff explained that they had two techniques, one high tech and the other rather simple. They had a soft x-ray machine, rather like the one used by picture restorers. It should reveal what was under the top layer. The other was to use a special solution to remove the tippex. They explained that the problem with this method was it could destroy whatever was underneath, especially if it were water-soluble. They asked Peter if he knew what sort of ink was used for the signature. Peter was sure it was a conventional biro and not a fountain pen. Peter was assured it should present no problem, as biro ink is stable even under water. The x-ray method gave a hazy signature, which was a little inconclusive, but looked like Gorring.

"You mean like the town on the River Thames," said Peter.

"Well not quite, I am pretty sure that there is a total of seven letters and the town of Goring has only six," came the educated response.

"So are you are going to try the other method?" Peter asked.

"Yes, straight away. You can watch if you want."

The technician pinned the document to a board so there would be no slippage and adjusted an anglepoise lamp to get the best lighting conditions. He then selected a fine brush, rather like the sort a watercolour painter would use. He dipped this in a solution of acetone and carefully brushed the tippex, taking the surface off a little at a time. It was time-consuming, because he wanted to remove the white tippex without affecting the signature underneath.

"Are you confident that it was signed with biro?" he asked Peter, "Because if so, I'll now switch to distilled water as the acetone may be too powerful."

"Almost 100% sure," Peter answered.

The technician took him at his word and changed from the solvent to water. It worked well and the signature, although a little hazy, revealed the true signature. It read, without question the name Goering. The name meant nothing to the young technician and Peter was happy to say little else. He thanked him for his valuable work and once the document was dry, took it away. Peter's appreciative, but restrained response to the technician belied his true feelings. In truth, he was totally exhilarated by this news. Somehow Peter had a suspicion, but no evidence, that Prof. Block was in fact the son of the notorious Hermann Goering, head of the Luftwaffe. It now all came together. Block had mistakenly signed his signature, as he would have done as a child and young man. Alternatively, he had done it deliberately. No one would ever know. The importance of the mistake or choice was huge. It meant that Peter now had the true provenance of the model railway. It had always been known that Reichsmarschall Goering was an avid collector of model railways. His personal collection had been hidden during the war and never seen again. That was until Peter had been to his son's house outside Magdeburg. The eight tea chests at Hadleigh Hall housed an historical treasure. One that could be the basis of unification between two devastated cities. Peter could hardly wait to get home that night to tell Mi Sun. His evening clinic passed in a cloud of amazement and euphoria.

Peter and Mi Sun returned to Hadleigh Hall the following weekend and unpacked just one of the tea chests. They selected a short piece of track, one engine, two carriages and a 20volt controller. They arranged a meeting for the end of the next week with the Director of The Imperial War Museum. Before the meeting, Peter made a lengthy phone call to an international lawyer. He wanted confirmation that a gift from the son of a former war criminal was acceptable. Would there be any unknown repercussions. He was assured that it was perfectly legal. Peter was satisfied.

His meeting with the Director of the Imperial War Museum was difficult at first because of the level of disbelief in Peter's story. However as Peter produced the evidence, piece by piece, especially the signature, the Director was eventually convinced. He asked for the address of the house outside Magdeburg, but Peter refused to give it. Peter took the view that it was the right of Prof. Block to remain anonymous. While Peter was still there, the Director made a couple of phone calls. Following these, he agreed to buy the complete set. The money would be used to underwrite the cost of appropriate memorials at both Coventry and Magdeburg. He even offered to provide advisors on the nature of these memorials.

The following year, The Imperial War Museum mounted a memorable exhibition. Hermann Goering's magnificent train set was displayed in its entirety in the Special Exhibition suite on the top floor. It took two months to complete the display and very soon became the most popular exhibit the Museum had ever produced. It was of interest to young and old and drew hundreds of new people to the museum. Such was the interest, that it was displayed for a full year.

On the 14th November of that year, exactly 32 years after 400 bombers had attacked Coventry, a distinctive memorial was dedicated next to Coventry Cathedral. The memorial took the form of two large photographs, placed side by side. One was of Coventry after the raid and the other was of Magdeburg following the RAF bombing on 16th January 1945. Alongside each photograph was an explanation in both German and English. Between the two photographs was a cross, made from metal fragments taken from British and German bombers. It was a fitting tribute to those who had lost their lives and homes in the devastation. On 16th January the next year, an identical memorial was placed next to Magdeburg Cathedral.

Hermann Block, nee Goering, had achieved his ambition to achieve a lasting relationship between the two cities.

CHAPTER 28
LEOPARD

On David's 29th birthday, he received another mysterious, unsigned card. It was of a leopard, but the colouring was not the deep orange and brown on the back, but much lighter. It was more like a dirty white colour, flecked sparingly with brown and black. The message, in its characteristic writing, read:

Dear David,

Happy birthday. Congratulations on your involvement in creating the Belsen Memorial.

This leopard is under serious threat and needs help in its preservation.

If you wish to save it, then your destination has to be Kyrgyzstan. I wish you well.

There it was again; the same phrase at the end of the unsigned message. David thought back to the number of times he had seen this phrase. It had been the start of so many exciting and fruitful adventures. It had started in North Wales with his discovery of the Roman baths, the cavern and the gold. Then finding the extra two verses to Blake's poem and finally the incredible quest for the lost painting. This time, though David was more than a little worried. He wasn't totally sure where Kyrgyzstan was to be found until he looked it up in his world atlas, his gift from Mr. Moran. He found Kyrgyzstan to be a remote and mountainous country in Central Asia, part of the vast USSR. The Tian Shan Mountains covered about 80% of the country and were largely unexplored apart from the few main passes meandering through them.

David spoke to his head of department at the Ordinance Survey and he was granted two weeks of leave, one unpaid, on the condition that he undertook some basic survey work while he was in Kyrgyzstan. He was keen for Laura to join him, not wanting to be away from her for too long. The matter was settled because she'd just found out she was pregnant with twins. She couldn't contemplate a journey of this magnitude, but gave David her blessing. It took a further month to make the necessary preparations.

David had one further task. He was desperate for more information on the leopard in the photograph. He took the photograph to London Zoo and they easily confirmed it was a snow leopard. They said the colouring was wrong, probably caused by over exposure of the photograph. They had none in captivity, but assured David they were indeed under threat. They explained that sightings were very rare and even to see one, let alone photograph it, would be quite a coup.

David took an Aeroflot flight to Moscow, followed the next day by the daily flight to the capital of Kyrgyzstan, Frunze. It was a miserable place, populated by a mixture of locals and Russians, none of whom wanted to mix in any meaningful way. From Frunze the road system was limited, but David managed to find an ancient minibus heading south. His aim was to get to the town of Naryn, which was in the centre of the country and seemed to be the nearest inhabited place to the Central Tian Shan mountains. After travelling for about 60 miles on a pitted and pot-holed road, the minibus stopped in a small village. It was clear the driver planned to go no further. David had bought a map at the airport and tried to show the locals the route he planned to take. There was much discussion amongst the men of the village and eventually an old Landrover was driven into the village square. David was forced to negotiate a ridiculously high price to make use of it, especially as he really had no idea how far the driver was prepared to go on his uncertain journey. He had little option but to accept the only offer open to him. He threw his two rucksacks in the back, determined to make the best of the situation. The drive south was difficult as a conventional road was non-existent. The Landrover negotiated stony and sandy tracks, streams, rocks and scrubland. It took a whole day to cover 100 miles, but the sight ahead was encouraging. Almost since he left the minibus, David could see the magnificent Tian Shan Mountain range ahead, growing ever closer and more daunting. That evening, David and his driver arrived at a small encampment, little more than a dozen gaily coloured yurts, a few horses and three yaks, roaming freely. The driver turned the vehicle around the way they had come, indicating to David this was the limit of his journey. David had no choice. The decision was clear. Using a calendar, David explained to the driver that he would need a return journey in one week. He seemed to understand, although David was unconvinced.

Once again the map came out and David showed the people in the village he now planned to head into the nearby mountains. His plans were met with a combination of mirth, shaking of heads, lack of trust and general indications of David's stupidity. Strangely, the photograph of the leopard seemed to cause particularly interest amongst the people in the village. They showed it around and pointed up into the forbidding mountains ahead. Their English was limited, but between them they managed two words, which all the locals could agree on. The two words were 'white ghost'. Peter was mystified, but could appreciate the spectral dimension of the off white animal shown in his picture.

David produced some American dollars and there was a sudden change in attitude. Over the next two hours, two horses were saddled and one of David's rucksacks was put on each one. A young man, Ozgan, dressed in bright but warm clothing, was assigned as a guide. Ozgan's oriental features, lacked the softness of most of his countrymen, and reminded David of a carving, whittled from a stick. David had never ridden a horse before, but fortunately the pace was steady and he soon became used to the rocking movement of the animal. There were times during steep descents when David felt decidedly uncomfortable and wondered if he would ever stay in the rough saddle. They were now higher than David had ever been before and he started to feel the effects of the rarified atmosphere. His breathing became labored, made worse by his tense muscles as he hung on to the constantly shifting seat. Just before they reached the snow line, the horses were tied loosely to a tree. They could be left to graze and would be safe until their return. David and Ozgan would carry on by foot.

That evening, now well above the snow line, they struck camp, with Ozgan seeming to be quite adept at coping with these conditions. He dug a snow hole for the two of them and lit a fire to melt water and to cook some basic rations. This was a totally new experience for David. He was uncertain whether he would cope with the cold and the rigours of these remote and inhospitable mountains. David was surprised how effective the snow hole was in keeping them warm. David was slightly embarrassed that he slept in a goose down sleeping bag, whereas Ozgan had little more than a blanket and his saddle cover made of a rather coarse fur.

The next day, the welcoming aroma of coffee being brewed over an open fire stirred David's flagging senses. There was no better way to revive the soul than the acidic, yet sweet taste from the strong, dark, freshly ground beans that Ozgan had produced from his saddlebag. The two continued to trek into the higher reaches of the mountain. By now all paths were left far behind and they were forging a new trail through the ever-deepening snow. Breathing became even more laboured and David had to stop every 10-15 steps to recover sufficiently before moving forwards and upwards. At the end of that day, David was exhausted and could do little to help Ozgan prepare a scant meal. The conditions underfoot were now rocks, covered by little more than drift snow. It was impossible to dig a snow hole, so David pulled out his small tent. They both struggled to erect it as the wind had increased steadily and it started to snow. At first it was light snow, but before long it became a total white out. They had already found some rocks to tether the edges of the tent and to the guy ropes, but the prospect of the tent surviving the snowstorm was in serious doubt. Once inside, the buffeting of the wind was quite frightening. They both knew that in conditions like this, there was only one option. They would stay in the tent until the storm blew through and they could risk going back outside. As the storm raged, Ozgan knelt and prayed to his God. David, although not a man given normally to prayer, did so quietly and privately.

The storm vent its anger unceasingly throughout the next two days and nights. The noise made it impossible to talk beyond a few shouted words; time seemed to extend to infinity. The two men could do little more than knock the snow off the tent from inside. To step out would have been far too dangerous in conditions like this. It was early morning of the third day in the tent when Ozgan woke David from his fitful sleep. The difference was striking. The howling wind had gone and the quiet of the place had produced, in its own way, an uncanny, almost eerie sensation. The two men, still dressed in their outdoor clothes, unzipped the tent door and looked out into the bleak and silent world. It was light, but the sun had yet to rise above the adjacent peaks. They looked around to assess the aftermath from the storm. Their first job was to move the snow piled up around the tent. As they did this, the sun slowly appeared and they could now see the pure white of the surrounding terrain. It was bleak and inhospitable. Both men, unused to such conditions, were in turn alarmed and impressed by the awesome features around them. The snow-covered mountains had a majesty of their own. The two just stared in silence at the fearsome, yet sublime panorama surrounding their little tent. As they stared, quite uncertain of their next move, David noticed a line of soft indentations in the snow. They looked more carefully and as the light improved, they could see that these were animal tracks. The size and shape meant the paws of a huge, cat-like beast could only have made them. The path of the tracks came down from way above them, right up to the back of the tent, and then returned to the height above.

"We had a visitor in the night," said David hesitantly.

Ozgan looked closely at the tracks.

"It can only be the white ghost," he said, his voice edged with alarm.

"So," said David, "with the weather as it is, this may be our only chance to catch a glimpse of our elusive quarry."

Ozgan was concerned. His culture had taught him not to step over the boundaries of certainty. He tried to explain to David that for generations people had talked of the white ghost. Yet none of his people had actually seen it. He, with his halting English, tried his best to explain that they were in the land of legend. Legend was to remain untouched. It was not to be disturbed by the self-interest of any man. It could only bring bad luck to venture into the land of legend. It was best to let it be. David tried his best to understand Ozgan's reluctance, but his own quest was even stronger. David struggled with the rift in their cultures, so suggested that Ozgan should stay with the tent and he would go on alone. This seemed to satisfy Ozgan's deeply held belief and with reluctance they decided to part. It was agreed that it would be no more than a day. David would follow the tracks, but would only carry provisions for the day and would return that night to the safety of the tent. David packed up a plastic emergency bag, his precious camera, his head torch, binoculars and a few emergency rations ready to last the day. They shook hands and David, now with crampons again firmly attached to his boots, set off uphill.

At first it was not difficult to follow the trail of animal tracks. The route was arduous. David often sunk up to his knees in soft snow. At other times the snow gave way to bare rock and he needed to scramble over the precipitous surface. After three hours, David was exhausted from the climb and had no option but to rest. There was now a light breeze and David found a spot behind a boulder to shield a little from the wind. He took out his binoculars and spent a few minutes scanning the horizon above the valley ahead. At first he could see nothing. Then his eye caught a few loose rocks, dislodged from high above, cascading down the mountain. He trained his binoculars on this, the only sign of movement in an otherwise featureless landscape. He looked just above the place where the rocks had been dislodged.

Then he saw it. Hardly perceptible, yet a slow, languid movement across the snow, revealed the faint outline of a big cat. It was so well hidden in the depths of the snow, that it was movement alone that showed its presence. When it stopped, it became invisible. It stopped; it disappeared. It moved; it reappeared. Slowly and serenely, the animal came down the mountain until it reached a path on the far side of the valley. At first David was mesmerized into immobility. He then pulled his camera from his rucksack and clipped on his telephoto lens. He rested his elbows on the surrounding rock and trained the viewfinder on the far valley. In doing this, David's attention shifted away from the snow leopard to focus on his camera. It took what seemed like an age, yet was probably only seconds, to find the wondrous beast again. There it was, still on the path. David could see it now with amazing clarity. Its small rounded ears and broad paws were beautifully adapted to the cold and snowy conditions. Its long, thick tail would give it balance as it leapt from rock to rock and would wrap around its body for warmth when sleeping. Most remarkable of all was its colour; almost entirely white with just the odd flecks of brown and black. It blended entirely with its environment. For a moment in time, David and the leopard were both cast in a cloak of invisibility. Their steps were silenced; their heartbeats in harmony; they were breathing the same still air. It was perfect.

For a fraction of a second it moved in front of a brown coloured rock and for the first time, David had a distinct outline. The shutter clicked. It moved again. David tracked it and the shutter clicked again and again. It stopped. It seemed to be rubbing its mouth on a rock as if either preening or trying to dislodge something from its teeth. David was uncertain. It moved again, very slightly. The camera clicked. David pressed the button again, but the camera fell silent. Surely he had more film. His camera was fully loaded. David had checked, but there was no response. David then remembered the warning. The batteries will die in the cold he'd been told. He undid the battery compartment and thrust the two batteries inside his coat. He waited. How long to rewarm them? He had no idea. He put them back in the camera and it came back to life. He trained the viewfinder once more on the path across the valley. He found the spot where the animal had rubbed its mouth. It had gone. He waited for fully thirty minutes. The snow leopard was not to be seen again.

The sun was starting to hide behind the towering peaks, but David was determined to reach the spot where he'd seen the leopard rub the side of his mouth. He wasn't sure why, but his intuition drove him on. He tried to maintain height, but had little option but to descend part of the valley and then work his way up the other side. It was difficult terrain, but David had confidence in his crampons and walking poles. After much effort, he made his way up from the valley floor to the path where he'd seen the leopard. He then followed the snow-covered and precipitously narrow path to the point where he thought the leopard had stopped. It was difficult to judge the exact spot, but luckily the tracks seemed to deepen at one particular place, almost as though the animal was gaining more purchase on the ground. This, David decided, would be the spot. He looked closely at the side of the path. There on the rocks, at a height of about three feet, were distinctive marks of rubbing or scratching. He took a knife and a plastic bag from his rucksack and scraped off everything he could from the surface of the rock. It was difficult in those cold and windy conditions to see exactly what he was collecting, but he thought it might include some animal hair or even a whisker. He wasn't sure, but knew that this wasn't the time for analysis. This would be best achieved later in a specialist laboratory. Anyway, he thought, time was now against him. The light started to fade fast; he needed to move. David retraced his footsteps and made his way back through the valley to the spot from where he'd photographed the leopard. He paused for a moment, took one look back and then pressed on towards the tent and safety. He could see clouds building up over the mountaintops and he feared the weather might change. The clouds darkened and this was soon followed by light snow. The snow, although light, very soon covered the animal tracks he was following to guide him home. He had taken a series of compass readings on the way up and these were now his best hope for a safe return. David's inexperience of these conditions was to take a heavy toll. He was unaware how the sun can melt the surface of the snow and refreeze, as it gets cold again in the evening. As he descended what was a safe route on the way up, his crampons slipped on sheet ice and he slipped a few feet. He tried to dig into the snow, but with no ice axe, it was hopeless. The short slip became a tumble and the tumble became a plunge. He plunged some 50 yards down a rocky slope until he came to a jarring stop. At first there was no sound apart from David's heavy and rasping breath as he recovered from the fall. Then the pain hit him. It came from his left ankle. As David looked down he could see it was at an unnatural angle, jutting far too far out to the left. He feared the worst. In a place like this, a broken ankle could be a killer. He gobbled down six paracetamol to try to relieve the pain. He kept his boot on to act as a temporary splint and used his plastic emergency bag to bind his ankle and lower leg as best he could. He had little option but to struggle on. Every time he put his left foot to the ground, the pain was horrendous. He put all the weight he could on his walking poles, but it made little difference. The only respite he could get was to try to lift his ankle clear of the ground, but this made progress almost impossible. In the end, he found that the best way was to drag his left lower leg behind him, usually using his left knee as a brace or in contact with the ground. This was less agonizing, but more exhausting and his progress was painfully slow. In the dark, his path lit only by the light of his head torch, the route was almost impossible to follow.

There were times when David felt utter despair and just wanted to curl up in the snow. There was a constant struggle for air. He developed a sore throat combined with an unbearable thirst. But David didn't have the means to melt the snow. His head was pounding uncontrollably. The thought of Laura and his unborn twins, gave him that little bit of extra motivation to keep going. As he neared the point where even his thoughts of home could no longer sustain him, he thought he saw, a long way in the distance, a dim light. This gave him a final surge of adrenaline and he struggled on for another 20 yards. Then he finally collapsed. He was totally spent, unable to move. He no longer cared. It was the end. As he drifted into unconsciousness, his final and mellow sensation was the spectre of a white ghost brushing past him.

He was being lifted, half dragged, half carried down the mountainside. David drifted in and out of consciousness. He was in the tent. A hot drink was put to his lips. His boots were off and he was in the heavenly depths of his sleeping bag. He swallowed more painkillers. He slept the sleep of utter exhaustion, despite the pain. As he started to recover from the shock of his ordeal, he knew it wasn't yet over. The two of them must get back to the village and away from the dangers of the high ground. It was going to be tough. As they took the tent down, Ozgan used the main pole to shape into a crutch for David. After a few steps it started to bend. The aluminium was too fragile for David's weight. There was no option but to use his walking poles and put all his weight on them as he walked, lifting his left leg at every step. It was slow going, but the two men made steady progress down the mountain, with Ozgan supporting David over the steepest parts. It took two days to reach the horses and a further two days to ride back to the village. As the horses worked their way down the rocky trail, a surge of pain marked every jarring step. He finished the last of his painkillers, and David, his ankle now a dull, throbbing pain, was reminded constantly of his fall. David had lost any sense of time, with each day merging into the next.

When they eventually arrived at the circle of yurts, there was no sign of the Landrover to take him back to Naryn. The villagers looked at his swollen ankle with interest. They took lichen from a nearby tree and it was cooked in a pot of water. When it became a paste, they smeared it on his ankle. Almost immediately, David felt the pain subside. His ankle was still swollen, so it was bandaged tightly with strips of cloth taken from the drapes in one of the yurts. He was given the rest of the lichen paste and told to spread it on his ankle daily. They waited optimistically for most of the day, and then the Landrover emerged, almost reluctantly from the surrounding hills. David was made comfortable sitting in the back with his foot resting on the seat. He thanked the villagers for their kindness, especially Ozgan. Before he left he turned to Ozgan to ask the question that had been intriguing him the most.

"Ozgan," he said, "you never told me why you left the tent that night and found me half dead on the mountain."

"It was the white ghost," he said, turning the palms of his hands and eyes to the heavens."

"The white ghost?" David questioned.

"Yes, David. That night I was about to go to bed when I heard a soft mewing outside the tent. I was very afraid, but opened the tent door a little and shone my torch into the dark. Her green eyes shone, no more than ten feet away. She moved in your direction then stopped. She looked back. She turned slowly away from me. Then she ran off up the mountain. For some reason, my fear left me. I followed her tracks in the snow and they led me to you. The white ghost saved you."

David now recognized the universal truth. Men need their strange animals, their myths and legends and old tales. These alone help to embody man's fears. Not so the immediate fears of the charging bull, but the fears outside oneself. The fears where mental courage and hope can be fought and conquered. David was relieved that the images in his camera were his alone. The legend of the white ghost was safe in the illusionary mind of Ozgan.

Back in Frunze, David went straight to the city hospital. His ankle was examined and X-rayed. There was found to be no breakage, but evidence of serious ligament damage; ligaments that had repaired well. The doctors found it unbelievable that the ligaments had recovered so quickly. In their professional opinion, ligament damage this extensive should take about six weeks to heal. He was considered lucky. David put his recovery down not to luck, but a strange poultice made from lichen. He knew the medical and scientific community would never believe him. He was given a light walking plaster and returned home on the first available plane.

Back home in Southampton, David recounted his strange and often frightening experiences to Laura. She was intrigued, pleased to see him home, but struggled to find the purpose of it all.

"All you seem to have," said Laura, "is some photographs of a snow leopard, no great difference from the one in the photo you were sent for your birthday."

"Not quite," said David, "I am sure the leopard I saw was different. It was almost pure white, with hardly any of the markings of a normal snow leopard."

David then removed the plastic bag from his rucksack.

"This is the only other evidence I have, although I doubt if it will add much to the mystery. It's the material I gathered from where the leopard had rubbed against a rock."

"And what are your plans for that?"

"I'll take it with the photographs back to London Zoo. They may have methods for identification."

The photographs were developed the next week and the quality was impressive. David had managed some excellent pictures of the snow leopard and regretted not getting more before the batteries failed. He took these and the contents of his precious plastic bag to London Zoo. He was asked to leave a copy of the photographs and the bag with the Zoo authorities. There were apparently two possible options. The first was that he had photographed a mutant snow leopard, a one off, a bit like an albino. The other, less likely possibility, was that he had indeed found a sub-species. The second option would be of much greater interest. It would be a find of major scientific significance. They also explained that, although it was in the early days of forensic analysis, the material he had brought back could help enormously in deciding which option was correct. He should find out in about a month.

David went back to work, still wondering if the whole expedition had been worthwhile. It very nearly cost him his life and to what benefit? A month to the day, he received a letter in an enveloped marked from the Zoological Society of London. He waited until Laura and he were together before opening it. It read,

Dear Mr. Clarke,

Thank you for giving us the opportunity to study the photographs and material you collected in Kyrgyzstan. The quality of the photographs suggested that you had found either a mutant specimen of snow leopard or a new sub-species.

The analysis of the material, using a new DNA technique developed at the Laboratory of Molecular Biology at Cambridge, has indicated the latter. As importantly, was the single whisker you retrieved. We now know that the base of the whisker, with the small amount of skin attached, is crucial in identifying species differences. It appears to be as specific as a single fingerprint.

We can confirm that you have observed and provided substantive evidence for a subspecies.

As the first person in the world to provide this evidence, you have the naming rights. Panthera uncia is the species name, and you could add a further Latin genitive term. Some people use their own name, others the area of the habitat. It is your choice.

As this find is such a rare phenomenon, I would be grateful if you could write an official report for the Journal of Zoology and present your findings at the next meeting of the Linnean Society.

I await confirmation of your willingness to do so.

With kind regards

Sir Henry Atkinson, Chair, Zoological Society of London

Prof. P.A.McIntire, Head of the Laboratory of Molecular Biology, University of Cambridge

David and Laura were stunned by the news and fascinated by the prospect of naming the new sub-species. They discussed options well into the night and eventually decided to give the honour to the one person who had made it possible. Not David, but the one who saved his life. The new sub-species was to be called Panthera uncia ozgani.

David's paper in the Journal of Zoology received critical acclaim and the more serious national newspapers took great interest in his story. His presentation at the Linnean Society meeting was his first opportunity to respond to questions about the trip. Inevitably there were a few doubters in the audience, but the combination of his photographs and the forensic evidence seemed even to satisfy them. It was a tradition for all new species or subspecies to be recorded in an ancient, leather bound tome, with the signature of the finder beneath. David Clarke joined a long list, which included such luminaries as Charles Darwin, Carl Linnaeus and Gertrude Jekyll.

During the dinner of the Linnean Society, David was able to broach the subject of conservation with a number of members. It was subsequently agreed that the Society should mount an expedition to Kyrgyzstan in the hope of capturing some cubs for breeding purposes. This would ensure the survival of the sub-species. It was planned for two years time and David was invited to be a member of the team. By then he would have two year old twins and he wondered if he could possibly leave them for as long as a month. He may have to leave them for even longer…

CHAPTER 29
CRICKET

The mid-summer cricket match at Hadleigh Cricket Club had been a tradition for over 70 years. The Viscounts of Culham for the last three generations had always captained the Hadleigh team. It had a mixture of players from the village, from Hall staff and a few 'ringers', county players who were invited to strengthen the team. It was in principle a fun event, but always played competitively. This year the visiting team was the Ordinance Survey team, on tour in Shropshire for a week. David was no cricketer, largely because his 'polio ankle' stopped him running but he had agreed to travel with the team as the scorer. It wasn't absolutely essential to have a scorer with the team, but David had a number of good friends in the side. It promised to be an enjoyable week, combining cricket with plenty of food and drink.

It was a glorious day in the Shropshire countryside. The setting, next to the Church of our Lady the Virgin, and surrounded by the low estate hills was perfect. The sky was blue, with the odd wispy cloud, and the sun so high at this time of year that the sightscreens were hardly necessary. The Ordinance Survey team won the toss and chose to bat first. Their opening pair stayed at the wicket for over an hour, but only managed to score 33 runs between them. The partnership was broken by a careless run out and during the next over the other opener was sent back to the pavilion clean bowled. As the morning progressed, the run rate increased slowly but steadily and by lunchtime, the visitors had scored 107 runs for five wickets. Both teams mixed happily over a light lunch of salad, a selection of cold pies and a dessert of Hadleigh Mess, a rather alcoholic variety of the better-known Eton Mess.

After lunch the cricket resumed its languid pace, with the visitors scoring steadily if not in any spectacular fashion. During a poor call, one batsman was scampering to reach the crease when his foot slipped and he twisted his ankle badly. He was helped off the pitch and ice was called from the bar to try to ease the rapidly swelling joint. David recalled his own injury in Kyrgyzstan and quickly realized this was far from a superficial injury. His colleague needed specialist treatment and arrangements were quickly made to take him to the nearest hospital offering emergency care. After this, the innings soon came to an end, with the visitors having scored a respectable 220 runs. The captain of the Ordinance Survey team turned to David and asked him to take the field. David was reluctant as he had little experience of cricket beyond enforced games during PE lessons at school. He also explained about his problem with running, but it was suggested that he could field on the boundary, well out of harms way. David reluctantly agreed and, after a short break, the Hadleigh team took the field.

Peter Culham, opened the batting with his father Neil. The pair put on a creditable 53 runs before Neil was caught behind the wicket after edging the ball to first slip. Peter scored another 20 runs before being clean bowled trying to hook over square leg. The match continued at a steady pace with successes on both sides. Towards the end, the visitors, needed the last wicket to win, but the score had crept up to a tantalizing 217 runs for the Hadleigh team. They needed just four runs to win the match, but the visitors only needed one more wicket. The last Hadleigh batsman couldn't resist the temptation to gain glory with a final flourish and hit a loose ball long and high. It sailed into the air and dropped out of the clear blue sky near the boundary patrolled by David. He moved as quickly as he could to the left as the ball dropped like a stone towards the boundary. David reached out and then, in spite of his ankle, leaped high in the air to grasp at the ball taking it in one far-flung hand. The small crowd watched in amazement at the brilliant catch. Then, as if watching in slow motion, David fell to earth and landed with the toe of one foot just touching the thick boundary rope. It was over. Hadleigh had won.

The Ordinance Survey team made a double line and clapped in the two batsmen. Hands were shaken and the two teams retired to the small pavilion for a late, but welcome, tea. It had been a superb game of cricket and everyone was enjoying the occasion.

"Bad luck, David" said the Ordinance Survey captain. "That was almost the catch of the century. And on your birthday as well."

"Your birthday," chimed in Peter Culham, from the other side of the table.

"That's strange, it's mine as well. A double celebration."

As he spoke, a huge birthday cake was carried in from the kitchen. It was covered in little icing cricketers, all arranged on a green iced surface.

"Plenty for everyone," Peter shouted, "but leave a couple of pieces for the two birthday boys."

The general hubbub of the cricketers was soon drowned by the rasping sound of the bar grill being opened. The scraping of chairs quickly followed this noise as some of he home team stood to fetch jugs of beer to toast the visitors and their own close victory.

A little later, Peter took David to one side.

"Great effort on the catch," said Peter, "No one would have complained if that rope hadn't caught your foot."

"Kind of you," David replied, "you know, haven't we met somewhere before?"

"Strange you should say that," said Peter, "I had exactly the same feeling."

The two men then had a long conversation trying to work out when or where it could have been. At last they both remembered the occasion.

"Of course," the two said almost together. "It was the colours dinner, " said David. "You got a blue for cross country and I got an honorary blue from the boat club."

"That's it," Peter confirmed, "now I remember. What a night that was. Do you remember the state the rugby club boys were in?"

"How could you forget?" David added, as the two of them shook hands.

"What did you read?" Peter said.

"Geography, and you?"

"Medicine. Strangely, I'm back at Cambridge now, working as a senior registrar. Are you all staying at the Culham Arms?"

"Just for the night. Then we travel on to play a team in Shrewsbury."

"Great, I've got a plan. To celebrate our joint birthdays, let's take up a helicopter. The views of this part of Shropshire are quite superb, especially on an evening like this. Are you up for it?"

David hesitated.

"I've never flown in a helicopter."

"Brilliant. Then here's your chance. It'll be fun. I'll pick you up later. No better still, let's have a quick shower here and go straight to the airfield. By the time we're back the party will have hardly got going. No one will even miss us."

So it was arranged. Ten minutes later, the two young men were in Peter's MG Midget heading for Boving Green airfield. On the way to Boving Green, they chatted about their time at Cambridge, reliving some of their experiences, perhaps with a modicum of exaggeration.

David was surprised to see that there was no one at the airfield when they arrived. Peter explained that it was quite normal. He knew the codes for all the gates and walked straight over to a small low building which seemed to be some type of flight office. Peter filled in a large book with his details, filed a brief flight plan and picked up two pairs of headphones. The pair strode over to one of two helicopters on a stand near the perimeter of the airfield.

"It's not a popular time to fly this late in the day, so I guessed we wouldn't have any trouble," said Peter. "If you wait here, I'll do a quick safety check and inspect the fuel levels. Then we'll be off."

"Is it really that simple?" said David, a little surprised.

"Oh yes. We pay a fortune to have these fellows serviced, they're always good to go."

The two climbed into the cabin and Peter, following a detailed safety manual, went through all the internal checks.

"OK. Switch your headset on and we'll get airborne. Without these things, you'll never hear a thing. That's the worse thing about the chopper, it's so bloody noisy."

Peter switched on the engines and looked all around carefully. He skillfully adjusted the collective, altering the pitch angle of the rotors and eased the helicopter into the air. Caressing the cyclic, a long stick between his knees, Peter adjusted the tilt of the craft, always in perfect synchrony with the foot pedals controlling the rudders. He made it look easy, but David was convinced it was an art based on considerable practice.

David found the ride quite exhilarating. They flew a sort of zigzag course around the area, picking out the distinctive features of the Long Mynd, Wenlock Edge and the Wrekin with ease. There was a bit of static through the headset, but David could hear Peter mentioning some of the small towns and villages as they flew along.

"Tell you what would be fun," David heard Peter say. "Why don't we land on the cricket field at Hadleigh? What a surprise that would be for the lads back there. Might even sober a few of them up."

Peter didn't even wait for a reply. His mind was made up. It took about fifteen minutes to fly towards the village of Hadleigh and David was the first to spot the steeple of the Church of our Lady the Virgin on the right hand side. He pointed it out to Peter, who skillfully flew the helicopter until it was about 200 feet above the cricket field. This was the very field that had just witnessed a day of most enjoyable competition.

It was then that the helicopter blew up.

CHAPTER 30
FIREBALL

No one actually saw the explosion. Those nearest were in the cricket pavilion, still socializing after the match. The noise was quite unbelievable, like a massive roll of metallic thunder, and the players rushed outside to see a blazing inferno in the middle of the pitch. Someone ran to nearby Hadleigh Hall to phone for the emergency services, but it was clear that no one could be saved. The fireball lasted for all of 30 minutes producing a ghastly pall of black smoke. The stench of burning plastic and rubber hung silently in the air. The putrid smell of charred flesh soon wafted across the burned cricket field. It lingered in the nostrils of those watching the gruesome scene. They were all witness to a spectacle of abject horror. The fire brigade and ambulance arrived swiftly but it was far too late. At first it wasn't even possible to see it was a helicopter that had caused the blaze, such was the level of devastation. All that could be seen was a twisted wreck of machinery, a jumbled mass of distorted metal. The fire brigade sent spumes of water on to the wreckage, and this turned the fire to steam and then smoke as the fire came under control. It was only then that a semblance of a helicopter could be seen. The cabin had simply disappeared. Any person or any thing inside had been literally cremated. It was quite the most appalling and shocking sight for anyone to see. Some of the cricketers were physically sick. It was the most hideous thing they could imagine. They knew it had meant a horrendous and macabre death. They just hoped it had been quick.

To add to the misery, the charred remains could not be moved. Everything had to stay in the centre of the cricket field until the aviation crash inspectors had finished their report. The next day three men in white protective overalls combed through the wreckage, more in hope than optimism. The two bodies were burned beyond recognition. In fact it was worse. The intensity of the flames had vapourised the cadavers to grey dust. Of course, the occupants were known. The logbook at Boving Green airfield said it all. Peter Culham and David Clarke were no more.

Laura, David's wife, was absolutely devastated. She could hardly bring herself to speak for a few days. She found some comfort in keeping herself busy with the twins. Her parents came to stay until she could start to make plans for the future. The pain never eased.

Mi Sun, Peter's wife, was horrified but more stoical. She had seen death and destruction in her own country and was more accepting of the traumas of life. Peter's parents went to stay close to her for a few days but found it more convenient to book into a local hotel. It gave her some comfort to have them nearby, but after a short time, she felt the need to face the future alone. The thought of returning to Hadleigh Hall, in full view of the crash site, was too much for Mi Sun. She only ever went back once, and that was on the day of Peter's funeral.

The aviation crash report took over a month and the inquest was postponed until its findings were made known. The intensity of the flames had destroyed all useful evidence. It was not even known if there had been an engine failure during flight or if an electrical fault could have ignited a fuel tank. There were no witnesses to the disaster, so no one knew if the craft had exploded prior to impact. The usual conspiracy theories were considered such as terrorist involvement. All were dismissed as fanciful. The only certainty was that the fuel tanks would have ignited to create such a fireball. There was no evidence from the airport records of inadequate servicing. Everything was in order.

The inquests, held independently as was the custom, could add little except provide the official cause of death. The coroner could make no particular recommendations because none were to be made.

At the end of the official proceedings, the coroner asked to speak privately to both sets of parents.

The Culhams met the coroner in a back room behind his office. They were still traumatized by what had happened, even after three months. They sat silently as the coroner turned to address them.

"Viscount and Viscountess Culham, there is something important I need to tell you both. Something surprising has only just come to light. Allow me to explain. As you are aware, your son was burnt beyond recognition. There was one other person with him. It was totally impossible to know which of the two occupants was sitting where in the cabin. We all hope and pray that both their deaths were swift. It is of little reassurance to you all, but the report suggests that this was the case. However there is something the report did not state because it was considered too sensitive. The crash forensic team found in the wreckage two tiny fragments of skin. They were found on different sides of the wreckage, implying that they were from different people. Normally of little consequence, but recent developments in forensic science have made it significant"

"Recent developments?" enquired Neil Culham.

"Yes. A Dr. Prentice at Leicester University is in the early stages of developing a technique to analyse DNA with reference to profiling individuals. It is hoped that in time the technique will allow, at some time in the future, to identify individuals from a microscopic piece of human material, from saliva even."

"I'm sorry, but I can't see where this is leading," interjected Neil Culham again, showing his frustration."

"Well, as I said, it is very early days, but some preliminary information has come to light. With your permission, Dr. Prentice has asked if he could keep this specimen and as his technique improves, he may be able to tell you more. Can I ask your permission now?"

Peter's parents gave their agreement. They had no real understanding of the implications of the request, but saw no harm in giving consent.

"And now to the sensitive matter that I mentioned earlier in this conversation. I have here an envelope containing the information that Dr. Prentice has provided to date. My earnest suggestion is that you take the envelope home before opening it. That is the best way for you to decide what action, if any, to take."

With that, the coroner stood up, took an envelope out of a drawer in his desk and gave it them. He shook their hands and left the room. The Culhams returned to Hadleigh Hall, intrigued, yet still in shock from the loss of their only son.

The Clarkes met with the coroner a week later and the inquest followed a similar pattern. The coroner, once again, repeated his condolences and requested a private meeting. As before, they were told about the two pieces of skin found at the crash site. Like the Culhams, they were told about the ongoing developments at Leicester University and handed an envelope. The only difference between the two meetings was that Maggie and Bill Clarke showed less frustration. They didn't interrupt the coroner, as Neil Culham was apt to do. They remained silent in their grief.

As suggested by the coroner, both sets of parents waited until they were home before opening the envelopes. Inside was a single sheet of paper, headed Biochemical Department, University of Leicester. It said,

To whom it may concern,

My preliminary analysis reveals that the two skin specimens may have come from different individuals. However, If this were the case, then these two individuals are closely related. The provisional DNA analysis implies that they were half brothers. I would wish to emphasize that this interpretation is totally dependent on the assumption that the two skin samples originate from different people.

Colin Prentice, Senior Lecturer

Both sets of parents were intrigued by this potential revelation. Celia Culham was quick to dismiss the suggestion as nonsense, although she of all people wasn't sure which of her former boyfriends could have been a father to Peter. Maggie Clarke was more circumspect. She accepted that David's biological father could have fathered other children. It was a topic that she and Bill had never discussed. They had built their lives on the present not the past. The implied coincidence was simply beyond belief. They all assumed that the skin samples were from the same person. Nothing more was said.

Celia Culham and Maggie Clarke had not seen each other for thirty years. As the inquests were independent, neither met, They were obviously aware that the two boys were born on the same day from their time at The London Hospital. Their dates of birth were not considered relevant to the inquests and were not revealed at the time. Celia and Maggie, privately and independently, knew that the two boys died on the very day of their 30th birthday. It was June 24th 1974.

CHAPTER 31
FUNERALS

Peter's funeral was held in the Church of Our Lady the Virgin next to Hadleigh Hall. On the evening before, Peter's empty coffin was placed in the church so the prayer vigil could take place. Close family, and a few people who knew Peter well, gathered to say prayers around the coffin. In the background, the organ played quietly, while the mourners stood in thought, lost in their personal memories. The priest read from the bible, his voice sometimes reduced to no more than a whisper with the emotion of the occasion. Celia asked Neil to say a few words, as she felt unable to speak. His eulogy was brief, accurate and spoken with a certain detachment. He read:

Peter was known to all of us here as a man of great charm and capability. From an early age, he loved to run and this reached its highest level when he was awarded a blue at Cambridge University. At Cambridge he studied medicine and went on to become a doctor of considerable distinction. His seminal work on oxygen therapy and his development of the pulse oximeter resulted in him being awarded the Holter Prize by the Royal Society of Medicine. But Peter's achievements went way beyond medicine. When he was still a teenager, something took him to Hamburg. There he managed to find some tapes and demo discs. With a little help from me, I think it would not be unreasonable to say that The Beatles were launched into their stellar career. Four years ago, Peter embarked on a totally different mission. Somehow he managed to discover what is now known as St Brendan's Isle hidden in the ocean, far to the west of Scotland. This discovery was not enough for Peter. His next adventure too him back to Germany, where he single handedly discovered a model railway, belonging to none other than Reichsmarschall Goering. If you haven't already seen it, it's still exhibited at the Imperial War Museum. Peter's short life was full of surprises and achievements. None of us know what he could have gone on to accomplish. God has chosen to take him early. God has chosen...

Viscount Culham stopped in mid sentence. It seemed right. The last act of the prayer vigil was for the priest to sprinkle the coffin with holy water and drape it with a white pall.

The next day at 12 noon the Requiem Mass was held, commemorating Christ's death and resurrection. This was of great comfort to the faithful at the funeral, believing that Peter was joining Christ in heaven. The first hymn was And Did Those Feet in Ancient Time, Peter's old school hymn, and the reading from the Old Testament was Psalm 100. The priest read from the gospel. He chose John 14, verses 1-6. It started Do not let your hearts be troubled and ended with I am the way and the truth and the life. Viscount Culham gave the eulogy once more, the one he had read at the prayer vigil the night before. This time he included a reference to Mi Sun, an omission that was pointed out to him overnight by Celia. The priest, once again, sprinkled the coffin, with holy water and incense. The final hymn was Praise My Soul, the King of Heaven.

The mourners then all moved out of the church and into the churchyard. Mi Sun, Celia, Neil and a few close family members stood by the grave as the priest committed the coffin to the ground. Mi Sun took a handful of soil and sprinkled it carefully over the coffin. Celia, her hand gloved, threw a handful of soil on the coffin and Neil followed her lead. All recited the Lord's Prayer and the priest chanted a final blessing. It was over.

As the mourners moved away from the churchyard, a tall man in a long black coat and standing alone, turned his back on the church. His dark glasses hid a solitary tear.

That evening the remaining family shared a sombre meal at Hadleigh Hall. Unsurprisingly it was far from a joyous occasion.

*   *   *   *   *

David's celebration of life was held at St Andrew's, Witchford, the church where he and Laura had married. The church was overflowing with family, friends and local people.

David's mother, Maggie, sat with Bill, slightly to one side After the introductions, the first hymn was O Lord my God! When I in Awesome Wonder. The family chose it because they knew David loved the second verse, which referred to woods, forests and mountains. One of the readings was also John, Chapter 14 verses 1-6, but at David's funeral, verse 27 had been thoughtfully added. It seemed an appropriate verse to add as a form of blessing. It read:

Peace I leave with you, my peace I give you. I do not give to you as the world gives. Do not let your hearts be troubled and do not be afraid.

Laura read the poem 'You can shed tears that he is gone, Or you can smile because he has lived'. It was heart breaking to hear her struggling with the words. There were times when she needed to pause to compose herself, but she coped with the emotion magnificently. David's mother, Maggie, sat with Bill, yet strangely alone with her thoughts. No mother should ever bury her children. The path of life should not be trodden this way. Maggie could only accept that this particular path had not been straight.

A friend from school recounted stories from David's time at King's Ely. One of the members of the blue boat at Cambridge, all of whom were there, recalled their times together. Both these accounts had flashes of humour, which lightened the occasion and made it more of a celebration of life than a sterile funeral. David's brother, Iain, talked about him as only brothers can. He recalled moments of family life, talked about David's love for Laura and his little twins. He stood at the front without notes and just talked as though he was with a group of friends. His eulogy was short and tried to reach to the core of his brother. He said:

David was a wonderful man in every way. He had a great capacity for love; for Laura, the twins, his family and virtually anyone who knew him. He had a zest for life in every way. He had a number of disappointments along the way, especially in his sporting life, but he rose above all that. He was an adventurer. Life, for him was one big adventure and he grasped it with both hands. He would go on strange missions to faraway places, but always find out something new or exciting. For some of these exploits, he won awards, but these meant little to him compared with the friendships he made along the way. It is sad that a person of such potential should die at such a young age, but it is not the end. Today is a celebration of David's joyous life. When we lose someone we love, we must learn not to live without them, but to live with the love they left behind. The memories David made with all of us will live on. Nothing can change the present, so we all should be glad that we were able to share a little of David, while he was still alive. Why don't we all stand together and clap David into heaven. The angels might even hear us.

The congregation welcomed the suggestion and applauded vigorously.

Other hymns were sung, including 'Thine Be The Glory', another of David's favourites, and finishing with 'Guide Me O Thou Great Redeemer.' This final hymn was sung with great gusto, those in the packed church knowing that this was what David would have wanted. Everyone was invited back to the church hall for tea and sandwiches. People who hadn't seen each other for years were reacquainted, more memories were shared and as people started to leave, the atmosphere was far from sad.

One person didn't stay for tea. He was a tall man, dressed in a long black coat and wearing dark glasses. He was cautious as he walked slowly away. He moved in a way that suggested his eyesight was failing him.

Laura had been given a casket of ashes by the air accident investigation team and arrangements were made to have then scattered in two places. One was at the river at Henley; one was at the start of the boat race course. Both places were chosen because they represented places where David had once wanted to be, but never quite made it. It symbolised David facing and surviving his personal demons. Those present at the scattering of the ashes were convinced that not only had he survived his demons, but had grown in strength as a consequence.

CHAPTER 32
DEATHS

Maggie, David's mother, had not been well for some time. She started to lose weight and after various consultations, was diagnosed with lung cancer. She went through the unforgiving treatment of chemotherapy and radiotherapy, which seemed to halt the disease. But not for long. She struggled constantly with her addiction of cigarette smoking. She knew it was stupid and very likely to have been the cause of her illness, but still found some perverted pleasure in the deadly nicotine. She cut down on her cigarette consumption, but couldn't stop completely for any length of time. It wouldn't have made any difference. Eventually the pernicious disease ravaged her lungs and body. She would cough violently and repeatedly. It was horrendous for the family to see her suffering, but there was little that could be done as the ghastly illness took its inevitable hold. She would cough up blood, trying to hide it in her handkerchief, but those close to her knew. As the cancer spread, she was given morphine for the pain, at first in small doses. It was never enough. Towards the end, she became bedridden. The family always hoped for recovery, but she knew in her own heart that it was not to be. A good friend, a health visitor like herself, nursed her at home. Her friend could do little more than offer the pain-relieving opioid in greater quantities to ease the pain. As her death became inevitable, Maggie was offered a large dose of morphine. It would kill the pain. It would shorten her life. She refused. She hung on to life's tenuous thread for hours longer. Her husband Bill and her son Iain were with her to the end.

As she slipped into the finality of fatal unconsciousness, her last words were "Where's David?" There was no time to give her an answer. Following that brief question, Maggie took a shallow breath. As she exhaled, the resonant rattle in her throat registered her last. She alone could choose the depth of her belief in a life to follow death.

After the funeral at the local Methodist Church, Bill asked Iain and his wife, Sandra, to help empty the house of Maggie's belongings. There were a few clothes and other items that could be sent to a charity shop. It was decided to burn the rest of her clothes and personal items. Bill wanted it that way. He had his memories. He didn't need Maggie's physical effects to live on with him into the future. The years of a happy, gentle marriage were enough. A marriage that had only just survived its early traumatic events during the times of war.

The cupboard drawers in the bedroom were emptied and the contents brought downstairs to the bonfire in the back garden. Laura and the twins had generously come over to help. The twins, totally unaware of the significance of it all, were enjoying the smells and sight of the bonfire. Laura was keeping a watchful eye on them when Sandra came down from upstairs and gave her a small packet.

"I think these may be love letters. I suggest you look after them," said Sandra. Laura looked at the bundle of letters, tied in a blue ribbon, with interest. Later that day, she undid the ribbon and sorted through a small number of letters. They were indeed love letters, mostly dated from just before the end of the war. Amongst one was a poem, written in a hand she vaguely recognised. There was also a photograph of a young man. She was shocked to see that she could have been looking at David. The hairstyle was slightly different, but in every other respect it was David. One of the letters had an address and was signed with the name Willard. She kept this one, the poem and the photograph. The rest were placed carefully on the bonfire. She watched as the faded memories of David's mother turned to ashes.

*   *   *   *   *

Celia loved fast cars. While in Rhodesia, she was driven around on official duties in an Austin Westminster. This she found far too sedate and much preferred her Sunbeam Rapier. With its rear wheel drive and a top speed of over 100mph, it was fun to drive, at least on the better roads of Rhodesia. Even this was not very sporty for Celia's taste.

On her return to England, Celia first enjoyed driving Neil's Triumph Herald Convertible. When the sun was shining and the roof was down, Celia loved the feeling of the wind rushing past her as she sped through the country lanes of Shropshire. She hankered after something a little racier and fell in love with an MGB GT V8 Roadster. Its low profile and sporty looks suited Celia's zest for life. The powerful engine meant that Celia was too often able to take risks and get away with it.

One damp day, with rotting fallen leaves on the road, Celia went into a bend too fast. She braked; the car lost its usual grip on the slimy surface. The car skidded to the centre of the road, Celia trying desperatcly to control the uncontrollable. She hit the brakes again and they locked. The rear end swung sharply to the right and off the narrow lane. The car hit a gatepost so hard that the impact stopped it dead. Celia's neck snapped back and she died instantly.

Celia's funeral was held at the Church of Our Lady the Virgin, between the Hall and the site of the fateful helicopter crash. A single wreath of alum lilies was placed on the coffin as it was interred in the church graveyard, in a plot alongside Peter's. Neil Culham, unlike Bill Clarke, kept many of Celia's personal effects. He needed these to relive his memories. He had no immediate heir; no one would follow in the illustrious Culham line. He kept Hadleigh Hall largely as it was when Celia was alive. He saw no reason to change. He had no plans for the future.

CHAPTER 33
LAURA

Laura brought up the twins alone as best she could. It was hard at times, but she put all her energies into giving them a loving home. As they grew older, the inevitable childhood diseases came and went. There was one particular condition that caused Laura some concern. One of the twins seemed unusually breathless at times. She went to the doctor, who was a little concerned that it could be juvenile asthma. She asked Laura about family history and she couldn't recall David ever talking about asthma in his family. She'd never had asthma herself. The doctor probed a little deeper.

"What about the grandparents?" she asked.

Laura's immediate reaction was to say no. Her parents had never mentioned asthma in the family and she had no recollection of Bill or Maggie Clarke ever mentioning it. Then Laura recalled the conversation she had with David on the evening of his 21st birthday. How he'd said that Bill Clarke was not his biological father. He'd said quite clearly at the time that he'd no plans to investigate further.

"I'm not totally sure," she answered the doctor, uncertainly but honestly.

"There may be some asthma on David's side, but I'm just not sure."

The doctor prescribed an inhaler, an aerochamber and facemask and showed her how to use it for the twins. She made it clear that it was a precaution if things ever got worse.

Laura was naturally worried about the twins' health and wondered if she should try to find out more about David's biological father. She strongly suspected that he was the one who signed himself Willard on the love letter to Maggie. There was one major obstacle in Laura's efforts to find David's real father. The man who had brought David up as his own was still alive. She knew that David had utmost respect for Bill Clarke. David would never have wanted to cause any upset. She, likewise, felt the same. If she really wanted to pursue this any further, it would have to be with extreme care and sensitivity.

Occasionally Laura would go back to the love letter, the only one she'd kept. The one with the vaguely familiar handwriting. The one that included an address. Perhaps this could lead her to David's real father, or perhaps a friend who could. Laura decided she would proceed with caution. She would make absolutely sure that whatever was done, it could never cause any discomfort to Bill Clarke. It was the least she could do.

Laura knew that her best hope was The London Hospital where Maggie had trained as a student nurse. The only address she had for Willard was the one on the love letter. It was an annexe of The London Hospital at Brentwood. It was a start. She had one other lead. While Maggie was alive, she'd kept in touch with an old nursing friend from her days in London. Her name was Sheila McEvoy and David had said that when he was younger, she'd come to stay for a time. David used to reminisce that he needed to give up his bedroom to Sheila while she studied at Cambridge. David then had to sleep in the same bed as his brother for about six months. He claimed that his mother used to put an old bolster between them to keep them apart. Laura worked out that it would have been when David was about ten. She also reasoned that there would have been few courses at Cambridge for a qualified nurse, perhaps it would have been some sort of professional training. She wrote to Cambridge University on the pretext of researching her own mother's past. She asked about the courses available in 1954 for nurses. When the reply came, she found her hunch had proved correct. There had been a course on midwifery in 1954 hosted by Homerton College. Laura wrote back to say that she was trying to trace a friend of her mother called Sheila McEvoy. Could they supply a forwarding address? She was in luck. The address was in Rottingdean in Sussex, not too far along the coast from where she now lived. Laura suspected it was the address of Sheila's mother, but she thought it was at least worth a try.

She wrote to Sheila, care of this Sussex address. A week later, she received a reply. It was from the post office and it was simply marked 'return to sender, not known at this address'. Laura was disappointed, but she was not one to give up so easily.

Laura's parents came over one weekend to see the twins and it gave her the chance to drive to Rottingdean. When she arrived, Laura parked just off the road going through the village and walked to the post office. The postmaster was new to the job, but when time allowed he promised to look at the old registers of electors for anyone called McEvoy. Laura explained she was only here for a short time and promised to return in an hour. She found a small teashop and enjoyed her favourite Lady Grey tea with a single, delicious buttered crumpet. On her return the postmaster still hadn't looked in his records, but promised to do so immediately.

"What was the name?" he said.

"McEvoy," came the reply.

"Ah yes, just give me a minute," and with that he disappeared into a room in the back of the shop.

Ten minutes went by and then he returned, wiping the odd crumb from around his mouth.

"I'm sorry, but we have no record of McEvoy as far as I can see."

Laura accepted she had wasted her journey and turned to leave. As she did, an elderly couple stopped her.

"Did you say McEvoy," one of them said, "There was a lady by that name around here. Used to live right up on the hill, quite near to the windmill. She had a lovely daughter, Sandra or Susan, I think."

"Sheila?" Laura asked. "Could it have been Sheila?"

"Quite possibly, yes Sheila sounds right. Of course old Mrs McEvoy is long gone now, but some of the old folk might remember her."

"Old folk?"

"Yes, the people who live in the residential home at the back of the original stables. It's called Abbeywood. Most of them would have been here at the same time as old Mrs McEvoy. It's worth a try."

Laura wasn't very optimistic, but as she was here in the village, she saw little harm in at least going to the home. She walked the short distance to Abbeywood and knocked on the door. A smartly uniformed orderly, who listened to her story with interest, greeted her.

"You've come at a good time. Most of our residents will be having high tea in the dining room. Do come in."

Laura followed the orderly into the residential home. It was a bright, cheerful place, smelling slightly of antiseptic, but spacious and homely. Laura was shown into the dining room. The residents were either seated in high back chairs or at the tables scattered around the room. Some of them were hunched over their meals, showing signs of limited movement, probably brought on by years of arthritis. Others were quite animated chatting amiably amongst themselves. Laura went first to the tables, where she could talk to four people at once. She asked if anyone remembered Mrs McEvoy and the response, once it eventually came, was consistently negative. Then she asked the individuals sitting alone. There was one lady in a wheelchair, who the orderly said was probably the brightest of them all, although apt to be forgetful. She was extremely helpful. She claimed to remember Iris McEvoy well and even her daughter Sheila.

"Yes," she said, " a lovely girl, Sheila. Went up to London, you know, during the war. Became a nurse, I think. Married an architect up Bournemouth way, but it never worked out. Sad really, nice girl."

"You don't by any chance have an address for her, in Bournemouth, perhaps?"

"Of course I do. I was a newspaper reporter you know. Never threw away any of my contacts. Never know when you might need them."

"And would it be too much trouble…"

No trouble at all. Just give my carriage a push to the lift and I'll show you my collection."

Laura pushed her wheelchair to the lift and along the corridor to her room on the second floor. The room was a complete shambles with piles of books and magazines covering every surface. There were old and new newspapers almost covering the floor.

"Sorry for the muddle," said the old lady, "haven't cleared up today. So much I need to read. Must keep up. Now what was it you wanted?"

"Sheila McEvoy's address in Bournemouth. You said you had it."

"Of course. Just pass me that address book will you. The one on the shelf over there. By the television."

Laura found an old address book under a pile of music manuscripts.

"Do you play?" Asked Laura, "You seem to have lots of music here."

"Only a little," was the reply, "I was very involved in amateur opera in my day. Could have been a professional, but stayed with the newspapers. Less travelling and more regular employment."

Laura handed her the address book.

"Who are we looking for?" she said.

"Sheila McEvoy's address, except you said she was married, so it could be under a different name."

"No problem. My cross referencing system is second to none. There you are. Sheila McEvoy, daughter of Iris and married to Harry Blakemore. Divorced in 1970 and now uses the name McEvoy. You see it's all here. Who did you say you were? I'll put you in my book."

"And does the old and new Sheila McEvoy have an address?" Laura asked, quite in awe of this lady's amazing reference system.

"Old and new? Oh I see what you mean. Was and now is, so to speak."

"Exactly."

"Yes, here it is. 43a Dean Park Road, Bournemouth. Sounds nice."

Laura thanked the old lady for her help, wheeled her back downstairs and left the residential home. It had been an interesting and fruitful day. Before she left the village, she arranged for the local florist to send a bunch of roses to the old lady. Sadly, Laura doubted if she'd remember her from the day before. Laura now had Sheila's address and in due course wrote to her asking if she could tell her more about Willard.

Sheila wrote back to say how sorry she was to hear about David and Maggie's deaths. She had known about Willard and his last name was Boulton. She thought he was American or possibly Canadian and she thought he had joined the army at the end of the war. In her letter she also counselled Laura to be careful about 'overturning too many well-worn stones'. Laura understood the metaphor and resolved to be patient with her investigations. She would proceed with utmost caution. Bill Clarke was, after all, her children's Grandfather. That meant a lot to her. The final paragraph in Sheila's letter was an invitation to meet. Sheila said she would be happy to try to answer any further questions, although she conceded there might be little more to add. Laura wrote a letter of thanks, adding that she would try to meet, but couldn't be sure quite when. The twins were still quite a handful.

The next summer, Laura, her parents and the twins, took a cottage near Christchurch. Her parents looked after the twins, and Laura arranged to travel the few miles to Bournemouth to visit Sheila McEvoy. Laura asked Sheila to tell her about the circumstances of David's birth. Sheila didn't quite appreciate the meaning of the question. Laura was hoping for some details about Willard's affair with Maggie. Sheila told Laura about the bomb blast and the way it had caused utter mayhem and confusion in the hospital. It was something for which Laura was totally unprepared and was surprised at the detail of Sheila's account and the significance she attached to it. As they parted, Sheila added one more piece of information. It was almost said in passing, but Sheila felt it had to be said.

"Laura," Sheila said as they reached the front door of her house. "There is just one other thing I feel the need to mention. It may be irrelevant, or indeed hardly worthy of mention. It is just something that happened during those tumultuous days during the blitz. You see the bomb blast caused immeasurable chaos in the hospital, especially in David's ward. This may come as a shock to you, or more likely you will ignore it totally. The truth is that none of us who were there could be sure, with absolute certainty, that David actually belonged to Maggie. There, I've said it now and perhaps I shouldn't."

Laura could hardly believe what was being said. She was stunned.

"What exactly do you mean, Sheila, David not belonging to Maggie?"

"There were two boys in the ward hit by the bomb and when it was all over, it was impossible to identify which was which. Evidently, one mother took one boy and Maggie was left with David. To this day none of us could be absolutely sure that the right child was taken. I appreciate that this sort of thing could never happen today, but you must realise it was total chaos. I'll be honest with you, Laura, I have no reason to believe that David was not Maggie's son. It's just that you said this investigation started because of family history possibly affecting the health of your twins. I felt it only fair to mention it."

Laura was astounded by this revelation. At first it troubled her, but then recognised that little could be done. Perhaps there was a way to be sure, but for the moment she had no idea how to find out. She would continue to find out more about David's real father. Perhaps this would shed light on the mystery.

Laura now had a name, Willard Boulton, and she knew that he was a student at The London Hospital in 1944. This information alone, should surely be helpful in her future enquiries. Laura wrote to The London Hospital, claiming she'd been asked to arrange a reunion for medical students who studied there during the war. She asked if a list of students could be sent to her. When she received the list, she was surprised to see the names of two students called Boulton. Willard graduated in late 1944 and Henry had graduated two years earlier. She then wrote back to the hospital and asked if they could provide any forwarding addresses for the two Boulton students. Henry had apparently returned to work in Canada in a remote, but developing part of Alberta. Willard had initially joined the British Army, but that was all they knew. There was no forwarding address. The hospital authorities suggested that Laura made contact with staff at Canada House in London. They may be able to assist in her search.

Laura was sensitive to the situation with Bill Clarke, especially as he was now alone, and took her time to plan the next move. The juvenile asthma seemed to be well under control, so she had no desperate need to trace David's real father. Yet all the time, the thought was there. She was interested in the truth, especially following Sheila's shocking allegation. The twins were growing up and still needed Laura's full attention, but when they both went to school for the first time, Laura had a little more time on her hands. She decided to pursue her quest a little further.

She took a train to London and went to Canada House, just off Trafalgar Square. It was an imposing building, with a row of Greek style columns along one side. Laura asked for help at the reception area and was directed to a member of staff, who listened to her request sympathetically. Laura's request was simple. Could the Canadian authorities give her the current address of either Drs Henry or Willard Boulton? Fortunately, Canada House kept a record of every doctor's surgery in Canada. The member of staff explained that it was to help any Canadian citizens who had health issues abroad. This way they could make contact with the Canadian surgery to access their health records. Laura was impressed with the efficiency of the country and said that one day she hoped to visit. There was no record of Willard Boulton running a GP practice, but Henry Boulton's address in Grande Prairie, Alberta was the same one she had been given by The London Hospital. Laura took her time, but eventually wrote to Dr Henry Boulton in Grande Prairie, asking for the address of his brother Willard. After several weeks, she received a reply. It appeared that the two brothers had at one time worked together, but more recently Willard had moved southeast to run a doctor's surgery in a small town called Red Deer. Henry had included a phone number and with some hesitation, she decided to ring the surgery. Laura was very conscious of the fact that Willard's love for Maggie was over 30 years ago and over time he could have remarried and had a family. She didn't want her private investigations to cause upset. She would be cautious and at least find out if he were married. She placed a long-distance call to Red Deer. Once again she pretended to be organising some sort of reunion. She asked the person answering the phone, presumably a receptionist, two simple questions. Was Dr Willard Boulton still working at the surgery and did he have a wife? The answer to both questions was yes. Laura left it at that.

Another couple of years went by and Laura busied herself with her growing family. During her quiet moments alone, she still wondered about Willard Boulton. After all, she reasoned, if he was the real father of her late husband and technically grandfather to her children, why shouldn't she know? Perhaps the time had come to try to make some sort of contact. She decided the best way was to write a cautious letter. It would be a letter that said just enough to interest someone, but avoiding any demand or commitment. If Willard chose to ignore it, then little harm would be done.

She wrote:

Dear Dr Boulton,

My name is Laura Clarke, widow of David Clarke.

David Clarke was the son of your former colleague, Maggie, nee Breakwell, from your time at The London Medical School.

You will be sorry to hear that David died on his 30th birthday as a result of a helicopter crash.

Two years ago, your former colleague, Maggie, died from lung cancer.

Should you ever be in Britain, it would be nice to meet.

With kind regards

Laura Clarke

Six months past and there was no reply. Then a letter came to Laura from Canada.

Dear Laura,

I am sorry to have taken so long to reply, but I am not very good at writing personal letters.

My job involves a lot of paperwork and, sadly, personal letters take second place.

Of course I remember Maggie Breakwell and I was saddened to hear of her death.

Likewise it was awful to hear of David's death. I do hope that you are managing.

There was a time when I used to visit England regularly, but not any more.

Should you ever be in Canada, it would be wonderful to meet up.

Best wishes

Willard

Dr. W.O. Boulton.

Laura, at least for the moment, decided to leave things as they stood. It was probably for the best. Now she had an address for Willard, she sent a Christmas card every year. She would occasionally include a photograph of the twins. It was her way of keeping some form of slender communication open. For now it remained slender. Time, with its perpetual habit of changing the future to the now, demanded some form of action. Laura was torn between causing Bill Clarke any distress and seeking the truth. Despite Sheila McEvoy's entreaty, she resolved that for her peace of mind, it would be impossible to remain in this state of constant unknowing.

CHAPTER 34
MI SUN

Mi Sun had moved back to live near London. She worked as a translator for a specialist book company, putting her knowledge of the Korean language to great use. While Peter was alive they had talked about the things that Celia had told him on his 18th birthday. One was the possibility that Willard Boulton was not his father. They had always planned to talk to Celia about it in more detail, but the time never seemed right. Now it was too late. After all, it was only a possibility that Willard was not Peter's father. It was something that Celia had mentioned, almost in passing. Willard had been abroad most of the time, but in every way he had been a good father. That was until his untimely death, when Peter was about six years old.

Mi Sun had no link with Willard. Peter, when he was alive, had almost no recollection of him. It seemed a fruitless exercise to try to establish the truth over Peter's parentage. There were times when Mi Sun wondered why she was even trying. It meant little sense, yet for some obscure reason she still wanted to know the truth.

Unbeknown to Mi Sun, she did have a link to Willard. It was sitting on top of the upright piano in her flat. It was one of the few items that remained from her short, happy years of marriage to Peter. It was his microscope, given to him by Celia when they first made a home together. Mi Sun remembered that the microscope had once belonged to Willard. She had no real interest in microscopy, but out of curiosity, took it down from the piano and examined it carefully.

She took out the brass microscope from its case and peered through the eyepiece. She could see nothing until she adjusted the mirror beneath the flat plate. It was only then that the light was reflected through the microscope lens and into her eye. It just gave a bright gold ring of light and nothing more. Looking again, this time more carefully, Mi Sun realised that something had to be placed on the plate. She plucked a loose bit of cotton from her dress and placed it carefully above the light source. As she looked through the lens, she could see it, but as she breathed it moved, distorting the image. She nearly gave up, but then noticed that inside the box was a storage compartment for glass slides. This, she now realised, was the answer. She needed to trap the cotton between two glass plates and that would keep it still. Carefully she took out the glass plates. They always seemed to be stored in twos, and she put them all on the table besides the microscope. There was only one pair that had nothing in them and these she used to trap her piece of cotton. It then worked beautifully and she could see the coarse detail of the cotton fragments. Mi Sun had never seen such detail before and was entranced. She looked at the other pairs of glass slides. One appeared to be a piece of either skin or even a sliver of onion. Mi Sun couldn't tell which. Another had the leg of some insect, possibly a spider or a fly. The final pair of slides had a single hair trapped between each piece of glass. Could this hair belong to Willard? Mi Sun could never remember Peter using the microscope since their marriage. Before that, it had belonged to Celia and had been kept at her home, Hadleigh Hall. There surely must be the possibility that Willard had used his own hair to make up the slide. This may be her only link with him. She resolved there and then to investigate further. This could tell her more about the man who she hoped would turn out to be Peter's father.

Mi Sun's only hope was to find friends of Willard's from his student days or perhaps afterwards when he was in the army. She requested the records from the Royal Army Medical Corps headquarters in Chivenham. Unfortunately, the Corps had served with numerous regiments and it was almost impossible to know which one Willard had joined. Mi Sun then thought she might be able to cross-reference the names of students at the London Medical School with the Royal Army Medical Corps. As she now lived in London, it was convenient to take a tube to Whitechapel and ask for the records directly from The London Hospital. Mi Sun asked to see the records of students from 1944, explaining that her father in law had been there at the time. The records clerk, somewhat surprised by a second request for the same information within a few months, provided the information without comment. It was not her place to ask why two young ladies should be so interested in the same cohort of students. Although there were over 50 students studying medicine at the University that year, only four were at The London Hospital. Mi Sun noted their names and then went back to the Medical Corps records. There were just three students who went on to join the Corps. Their names were Willard Boulton, Harry Ames and Jim Driver. There was a chance that Harry and Jim would have been friends with Willard. They could possibly provide more information about him, at least when he was younger.

Mi Sun's next visit was to the British Medical Association's head office in Tavistock Square. The impressive building had an attractive central courtyard. The staff could enjoy moments of peace there, away from the busy streets outside. The records were sparse, but gave Mi Sun some crucial information, particularly the most recent addresses of Dr Driver and Dr Ames. Dr Boulton had never been a member of the BMA. This didn't altogether surprise Mi Sun, as Willard's time in the army would have covered all his medical insurance needs. Mi Sun felt she was making progress, but was still unsure of the real purpose of her mission.

Dr Harry Ames was a GP in the small town of Great Missenden, on the fringes of the Chiltern Hills. Mi Sun wrote to him initially, but thought it would be more helpful to meet him personally. Letters could be too guarded. Face to face contact gave the opportunity for a proper dialogue. She took the train from Marylebone station and arrived towards the end of morning surgery. Dr Ames was the senior partner in a practice based in the main part of town. He was middle aged and had a lively, sunburnt face as though he spent time out of doors. He wore a white shirt with a striped tie and a well-fitted tweed jacket over charcoal grey trousers. He shook Mi Sun's hand firmly and suggested that they had a sandwich in the local caf . Once they were seated, he asked Mi Sun why she'd asked to meet him. Mi Sun explained about Peter, what had happened and how she had this deep-seated yearning to know more about Willard. Dr. Ames explained that although he knew Willard, he was not so much a close friend, more of an acquaintance. They had different interests at University and weren't always in the same lodgings. He reminded Mi Sun that times were strange during the war, with much more movement than today. He explained that people rarely stayed in the same place for more than a few months. He said he was fairly sure that Willard had signed up for the British Army as soon as he graduated. After that they had lost touch. He also said that Willard's close friend was Jim Driver and perhaps she could contact him. Mi Sun explained she was hoping to see Jim soon. As they parted, Dr. Ames mentioned one other thing, which he thought may be of interest.

"There was one strange thing as I remember," he said. "I was involved in transporting two new born babies from Great Ormond Street to the London Hospital. I remember now distinctly, even mentioning it to Clare, now my wife. Never even thought of it again until just now."

"Yes?" questioned Mi Sun, her interest now increasing dramatically.

"Oh I'm sure its pretty meaningless, but one of the children was seen later with an unusual scar on its right heel. It just didn't seem to fit with its other injuries."

"Other injuries?"

"Oh yes, these little babies were pretty messed up. They had been in a ward at Great Ormond Street when a bomb hit it. They were lucky to live."

"And why are you telling me all this?"

"Well, this is the thing. I have a feeling that Willard Boulton might have married the mother of one of those children. I don't know for sure. I wasn't invited to the wedding or anything. It's just a vague feeing. I may be totally wrong."

"So there's nothing else you can add about Willard?"

"I'm sorry, Mi Sun, but it was over 30 years ago. A lot of water under the bridge since then."

"I understand," said Mi Sun with some resignation, "well thank you anyway."

They shook hands and parted. Dr. Ames back to his afternoon surgery and Mi Sun to her train and her thoughts.

On the journey home, Mi Sun could make no sense of the comment about the heel scar. It would have to wait.

Mi Sun's next visit was potentially more difficult. Dr Jim Driver's most recent address according to the BMA was in the town of Peebles in Scotland. It was hardly the place that Mi Sun could visit easily without making a lengthy trip. This helped her decide a letter would be the best option, at least to start.

She wrote and explained about Peter, expressing her wish to know more about Willard. Jim replied, without giving anything away, and asked after Celia. Mi Sun wrote again telling Jim about her accident and death and explaining that her second husband, Viscount Culham was still alive. Jim then wrote that he would welcome the opportunity to talk to Mi Sun. He mentioned that the following month he was in London for a few days at a conference and hoped they could meet.

The conference programme gave Dr. Driver a free half-day. He invited Mi Sun to meet him at The Caledonian Club in Belgravia, where he was a country member. They met for afternoon tea in the drawing room and were served with a selection of sandwiches and fancy cakes. Jim Driver was dressed in a dark blue lounge suit with a pale blue shirt and a tartan tie. In spite of being in his mid 50s, he looked remarkably athletic and had an open honest face, which Mi Sun found appealing. As they sat down, Jim pulled out Mi Sun's chair for her, showing a certain old world charm, which added to the friendly atmosphere. The room itself had space for just five tables, each with four chairs. The walls were hung with tartans and one had a number of mounted stags heads, adding considerably to the Scottish atmosphere of the club. There was no one else taking afternoon tea, although a few ladies could be seen playing bridge next door, in the members' room.

Mi Sun and Jim Driver engaged initially in small talk about the building, the conference and the weather. When this had run its course, Jim turned to Mi Sun, saying,

"So tell me, why am I sitting here with an attractive young lady?

Mi Sun blushed slightly, but retained her composure.

"Well, you know from my letters that Peter, my husband, was sadly killed in a helicopter crash and several years later, his mother was also killed."

"Of course. It came as a great shock to hear all this, but nothing compared with the horror it must have been for you."

"The thing is, I would welcome the opportunity to get to know more about Willard, particular when he was a student with you."

"Oh I could talk all day. We played in the same rugby team, The London Medical School team. He was a second row forward, a specialist line out jumper. I played on the wing. He always joked that we wingers liked to keep our shirts clean. We went to dances and things with the other students. There were hardly any ladies training to be doctors in those days. We would meet up with the nurses and have a rare old time, the war permitting of course. We couldn't get out of London because of the rationing, but we organised dos at the hospital lodgings. I can't recall how he met Celia, but she was a cut above most of the girls. Always dressed smartly, a great looking girl, quite a catch."

"And were there other girls?"

"Oh yes, we all had lots of girlfriends. It seemed to be the thing during the war. You could never be quite sure if anything would be long term back then. It was a strange time. Of course when the war ended, then people settled down more, just as Willard and Celia did, at least to start with."

"Was there anyone else, perhaps special to Willard at the time?"

"I seem to remember a girl called Maggie. He was sweet on her for a little while. No idea what happened to her."

"And what happened when you both graduated?"

"Willard and I joined the Royal Army Medical Corps. We both went overseas, to Northern Germany. The war was almost over when we joined up, but it was still pretty harrowing."

"Harrowing?"

"Yes, Willard and I were the first medics into a Nazi concentration camp. It was ghastly. It still upsets me, even today."

"I'm sorry. I appreciate your time there must have been horrendous. I don't want to cause any distress by reliving it in any way. Shall we move on?"

"Of course. I left the army as soon as the war finished, but Willard stayed on. He spent a few years in Germany and was drafted to Korea in 1950. Before that he married Celia. I was his best man."

"So when was that?"

"Willard married Celia in April 1945, Peter was about nine months old as I recall. Of course Willard was away abroad for the early years of their marriage. Hardly ideal. Celia should have gone with him, but she wouldn't leave England."

"And was the marriage rocky before Willard's death?"

"Very much so. Celia had numerous affairs. Once Willard went home to find her with another man."

"And Peter was about six years old when he died."

"Sort of."

"What do you mean 'sort of'?"

"Well it's a bit difficult for me to explain. What died was the marriage."

"And?" Mi Sun questioned.

"Oh hell, I suppose I'll have to tell you."

"Tell me what?"

"What with Celia and Peter both dead, I guess it no longer matters."

"I'm sorry Jim, I'm not following you."

Jim poured more tea, slowly and deliberately. He put the teapot down and pulled his chair in closer to Mi Sun. He placed both hands together with elbows resting on the table, almost as if in prayer.

"OK Mi Sun. What I'm about to say will shock you. Please don't ask for details. Only one person should provide those and it's not me. Are you ready?"

"I think so. Jim you look really worried."

"I am worried, because I'm struggling to imagine the consequences."

Mi Sun stretched across the table and clasped her own hands around Jim's.

"Go on," she said quietly.

"Willard is still alive. He didn't die in Korea. It was all a fake. He had good reasons. He just needed to start a new life. A life without Celia."

Mi Sun unclasped her hands from Jim's in undisguised horror. She gripped the edge of the tablecloth. Her breathing was rapid at first. She could feel her heart beating in her chest. She said nothing at first, then as her breathing came back to normal; her emotions fluctuated between anger and doubt. At last she spoke.

"Are you telling me that Willard abandoned Peter, leaving him without a father?"

"On the face of it, anyone would think that. Willard had good reason. Peter was brought up in a stable family with Neil and Celia. He did well, I believe"

"I'm sorry Jim. I'll need time to take all this in. Why did you have to tell me this? It changes everything."

"I realise that. Mi Sun, in fairness you came here to find out about Willard. The next move is yours to decide. You can treat Willard as an ogre who abandoned Peter, or you can find out the true reason. The choice is yours. Remember, Mi Sun, I will be forever indebted to Willard. Now is not the time for details, but many years ago, Willard saved me from murdering someone."

Mi Sun sat in silence. She couldn't think clearly. It was all too much of a shock.

"What I suggest," said Jim, "is that you think carefully about the implications of what you've just heard. Let's leave things be for now. If you do decide to make any contact with Willard, then I can help you. But not right now. Give yourself thinking time. You have my address."

"Thank you, Jim."

Mi Sun forced a smile, although she was far from happy. They shook hands and Jim helped her to stand by walking around the table and easing her chair backwards. Ever the gentleman, she thought.

When Mi Sun returned home, she could think of little else but the implications of this news. The possibility of Willard still being alive seeped into her very soul. Why had he abandoned Peter? How could anyone do such a thing to a young child? It was unfathomable. Perhaps the answer was easier than she thought. Perhaps Willard wasn't Peter's father after all. This might be reason enough. Mi Sun decided to renew her efforts to resolve this outstanding dilemma, Peter's true parentage.

It was about this time that the newspapers were reporting how criminals were being profiled by material left at the scene of the crime. A new technique was in the early stages of development. It was called DNA analysis. Early results looked promising. The newspapers had said that with more research it might be possible to establish whether a particular person had been involved. The lead researcher was a Professor Colin Prentice at Leicester University. Mi Sun wrote to him, explaining her situation and asking for help. She told Prof. Prentice that she had a single strand of hair. She asked if this could be enough material for his DNA analysis. When he wrote back, his letter was full of caution. He explained that his research was progressing slowly. He said that he newspapers had overplayed the certainties of his techniques. However he was pleased to help and if the strand of hair could be delivered in good condition, he would try his best. Mi Sun arranged to have the glass slides containing the hair packed carefully and posted to the Biochemical Department at Leicester University.

Several weeks later, Mi Sun received a reply from Prof. Prentice. He explained that they had undertaken an analysis of the hair she sent him and now had a very basic DNA profile. It meant very little on its own. What he now needed was a sample from the person with which she was trying to compare. If the hair were from her husband, then something from the father would be necessary. This would be the only way to indicate their relationship. If, on the other hand, the hair were from the father, then something from her husband would be necessary. Mi Sun had nothing but the single hair, which could have come from Willard. She was desperate to think of something from Peter, which could be used for DNA analysis.

It had been three years since his untimely death. Life had moved on. When he had died, Mi Sun had kept none of his clothes. She had photographs, his books, ornaments and other items they had bought together. None of these seemed remotely suitable and everything else they had shared had been cleaned or washed, often several times. She was at a loss. She was lying in bed one night, reflecting on her loneliness, when she thought of the one unwashed item. It was stored at the back of the wardrobe. She could not part with it. It was too precious. It was her wedding dress.

Mi Sun thought back to her wedding night. How she couldn't bear to take it off; it meant so much to her. The beautiful, light purple hanbok embroidered in pink. How Peter had kissed every part of her body through the fine silk. It was only then that he had slowly untied the bows and undone the silk-covered buttons. As each bow was untied and each button undone, Peter had paused. He had kissed each pore of her skin as it was exposed to his touch. It was the most delicious experience ever. It seemed like a lifetime before she was fully naked. Every part of her body was singing with desire. The dress dropped to the side of the bed as Peter and she made gentle and quite unforgettable love. She slept; the memories spiralling in her dreams like a whirlpool in river.

She awoke with renewed determination. Her wedding dress was the only option. She would lend it to the laboratory at Leicester. Although it was her only physical link to Peter, it was also her only possible link to Willard. As she folded the dress, her sadness returned. Mi Sun insisted on delivering the dress to Leicester herself and handing it over personally to Professor Prentice. He promised faithfully to take care of it and make absolutely sure the process he had developed would not damage a single stitch.

A month later a letter came from Prof. Prentice by recorded delivery. It was headed the Biochemical Department, University of Leicester. It read:

Dear Mrs Culham,

Thank you for the opportunity to examine the dress you delivered to my laboratory. Although the dress is approximately seven years old, we were able to extract a small amount of suitable material for analysis. I wish to stress before giving you my conclusions, that what we have achieved is at the cutting edge of current science. We have had very few opportunities to validate our techniques, so there could still be the possibility of false positives and false negatives. Forgive the scientific jargon, but this essentially means that we cannot be 100 per cent correct in our assumptions.

However, I can report that we are reasonably confident in our analysis. The two items you have subjected to analysis are either a) from the same person, or b) from the same bloodline. As the wedding dress is clearly only associated with you and your late husband, it means that the hair sample is the only contentious issue. It could be either from your late husband or his father. Of that I am confident.

I do hope that this information is of use to you. Please do not hesitate to contact me again should that be necessary.

I have made arrangements to keep the dress in a secure place for your collection.

Yours sincerely,

Colin Prentice

Professor of Forensic Biochemistry.

Mi Sun was ecstatic and relieved. She now knew that Willard was Peter's father. This was a major breakthrough in her quest for the truth. The hints from Celia at Peter's 18th birthday were totally unfounded. Mi Sun just couldn't understand why she even suggested the possibility that Willard was not Peter's father. She could have said nothing and avoid the entire trauma that followed. Perhaps it was some twisted plan to distance Peter from Willard. It would remain a mystery.

Jim Driver had suggested that Mi Sun took her time to decide on her next move. Should she try to find Willard, wherever he was, or just let things stay as they are? She was undecided until another letter arrived from Leicester University.

Dear Mrs Culham,

I apologise for this letter arriving unsolicited. However a member of staff in my department has found something, which you may find of interest. You will recall at the time of your husband's death, a fragment of skin was retrieved from the crash and sent to my lab for investigation.

At the time (I signed it Dr Prentice, because this was before I became a Professor), I indicated that the two skin samples could have been from half brothers. Once again, I do need to reiterate that these statements are made on the assumption that the skin samples were from **different** people. If this is the case, then our re-analysis, using the latest techniques, gives greater credibility to the following possibility.

This must logically infer, that the father of your late husband could have been the same person as the father of the other person in the helicopter crash.

I do hope that this information helps you in your wish to gain clarity over this matter and does not cause you further anguish.

Yours sincerely

Colin Prentice

Professor of Forensic Biochemistry

Mi Sun absorbed this second letter with fascination and intrigue. She was fascinated by the findings from the laboratory and intrigued by their consequences. It was just an unreal coincidence that the two young men killed in the crash were both fathered by Willard. It could not be true. The explanation was simple. The skin samples were from one and the same person.

Yet at the back of Mi Sun's mind, there was always the possibility. She would need more time to consider her next move. If indeed, there was to be one.

CHAPTER 35
DECLINE AND FALL

Bill Clarke started to decline in the early winter of 1981. He still rattled around in the old family house in Witchford. He would spend his time listening to his favourite classical records, a little gardening, working for the British Legion and a fairly regular visit to the local pub, the Cross Keys. A few friends would very occasionally come round for the evening and he would generously fortify them with alcohol. Whether it was the free alcohol or the company was difficult to discern. Since Maggie's death five years earlier, he had coped in his gentile, rather unkempt manner, on his own. The family home was far too large for one person, but he had no inclination to leave. He had planned the house and had it built to his own specification, so memories were etched into every brick. When it was built 30 years before, it had been designed in a relatively modern style. It had a substantial open plan layout and floating stairs out of the main room. Such a family home, now architecturally dated, was difficult to keep clean and in good repair. As the years went by, Bill was less inclined to attend to cleanliness or maintenance. In spite of this, his son, Iain, would visit him every week without fail. Iain, his wife Sandra and the two children, Freddie and Poppy, would arrive every Saturday morning for a coffee and stay until lunchtime. In the early years after Maggie's death, Bill would produce a salad with cold meat for them all. Even this became more difficult as he declined and the family would only stay until just before lunch.

It was difficult to attribute Bill's decline to the loss of Maggie or David. The life of a man living alone for five years, especially one so dependent on his wife, could never have been easy. Such a scenario sometimes questions the purpose of life, yet it would have been unfair to suggest that Bill's life lacked purpose. He had four grandchildren in Poppy, Freddie and the twins. He was chairman of the local branch of the British Legion, which was a hive of activity around November 11th. The rest of the year little happened to vary his settled, but rather mundane existence.

As the years wore on, Bill would struggle to get up some mornings, especially in the cold winter months. He had always suffered from a skin condition called psoriasis. This was uncomfortable, needed regular personal treatment with an unpleasant ointment and was thoroughly wearing. As it was in part related to catching malaria in Burma, it was a permanent reminder of the awful consequences of war.

It was no wonder that Bill would suffer from bouts of depression. He would sometimes replace proper food with alcohol. There was little anyone could do, in spite of offers from family and friends. This situation could have continued for many years, but a fall accelerated his decline. He had been unsteady on his legs for some time and the fall was no surprise. He broke his hip and was taken to hospital by ambulance in a sorry state. While in hospital he developed a viral infection, complicated by pneumonia. Unable to move, it was difficult to treat and in spite of antibiotics, he died three weeks later.

At his funeral, his granddaughter, Poppy, read a most moving poem. It described the man, his shambling gait, and the love of his remaining family.

The members of the British Legion were acutely aware of their fallen comrades. Those that remained had by their humble efforts earned a level of respect and gratitude, ensuring that memories would remain. Bill Clarke was one of their own. They lowered their banner in homage.

Laura knew that his greatest contribution was to bring up a son who was not his own. A son who, in spite of what had happened, he treated equally in every way. It was the measure of a truly noble man.

CHAPTER 36
HUNT AND FALL

Viscount Culham's death was altogether different. It was slow and painful.

He had retired from his position as Governor-General of Rhodesia when it became independent. Since then he had concentrated his energies on his business enterprises and improvements of Hadleigh Hall and the Estate. He was honoured to become Lord Lieutenant of Shropshire, the Queen's representative in the county. He had the occasional liaison with other women after Celia's death, but nothing too serious. He had always enjoyed the company of women, but a second marriage was unthinkable. In spite of his best efforts, the estate was in decline and he knew that the imposition of death duties would leave but nothing but hardship for another wife.

The Boxing Day hunt was an established tradition at Hadleigh Hall. The Hadleigh hunt, of which he was the master, would meet at ten-o-clock on Boxing Day morning every year, in the car park of the Culham Arms. On this clear, bright, cold morning, it was a colourful and dramatic occasion. The stirrup cup was passed from hand to hand and there would be a distinctive air of merriment amongst the assembled huntsmen. The horsemen, in either red or black jackets, would look resplendent, especially mounted so high above the watching public. The brown and white hounds would be milling around excitedly. The ancient Hadleigh horn would sound for the start of the hunt and they would be off. The onlookers would either head into the Culham Arms for a post-Christmas drink or home to the warmth of their coal fires.

The hunt would head into the Hadleigh Estate, but the fox might have other ideas. It was quite common to charge over the fields of local farmers and sometimes into the open gardens of local villagers. Once a fox was scented or spotted, it became a free for all. The usual discipline and control of man and beast were lost in pursuit of the quarry. Horses were encouraged to take the direct line, whatever the consequence. On Boxing Day, 1983, the consequence was momentous. Neil Culham was in the middle of the pack of hounds when the bugle sounded for the sighting of the fox. Neil urged his magnificent steed in hot pursuit. The horse made good ground on its quarry, but the fox ran through a narrow gap in a hedge. Neil followed and the horse had little option but to jump the hedge. Neil steadied for the jump, but an unseen ditch the other side brought the horse down, throwing Neil clear. The pain in his lower back was excruciating and he drifted in and out of consciousness. He tried to move but couldn't even crawl. When help arrived, it was clear that the injury was serious. It took time to return to the Culham Arms to phone for an ambulance and a helicopter was despatched from RAF Cosford. Before long he was airlifted to hospital in Shrewsbury. His injuries were thoroughly assessed and he had suffered a bleed on the brain, which affected his speech. All Neil could manage was a muffled whisper, making him barely intelligible. Far more important was the damage to his lower spine, leaving him paralysed from below the waist.

After months of physiotherapy, he returned to Hadleigh Hall, a man now bereft of his former stature, both physically and emotionally. Neil was moved to a nursing home, reliant on a team of carers and hated the lack of independence. At first friends and acquaintances would visit. Mi Sun would travel over from London and sit with him whenever she could. Over time the visits came less frequent and Neil lost interest in everything. He just wanted to die. Eventually he resolved to take his life. He saw no point in continuing the way he was. To Neil, his existence simply lacked any purpose.

He asked his carers to bring him some mementos from his own grandfather. They included an old cut-throat razor, which he hid in his wheelchair. Normally he'd have a glass of wine with his evening meal and either a single whisky or port to follow. That evening he asked that both bottles were left on the table beside him. He drank steadily for the rest of the evening. It was a blessed relief from the miserable life he now endured. At midnight he took the razor and slashed both his wrists. The blade then went to his neck, but he hadn't the strength to inflict anything more than a superficial wound. He lay slumped in his wheelchair, bleeding profusely from his wrists until the dawn light suffused the room. His injuries were serious, but not sufficient to cause death. He was rushed to hospital and placed in intensive care. No one could honestly tell if his attempt was a failed suicide or a cry for help.

At first his recovery was steady. Then, in spite of constant care, his injuries deteriorated. Sepsis had set in. At first the staff were hopeful they had the condition under control. It was not to last. One by one his vital organs closed down. The doctors tried their best to save him, yet deep down they knew they were fighting a losing battle. Mi Sun, Neil's only known relative, was contacted and she arrived the next day. Neil slipped into a state of unconsciousness just before she arrived. As she sat by his bedside, he looked so fragile. The numerous tubes and wires attached to his body added to the feeling of despair, his life supported by little more than gases and fluids. The once vigourous man she remembered was no more.

A priest was called to administer the last rights. Mi Sun welcomed him to Neil's bedside and stood back. The priest gave the apostolic pardon to Neil. He asked for forgiveness, as Neil was unable to confess for himself. The priest then anointed Neil with oil as he read a passage from the scriptures. Finally he prepared the Eucharist. He touched the wafer and the wine to Neil's lips. At this point in the final communion, Neil, for the first time in hours, opened his eyes. He looked unblinking at the priest. He then took a deep breath, closed his eyes, sunk back into his pillows and died. The priest turned to Mi Sun.

"It was a sign of his faith," was all he said.

The funeral was held in Hadleigh Church, next to the Hall. It was attended by a number of friends and acquaintances from home and abroad. Six men from the Hadleigh hunt carried the coffin into the church. The eulogy referred to the tragedy of Celia and Peter. How he had weathered the storm with courage and fortitude. The priest assured the congregation that Neil would join his wife and son in the place reserved for him in heaven. He explained how Neil had held strong to his Catholic beliefs, right to the very end.

Neil's adopted son, Peter, had once held similar beliefs. That was before his traumatic experiences at Downthorpe. It was probably for the best that Neil was unaware of such things. If he had known, Neil's own faith could have been sorely tested. There are times when certain life events are best kept private; to share does not always bring closure.

CHAPTER 37
FOUND

The deaths of Bill Clarke and Viscount Culham made a huge difference to the attitudes of Laura and Mi Sun. Previously they had both been cautious in their quest to find Willard. They were both desperate not to upset their respective fathers-in-law. As far as they were aware, their late husbands had been quite happy in childhood and had always had supportive parents. To introduce a person from the past, for whatever reason, was something that had to be treated with great sensitivity. Now things were very different. They independently resolved that the time was right to try to make contact with Willard. Possibly, if he would agree, to go so far as a meeting.

* * * * * *

Laura had been having a rather stilted correspondence with Willard over the years. It had amounted to nothing more than a Christmas card, occasionally including a photo of the children as they grew up. She had little more than a name, an address in Canada, a poem and a photograph of a 25 year old man. A photograph that brought memories flooding back of her David. The last, brief letter from Willard had invited her to visit, if ever she were in Canada. Perhaps the time had come.

* * * * *

Mi Sun knew that Willard lived in Canada, but had no address. The forensic evidence from Leicester University implied strongly that Willard was Peter's father. She was confident that Jim Driver would give her his address. This alone would be enough to trace him. It didn't resolve the possibility that Peter had a half brother, but only Willard could answer that. She decided that she really did need to know. Perhaps the time had come.

She contacted Jim Driver who was pleased to give her Willard's address in Canada. He still expressed caution in her resolve to find Willard, but her mind was already made up. She wrote to Willard at his surgery address, the only detail that Jim could supply. Like Laura, years before, she decided to adopt a very discreet approach. She knew that Celia had officially dissolved the marriage, but she had no idea of its legality in Canada. It was complicated. She didn't even know if Willard had remarried. She wrote:

Private and Confidential

Dear Dr Boulton,

My name is Mi Sun Culham. I was married to your son, Peter, until his death in 1974.

You will be sorry to hear that your former wife, Celia, also passed away two years later.

I am writing to you in the hope that we could meet.

It would be a wonderful opportunity for me to understand better certain aspects of Peter's early life.

It would also give me an opportunity to share with you my short time with Peter.

I do hope you will agree to my request.

With kind regards

Mi Sun

Mi Sun Culham

After six weeks, Willard wrote back.

Dear Mi Sun,

I was so sorry to hear of the death of my son Peter and Celia Culham.

It would be an honour and a pleasure to meet you.

There are many things that need explanation and telling you would be a great privilege.

Should you be able to come to Canada, that would be wonderful as I no longer travel far.

Please let me know when it would be convenient for you and I will make the arrangements.

Kind regards

Willard

Dr W.O. Boulton

Mi Sun was due to give a paper on 'Teaching English as a Second Language in South Korea' at an international conference on linguistics in Toronto the next June. She made arrangements to travel to Edmonton the day the conference ended on June 20th. Her team leader at the Institute of Linguistics, based in London, was happy for her to extend her trip by a week. She deserved a holiday, and where nicer that western Canada? The conference had been a great success and her paper well received. The journey from London was tiring and the evening sessions at the conference, coupled with her jet lag, had left Mi Sun exhausted. She was anxious as she took a taxi to the airport in Toronto. She wasn't sure whether she'd done the right thing to arrange this meeting. It was too late now. Willard had agreed to meet her at Edmonton airport. The die was cast, but she still felt uncomfortable. How could she cope with the man who had so cruelly abandoned her Peter? Not just walked out on him, but at such a young age; the tender age of six years. She caught flight AC175, leaving Toronto at midday.

* * * * *

Laura had no ulterior motive to be in Canada. The twins were now aged twelve and had grown out of the childhood asthma that had been the start of her quest to find Willard. She simply had a deep-seated desire to know the man better. The man who had once been in love with David's mother. Was that so unreasonable? She thought not. The children were becoming quite independent and Laura's parents were happy to look after them for a week or so. They had encouraged her to meet Willard. Apart from the children, it was one of her few links with David. She arranged to take a train from her home outside Southampton to London and fly directly to Edmonton. The date was set for June 19th and Laura was excited by the prospect of meeting David's true father at last. She had so much to tell and so much to learn.

The journey was horrendous. Laura had arranged for a taxi to pick her up from home at 5.30 am so she could catch the early train to London. By 5.45, there was no sign of it and Laura phoned the taxi company for an explanation of the delay. She could tell by the drowsy voice that the person answering the phone was still in bed. He promised to be around as soon as possible, but it was 6.30 before the taxi arrived. As they drove sedately on the four-lane motorway to the station, Laura noticed that the speedometer never registered more 40 miles per hour. She explained to the taxi drive she was running very late for her train. As she said it, a ghastly crunching sound came from the bowels of the taxi and it drew to a grinding halt. Laura had no time for an explanation. She grabbed her suitcase and marched away from the, now smoking, taxi. As she stood on the motorway, she faced the realism of not only missing her train, but being abandoned on an unfriendly and pedestrian-free motorway. Cars were racing by in the outside lane at well over 70 miles an hour, so her outstretched arm was more than useless. She was still only a few miles from home and was nearly in tears. As she started to give up hope, a car slowed down and pulled in just ahead of her. The car already seemed to be full, but Laura was invited to squeeze in behind the driver. She passed her hand luggage to one of the two people already in the back, and perched her suitcase precariously on her knees. The driver appreciated the urgency of her trip and took her directly to the station. It was only as she left the car that Laura realised that the other passengers were travelling to the local airport. This had truly been a Good Samaritan. She had missed her intended train and was forced to wait another two hours for the next direct train to London. As it pulled into Waterloo station, Laura realised that she now had insufficient time for her transfer to Heathrow airport. There was little she could do. Once at the airport, she had two options, either to wait until the next day, or reroute via Toronto. She chose the latter, as at least it meant she was on the way. She just had time to ring home, telling her parents that nothing could have been worse than the start of this particular journey. As she settled into the flight to Toronto, she tried to relax, but after such a traumatic start, it was almost impossible.

The flight was tedious and lengthy. The noise of the jet engines prevented Laura from getting any sleep. She could think of little else but her meeting with Willard. How would it work out? Would it be a success or a total disaster? The stopover in Toronto was in a cheap hotel, just outside the perimeter of the airport. The state of the room mattered little to Laura, as all she desperately needed was a bed for the night.

The last thing she did that evening was to send a telegram to Willard, explaining the delay and telling him when she expected to arrive in Edmonton. He replied, telling her that it was not a problem. Meeting her at the new time would be quite convenient.

She had time the next morning to buy a shirt for each of the twins. She chose one with a glorious, red maple leaf emblem. The maple leaf would mean nothing to the boys, but she knew they'd be pleased. After her modest shopping, she headed back the short distance to the airport. She caught flight AC 175, leaving Toronto at midday. The flight was not full. In the three-seat row, there was only one other passenger, already seated by the window. Laura settled down in her allocated aisle seat, smiling politely at the lady in the window seat. She looked East Asian, possibly from China or Japan. Laura noticed she was reading a book in English. It was one of Laura's favourites, 'Lorna Doone' by R.D. Blackmore. The tale of love set in the wilds of Exmoor had excited her from the moment she first picked it up at the age of fourteen. She approved of this lady's choice. When the meal came two hours later, Laura needed to pass the tray to the lady in the window seat. She smiled a thanks and Laura mentioned the book.

"I see you are reading, 'Lorna Doone', always one of my favourites"

"I'm enjoying it tremendously, the description of the countryside around Tiverton is quite exceptional. I would love to go there," answered Mi Sun politely.

"I don't know that area either," Laura added, "perhaps one day I'll make it also."

"Are you familiar with Edmonton?" Mi Sun asked.

"Not at all. It's my first time."

"It's the same with me."

"Are you going there on business?"

"Not really, more of a private visit."

Laura didn't want to intrude, so left it at that.

"I've been at a conference in Toronto and took this opportunity to travel to Alberta," added Mi Sun.

"I'm told it's a beautiful area, wonderful lake and mountains."

"Not quite 'Lorna Doone' country."

Laura smiled.

"Do you have people to show you around?" Mi Sun added.

"I'm not sure how much travelling I'll be doing, but at least I'll be met at the airport."

"I'm a bit the same. Meeting someone to start with, but not sure what will happen after that. I believe the English word is serendipity."

"Sounds fun, although perhaps a little uncertain."

"I'm sure it will be worth it. A little adventure can do no harm."

Laura reflected on David's adventures. They were quite possibly the making of him.

Mi Sun, likewise, recalled Peter's adventures. Although she hadn't shared in them directly, she knew it had been his very essence.

The hostess was asking for their empty trays. The two women took this as a natural break from their brief conversation. Mi Sun back to her book and Laura back to her thoughts.

The flight seemed never ending. Neither woman had realised the flight from Toronto to Edmonton was about half the distance from London to Toronto. They had both had enough of flights by the time the captain asked everyone to prepare for landing. They left the plane together but were separated after passport control. They met up again as they waited by the carousel, ever watching for their suitcases to come tumbling out of the murky depths of the handling bay. The two walked through the duty free green route of customs, both with that strange sense of guilt, yet for no reason at all. They walked through the automatic doors, which thrust them into the throng of people waiting to greet the arriving travellers. Laura turned to Mi Sun and held out her hand. Mi Sun took it, smiled and wished her a great trip. The two women then looked around the arrival hall in equal anticipation.

Dr Willard Boulton was standing a little back from the main throng. He was tall and wearing a long black coat. His wife was on tiptoes, scanning the crowd as they moved forward.

"Wait here, darling," she said, "I'm sure I've spotted one of them."

She moved rapidly through the spreading mass of people as they all sought their friends, drivers and routes to public transport. She was alongside Mi Sun in a moment and gently tugged her arm.

"I do hope that you're Mi Sun, because if not this is very embarrassing, " she said.

Mi Sun smiled.

"I am indeed. Lovely to meet you. By the same token, I trust you're Mrs Boulton?"

"Absolutely, I'm Sheila. Willard is standing over there by the news stand, where we agreed to meet."

With that, Mrs Boulton steered Mi Sun through the slowly moving mass of expectant humanity to meet Willard.

"Willard this is Mi Sun," she said once they were together.

Willard gave a broad smile. So reminiscent of Peter thought Mi Sun. He bent to accept a kiss and Mi Sun responded by touching her lips on his cheek.

Laura, meanwhile, was trying to find the same news stand. As she approached, she was staggered to see the woman standing there. She knew that woman. The jet lag had jumbled her thoughts, but then she suddenly regained focus. She looked again to confirm her confused mind. Was it really? Yes, she was quite sure. It was Sheila McEvoy, the friend of Maggie from Bournemouth who had given her Willard's surname. Sheila was alongside Laura in an instant.

"Lovely to see you again, Laura," she said. "Sorry for the shock, but I thought it best this way. Come and meet Willard, my husband."

With that, she took Laura's arm and led her the few yards to where Willard and now Mi Sun were standing.

"This is Laura, darling," she said.

Willard held out both his hands and took Laura's in a firm, steady grip. He bent slightly and Laura kissed him gently on the cheek.

"Mi Sun tells me that you two have already met on the plane," said Willard with a broad smile.

Laura noticed the dimples in his cheeks, so reminiscent of her memory of David. Mi Sun was the first to react as Laura was still taking in the amazing and somewhat disturbing coincidence.

"Well not exactly. We did sit together, but have not been introduced properly. I'm Mi Sun Culham, widow of Peter, Willard's son."

"And I'm Laura Clarke, widow of Willard's son, David."

Willard beamed, looking from voice to voice as they spoke.

Laura and Mi Sun now looked again at the man standing in front of them. He was in many aspects a more mature portrayal of their own husbands. His bearing and presence was of a person of distinction, tinged with an air of resignation. A man whose past and present were not quite aligned.

"Let's go home," said Sheila, "we've so much to talk about."

She took Willard's arm and led the way, steering him skilfully through the crowd towards the exit doors.

It was then that the two girls suddenly, and at exactly the same time, realised something. Something important and slightly shocking.

Willard was blind.

CHAPTER 38
BACKGROUND

The journey to Red Deer was bewildering. Sheila Boulton drove, with Willard seated in the front. Mi Sun and Laura sat in the back of the car; two ladies who had only just met; two ladies who were utterly confused. They were unsure of their place in this extraordinary situation. Conversation was light and not very specific. It kept to the journey they had both had and the weather in Canada and England. After less than an hour of driving, Mi Sun and Laura were struggling to stay awake. The effect of crossing so many time zones to get here was taking its toll on them both. They tried to stay alert but it was impossible. Willard and Sheila were understanding and let them sleep. When they arrived at a suburb of Red Deer and turned into Willard's drive, they struggled to wake. Willard suggested they had a hot drink and go straight to bed. He promised they would have every opportunity to talk in the morning. Laura and Mi Sun shared a comfortable twin-bedded room. This arrangement pleased them, as they knew there were likely to be many things to discuss privately amongst themselves, but now was not the time. Unpacking no more than essentials they showered and went to bed. In spite of their confusion, anticipation and uncertainty, they both slept soundly.

As the two came down for breakfast the next day, they noticed that Willard was busy preparing breakfast. In spite of his blindness, he was managing to make tea, boil eggs and cook toast. There was a wicker basket full of fresh muffins, the delightful smell suffusing the kitchen. As the meal finished, Willard took control of all the clearing up. Mi Sun and Laura were amazed at his competence. Sheila was quite content to let him do exactly what he could. She rarely intervened. After breakfast, now with everything cleared away and a pot of filter coffee simmering, they all sat down together. It was then that Sheila excused herself. She claimed she had some important business to attend to and would leave the three of them to talk. Willard started.

"Thank you both for coming. I have not been on top form recently, so the timing is perfect. I do hope that for you both to arrive at the same time was not too much of a shock. It wasn't planned this way, but I'm really glad it's worked out like this. It gives me the opportunity to explain things to both of you and feel free to ask questions, either together or separately. Would you be happy for me to talk initially and for you to ask questions later?"

Both Laura and Li Sun nodded in assent.

"Peter and David were both my sons, my only sons. That they should die together in that ghastly helicopter accident was more than tragic. Why God had to be so vengeful on two bright and promising young men is beyond my comprehension. It is not for me to explain God's purpose, but I have spent the last twelve years wondering why. Is it retribution for my own sins? I guess it is something I will only understand fully if, or hopefully when, I meet my maker. Part of the great tragedy is that those two fine men died, not knowing they were brothers.

I think it best if I try to tell you the whole story, at least from my perspective. You'll have plenty of time to ask questions later and I will try my utmost to answer them all.

First I recognise that the path I chose was not always right. Some say that regret is a wasted emotion. However there are certain aspects of my life that I regret deeply. It is what it is. Nothing can change. All I can do is try to explain my actions. It will be up to you to form your own opinions, good or bad.

Let us go back to the summer of 1943. We were at war with Germany and the situation in Britain was looking grim. I was a Canadian medical student training at the London Medical School. We saw the war close up in the east end of London, what with the Luftwaffe bombers and then later the dreaded V rockets. Life was unusual. Friends were being killed at home and in all the theatres of war. Relationships were more temporary, more intense. Possibly difficult for you to understand because, thankfully, you have both lived through a period of peace, at least in Britain. I was engaged to Celia, your mother-in-law, Mi Sun. We had a form of love. Yet, in a strange way, it was more an expectation of our parents. We had known each other, through our families for years. Although I am Canadian by birth, my father and family had lived in London for many years. Celia and I had met each other regularly through numerous social engagements. It seemed logical for us to get married in due course. Celia had always been, how could I put it, a flighty girl. She enjoyed the company of many men. I had hoped that she would change if and when we settled down together.

It was about that time that I met Maggie, your mother-in-law, Laura. With Maggie it was different. She was a nurse; apparently a single woman and we fell deeply in love. When this happened, I had every intention of breaking off my engagement to Celia. To my utter shame, I did not. Maggie and I had a full and intimate relationship throughout the late summer of 1943. It would have been in November

250

of that year that Maggie told me she was pregnant. I was desperate to marry Maggie, but she then hit me with a bombshell.

Maggie was already married. What you both have to understand is that to train as a nurse at The London Hospital in those days, you had to be single. Difficult to comprehend these days, but that's the way it was back then. Maggie had registered as a single woman and had been accepted as such. Her husband, Bill Clarke, was away in Burma fighting the Japanese. He came home on leave probably only once or twice during the war, so it wasn't difficult to maintain the deception.

I asked Maggie to marry me, which would have meant divorcing Bill. Maggie, to her credit, wouldn't do it. She felt it only fair to wait. She wanted, at the very least, to talk to Bill directly. She planned to wait until he returned from the Far East. The whole situation was complicated by the fact that the baby was due in June and Bill didn't return from Burma until long after that.

At the same time, Celia would visit me occasionally and we continued to make love. Clearly I was careless or, you might consider, callous. The outcome, as you now know, is that my fianc e, Celia, and the person I truly loved, Maggie, were pregnant at the same time.

I am sure it makes little difference to your low opinion of me, but I did try to resolve things. Maggie had returned to her parents' home in Gloucester. I cannot be sure, but I think it was her father who prevented any contact. I tried my best, but it was impossible to communicate with Maggie at this time. All my letters were returned or unanswered and my phone calls were never put through to Maggie. I didn't even know the exact date that our child was to be born. Not until that fateful night of June 24th 1944. We will go back to that date later.

As far as Celia was concerned, Mi Sun, we made arrangements for her to have her baby in secret. It was her wish. She was to have her baby at the Portland Hospital in London. It was the best we could do.

You both need to appreciate that back in 1944 an unmarried woman with a child was considered very differently from today. Clearly it happened and, during the war years, more commonly. However the stigma still remained, whatever your background.

I never found out where Maggie's son was born. By dreadful coincidence, both babies were transferred to Great Ormond Street Hospital on the day they were born. I was working there as an acting registrar. In those war years, hospital ranks were blurred and training was often accelerated. It was by pure chance I found out that the two babies, both my sons, were there at the same time and in the same ward."

Mi Sun and Laura listened to this account in amazement. It just seemed a most implausible coincidence and hardly credible. Yet here was a man, a man they had no reason to doubt, telling it to them both. It was clear he found the telling uncomfortable. It was also clear that it had to be said. As they sat there mesmerised by what they were hearing, the tension was broken. Sheila was knocking quietly at the door. She came and in looked at Willard with concern.

"I do hope you're not overdoing it, darling," she said fondly. "I've brought you all fresh coffee as you've not touched the last lot. Perhaps it's time for a short break."

Willard agreed and he relaxed back in his chair as the coffee was handed to him. He did look tired. More than tired, he looked sallow. Perhaps the telling was affecting him deeply. Sheila noticed these things and was concerned. Once again she left them alone.

During the break, the two younger women had another chance to take in their surroundings. The room was bright and airy, the large windows giving plenty of light. It felt organised but comfortable. Not untidy, but definite 'lived in'. There were a number of bookshelves, containing medical texts, travel books and novels. One shelf was dedicated to audiobooks and tapes, presumably for Willard to enjoy when he wasn't listening to the television. On a coffee table next to one of the chairs was a tape player with a pair of headphones attached. Laura and Mi Sun could see that despite his handicap, Willard was far from idle. He returned to his story.

"The next part of the story will make you shudder with its apparent inhumanity. I'm sure you already have a pretty dim view of me as a person and this will make it worse. For some reason, I had a powerful sixth sense of impending doom. To this day, I cannot explain it. I somehow knew, quite inexplicably, that the future was going to be complicated. I couldn't say how or why. I just felt that certain action was needed and I took it."

"Action?" said the two women. It was a question, not a statement.

"Yes," Willard continued. "I don't expect you to understand, although the passage of time has proved me right. I sensed that whatever was to happen in the future for these two boys, I would not be able to keep close contact with both of them. Something dramatic had to be done for me to know which was which. I meant forever. There was only one course of action I could think of at the time. Perhaps I wasn't thinking straight. I don't know. Most people would say it was horribly cruel to inflict pain on someone so young. I gave one of the boys a local anaesthetic and sliced the flesh on the inside of his right heel. It couldn't be superficial because that would heal without a scar. My medical training told me the correct depth to slice through the living flesh."

Laura gripped the arms of her chair and Li Sun nearly fainted.

"I sutured the wound, treated it as best I could, and made absolutely sure that all was well. It may be no comfort to you, but no child of that age will ever remember what had happened. I returned every few hours to give further local anaesthetic. I was sure that the little boy, one of my own sons, would experience very little pain."

"How horrible," shuddered Laura, "to think that you could do this."

"How calculating," added Mi Sun.

"I accept all you say and you could both add how unnecessary. Each child would normally go to its own mother and there would have been absolutely no need for such drastic action."

"So why?" shouted both women, almost in unison.

"As I said earlier, it was a sort of sixth sense. It was almost a foreboding of some sort of impending doom. Perhaps doom is too strong a word. Adversity may be better. I don't know. I cannot explain more than that. I'm not sure if either of you know what happened next, but my intuition seemed to be right."

Mi Sun and Laura looked blank. There was no reason for either of them to have known what happened on that fateful night.

"At just before midnight on the day David and Peter were born, a German bomb hit Great Ormond Street Hospital causing untold damage. It was utter devastation. We lost all power and at first we all thought that everyone in the ward including the two children had been killed. It was then that Sheila, who was badly injured, heard the faint cry of babies. I managed to crawl through the blackened debris and smoke to get to them. I was able to pull their incubators clear. They were extremely lucky. I think the incubators probably saved their lives. Their injuries were serious, but largely superficial and we then transported them to The London Hospital so they could recuperate. In time, the two boys went to Celia and Maggie. The adversity or complication became apparent when Celia took one of the boys without consulting the hospital authorities. Neither child could be identified anyway. They looked identical. In fact the staff at The London called them the twins. The only distinctive feature was the scar on the heel of one of the boys, the scar I had inflicted. As far as I was aware, no one had noticed it.

As I told you earlier, I lost contact with Maggie totally. She brought up David with her new family and as far as I am aware did a great job. I am sure he had a happy life. Sadly far too short.

Celia and I were married in early 1945 and soon afterwards I was posted to Northern Germany. It was there that I was subjected to the abject horrors of Belsen."

Mi Sun said nothing. She'd heard about Belsen, but didn't appreciate that the concentration camp mentioned by Jim Driver, was the one named Belsen.

Laura remembered vividly David's account of the visit he'd made to Belsen when the memorial was dedicated. She also remembered that David had corresponded with a Canadian doctor about the memorial. David had mentioned the brief meeting with him at Belsen. Was it possible that she was listening, right now, to that self-same doctor? This story was full of strange coincidences, but surely this was one too far. Her thoughts were interrupted as Willard continued.

"I stayed in the army and could do very little to keep any sort of regular contact with David. I made the occasional gesture such as sending both boys a toy bear, but doubt if it made much difference."

"Your quite wrong there," Laura interjected. "David loved that bear. We still have it in the boys' room. They used to play with it when they were younger."

Willard, looking drawn, continued.

"It became increasingly obvious that Celia had returned to her old ways, in spite of our marriage. She had a series of affairs. I can't totally blame her as my work in the army kept me overseas and we were together rarely. On the short times we were together, the spark had gone from our marriage. It was the last straw when I came home on leave and found her in bed with one of her lovers. I wanted a divorce, but Celia's Catholic faith wouldn't countenance it. Shortly afterwards, I was posted to Korea."

Mi Sun and Laura were mesmerised by this account. They waited with anticipation to the next intriguing chapter.

"During the defence of Kapyong Valley, I was seriously wounded. I was evacuating our boys from the front line. Shrapnel from what is now called an IED hit me with full force. It was basically a booby trap bomb hidden underground. I was taken to a field hospital and although most of my body was a mess, my eyes suffered the most. I wasn't totally blinded at the time. Perhaps if I had been in a modern hospital with top ophthalmic facilities, things could have been different. But they were as they were. I still had very limited vision, but the doctors knew that deterioration was inevitable. I was told I would eventually go blind. The timescale was the only unknown. It was then I recognised it would be impossible to return to any sort of normal life, especially with a woman who no longer loved me. I don't expect you both to understand, but this was the reason I faked my death in Korea. It gave me, selfishly I admit, the opportunity to start a new life. A life I had hoped would serve some useful purpose beyond an unhappy one with Celia. It wasn't too difficult to arrange it with the help of my best friend, Jim Driver. I tried my utmost to provide well for Celia. I arranged a monthly allowance for the rest of her life. Jim assured her that it was my army pension. I knew she was the sort of person who was unlikely to enquire too deeply. The main thing was that it was paid into her bank account on a regular basis.

Jim arranged to meet her soon after the so-called report of my death. He continued the subterfuge by returning most of my belongings. These included my old microscope."

"The microscope," said Mi Sun, "it was given to Peter on his 18th birthday. There are questions I need to ask about that microscope."

"Why don't I finish my side of the story and then I would be happy to answer all your questions. Does that seem reasonable?"

Both young women agreed.

"At every birthday, I sent an anonymous card or gift to both boys. I suspect that Maggie might have guessed the sender. Celia, on the other hand, would have been perplexed or disinterested. I don't know. What I did know is that Celia married Viscount Culham just a year after my death was reported. I was pleased about this, as I was confident that Peter would be well looked after, at least financially. Peter then moved into a stratum of society way beyond my means. He was still my son, but I just hoped he would be fine."

At that point, Willard lost a little control in his voice and he lapsed for a time into silence. Sheila was busying herself in the kitchen and noticed his momentarily lapse. Sheila suggested that Willard took a short break. She said that Willard found it an effort to talk for too long. The four of them had a light lunch of salad and cold meat. Willard, as before, brought the cutlery and crockery from the kitchen and cleared away after the meal. After they had eaten, Willard continued his story.

"Now, where was I?" he said

"Birthdays," Laura volunteered, "You mentioned the bears."

"Oh yes, but first I need to tell you that I had by now left the army and returned to Canada. My own father, the grandfather that Peter and David never knew, had immigrated to Britain. He was a successful psychiatrist with rooms in Harley Street. In the early days I visited him from Canada. After he died, I had no reason to go back to Britain.

I started my new life in Canada at a small practice in the developing town of Peace River. In those days it was very primitive. A GP was expected to undertake a range of procedures that would only take place in a hospital today. It was tough but rewarding. I delivered numerous babies at their homes. I regularly performed appendectomies and often had to reset limbs manually. I became especially interested in spinal manipulation, something that wasn't affected too much by my partial sight. Of course, I couldn't drive, so certain things were pretty limited. I forgot to mention that by now I was remarried. My wife, Ruth, was an absolute godsend. Sadly she died at about the same age as Maggie. Far too early, far too early."

Willard stopped for a moment, the memories clearly very painful for him. Mi Sun and Laura were entranced and had no intention of stopping the flow. They waited for him to carry on.

"After a few years, I left medicine and went into politics. Within a short while, I became a member of the state legislature. This is equivalent to what you call an MP in Britain. My eyesight, as predicted, was deteriorating rapidly. I was officially registered blind. I couldn't see faces clearly, but could just about manage to get around. Often with help. In fact I was the first registered blind politician to hold high office. Whether it was sympathy for my situation or something else, I don't know, but I was promoted to ministerial rank. I became the Minister for Housing and Infrastructure Affairs. It was a hugely exciting time. It involved numerous visits to infrastructure projects throughout Canada. I even met the queen on one occasion when she opened the dam at Bow Lake, providing power for Red Deer. They were heady days. It would have been about this time when Laura first made contact with me. I accept the charge of utter selfishness. However for a Minister of the Crown to be known to have fathered a child out of wedlock would have been political dynamite. This was in part, I guess, why I took so long to answer your letters, Laura. I was well aware that Peter and David had died in that ghastly crash in 1974. It was to my personal shame I thought it better to delay meeting you both face to face until I was well out of politics.

Partly because of my blindness and partly because of your attempts to contact me, I resigned from politics. I then went back to medicine, spending more of my time in administration. In addition to working in hospital management, I continued my work in spinal manipulation. You would be surprised how many physiotherapists and osteopaths are blind. I am proud to say that over the years I have managed to cure many people of back problems. The pain and depression caused by sciatica is huge and I am pleased I was able to play my part in helping so many sufferers. I admit there were times when I missed the excitement of politics, the proximity to power. Yet I quickly learned that blue jeans are as comfortable as a lounge suit, that my old books are far more interesting than affairs of state and the cushions in my old chair at home are far more relaxing than the upright, leather-bound seats of the Senate.

I've talked far too long. I realise that you will both have lots of questions. I would welcome a rest and then perhaps we could eat together later. Then I would be happy to answer your questions tomorrow, when I've had a good night's sleep. Can I suggest that the two of you take a walk around the town? There is plenty to see. The bison park is fascinating."

Willard was looking drained and the two women thought his advice admirable. They had been indoors for far too long and welcomed the opportunity to get outside and enjoy the midsummer sunshine. They took a local bus into Red Deer and started by seeking out the visitors' centre. It was very impressive and organised minibus trips out to the bison park. They learned all about the Cree people, the first community living in the area.

They returned in time for the evening meal, which Sheila had arranged as a sort of celebration of living. Grace was said reverently before the meal. Thanks were given for those missing and red wine was served and glasses were raised for special memories. Willard asked both Laura and Mi Sun to recall the happy times they'd had with David and Peter. It was clear he enjoyed hearing their stories. Soon after the meal, Willard excused himself and went to bed. The ladies talked for a while; then Sheila said good night and followed Willard upstairs.

Laura and Mi Sun both agreed that Willard seemed unwell. They had so many questions to ask and hoped he'd be able to answer them in the morning after a good night's sleep. Where did Sheila fit in? How many of the quests and missions that Peter and David had grappled with, were initiated by Willard? They both hoped the next day would reveal everything.

CHAPTER 39
QUESTIONS

The following morning after breakfast, the discussions continued. This time Mi Sun and Laura took the initiative. They were desperate to have their many questions answered.

"Willard," said Laura, "yesterday you started to tell us about the birthday cards and presents. They were often the start of strange, difficult, but ultimately fulfilling quests. Why did you choose to do this?"

"As an absent father, I could do little to influence the boys' lives. With some of the birthday cards, I gave clues to experiences and adventures, which I hoped might help to mould the boys' personalities. Parents would clearly be a major factor in their development, but I tried to give them opportunities beyond the experiences provided by their homes. I knew that both boys were in quite secure families. They both had parents who loved them in their own way. I just tried to add an extra layer of interest for both David and Peter. It was up to them how, or indeed if, they would respond. I wanted them both to take responsibility for their actions, whichever way it might lead. I just gave a little stimulus. It was a totally inadequate substitute for being able to walk alongside my two boys.

I was careful to ensure that it became their choice and theirs alone to start these missions. One of the great and well-established tenets of moral philosophy is freedom of choice. I think in almost every case, I made the first stage some little conundrum they needed to answer before they could start. I didn't want to dictate or prescribe. I wanted to guide, to influence a little. They could easily have rejected each and every one if they chose."

"So in some way, you were responsible for Peter's personal development," said Mi Sun.

"Only in part. Character and personality are essentially your own. I just tried to provide the odd opportunity or encouragement along the way. Of course, as I said before, it was nothing compared with the impact of their parents. I may have helped a little. I suppose in all honesty there was also a level of personal interest, even fulfilment. I was not able to do any of the things that David and Peter did, but through them I did them all."

"So David's adventurous nature came, at least in part, from you. You initiated his pursuit of the snow leopard, his obsession with the painting, Blake's poem and all the finds in North Wales. But how on earth did you know about these things?"

"The Roman thermal baths near Conwy were purely chance. I had been on holiday as a youngster in the area and had sneaked into that particular farm looking for apples with my older brother. We found the cave, long before it had been blocked up with builders' rubble. I was very young, probably eight or nine. What I saw meant nothing to me then. It was as I grew older and studied Roman history at school that the significance of the cave started to come to light. I never had the opportunity to return and so it was an ideal mission to offer to David. The underground mine workings near Blaenau Ffestiniog were well known in the area when I was young, but the work stopped at about that time. Yet there had been gold mined in that area in small quantities for centuries. The cavern was a totally original find by David. Yet strangely, there had always been legends about it. My wife, Ruth, was Welsh and from that area. She told me some of the sagas and legends of the North Wales community. Of course you always take these things with a pinch of salt, but David found the truth.

Goering's model railway and the hidden paintings both came about from my time in the army. Remember I was stationed in Germany before I went to Korea. I leaned to speak German well, which gave me a real advantage. Immediately after the war we had some very senior members of the Wehrmacht under interrogation. I learned a great many secrets."

"But surely they were not going to give away information as valuable as the paintings?" said Mi Sun, a little surprised.

"Certainly not. Not under conventional interrogation. This was the clever bit. Prior to Nuremberg, we put a number of the senior staff together in a private house, guarded well from the outside to avoid any escapes. They were treated extremely well and had access to good food and even vintage wine. They were an arrogant lot and assumed it was because of their high rank. What they didn't know was that every room, even the toilets, were thoroughly bugged. We had people recording and transcribing every single thing they were saying. They thought they were talking in private, but with a few drinks inside them, tongues were often loosened. Most of the useful material was about military strategy, but not all. I was able to sift out some of the more personal items. It was like a verbal jigsaw puzzle, but over time I managed to connect the pieces. This was the way I found the exact whereabouts of the paintings and the original location of the model railway."

"So why didn't you retrieve them yourself?" Laura asked.

"That's easy to answer. I was posted to Korea. After that as you know my life took a very different course and I went back to Canada. I knew that I had two boys growing up, who one day might be attracted to the proposition of finding them. I was prepared to wait for the right moment."

"But what about the snow leopard," said Laura, remembering the traumatic time that her David had suffered finding it. "That sub-species had never been seen before."

"No, not by anyone from the west. But don't forget the British Army had troops from Nepal, the Gurkhas. Sometimes the talk would come round to mysteries and myths of the, so-called, yeti. Most of the Gurkhas had little time for that particular tale, but the white ghost, the white snow leopard was a different story. The snow leopard's habitat was exclusively the Himalaya, but not necessarily confined to Nepal. The Gurkhas heard from other people, especially those in Kyrgyzstan, how they had also reported a white ghost. I was confident that this was the more likely place and directed David accordingly. Of course, I had no idea that the whole exercise would be so precarious."

Sheila was insistent that Willard had a break from the questions, but realized her two guests needed to have answers to their many questions. They had coffee together while Willard went to his room for a short rest. While he was resting, the younger ladies took the opportunity to talk to Sheila alone.

"Sheila," said Laura, "do you mind telling us how you came to be involved with Willard?"

"Of course," she replied. "It's no great mystery. You've heard Willard describe what happened on the night of the bomb at Great Ormond Street. It was sheer luck, although to be honest, I was at death's door. I heard the plaintive cries of the two boys and that was when Willard went back into the ward to rescue them. It took me a long time to recover, but as you can see I'm fine now. I had totally lost touch with Willard after that. I spent some time with Maggie and David when I was studying at Cambridge, but a former lover was hardly a suitable topic of conversation. It was after your visit, Laura, when we met back in 1977, that I thought it prudent to contact Willard. I suppose in part it was to warn him you might be trying to make contact. Anyway, I had some of the misgivings you had, especially not knowing if he was married at the time. It turned out that his first wife, the one he talked about from North Wales, had died some years earlier. Strangely at the same age as Maggie. To cut a long story short, we wrote to each other and after quite a short time we met. We were married seven years ago. It was quite special for me, because my first marriage ended in divorce and I never expected to find a man like Willard. We both took the view that just because we'd lived our lives separately, it didn't mean we hadn't a life to live together. We've had a very happy time and feel truly blessed.

After lunch, Willard was happy to continue his explanation of his involvement with the two boys. He looked better for the rest.

"What about Peter," asked Mi Sun, "you must have also influenced him with those birthday cards?"

"Possibly less than David," he replied. "I certainly had no influence on his success as a doctor and his impressive breakthrough in the treatment of respiratory conditions. The use of oxygen under high pressure, his development of the oximeter and his positive pressure device was all down to his own ingenuity."

"I remember he told me about his involvement with the early Beatles material. Something about a visit to Hamburg."

"Once again it was a lucky break for me. I was on leave in Hamburg while I was in the army in Germany. I went to the Top Ten nightclub and got to hear the Beatles or the Beat Boys as they were in those days. They were mainly the backing group for Tony Sheridan, but they did a few sessions on their own while I was there. I thought they were something special and was hoping that Peter's little mission might confirm my opinion. It was his incredible detective work that ended up with Astrid Kirchherr giving him those tapes and demo discs."

"But what about the island Peter found. That couldn't have been one of your lucky breaks"

"I confess I did know about the island in the North Atlantic off Scotland. Jim Driver, my partner in crime in the Medical Corps, had a brother in the Merchant Navy. During the war his brother had run the gauntlet of the Atlantic convoys. He told Jim of this island always hidden in cloud deep in the ocean. Evidently one of the merchant ships had been caught in a violent storm and driven much further south than the planned route. At the time it seemed of little consequence. As I thought more about the legend of St Brendan, I just wondered if there could be any connection. It was a ridiculously long shot, but certain features somehow seemed to fit. I found it hard to believe that an island of this magnitude could exist without any regular sightings. I suppose in part it was because it was of no strategic importance. The upshot is the Ordinance Survey now officially records it. I have noticed that if you buy a map today of the Western Isles of Scotland, they still don't add it in, even as an inset, like St Kilda. Too far out I suppose."

"That leaves the poem," said Mi Sun, hardly believing these incredible explanations from Willard. "How could you have possibly known about that?"

"The truth is," Willard answered, "I didn't. It was another of my questionable hunches. I had studied Blake at school and his attitude to God was indeterminate. This poem was one we studied in the sixth form and arguably one of his best known. Many scholars consider this poem as a vindication of his antipathy towards God. I don't know why, but it just didn't sit right with me. Even the length of the poem, just three verses, seemed inconsistent with his other works. I just wanted confirmation that Blake really felt that way about God. That he hadn't recanted in some way and expressed his feelings properly towards the end of the poem. David proved me right and I shall be forever grateful for that. It has put my confused mind over Blake at rest."

"Thank you Willard, for putting our minds at rest," said Mi Sun. "We were both fascinated to know how our husbands became so involved in such a variety of activities throughout their lives. We're sure it made a very positive difference to them as people, the men we loved. In fact in my case, I would never had met Peter if it hadn't been for one of his quests – the one to find your non-existent grave."

"It was the same for me," added Laura, "the only reason I met David was because he was in a bookshop looking for a map for North Wales. But Willard, there are still two other questions you've left unanswered. You've told us a lot about your life both before you came to Canada and while here. But you haven't explained how you knew all about Peter and David while they were both alive."

"That wasn't too difficult. When I became a member of the legislature, here in Canada, it opened many doors. The ministerial office has access to extensive intelligence. The people involved all sign a secrecy act, so any request I had would stay with them and them only. At intervals, I would make enquiries of the two boys and receive regular updates. Some of the things were easy because of the awards and plaudits they both received. Other things were more difficult. As part of the Canadian Legislative Information Bureau, all the British newspapers were scanned daily for information on all manner of things. The terrible news of the helicopter crash clearly made the headlines. When I heard the ghastly news, I rearranged my schedule and came over to England as soon as the funerals were arranged. I was there for both."

"You were there for the funerals," Laura and Mi Sun cried out in unison and disbelief.

"I was and they were the saddest two days of my life. Of course I couldn't make myself known and my blindness made it doubly difficult."

The two women went quiet. It was difficult taking all this in. They were both stunned into silence, lost in their own thoughts.

Laura was the first to recover.

"Now I see," she said. "I was told later that one of the mourners at St Andrew's was alone and left immediately after the service. A tall man in a black coat. That was you Willard!"

"It was and exactly the same happened at the church at Hadleigh Hall. I was present at both funerals. Of course nothing could compare to your grief, but it helped me come to terms with the loss of my only sons.. The eulogies, in both cases, helped me appreciate the individual lives of David and Peter."

It was clear that Willard was struggling to talk about his distant involvement all those years ago as the melancholic memories came flooding back. After a minute or so, he regained his composure.

"There were, of course, happier times. I managed to witness both of your marriages."

You did," Laura cried out in amazement.

"How did you know?" added Mi Sun.

"In your case, Mi Sun," Willard answered, "it was not too difficult as your engagement was announced in The Times. Laura and David's wedding was less easy, but I guessed you were likely to marry in Witchford. My intelligence people kept a marker on the banns in that parish and eventually it paid off."

"So tell me, Willard," said Laura, quite stunned by the revelation, "did you have a guide dog at the time?"

"I did indeed. Good old Muddle."

"I remember her outside the church door as I went in. A beautiful golden Labrador."

"She was my constant companion until she died just over seven years ago. I was tempted to get another one, but then Sheila came into my life. She's a much better driver than a guide dog!"

"I can't remember seeing a guide dog at our wedding," Mi Sun added. "How did you manage then?"

"In between your weddings, I returned to Canada and old Muddle started to suffer from a touch of arthritis. I didn't think it fair to travel that distance with her a second time. I arrived and left Hadleigh Hall in a taxi. You both looked absolutely stunning at your weddings. Perhaps you could send me a photograph?"

Mi Sun and Laura promised to do so and then returned to their questions.

"Willard, what you haven't shared with us in any detail is your personal feelings about the way everything has turned out. You've explained your involvement, but not your sentiment. Do you have any sense of disappointment, contrition or self-reproach, even?"

"But of course, I've had to learn to live a detached life. Detached from my own flesh and blood and it's not been easy. As I've said before, regret is a wasted emotion, but it doesn't mean to say I'm totally lacking in feeling. What I have learned to accept is that human beings, by their very nature, are complex, often contradictory, variable and inconsistent. It is wrong to form a firm opinion of another person until time has been spent in their presence, in numerous settings and at numerous times of day and night. This was never my privilege with David and Peter and this makes me sad. We are all, in many ways, a product of our history and your two lovely husbands were no exception. Peter and David died too young to be fully formed in many ways. But what I have seen and what you both know is that they had both reached a personal framework of living. We all eventually reach that state, through the numerous actions and interactions, through the major and minor events of our lives, through the people we meet and the things we see. Life's important experiences do not have to be the momentous episodes; they can equally be the apparently unimportant. They can be planned or impromptu. These things do not matter. As I've got older, I've started to appreciate better our part in life, however modest. It is essentially to reach a point of true contentment. Only then can we expect to live in peace and die in peace. It is contentment that gives meaning to life.

David and Peter both had an impact on the lives of many, not just on you and their families, but also on the wider world in so many ways. Their fingerprints can never be wiped away from the numerous little marks of kindness they left behind. Their lives have shaped the future, in ways, perhaps, yet unknown. My influence, for what it was worth, is now long gone. It is now your responsibility to ensure that their legacies live on. I wish you well."

The two women remained silent as they absorbed Willard's words. Eventually one of them spoke.

"Willard, you have tried to explain the bewildering business of the scar on David's heel."

"David's heel," Willard stated. " Forgive me, but don't forget that I did such a seemingly offensive act before either child was named. It was little more than a premonition at the time. One that, as it turned out, was horrendously correct. No one could have possible predicted that one mother would take a child without consent. A child that she had no way of knowing if it was truly hers."

"Absolutely," said Laura, "but there is no question that David was the one with the scar on his heel. It itched a little in cold weather, but otherwise it was of no consequence. David always assumed it was caused by some childhood injury."

"I'm relieved to hear it was of no physical consequence, but its overall importance is without question," said Willard. "You will recall that Celia took one of the boys away and Maggie was left with the other. I appreciate that such a thing is virtually impossible today because of arm and wristbands on newborn babies. But it was very different then. People were living every day during the war on a permanent knife-edge. Bombs were dropping daily and there was less chance to get every correct procedure in place. I realize that you both need to know the truth and I will tell you. However although it's not late, I'm feeling exhausted. It can wait until tomorrow. I promise I'll tell you then."

Sheila had been busy in the kitchen and could hear Willard's last comment. She took this as her cue and came in to join them. Willard looked drawn and listless as she helped him to his feet. She smiled at the girls. Without further comment, she took his arm and let him lean on her as she steered him slowly to his room.

That evening, the three ladies were pleasant, yet placid company for each other as they shared a light meal. It was a quiet and thoughtful time together. There was an air of expectancy, but each for different reasons.

CHAPTER 40
TRUTH

After Willard had retired to bed, the three ladies sat together recalling the events of the day. Mi Sun and Laura were still slowly coming to terms with the manner in which Willard had influenced their husbands. They were both so pleased that over the years he had been a remote, obscure, yet ever-present guide on the fortunes of the two men they knew so well. He had initiated amazing life experiences, all of which were quite unique. They were truly grateful. Willard's distant involvement had made Peter and David much more into the people they had become. The people they loved.

There was still the one big question he hadn't answered. As Peter was growing up with Celia, Willard must have seen that there was no scar on Peter's heel. Even then he must have been fully aware of any error at the hospital. He must have known which child Celia took and whether it was really her own son. The truth was unlikely to change their present lives a great deal. Yet both Laura and Mi Sun felt they had a right to know. Who were the true mothers of David and Peter? They had discussed it between themselves and both felt a genuine, deep need. They realised that the truth could cause relief or dismay, comfort or distress. Nonetheless, for some strange, insoluble, innermost feeling, they felt this mutual desire to know.

"Sheila" asked Laura, "what Mi Sun and I cannot understand is how Willard knew which child belonged to which mother after the bomb blast? He said they were like two peas in a pod. The staff at the hospital and their own mothers couldn't tell them apart, so how could he?"

"What you forget is that Willard was able to find out the circumstances of them both being at Great Ormond Street in the first place, just before they were transferred to The London Hospital. He knew that one of them reached full term, but was jaundiced. The other was premature. Strangely, in spite of this, the two babies were almost exactly the same weight. The key was the small blood sample he took when he caused the scar. He had it analysed and there was clear evidence of elevated bilirubin, a sure indication of jaundice. Remember that after the bomb blast and the rescue of the two boys, Willard was incapacitated for some time due to excessive smoke inhalation."

This new information was sufficient for Mi Sun and Laura. The story was almost complete. Willard had promised. For good or for ill, they would know in the morning.

Sheila excused herself, saying that she needed to make up the coal fire in Willard's room. Before she did, she confided in Laura and Mi Sun.

"You must have noticed," she said, "that over the last few days, Willard has been a little unwell. "I appreciate that because of his blindness, you have made certain allowances. But I can assure you that under normal circumstances he would have been much more alive to our discussions. He is normally a man full of life, almost unstoppable. The truth is that Willard has spent the last three months in a local hospice. He has advanced pancreatic cancer and is unlikely to survive for more than a few months. He returned here from the hospice purely to meet you both. It was his wish alone and I know he has been so grateful to be able to talk to you. With memories like his, both disappointments and successes, it has been a delight to meet you both. He told me last night that talking with you has been his greatest joy."

Sheila kissed both Mi Sun and Laura goodnight and went to her room.

In the morning, the three women were up as usual for breakfast. They were surprised that Willard was not with them, bustling around in his normal way trying to be helpful. There was an air of anticipation for both Laura and Mi Sun. They were waiting for the final piece of a lifelong puzzle to be put in place. The maternal mystery was about to be resolved.

"I don't know what's keeping him," said Sheila. "As you know he's always up and about at this time, in spite of his blindness. I'll give him until the end of breakfast and then I'll chase him," she added.

"Could he be reluctant to tell us the truth about Celia and Maggie?" Mi Sun enquired with a degree of hesitation.

"Absolutely not. He promised he'd tell you. And he will; in his own time."

Breakfast was over, still with no sign of Willard. Sheila went upstairs and into Willard's room.

Willard was lying on his bed in a silk dressing gown. He was very still. Sheila bent over and felt his pulse. There was no question. He was dead.

Sheila found a single sheet of paper clasped in his left hand and resting over his heart. She carefully and gently prized open his hand and loosened the white note of truth. She read in neat, bold letters.

'THE CHILD WITH THE SCAR, DAVID, WAS THE SON OF CELIA.
I HAVE BEEN THE SHAMEFUL CAUSE OF TWO LIVES OF THOROUGH DECEPTION.
MAY GOD FORGIVE ME.'

Sheila crumpled the sheet of paper into a ball. She placed it carefully on the dying embers of the fire. She watched as, at first, the edges of the paper turned brown and then lit. The truth turned to flames. The smoke of a lifetime of secrecy streamed slowly upwards. The remnants of each particle of paper would shortly join the atmosphere above. An atmosphere that held all the hopes, failures and successes of so many lives. Soon there was nothing left but an enigma of ashes.

She turned and kissed Willard lightly on his forehead. She said a silent prayer.

Sheila closed the door and, with an air of finality, she went downstairs and sat with Mi Sun and Laura.

"He kept his promise," she said quietly. "This morning, he wrote in a clear hand that the child with the scar, David, was Maggie's son. Things were just as you remember them. Nothing has changed. It was his final action. He was content and at peace. It was then that he died."

The date was June the 24th.

CHAPTER SUMMARIES

1. Births – June 24ᵗʰ 1944 – two boys are born on the same day, in different places   and in different circumstances.

2. Devastation – June 1944 – the consequences of a bomb damaging the hospital where both boys are in the same ward.

3. Phoenix – June 1944 – the boys are found and transferred to another hospital.

4. Restoration – July 1944 – the babies survive and are visited by their mothers.

5. Certificates – July 1944 – Maggie registers her child and Willard and Celia marry.

6. Liberation – April 1945 – Willard is sent to care for the survivors of a concentration camp.

7. Separation – January 1946 – Maggie and her husband are temporarily reunited at the end of the war.

8. Rescue – November 1947 – Maggie rescues a woman drowning in a canal.

9. Affairs – 1951 – Celia has a number of affairs.

10. Death – April 1951 – Willard is killed.

11. Lost Child – June 1952 – Peter goes to a prep school.

12. Illness – June 1955 – David suffers a serious illness.

13. Cathedral - September 1955 to June 1962 – David studies at secondary school.

14. Downthorpe – September 1957 to June 1962 – Peter studies at a boarding school and is sexually assaulted.

15. Eighteen – June 1962 – Peter celebrates his eighteenth birthday.

16. Mission – August 1962 – Peter travels to Korea.

17. Music – September 1962 – Peter seeks a band in Hamburg.

18. Spa – September 1962 – David discovers an ancient spa.

19. Cavern – September 1962 – David goes underground.

20. Colours – May 1965 – Time spent at University.

21. Poem – June 1965 – David explores Blake's poetry.

22. Oxygen – 1968 – Peter develops medical instrumentation.

23. Revenge – 1969 – Peter has the opportunity to exact revenge.

24. Island – 1970 – Peter discovers an unknown island.

25. Marriage – 1970 – Peter and David both marry.

26. Painting – 1970 – David finds a missing painting.

27. Train – 1972 – Peter 'liberates' a model railway.

28. Leopard – 1973 – David hunts for big cats.

29. Cricket – 1974 – David and Peter play in a cricket match.

30. Fireball – 1974 – An explosion causes two deaths.

31. Funerals – 1974 – Two funerals take place.

32. Deaths – 1976 – The mothers of Peter and David both die.

33. Laura – 1977 – Laura starts to investigate the past.

34. Mi Sun – 1977 – Mi Sun also starts investigations.

35. Decline and Fall – 1982 – David's father dies.

36. Hunt and Fall – 1983 – Peter's father dies.

37. Found – 1984 – A visit to Canada.

38. Background – 1984 – History unfolds.

39. Questions – 1984 – Questions are asked.

40. Truth – 1984 – Questions are answered.

A NOTE ON THE AUTHOR

David Brodie was most recently the Professor of Cardiovascular Health at Bucks New University and previously held a Personal Chair at The University of Liverpool.

During his academic career he published six academic texts and over 200 journal papers. He was awarded a DSc in 2011 in recognition of 'distinguished, original research work' over a twenty-year period.

He started to write this novel whilst recovering from Covid-19 in March 2020. When not writing, he enjoys jogging, rowing, family times with children and grandchildren, bridge, U3A and Rotary. He engages in fund-raising activities in the UK and abroad. He loves a challenge, with one of his most recent being to establish 12 children's libraries in primary schools in Nepal. This involved him in carrying the books to remote, mountainous areas; many days walk from the nearest road. The front and back cover photograph of this book was taken on one of these trips.

He has recently written a number of children's books, all available from OK Our Kids (www.okourkids.org.uk).

He lives with his long-suffering wife of 50 years, in South Buckinghamshire, UK.

Other of his non-academic books include 'Treacherous Games', (available from Kindle and Amazon), 'Beggar on a Bicycle, 'Purple Pup Goes Swimming', 'Purple Pup and the Coat of Many Colours', 'Purple Pup Meets Sad Sally' and 'Purple Pup and the Flying Hats'.

Printed in Great Britain
by Amazon

29815042R00150